Acclaim for Pepp

T0054127

POSITIVELY, PENELOPE

"Basham is a rising star. *Positively, Penelope* is humorous and touching, and everything you want in the perfect summer read. Don't miss this one."
—Rachel Hauck, *New York Times* bestselling author of *The Wedding Dress*

"What do you get when you combine a lovable heroine with characters who have mastered the art of witty banter? A charming read. And that is what *Positively, Penelope* is."
—Sheila Roberts, *USA TODAY* bestselling author

"This book is a positive delight from the first line to the last. I adored Penelope in Izzy's book, and she screamed for her own book, so I couldn't wait to dive into the pages of this novel. Oh my goodness, it was a true, laugh-out-loud joy to read this book. The story was filled with twists and hiccups, but there was also such delight and fun. And fairy tales. And princesses. And Julie Andrews. And Gene Kelly. All the things I adore. In one place. And the kissing. Pepper does enjoy writing kissing books. I highly recommend this sweet, fun, romantic romp of a book. It was wonderful!"
—Cara Putman, award-winning author of more than 35 novels, including *Flight Risk*

"Like the character Penelope herself, this entire book radiates sunshine and magic. The banter between Penelope and her siblings kept me smiling. The theatrical references kept me humming and tapping my toes. And the overall joy that Pepper Basham exudes with her unique writing style and voice kept me engaged in a story I never wanted to leave. Simply put, this book is supercalifragilisticexpialidocious."
—Becca Kinzer, author of *Dear Henry, Love Edith*

"You won't want to put this book down! Pepper has a way of creating characters who are disarming and charismatic in all the best ways, while still reflecting our inner-selves. Her stories are charming and witty, and I've never laughed so much while reading! You'll walk away with more joy than you came with and a heart full of assurance and encouragement about the power of our heavenly Father's heart for your love story."

—Victoria Lynn, author of *The Chronicles of Elira*, *Bound*, and *London in the Dark*

AUTHENTICALLY, IZZY

"*Authentically, Izzy* is an absolutely adorable, charming, sweet romance that genuinely made me laugh out loud. A wonderful escape you're sure to fall in love with!"

—Courtney Walsh, *New York Times* bestselling author

"*Authentically, Izzy* is witty, endearing, and full of literary charm. Grab your favorite blanket and get ready to snuggle into this sweet book that will make you believe your dreams will find you."

—Jennifer Peel, *USA TODAY* bestselling author

"I can't remember the last time I've read such a truly wonderful romance. Basham's *Authentically, Izzy* was smart, funny, and adorably bookish. I smiled all the way through and finished it with my cheeks hurting. All the *Lord of the Rings* references were the cherry on top for me. Izzy and Brodie have officially overtaken Jane Eyre and Mr. Rochester as my favorite literary couple. You have to read this book!"

—Colleen Coble, *USA TODAY* bestselling author

"Pepper Basham is at her witty and charming best throughout the pages of this bookish delight! Fans of Katherine Reay will feel right at home between the covers of this epistolary treasure. Featuring a perfectly sprinkled smattering of Tolkien, *Authentically, Izzy* proves that the best reality sometimes begins with a little bit of fantasy. I hope you have as much fun with this one as I did!"

—Bethany Turner, bestselling author of *The Do-Over*

"In *Authentically, Izzy* author Pepper Basham has created a delightful cast of characters who quickly become your friends. Izzy beautifully captures the nerd in all of us who adores books and stories—sometimes more than real life. When a family member decides Izzy needs to live her own story, it sends Izzy on a fun romp that leads to a sweet, sigh-worthy romance. Grab this one today!"

—Jenny B. Jones, bestselling author of *There You'll Find Me* and *Sweet Right Here*

"This book was so much fun! I was drawn into the story from the beginning and loved the emails and text messages between Izzy and her cousins. What was even more fun was seeing how Izzy and Brodie's relationship grew from a few funny messages to a sweet relationship. I loved how Izzy grew throughout the story and learned to love herself and find her own strength and love. And her cousins were a hoot! Luke was my favorite cousin. His emails and text messages kept me in stitches. I highly recommend this fun and romantic book!"

—Amy Clipston, bestselling author of *The View from Coral Cove*

"You don't see enough epistolary novels these days, so the format of this being told almost entirely through emails appealed to me straightaway, and I wasn't disappointed! We follow librarian Izzy as she meets perfect-sounding bookshop owner Brodie online and wonders if he's too good to be true. Filled with the wonderfully warm cast of Izzy's family, and the swoon-worthy email exchanges with Brodie, I absolutely loved reading this book and felt like Izzy was a real friend rather than a book character! A book written by a book lover, about a book lover, for book lovers everywhere! I loved it! In fact, the only issue with this book is that my to-read list has grown exponentially from Izzy and Brodie's recommendations! It's a book lover's dream read!"

—Jaimie Admans, author of romantic comedies

Positively, Penelope

Other Books by Pepper Basham

CONTEMPORARY ROMANCE

Stand-Alone Novels

Authentically, Izzy

The Mistletoe Countess

Hope Between the Pages

The Red Ribbon

My Heart Belongs in the Blue Ridge: Laurel's Dream

Mitchell's Crossroads Series

A Twist of Faith

Charming the Troublemaker

A Match for Emma

A Pleasant Gap Romance Series

Just the Way You Are

When You Look at Me

Novellas

Second Impressions

Jane by the Book

Christmas in Mistletoe Square

HISTORICAL ROMANCE

Penned in Time Series

The Thorn Bearer

The Thorn Keeper

The Thorn Healer

Novellas

Facade

Between Stairs and Stardust

Positively, Penelope

a novel

PEPPER BASHAM

THOMAS NELSON
Since 1798

Published in Nashville, Tennessee, by Thomas Nelson. Thomas Nelson is a registered trademark of HarperCollins Christian Publishing, Inc.

Published in association with William K. Jensen Literary Agency, 119 Bampton Court, Eugene, Oregon 97404.

Maps by Lydia Basham.

Thomas Nelson titles may be purchased in bulk for educational, business, fundraising, or sales promotional use. For information, please email SpecialMarkets@ThomasNelson.com.

Scripture quotations are taken from the Holy Bible, New International Version®, NIV®. Copyright © 1973, 1978, 1984, 2011 by Biblica, Inc.® Used by permission of Zondervan. All rights reserved worldwide. www.zondervan.com. The "NIV" and "New International Version" are trademarks registered in the United States Patent and Trademark Office by Biblica, Inc.®

Publisher's Note: This novel is a work of fiction. Names, characters, places, and incidents are either products of the author's imagination or used fictitiously. All characters are fictional, and any similarity to people living or dead is purely coincidental.

Library of Congress Cataloging-in-Publication Data

Names: Basham, Pepper, author.
Title: Positively, Penelope: a novel / Pepper Basham.
Description: Nashville, Tennessee: Thomas Nelson, [2023] | Summary: "Told mostly through letters, texts, and email, this contemporary romance will charm its way into hearts as Penelope rescues a theater and discovers her true self in the process"—Provided by publisher.
Identifiers: LCCN 2023005306 (print) | LCCN 2023005307 (ebook) | ISBN 9780840715203 (paperback) | ISBN 9780840715340 (epub) | ISBN 9780840715388
Subjects: LCGFT: Romance fiction. | Novels.
Classification: LCC PS3602.A8459 P67 2023 (print) | LCC PS3602.A8459 (ebook) | DDC 813/.6—dc23/eng/20230210
LC record available at https://lccn.loc.gov/2023005306
LC ebook record available at https://lccn.loc.gov/2023005307

Printed in the United States of America

23 24 25 26 27 LBC 5 4 3 2 1

*To Dr. Broadway, who not only let me pick her
brain about all things theater but also encouraged
me with her excitement for this story.
Thank you, Kristin.*

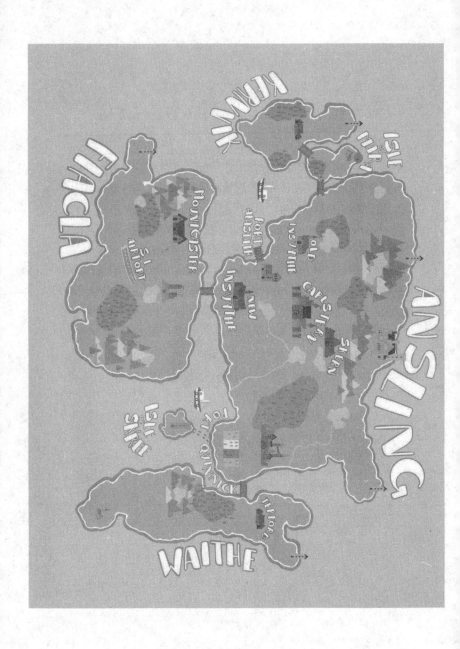

PROLOGUE

Dear Reader,

I've always lived by the adage that "a spoonful of sugar helps the medicine go down." In fact, I've found that leading with positivity is a great way to face any situation in life, even if my older siblings doubt my logic just because I like to dress in costume—I work in theater, it's a part of the job . . . most of the time. I mean, there are occasions when I dress in costume for fun, but who can really ignore a perfectly amazing pair of shoes and a vintage hat?

But being the baby of a somewhat well-adjusted family does not make one spoiled. Or wrong all the time, though the elder siblings may argue to the contrary.

In fact, being a faithful observer of older siblings could be said to make the youngest more prepared to avoid the possible missteps she's seen her siblings make.

But then again . . . it may not help at all.

Especially when said—quite attractive, somewhat witty, and definitely single—youngest sibling ends up on an island surrounded by strangers with an impossible job: to save a historic theater.

And of course, there's a little girl who very much needs a Mary Poppins in her life, or a Maria von Trapp.

And two very single men who may be vying for this particular sibling's heart.

Until they are not.

And a few Chris Pine references, but I'm not apologizing for that.

And some life-threatening escapades on a bicycle.

Plus a sea monster.

But don't let me frighten you away. It's a good story. Mostly. Except for the mole.

Penelope

PS: Sometimes a girl just wants to be rescued now and again. Why is that so wrong?

PPS: I do *not* sing too much. No matter what Luke says.

CHAPTER 1

From: GK
To: JA

Glad to know you'll be arriving in Skymar tomorrow. Most people prefer the larger island of Ansling, but I've always had a soft spot in my heart for Fiacla because of its preponderance of ruins, friendly natives, Troir Head with one of the oldest lighthouses on the islands, and the city of Mountcaster. But mostly because it's home. I'm not certain where you will be staying for your job here, but if you get a chance to visit Mountcaster, it is worth at least a two-day trip for the buildings alone. Fantastic craftsmanship and history, as well as some of the best seafood on the island. There are two cathedrals, a lovely park in the center of the city, and the extraordinary Avelynn Palace. My brother enjoys the hiking trails as well, but I'd rather be within the magical world of theater.

You may even get the chance to meet some of the online theater troupe, but the ones who wish to remain unseen will simply continue to hide behind their online pseudonyms. I've found the anonymity to be particularly beneficial when one wishes to avoid former romantic disasters. But those in the online theater group usually have in-person meetings throughout the year, so the choice is up to you. Continued anonymity, or enjoy the company of possible new friends (or enemies . . . you know how it is in theater. You never really can tell until auditions begin).

But since you and I have been privately corresponding for the last month, I feel fairly safe in saying I wouldn't mind meeting you in person. In the meantime, keep in mind that I'll be happy to give any guidance as you acclimate to the wonderful world of Skymar. But for now, I shall remain,

Your anonymous friend,
GK

. . . .

From: Penelope Edgewood
To: Izzy Edgewood, Luke Edgewood, Josephine Martin
Date: August 27
Subject: I'm here!!

My plane just touched down in Skymar! I'm so excited. And particularly grateful that I packed an equally adorable outfit in my carry-on bag since I have chocolate handprints on my blouse in two highly obvious places. It's a white blouse, which makes the prints all the more obvious, so my plan is to pull my sweater closed at the front while trying to hold my bags and navigate the airport until I can find a bathroom.

What an introduction to Skymar! But the views out the window are so lovely. I can't believe I have over three months to intern with one of the most historic theaters on the island! Beginning of December may sound very far away, but I'm sure it will come much too quickly!

The emails from Matt Gray, the business manager of the theater, haven't given a whole lot away on how I can help the marketing team at The Darling House, and their online presence doesn't really tell me much either because . . . it's practically nonexistent (which may tell me all I need to know about how to help), but from my rather extensive online search, they have an incredibly rich history of high-quality plays and musicals!

Anyway, we are disembarking, so I'll let you guys know more later.

One of the other managers of the theater is supposed to meet me at the airport. I'm guessing it's going to be the one who is more of the PR person, Alec Gray. His photo *is* on the website and he's very dashing! I think he and Matt must be related. There are several references to "the Gray Brothers" on the website . . . if you very carefully read the fine print on the very bottom of the Contact Us page. Anyway, Alec Gray looks like Chris Pine. I'm including the website link for you to see for yourself.

Love,
Penelope

PS: I wonder how different the island of Fiacla is from the other Skymarian Islands!

PPS: Brodie is coming to see me on Saturday! Did I tell you that? Oh, Izzy! I'm so glad you'll be here in a few months! I'm sure he'd much rather see you than me!

PPPS: Do you think "the Gray Brothers" sounds like a pair of gangsters or am I allowing my recent viewing of *West Side Story* to influence me?

. . . .

From: Izzy Edgewood
To: Penelope Edgewood, Luke Edgewood, Josephine Martin
Date: August 27
Subject: Re: I'm here!!

Maybe I'm asking the obvious, but . . . why do you have chocolate handprints on two "obvious" places on your blouse?

I'm not sure why, but "the Gray Brothers" sounds so much more like a group of gangsters than Brodie's family at Sutherland's Books ever did. And I hope someone is meeting you! Please say you're not alone, Penelope!

Concerned,
Izzy

PS: Survive for a few days, cousin! Please? Then Brodie can rescue you from gangsters in person on Saturday.

PPS: Any movie/musical you watch influences you, Penelope. Recall *Sweeney Todd* and how long it took you to go to the hairdresser after that.

· ·

From: Luke Edgewood
To: Penelope Edgewood, Izzy Edgewood, Josephine Martin
Date: August 27
Subject: Re: I'm here!!

I'm just wondering why someone would waste perfectly good chocolate. Unless Skymarian chocolate isn't so great? Oh wait, this was airplane chocolate. It all makes sense now.

Luke

PS: *Sweeney Todd* was actually a musical I liked. But not the singing parts.

· ·

From: Penelope Edgewood
To: Izzy Edgewood, Luke Edgewood, Josephine Martin

Date: August 27
Subject: Re: I'm here!!

I just got off the plane and wanted to send a quick response about the chocolate fiasco. It really was nothing. A mother of two small children was having a difficult time managing the baby during the flight and her three-year-old started crying due to the turbulence, so I offered to help. Needless to say, as the mother was handing the three-year-old over to me, I didn't realize he had chocolate-covered fingers, and then we hit turbulence, he fell forward, and I can only assume he grabbed onto the most obvious and available parts of me. My squeal caused the flight attendant to come running in our direction, but by the time she arrived, I'd calmed the little guy down with a fun spinning toy I pulled from my Mary Poppins bag. (I did NOT pull out my stuffed otter. Chocolate does not wash off of him as easily as the spinning toy.)

Penelope

PS: Izzy, you didn't tell me how lovely the airport is here in Skymar. Except the playground. For some reason there is a giant toy sea monster in there for children to ride. Why would they make something like that? Don't they know they are contributing to children's nightmares? I avoided eye contact with it.

PPS: I refuse to respond to the *Sweeney Todd* reference no matter how much I enjoy the theatrics of Johnny Depp and Helena Bonham Carter.

• •

From: Luke Edgewood
To: Penelope Edgewood, Izzy Edgewood, Josephine Martin

Date: August 27

Subject: Re: I'm here!!

I bet one of the gangster brothers could protect you from the fake sea monster.

Luke

PS: Or you could pull a sword from your Mary Poppins bag.

Text from Luke to Izzy: If Penny-girl ever questions whether I love her, please remind her that I actually respond to her ridiculous emails.

Izzy: I'm so glad you do! It reassures me that your dear little sister really DID write what she wrote. I'm not going crazy.

Luke: Says the woman who is packing up her life in a few months and moving to a foreign country that has five months of winter.

Izzy: You're just jealous.

Luke: Iz, you can have Brodie. He wears too many sweater vests for me.

Izzy: My boyfriend would not trade me, even if you can speak Klingon. I'm a much better snuggler than you. I was talking about you being jealous of the winters. You love winter.

• •

From: Izzy Edgewood

To: Penelope Edgewood, Luke Edgewood, Josephine Martin

Date: August 27

Subject: Re: I'm here!!

Penelope,

It's a good thing the sea monster is safely fake so you don't have to worry about him. Besides, it's just some fun thing Skymar uses for marketing to the tourists. I can't remember where that particular sea monster is featured most, but there's a place somewhere on Ansling where he supposedly makes his appearance.

And I will forever be amazed at what you carry in that magical bag of yours. Why on earth would you have a spinning toy?

BTW, Penelope, are any of the new friends you've made through that online Skymarian Theater Troupe going to meet up with you while you're there? Since you've been emailing them for a few months, maybe it will be an easy way to make new friends.

Izzy

Text from Luke to Izzy: Iz, Penelope can make friends with a tree. By the end of the day, she'll probably have the gangsters joining her in a musical rendition of something with sparkles and fairies, and the sea monster asking to wear that crown she carries around in her bag all the time. I don't try to make sense of it because there is no sense to be made.

- -

From: Penelope Edgewood
To: Izzy Edgewood, Luke Edgewood, Josephine Martin
Date: August 27
Subject: An underappreciated Mary Poppins rescue

Oh dear! I have so much to tell and most of it is very good. Well, part of it. The dimples part. And the scenery, but as you three know, I do try my best to make rainbows out of rain!

Do you remember how Grandma Edgewood always used to say that I had a remarkable gift of making a first impression? (Now that I think about it, I'm not sure whether she meant that as a positive thing.)

Anyway, I gathered my bags and made it through customs, and apart from one of the security workers mistaking my curling iron for a weapon and another one insisting on checking my shoulders (since they beeped as I went through the security scanner), all was well. I'm not quite certain how shoulders can be dangerous for airport security, but I've seen dance moves where the shoulders give off risky vibes. (*Grease*, *Moulin Rouge!*, to name two.)

It was very crowded as I searched the waiting area for Mr. Gray. Of course, I expected some sort of colorful banner with my name in neon but didn't see anything to give me a clue to someone waiting for me. Plus, I couldn't understand half of what the people around me were saying. As you can imagine, I'd already made out my game plan if no one arrived to pick me up. I'd even printed it out in case Wi-Fi was disabled due to some horrible situation involving whatever island problems can disable Wi-Fi. So, with bags in hand, I marched toward the "dros" and buses—which is taxis and buses, BTW. (I downloaded Translate Now to my phone and the app actually has Caedric!)

Before I'd even made it to the taxis, some man who looked a little like Doc What's-His-Name from *Back to the Future* approached me. I think my eyes must have gotten really wide, but not because I was afraid of him; it's just he wore a constant look of surprise and you all know how I sometimes imitate other people's facial expressions without knowing it. Anyway, he asked if I'd rather take the ferry to the main island instead of a taxi because "it's much more scenic," but I quickly told him I planned to stay on Fiacla instead of going to Ansling right away. (There was no way I was going to tell a complete stranger that I'm petrified of boats!) But I feel it was very providential that I stopped to talk to this ferryman because I might not have heard it otherwise.

Someone was crying, and not just anyone! A child. I'm particularly sensitive to crying children, as you all will remember, since I was so good at crying myself. As the youngest in the family, I ended up getting the brunt of the teasing, not that I'm pointing fingers or anything. (*Luke.*)

Not too far away sat a little girl crying. She was the most adorable creature. Golden curls in two pigtails, a checked jumper, and the most fantastic patent leather shoes known to man . . . er . . . woman. Mother would have adored them. I immediately thought of Shirley Temple. At any rate, I tugged my cloche hat more tightly on my head, took a firm hold of my Mary Poppins bag, grabbed my suitcase, and dashed toward the little damsel. (I instinctively knew she needed help. I've always been in tune with children.)

When I sat down beside her, I immediately pulled my Peter Pan handkerchief from my bag—you know, the one with Tinker Bell on it—and offered it to her. She stared at it long enough to stop crying and then took it, but not before shooting me a confused look. Maybe she'd never seen such an excellent handkerchief.

Within one minute, I found out she had lost her father in the crowd, dropped her milkshake on the floor, and then run away to hide in utter shame from not only the loss of the milkshake but the chocolate stain now donning her jumper. I feel certain that she is my spirit animal.

I offered her a peppermint and asked whether I could help her find her dad. Her face immediately brightened into double dimples! Can you believe it? And she told me that her name was Iris. After I did a quick check on my phone for any shop within the airport that sold milkshakes, Iris took my hand and we started walking through the airport toward Skremtik, which evidently means something ice cream-y.

Now here's the part where the villain shows up. Though he mistakenly thought I was the villain. Ridiculous, really. What villains wear red cloche hats and Nine West pumps? A female villain would definitely be in Valentino or something expensive like that. We'd barely made it to the food court (or whatever they call it in Skymar) when someone grabbed me by the arm and nearly sent me teetering into some fish shop with the logo of a hat-wearing squid. I expected some older man with a grumpy brow and a voice like he'd chewed on glass, but instead I came face-to-face with a man, probably in his late twenties-ish, who looked a lot like that man Izzy likes to stare at in the movie *Austenland*. You know? The one who plays the Darcy character. He had the grumpy countenance for certain, and there was a bit of a wave to his brownish hair.

Do you remember that character, Izzy? Not the captain or the barn guy. The other one.

Penelope

PS: The fish at the squid place was very tasty.

PPS: GK from the Skymarian Theater Troupe has sent me some good notes but I'm not sure I'd call her a friend just yet.

I don't even know her real name. Only the initials *GK*, as the whole online group has a strict rule about sharing real names in the forum—a rule I appreciate. No real names and no real photos. Though if they choose to forsake anonymity, there are opportunities to meet in person too. I gladly chose the initials JA. Not for Jane Austen, as you may think, Izzy, but for the undeniably charming and delightful Julie Andrews.

. . . .

From: Izzy Edgewood
To: Penelope Edgewood, Luke Edgewood
Date: August 27
Subject: Re: An underappreciated Mary Poppins rescue

Penelope,

I love you to pieces but would you PLEASE finish the story? You left us with the idea of a man accosting you as you helped an adorable little girl through the Skymarian airport. Do you realize that you have a tendency to not finish your stories?

Izzy

PS: I'm leaving Josephine off this thread because I really don't want to alarm her with my obvious concern for your SAFETY!

PPS: The character in the movie's name is Henry Nobley. His name is Henry in the book too. The book is better, as most books are, but the movie provides some great visual inspiration, a.k.a. JJ Feild and Ricky Whittle.

. . . .

From: Luke Edgewood
To: Izzy Edgewood, Penelope Edgewood

Date: August 27
Subject: Re: An underappreciated Mary Poppins rescue

Penny-girl,

Brothers tease sisters. And I'm pretty sure I didn't tease you beyond what any other self-respecting older brother would do. You had a tendency toward crying no matter what happened. Most of the time I didn't have to say anything.

Besides, I think you must have enjoyed crying since, as I recall, you took photos of yourself crying so you could see if you were a "pretty crier."

How long ago was that? I can't remember. Last year?

Izzy, I'm more worried about the stranger's safety than Penelope's. My foot has been on the heel-side of Penelope's fancy shoes. If she's really mad, the guy won't be able to walk without a limp for a week. And of course, she has the sword in her Mary Poppins bag. She's fine.

Luke

PS: I'll refrain from stating why you are so in tune with children.

PPS: Didn't you go on a cruise with Mom a few years ago? I recall you loved it. Wasn't that on a boat?

Text from Penelope to Luke: Boats and ships are not the same thing. Cruise ships are like little floating cities. If you want to look at the water you can, but for all intents and purposes, you don't even have to know you're floating and still have a marvelous time.

Luke: You're on a "floating city," which pretty much means . . . boat. You're technically still floating. In fact, the whole island you're on right now could be considered a really big boat.

Penelope: No. Boats mean that you are right next to the water and can look down into the depths without knowing exactly what is going to be staring back at you. There's very little distance. It's much easier for a sea monster to sink a boat.

Luke: I have no response to that logic. At all. Probably ever.

From: Josephine Martin
To: Penelope Edgewood, Izzy Edgewood, Luke Edgewood
Date: August 28
Subject: Re: I'm here!!

Penelope,

I'm so glad your visit has started off relatively well, except for the airport fiasco and the chocolate blouse. Do be careful of eating at airports. I've had several experiences with those eateries that left very unpleasant results. And being in a foreign place only makes the negative possibilities greater in every way. You know that you can always come home if things turn out to be less than you were hoping.

I saw Jacqueline Morrow Crenshaw in town yesterday and she was asking about you. I told her you'd graduated and what you were doing in Skymar with the theater. She was incredibly interested, Penelope, because she is looking for a younger, passionate person to be the executive director for the reopening of the old Ashby Theater! You know, after her husband died, she gave up on the productions and let the building fall into disrepair, but she's hired Luke to help renovate it and is looking for "young blood" to revitalize the love of arts in the Ransom community.

Do you realize how perfect this is? Ransom is only a half hour away from Mt. Airy, Penelope! You could have your dream of running your own theater! And be close to home while doing so! I gave Jackie your email address and told her you would be ecstatic about her contacting you. After all, she did start you on your theatrical career all those years ago.

By the way, I never realized how wonderful it is to run errands and spend long minutes talking to people you meet in normal places, like the grocery store or the bank. I had an entire hour on my own while Izzy watched the twins. It was marvelous . . . until I realized the odd spoiled-milk smell was not from the diaper bag but was indeed from a spot on the shoulder of my blouse.

I don't think I'll ever smell fresh air again. The twins are two months old and I can't remember what anything smells like without a hint of spoiled milk tainting it. Mother tells me I'll be able to smell fresh and clean again, but I have my doubts.

Anyway, don't be surprised if you receive an email from her very soon. As she said, you were one of the best stage assistants and performers she'd ever had come through Ashby's. It sounds very much like a sure thing to me.

Love,
Josephine

· ·

From: Penelope Edgewood
To: Izzy Edgewood, Luke Edgewood

Date: August 28

Subject: Re: An underappreciated Mary Poppins rescue

Do I really stop in the middle of a story? Well, I don't think it's something I commonly do, but with all the excitement, how can you blame me? Let me attempt to summarize the full experience so that you will know that Iris, the grumpy stranger, and I all survived, even if the grumpy stranger continues to be . . . grumpy.

I turned to the Henry Nobley–looking man and he had the nerve to accuse me of trying to kidnap his daughter! Kidnap! I was carrying a Mary Poppins bag! How could he even think such a thing? Mary Poppins may offer tremendous adventures to children, but she doesn't kidnap them! After a rather intense conversation where I might have used unladylike language and even threatened him with my nail file, Iris intervened with the full story and the stranger growled out an apology and offered to buy my lunch (thus the comment about the squid shop).

You will not believe it, but the grumpy stranger is Matt Gray, the business manager / accountant of The Darling House (clearly not Alec Gray, the PREFERRED option, I'm sure). Mr. Gray didn't seem in a mood to have a polite conversation. In fact, he reverted to more grunts and grumbles than words while Iris and I enjoyed a delightful discussion about Disney princesses. (I asked her how she spoke English so clearly and fluently, and her grumpy father informed me the schools in Skymar begin English-speaking classes at the start of their education.) Anyway, Mr. Gray didn't like princesses and absolutely refused to allow Iris to wear the princess hat I'd brought with me, saying (and I can't even believe this), "Don't fill my daughter's head with fluff and nonsense." After which he continued to lecture me on the harm of teaching girls about fairy-tale romances, glass slippers, and happily ever afters!

If I could have found my voice, I would have given him a severe tongue-lashing on the not so happily ever after of certain fairy-tale villains, but I didn't want to frighten Iris. No wonder the little girl was crying! Besides being lost in an airport, her grumpy father had stolen magic from her childhood. No one had read *Cinderella* to her! Ever! Can you imagine? And she is seven years old!

Well, I can tell you one thing for certain—there is someone in her life for the next few months who will be happy to introduce her to all sorts of fairy-tale "fluff and nonsense." Her father could use a bit of it too. No wonder the theater suffers from a gloomy online presence and a foreboding financial future. You take away the wonder of childhood in any place and there's an immediate loss of something beautiful. Especially in a theater!

The Darling House needs some childish magic, and I'm just the woman to bring it. A self-appointed joy-bringer. What could go wrong with a good-hearted start like that?

Positively,
Penelope

PS: "Gray" certainly matches the overall outlook of SOME people I met today!

PPS: At least Grumpy Gray has set me up in a charming apartment. The building looks like it used to be a garden house for a nearby estate. They call it a *cottage*. I'm sending photos. Do you see the tower? It's the main BEDROOM!!!! I am a princess!!!!

• •

From: Izzy Edgewood
To: Penelope Edgewood, Luke Edgewood

Date: August 28
Subject: The rest of the story?

Penelope,

I'm assuming there was a part to your story where you actually got into a car and rode to your cottage. Are you sure you want to start a professional relationship with a personal objective to sprinkle fairy dust into the life of a man who may not respond positively to your brand of joy?

I am ALL for bringing magic to a place. You'll remember that's how I felt about Brodie's family's bookshop when I arrived in Skymar, but Brodie was *willing*. Your Mr. Gray doesn't seem to give off those vibes . . . unless you actually FINISH your story and he improves upon better acquaintance.

I feel there is no need for me to remind you about the many literary examples of such a change.

Izzy

PS: Your place is the cutest gardener's cottage I have ever seen. Are you staying near the city or in a suburb? (See? These answers probably would have come out if you'd given the rest of the story.)

Text from Luke to Penelope: How can you expect anyone with the last name Gray to be a cheery sort of person? This is called foreshadowing.

Luke: PS: Is it wrong if I am rooting for Grumpy Gray?

CHAPTER 2

Skymarian Theater Troupe •

From: HJ
To: JA

Happy to hear you've arrived in Skymar, JA. Several of my friends and I are meeting at one of the local pubs tonight. I know we maintain anonymity online, but if you want to have some real fun, PM me. Acting is only one of my many talents.

From: GK
To: JA

JA, whatever you do, don't take HJ up on the offer. I know who he is and he's not to be trusted, despite the fact that his initials are based on one of my favorite modern actors. And never agree to watch his cat. There are things that keep people up at night. His cat is one of them.

• •

From: Penelope Edgewood
To: Izzy Edgewood, Luke Edgewood, Josephine Martin
Date: August 29
Subject: Introduction to Fiacla

I woke up to a beautiful day in Skymar, and it fueled my optimism for all the possibilities. As you can imagine, it took a long time to go to sleep last night. I had to write in my journal, of course, and then take more photos, and then begin a list of things I want to see during the first week while in Fiacla. Today is a free day for me to get settled and so I'm sending a quick message to you all to let you know all is well, I'm safe in my princess cottage, and I have plans to travel into the nearby village (which I believe is called Kelna) and explore.

I'm going to see if I can sneak over to the theater and scout it out before my official intro tomorrow. Doesn't that sound like something a spy would do?

Penelope

PS: I can see a mansion from my bedroom window. What if royalty lives there and I happen to meet the heir to the Skymarian throne as he's driving by on his motorcycle with his leather jacket and he decides I'm the woman to share his title and his future?

PPS: Redheaded royalty can be pretty popular, I hear.

Skymarian Theater Troupe ●

From: JA
To: GK

Thanks for the warning. He definitely gave off a few of the jerk vibes from previous emails on the loop, so I really appreciate you confirming my initial thoughts. Why can't men be like the classics? You know what I mean? The good ones? Even if they stumble around wide-eyed like Cary Grant in *Arsenic and Old Lace,* or are a little desperate and tricky like Monty from *A Gentleman's Guide to Love and Murder,* there's something appealing about a man in a fedora with a bit of class for backbone. Don't you think? Though to be perfectly candid, I do wish for a man to have actual conversations with. Most of the guys I've dated treat me as if I don't have a brain at all. Just because I care about my appearance and give off a usually joyful disposition, why do they automatically think I'm an "easy" conquest or don't know how to tie my own shoes? (BTW, I'm an expert shoe tie-er. I wear oxfords.)

Happiness does not equal stupidity. (I bring Maria von Trapp to your attention as exhibit A . . . and, well, Julie Andrews overall.)

Sure, I'm usually pretty happy and content, but I've not always been this way. Kids can be pretty mean to stutterers. And just because I'm not desperately looking for Mr. Right doesn't mean I'm not interested in finding him. I have a list for just that occasion, too, but it all boils down to finding someone who listens and laughs and loves well. If he sang and danced and occasionally used words like "darling" and "my dear," I wouldn't mind either. A fedora and/ or bow tie might be nice too.

Anyway, sorry for the long note. I'm off to explore! Have a wonderful day!

. . . .

From: Luke Edgewood
To: Penelope Edgewood, Izzy Edgewood, Josephine Martin
Date: August 29
Subject: Re: Introduction to Fiacla

Penny-girl,

Why does your "prince" sound like he just stepped out of *Grease*? And why am I sick to my stomach at the fact that I actually know what the guy from *Grease* looks like?

Sisters!

It's time to watch all five Rambo movies and grill steak.

Luke

From: Izzy Edgewood
To: Luke Edgewood, Penelope Edgewood, Josephine Martin
Date: August 29
Subject: Re: Introduction to Fiacla

Luke,

Noooo!! Please, not the Rambo movies. You'll be quoting them for weeks and resort to wearing a headband and making strange upper-lip movements.

On Rambo strike,
Izzy

From: Luke Edgewood
To: Izzy Edgewood, Penelope Edgewood, Josephine Martin
Date: August 29
Subject: Re: Introduction to Fiacla

Desperate times call for desperate measures . . . and a survival knife.

"Whatever possessed God in heaven to make a man like Rambo?" For men who have sisters. That's what.

Luke

From: Penelope Edgewood
To: Luke Edgewood, Izzy Edgewood, Josephine Martin
Date: August 30
Subject: Re: Introduction to Fiacla

I can't respond at length right now because I'm currently waiting in line at a pastry shop. It's the cutest place ever, with rose and gold themes. Izzy, you would adore it. And the smells? Delightful. I'm grabbing a quick snack before I walk from here down a footpath to a place called Elowyn's Tower. AHHH!!

Penelope

PS: Luke, I'm certain God made women like the illustrious Audrey Hepburn to combat flannel-wearing woodsmen like you.

PPS: There was a note on my kitchen table this morning that suggested I ride a bicycle into town, and said bicycle was waiting outside the cottage. Despite the loveliness of the pink, vintage, basket-donned bicycle, as you all know, I can't ride one and my eyes started watering at the thought of trying to ride one again. Therefore, I suppose someone is going to have to provide another means of transportation because bicycles and I have never worked, though I've had this lifelong dream of riding one down a lane with my skirt flapping in the breeze like Julie Andrews does in *The Sound of Music*. Sigh. I suppose some dreams will never be realized.

Text from Luke to Penelope: Lest you forget, sister dear, a
  flannel-wearing woodsman saved Red Riding Hood and he
  likely used a survival knife to do so. Not to mention very real
  men like Daniel Boone and Davy Crockett likely wore more
  rugged apparel (how's that for using your fancy lingo?).
Luke: Also, we woodsmen have our uses, and sometimes we
  kill a bear when we're only three and then later become
  a congressman. Are these two things related? Maybe
  or maybe not. But I bet the bear was the least of Davy's
  problems after becoming a congressman.

Penelope: When I think "flannel-wearing woodsman"
in regard to you, my thoughts go more toward Jed
Clampett or one of the Darling boys from *The Andy
Griffith Show*. They seem more your speed. *smiling
sweetly and eating a chocolate croissant ruthlessly*

Luke: "Don't push it, or I'll give you a war you won't believe."

Penelope: Stop with the *Rambo* quotes or I'll start quoting
Legally Blonde.

Penelope: BTW, look at this amazing view from Elowyn's
Tower! This place truly is like stepping into a magical
land! "Second star to the right, and straight on till
morning" stuff!

Luke: The view is great. Was the quote from *Star Wars*?

Penelope: Ugh. You are such a Neanderthal sometimes!

· ·

From: Penelope Edgewood
To: Luke Edgewood, Izzy Edgewood, Josephine Martin
Date: August 30
Subject: An adventure and a mystery

So, after visiting Kelna and Elowyn's Tower (photos attached),
one of the natives at the cutest little consignment shop in the
world suggested I travel to the largest city on Fiacla. Mountcaster
is its name *and* it's where I'll be working at The Darling House
(my online contact suggests Mountcaster too!). When I found out
that it was only a fifteen-minute drive, I paid a taxi and decided
to get a first glimpse.

In anticipation of a stellar adventure, I wore my navy detective
hat like the one Bonita Granville wore in the 1930s Nancy Drew
series and made sure to take my camera for photos instead of
only my phone. I still can't get over how much this place looks

make-believe. The ocean cliffs, the stone houses, the narrow lanes, and the rolling green hills, with enough mountains in the distance to make me miss home! I keep looking for fairies poking out from behind one of the picturesque stone walls or a mermaid splashing up on the rocks at the sea's edge. Oh my!

I don't think the GPS is accurate around here, BTW. My taxi driver got me to Mountcaster much faster than GPS would suggest, and he didn't join me in singing "Part of Your World" once. I wasn't singing it loudly, of course, but he seemed to understand the music because he began shaking his head very slowly in rhythm to the song.

Anyway, I got to spend only a few hours exploring Mountcaster before returning to my little cottage for the night, but in the process I had one job offer, took a sneak peek at The Darling House (you guys, it's like one of those old buildings that needs lots of work but you can feel the personality oozing from the walls like magic), received an unsolicited marriage proposal from a mime, and almost adopted a dog.

I'm exhausted but deliriously thrilled about tomorrow. I just had dinner at this wonderful Italian restaurant called Rosemary & Thyme and am using their Wi-Fi to message you while I await my taxi—oh, but here it is. I'll tell you more later.

Penelope

PS: There's a newer theater in town called Emblem Studios. They have acting and dancing lessons, but I don't think I'd want to work there even if they offered lots more than I'm making for the internship. Something about the guy with the sinister eyes gave me chills, no matter how expensive his suit was.

PPS: He'd look great in a fedora, though. Very gangster-ish.

From: Luke Edgewood
To: Penelope Edgewood, Izzy Edgewood, Josephine Martin
Date: August 30
Subject: Re: An adventure and a mystery

Penny-girl,

Do you ever reread your emails and think how your family may respond to some of your information . . . or lack of information? I'm just curious.

Luke

PS: If a house is oozing anything, I'd be concerned.

PPS: The mime makes sense, but very quietly.

From: Izzy Edgewood
To: Penelope Edgewood, Luke Edgewood, Josephine Martin
Date: August 30
Subject: Re: An adventure and a mystery

Penelope,

As you well know, I am a big proponent of stories. I particularly like them when they're complete. Would you be a dear and FINISH THE STORY? What sort of job were you offered upon meeting someone for the first time in a foreign country? (I can think of three possibilities and none of them are complimentary to you.)

And . . . a mime? What is that about? Oh gracious, maybe I should find a way to get over to Skymar before December so I can ensure your survival, or at the very least find out what is going on with the mime, the dog, and the sinister mister. (Good grief, why does this sound like a really strange movie by some director with an unpronounceable last name?)

BTW, the website for The Darling House IS ancient and Emblem Studios is definitely not. Wow, how did you find a creepy guy in a suit from that place? It looks like a high-end, monochrome glass house. Oh wait, that's probably the perfect place for a creepy guy in a suit. I've read my fiction and seen enough modern movies!

Izzy

PS: I've sent Brodie your address so he can come check on you if I don't hear from you within two hours.

PPS: I always get concerned when you wear that hat.

• •

From: Penelope Edgewood
To: Luke Edgewood, Izzy Edgewood, Josephine Martin
Date: August 30
Subject: Re: An adventure and a mystery

The only redeeming quality of Matt Gray is his daughter! I don't know what the man was doing outside my cottage when I showed up, but he seemed annoyed that I had kindly left the bicycle behind. I think he actually expects me to ride it to work on pretty days. His first response was, "It's barely a fifteen-minute ride along the countryside. An excellent way to start and end the day." I'm sure he's joking, although he doesn't seem the joking sort. In fact, the only time he smiled the whole drive from the airport to my cottage yesterday was when he spoke to Iris. It was a nice smile but completely disappeared when he looked at me. I can't understand why. I'd worn my beret. Who frowns at a lovely lavender beret? Maybe he doesn't like the French or lavender.

He seemed utterly surprised that I'd gone into Mountcaster when I was "supposed" to be recovering from jet lag. THEN he didn't believe me when I said I didn't have jet lag, or at least I interpreted his wrinkle-lipped scowl to mean the same thing. The only saving grace was that Iris was there, so as Grumpy Gray took a phone call, Iris and I made crowns out of the lovely pink flowers in the garden near the cottage. The pink crown looked perfect among her soft, golden curls, and even her grouchy father seemed to soften for a split second of admiration before encouraging Iris to move toward her bicycle so they could ride home. Who knows where they live if he's encouraging a complete stranger to ride fifteen minutes into town every day! Just for spite, I almost told him about my job offer but decided he didn't deserve to know.

At any rate, I was in Emblem's lobby looking at their framed production posters on the walls (they've done a lot in their four years as a studio), and a woman in a perfect pinstripe pantsuit came up to me and asked whether she could help me. She was nice in a reserved sort of way. And I'd wager she has an important position because of the size of her heels. Anyway, she seemed very interested in why I was in Skymar and then returned to her desk to answer her phone. A few minutes later a man named Niles, or something like that, approached me in the lobby, asked a few questions, and then made some comments like, "The Darling House has a much too old-fashioned mindset to really take your ideas into account. We appreciate innovation and insight here at Emblem and are always looking for individuals with creativity, spunk, and ingenuity." Then he proceeded to outright ask me if I'd be interested in transferring my internship to Emblem . . . with a sizable increase in salary.

Well, I smiled, declined his offer, and left the building. As you all well know, I'm loyal to a fault, even if it means I'll have to wait a little longer before I completely update my wardrobe to match everything to Audrey Hepburn. I rushed out of Emblem so fast I ran headfirst into a street mime, or at least that's what I thought he was because he was dressed in all black and held a sign that read "Will You Marry Me?" He didn't say a thing, just stared at me, so I sweetly declined. He grinned—you know, that tight smile like he wanted to say something but clearly couldn't—then he ran up the street to catch a crowd of people all dressed as if they were going to a party. They must have been glad to see him, because there was a great shout of happiness when he reached them and some woman flung herself into his arms. I'm so glad he's not alone.

A very adorable dog followed me to the restaurant and then to my taxi. He's a lovely mix of some sort of shepherd and I'm already calling him Jack. Maybe I'll see him again tomorrow and discover whether he has an owner. The sweet thing seemed to be wandering aimlessly so, of course, I gave him my leftover chicken parmesan before getting into my taxi.

BTW, I'm going to do a bit of research tonight on Emblem Studios. Mr. Gray said he'd provide me a packet on The Darling House's history tomorrow during my orientation, so I have high hopes the information will spur my creativity. I didn't have time to visit the inside of The Darling House before returning to the cottage—not with the job offer, dog, and delicious Italian dinner. So I will tomorrow, and to quote *Annie*, "it's only a day away."

Penelope

PS: I quietly taught Iris the song "A Dream Is a Wish Your Heart Makes" while we were braiding flower crowns. She has a lovely voice, even with that tiny lisp. I also told her the story of Rapunzel. She particularly liked the idea of a horse with an extreme personality.

· ·

From: mgraydarlinghouse
To: Penelope Edgewood
Date: August 30
Subject: Tomorrow

Miss Edgewood,

I will come around with my car to collect you at the cottage at half past seven in the morning. We will take Iris to school first and then continue to the theater. After work on Thursday, please reserve some time for us at your cottage. Iris is adamant about teaching you to ride your bicycle and, as she is rarely adamant about things, I am inclined to allow her this opportunity if you are amenable to it.

In response to your earlier question, which I feel I did not answer to your satisfaction, and after a brief online search, I have discovered our usual style of dress at The Darling House is business casual, unless there is some sort of special occasion or workday, at which time we would adjust accordingly. Hats are not frowned upon but are not commonly worn by most of the staff except in winter or at the seaside. I have no opinion on shoes but trust you to wear what will be most comfortable for your occupations of the day.

Some people bring their lunches, some order in, and others visit nearby bistros, cafés, or restaurants during their lunchtimes.

Mrs. Lennox, our administrative assistant, will be happy to provide you with recommendations during your orientation tomorrow; however, tomorrow you will have lunch with me and my grandfather, Lewis Gray, who retains ownership and oversight of the theater.

You will also have the opportunity to meet my sister, Gwynn, on Friday, and my brother, Alec, in a few days once he returns from a business trip.

Your essay regarding marketing and theater, along with your sterling references, secured your position here, and we look forward to seeing how your brand of vitality will bring life back into the dusty corners of our beloved theater.

Sincerely,
M. Gray

CHAPTER 3

Skymarian Theater Troupe ·

From: FA
To: Skymarian Theater Troupe

Hi, all! It's time for the monthly Fiacla group meetup. As usual, we will offer a somewhat central location so that no one has a terribly long drive from across the island. I know some of you wish to remain anonymous and that is fine, but for those who are interested in some in-person time with other theater lads and lasses, we'll be meeting at Orkney's in Mountcaster Friday next at eight in the evening.

If you're involved in a fall production or are teaching any courses, please feel free to share your information in the loop or bring it with you on Friday. And welcome to any newbies. I think JA is our only one, so welcome, JA.

From: JA
To: GK

I adored Mountcaster! Thank you for recommending it. I went yesterday for a very quick visit but hope to have more time outside of work this upcoming weekend to explore a little more. Everything holds an old-world charm. It's like I've truly stepped into *The Sound of Music* with these beautiful buildings and occasional spires shooting into the sky, a church bell ringing in the distance, a few cobbled streets, and all of it surrounded by rugged mountains along one side. It's very difficult not to stop and stare on a regular basis. Do you ever feel like you want to get a Vespa scooter and drive through the streets like Audrey Hepburn in *Roman Holiday*? Oh, I wish I'd packed my outfit that matches hers in the movie!

I feel certain I frightened a few people with my amount of staring . . . and perhaps with an excited squeal or two. The fountain in the center of town is magical. It reminds me of one of my favorite parks back home in a town near where I grew up. The town's called Ransom and it has a fountain in the middle of the square too. Not as grand as the one in Mountcaster, nor as old, but wonderfully quaint.

I think I'll attend the theater troupe's get-together in two Fridays. Have you ever been? I would love to make new friends, especially of the "dramatic" variety. I start my job this morning and am sure I'll make some new friends there as well, but I would love some outside of work, you know? It's much safer to bemoan the ills of a job to outsiders than, very unwisely, share those misgivings within the ranks. Especially since I will be a new hire and have no allegiances yet.

Curiously, do you think hats are out of fashion in Mountcaster, or Fiacla in general?

. . . .

From: Penelope Edgewood
To: Izzy Edgewood, Luke Edgewood, Josephine Martin
Date: August 31
Subject: The Darling House

Izzy,

You know that movie you showed me about a creepy manor house? I can't remember what it was called, but there was something important about a key and Colin Firth. Anyway, The Darling House gives off a little of the creepy-manor-house vibe just because it has so many unused spaces. And a lot of old

lighting. But there are SUCH good bones there. Vintage style
with an almost Victorian look. Lots of embossed fixtures and an
ornate ceiling in the lobby. I'm sending a photo.

Okay, I'm going to try to give a FULL story while I'm on my break.
I have lunch with Mr. Gray and his grandfather in ten minutes, so
I'll make it snappy. From what I understand, The Darling House
is the oldest existing theater on Fiacla and one of the three
oldest in Skymar. Isn't that wonderful? You all know how much I
love old things. However, this type of old thing is more "sad and
desolate" than "classy and square-toed shoes." There are lots of
dark hallways that lead to rooms "we haven't used in over five
years" or storage closets that "haven't been opened in a long
time." Evidently, the owner of the theater, Mr. Lewis Clarkson
Gray, lost his beloved wife almost five years ago after having
lost his only daughter the year before. His wife had inherited the
theater from her grandfather, the original owner and builder
of the place. The reason he built it is wonderful and I will share
more later when I have a chance. As soon as I learned about it, I
knew I belonged here for this very moment.

The theater used to have four performances a season, performed
mostly by a mixture of community-theater actors, children's
theater, and touring companies (which came twice a year),
but their pattern over the past few years has been fewer
productions that are more sporadic. They don't even have a solid
performance schedule, which doesn't help with advertising or
ticket sales. Also, The Darling House performs *Peter Pan* every
November. It's a tradition that goes back to the very foundations
of the place, and despite my love for the reason, the marketing
side of me has seen the numbers. Tradition is not in Peter's favor.

BTW, for those who are not familiar with theater business, even two shows a season for such a theater is not viable long-term. It's a miracle they've kept things working as long as they have. I got the hint from overhearing a few conversations that there is family money keeping things afloat . . . but that's running out quickly.

Oh, Mr. Gray just texted me to meet him in the lobby, so I've gotta run. I'll let you know more later.

Love,
Penelope

PS: I'm already dying to give the secretary a makeover. She'd look fantastic with a little eyebrow pruning and some work with her hair. Curls like those really deserve some direction. From the way she wields a pen, though, I'm a little nervous to make any suggestions. I guess I'll have to soften her up with baked goods first before I broach the subject.

· ·

From: mgraydarlinghouse
To: Penelope Edgewood
Date: September 1
Subject: Singing

Miss Edgewood,

It has come to my attention that there is a sudden increase in singing within the theater. I understand that singing is quite typical during showtimes and rehearsals, but since rehearsals will not be starting until next week, I believe the singing may be coming from your general direction. I'm not certain where you are accustomed to working, but during business hours, we try to refrain from such musical enthusiasm outside of rehearsals. And yes, I am aware that you closed the door to your temporary office in order to subdue the sound. Since my office is down the hallway from yours, I can assure you that closing the door didn't work.

On another note, Grandfather sends his apologies once again for missing our lunch appointment. I should make you aware that Grandfather often hopes to fulfill such commitments and then finds the idea of socializing too much for him. He's struggled since my grandmother passed and some days are more difficult than others. I appreciate your ready understanding in this matter.

See you at five for the drive home.

M. Gray

Text from Luke to Penelope: Do you even watch your videos before you send them? There's a full minute of the phone pointed at your shoes while you talk to a man about a bridge.

Penelope: Really? Well, it was a very interesting bridge. And at least I wore great shoes. Much better than what you see all day long as a carpenter, anyway.

Luke: I'm currently building a stone patio off a cliffside house with the Blue Ridge Mountains on the horizon. My view is better than your shoes.

Penelope: I love those mountains. And my shoes.

. . . .

From: Penelope Edgewood
To: Izzy Edgewood, Luke Edgewood, Josephine Martin
Date: September 2
Subject: The story

Well, actually, I have a lot of stories from the past two days. (Plus I received that email you were talking about, Josephine. The one from Mrs. Jacqueline Morrow Crenshaw. I haven't read it yet and am not sure I have the emotional energy for it tonight because this day lasted two weeks, but I will read it tomorrow.)

First things first, the story behind The Darling House! Mr. James Everett saw the debut of the stage production of *Peter Pan* when it came to London and the experience made such a mark on him (as he'd just lost his mother a year before) that he determined he'd one day create his own theater. Mr. Everett survived the hardships of World War I, and like so many other creative men who came through that war (Izzy, you would know of which authors I speak since two of them are your favorites), he turned the trials into something magical and built The Darling House. The theater then passed on to his granddaughter, Lorianna Gwendolyn McKay, who married Mr. Lewis Clarkson Gray. By all accounts, Mr. Gray, who loved his wife dearly, also adored her theater, and the two of them saw wonderful careers of both performances and classes (his wife was a dance instructor). I don't know much about the productions that the theater has performed long-term, but I plan to do my research starting tomorrow. Research is vital in creating an authentic marketing strategy, but I can already tell this is going to be a delicious mystery. My scalp is tingling at the possibilities.

From what I understand, when Lorianna Gray died, something in the magic of The Darling House died too. The plays became less frequent, Mr. Gray pulled himself away from the public eye, and a steady decline of The Darling House has led to its current gloominess and . . . quiet. Oh, you haven't known quiet until you've stood on an empty stage in an empty theater and stared out into the shadowed seats. Doesn't the idea just send a shiver through you?

And here I am! Me. Like my very own Esther moment for such a time as this. No, there are no kings nearby—or at least ones associated with this theater. Neither are there devious Hamans, or at least I don't think so—most men here have Scottish or Norwegian name derivations—but there is a lonely theater with a bunch of sad-faced workers who are in desperate need of a great deal of . . . possibilities. (There isn't even music playing in the offices around here. It's a little scary-movie-like.) I'm supposed to meet the rest of the "team" tomorrow, sans Alec Gray. He's scheduled to arrive back from a work trip this weekend.

So there's the first finished story. Isn't it all so exciting?! Since I'm planning to do some sneaking around the theater tomorrow, I decided on the perfect hat to wear for courage. My large-brimmed bowler like Diane Keaton wears in *Annie Hall*! I'm afraid anything from *My Fair Lady* wouldn't fit through the doors, except maybe the adorable pink one she wears when Freddy sings to her. Sigh. What a voice! All he needed was a little more backbone.

Penelope

PS: I'm going to hold out for backbone. I think that's an excellent characteristic for the leading man of my life.

PPS: I'm considering going to the beach on Saturday. You know how I love watching the waves from a safe distance. Though I can see a lake just beyond the tree line, so I may venture there first. What a magical place!!

PPPS: The Darling House has beautiful bones. But it needs a makeover as badly as Mrs. Lennox. I'll start with her first, though.

From: Luke Edgewood
To: Penelope Edgewood, Izzy Edgewood, Josephine Martin
Date: September 2
Subject: Re: The story

Penny-girl,

I'm glad you've raised your expectations from slugs, jellyfish, and spiders to creatures with actual backbones as possible lifelong partners. It shows real growth.

Luke

PS: Maybe you could include "mammals" as a deciding factor too. Just think of the possibilities!

Text from Penelope to Luke: You're hilarious. I know why you identify with all the mammals. The hair. Gross. You might actually look like a leading man if you shaved once in a while.

Luke: I can list a few very fine leading male specimens who wear hair quite well.

Penelope: I wasn't talking about King Kong or Bigfoot.

Penelope: Ack! Stop texting me photos of the Chrises with beards. (You know I have a weakness for Chris Pine . . . and Chris Evans.) I refuse to agree with you.

Luke: And yet, I bet you saved the photos to your phone.

Penelope: I hate you.

From: Izzy Edgewood
To: Penelope Edgewood, Luke Edgewood, Josephine Martin

Date: September 3
Subject: Re: The story

Penelope,

I'm still waiting to hear about the bicycle lessons from today. Sorry if I seem overly invested, but I tried to help you learn how to ride a bike in the first place and I'd really like to see this accomplishment through, even if it's through the success of someone else. Please say you haven't given up again! If you were able to learn how to wear that pink bunny suit from *Legally Blonde* on stage in front of a pastor and his entire youth group, I think you can do anything.

The history of The Darling House is fascinating, beautiful, and sad! *Peter Pan*, the death of their grandmother, a reclusive husband, a "shadowed" theater! It's everything a fantastic story needs. Do send more photos when you can!

As far as movies with Colin Firth and a key? I'm stretching my memory, but could you be talking about *The Secret Garden*? Colin Firth is only in the teeniest part of the ending of that movie! Unless you mean the more modern one, and we do not speak of it. So I'm assuming you mean the older version. I'll send you a link for confirmation.

You're right about their website. It's atrocious! Much worse than Sutherland's Books even, and I thought that web presence was bad when I first started working on it. There's so much potential for a theater site, though. Let me know if you'd like to brainstorm. I know we have a six-hour time difference, but since I've already worked out video chats with Brodie on a regular basis, I'm sure we can easily set something up, especially since you're a night owl. Let's plan one for Saturday. What do you say?

I've pulled out my favorite copy of *Peter Pan* so I can reread it and feel somewhat connected to your adventure. Here is one of my favorite quotes from this classic: "All the world is made of faith, and trust, and pixie dust." Sigh. How lovely! I can't imagine anyone more suited to bring pixie-dust magic back into a dying theater, Penelope! It really sounds absolutely perfect for you, and a possible mystery to boot.

Izzy

PS: Are you still meeting with Brodie on Saturday?

• •

From: Penelope Edgewood
To: Izzy Edgewood, Luke Edgewood, Josephine Martin
Date: September 3
Subject: The bicycle story

Oh, Izzy,

As much as I adored playing Elle Woods, I would never want to reprise that role. I certainly hope I've moved beyond the bunny outfit with the same character growth as Elle, though I still admire all the wonderful shoes she wore and a few of the suits. I'm a flare-skirt girl myself.

As far as how the bicycle lesson went . . .

I rode back to my little cottage with Mr. Gray, and though he was mostly quiet, he did answer some of my questions related to the logistics of the theater and the history. His face softened a little from its usual intense seriousness when he spoke of his grandmother Lorianna. Matt's sister carries Lorianna as a middle name. Gwyneth Lorianna. Isn't that beautiful? I asked Matt what his sister's favorite musical or classic movie was, but he really struggled with answering. Perhaps they're not as close as we all are. He was able to provide her eye color. A pale gray-blue (I suppose they're like his). He also mentioned that Gwynn is in her last semester of college and pursuing a double major in marketing and business! Isn't that wonderful? It means whatever I start at The Darling House can be carried over by Gwynn!! Assuming she'll want to pursue a career at the family theater.

Now here's the real rub! I truly think Matt Gray didn't believe me when I said I couldn't ride a bicycle, so I actually had to PROVE it by stumbling like an idiot for a good ten minutes. When he gave me a rather incredulous eye roll (because I'm certain he assumed I was being extra dramatic! I love theater, but I am not extra dramatic about bicycles), I was compelled to tell the entire story about what happened when I was seven and the atrocious bicycle accident. I mean, how was a little girl who already struggled with talking supposed to focus on riding a bicycle again after all that? Not only was I a stutterer who hadn't grown into her ears, but I was missing three of my front teeth, had a busted lip, a swollen nose the size of a tomato, and two bruised eyebrows. E.T. had nothing on me, with or without the wig. Not to mention that I limped for two whole weeks afterward. I barely made it through that year without having a complete breakdown, let alone learning how to ride a bike. Though that's the year I discovered my singing voice, so I can't say it was all bad.

For some reason, Grumpy Gray offered another lesson tomorrow. I think he must be one of those men who, when determined, will stop at nothing to prove his point. Kind of like you, Luke. I will never forget what you did with spaghetti noodles. I don't think Mother ever recovered. I can't remember the last time she cooked spaghetti.

But it means I get to see Iris again, so I don't mind. I don't know why Matt seemed so frustrated at me holding on to his arm while I attempted to ride the bike. I let go in plenty of time for him to keep his balance, and I must say, I prefer his wide-eyed look of shock over his usual frown. But no wonder he's grumpy. Anyone who is against fairy-tale talk, singing in public, dancing on the sidewalk, and general hat wearing has to be a sad sort of person.

Iris was a wonderful cheerleader, however, so I kept trying for her sake. Did I tell you that there is no Mrs. Matt Gray? I don't know him well enough to ask about the story, but he's divorced, and evidently, Iris's mother isn't in the picture. Does that sound strange to you? How could a mother not be a part of her daughter's life? I'm going to try very hard not to allow the curiosity to keep me awake tonight, but . . . well, it is a curious thing.

Anyway, I'm staring out the window of my tower and watching the sunset over the roof of the manor house on the other side of the forest. Isn't that such a wonderful sentence?! And it's not a fairy tale but REAL.

Penelope

PS: Do you think people who are referred to by three names are more intimidating than other people?

PPS: Josephine, you haven't sent any pictures of the babies ALL DAY LONG!! When can we video call? I don't want them to forget me while I'm gone.

PPPS: Brodie's coming on Sunday! We're meeting after church and he's taking me on a tour of Fiacla!

Skymarian Theater Troupe •

From: GK
To: JA

I don't think hats should ever be out of fashion, so don't let your new employer intimidate you. You strike me as someone who is confident in herself, so I think your employer should be fine with that.

I haven't met with the theater troupe in a long time because I'm rarely in town when they meet and I have a few folks from the group that I don't want to see (former romantic ties are extremely inconvenient at times). But I'm sure you'll find a few kindred spirits, or at least a few fun acquaintances, among the lot.

MacDougall for Hire in Mountcaster has all sorts of small and large vehicles. I imagine they'd have a scooter or two as well. You must wear a neckerchief when you take your ride, or at the very least large sunglasses.

As we get to know each other better, I will be curious to hear about your job. Are you a performer as well as a movie/musical enthusiast?

• •

From: Izzy Edgewood
To: Penelope Edgewood, Luke Edgewood, Josephine Martin
Date: September 4
Subject: Re: The bicycle story

Penelope,

I think Matt may have a soft spot for damsels in distress, if you ask me. Either that, or he's wrapped around his adorable daughter's finger and SHE has a soft spot for damsels in distress. I wouldn't be too hard on Matt Gray. It sounds like he could use a little of your positivity too. I mean, if you think about it, he's

43

lost his mom and grandma in less than five years. Those sorts of losses linger and sometimes distort our views. Besides, most of the time people have reasons why they act the way they do. He's a single dad for *some* reason. Maybe there's a broken heart beneath all that fairy-tale hate, so your faith, trust, and ever-present . . . enthusiasm may be what he needs even more than you needing to ride a bike.

He has to have a little bit of patience and charm to convince you to try to ride a bicycle again, though, so there is that.

Izzy

PS: Let go of Matt next time you practice riding. Trust me, you're supposed to do that.

PPS: Oh, I'm so glad Brodie's coming to hang out with you. I'm sure he'll be quietly encouraging in his wonderful way.

• •

From: Luke Edgewood
To: Penelope Edgewood, Izzy Edgewood, Josephine Martin
Date: September 4
Subject: Re: The bicycle story

Izzy! Maybe I put too much faith and trust into your words. You're encouraging her to pour her fairy-tale enthusiasm on some poor single dad who has a dying business to save? Of course, if he's spending his afternoons trying to help Penelope ride a bike, then he has more free time than I realized . . . and perhaps he's crazier than I thought too. (And since he works in a theater, I already thought he was pretty crazy.)

Luke

PS: Brodie will bring sense.

PPS: Common sense is better than pixie dust. Prove me wrong.

Text from Penelope to Luke: Maybe common sense AND
   pixie dust are the perfect match?
Luke: You talk nonsense. Just like wizards. Except Gandalf. I
   have to support Izzy in that.

• •

From: Penelope Edgewood
To: mgraydarlinghouse
Date: September 4
Subject: Centennial???

How could you not have told me that this year is the centennial
of The Darling House's opening? *This* December before I'm due
to leave! I'm sure I don't need to tell you how FANTASTIC this is!!
It's the additional MAGIC we need to bring this theater back to
the public's attention. I am THRILLED beyond words!

Is there a place within the theater where I can locate some old
props or historical documents or anything else that will give me
some ideas of the theater's past life? I MUST find out more about
Peter Pan's influence and your grandmother's involvement and
so many other things. These will all make my job easier AND your
product even better! Story is vital to creating so many things,
but definitely for helping the world fall in love with The Darling
House all over again.

How, you might ask? Because story is the key to what we bring
to the stage, how we present ourselves online, and even how

we engage with one another. We all have stories, but in our hearts, we all LOVE stories. (Even if it takes some of us longer to admit it . . . kind of like a smile. Some people need more encouragement to smile than others, but you should really know a smile makes all the difference.)

I'm sending a list of ideas for the website. Please let me know whether these are what you had in mind.

Penelope Edgewood

PS: The thrift store down the block from the theater had a pair of silver shoes that looked like Iris's size. Would you mind if I bought them for her? Every little girl needs a pair of shiny shoes.

PPS: I already bought them.

• •

From: mgraydarlinghouse
To: Penelope Edgewood
Date: September 4
Subject: Re: Centennial???

Miss Edgewood,

With the many expectations of this position, I'm afraid the idea of the centennial completely slipped my mind. Please take whatever liberties you need to research the theater if you believe the idea of a centennial celebration will help matters. There are a great many unused storage rooms by the grand theater, and though I have not been in them in years, I understand that some paraphernalia from decades ago are housed there.

As far as the website, you were brought on to update those

things, so I expect you to know what is best. I have no interest in micromanaging you and trust you to run ideas by me as you see the need, though I do not believe pink is the preferable color to use. When Alec arrives, you can also seek his counsel, but for the most part I entrust you to do what you have so valiantly declared your "calling" for The Darling House: bring magic back.

See you at five for the drive home.

M. Gray

PS: Do you use capital letters to draw attention to what you're writing or to share heightened emotion? Since you use both so liberally, I feel I ought to ask to clarify for future correspondence.

PPS: Also, if capital letters are to convey emotions, I believe your abundant use of exclamation marks may be redundant.

CHAPTER 4

From: Jacqueline Crenshaw, The Ashby Theater
To: Penelope Edgewood
Date: September 4
Subject: A new adventure?

My darling girl,

I was so delighted to run into your sister this week as you've been much on my mind, and I hadn't any way to contact you. It's been too long since I saw you. When my dear Peter passed, I'm afraid I lost touch of so many things. Finances, logistics of the business, and even everyday life seemed all too much of a burden to bear and something had to go. I couldn't manage the theater without him, as you know. My heart just wasn't ready.

About six months ago, I was going through old photos and papers, and I discovered a letter you sent to me after Peter's death. It was filled with your memories of me and him and our theater. Some of your joy and hope must have spilled over from those pages, because it seemed to awaken my heart and imagination from what felt like a shadowy slumber. You seemed to speak directly to a part of me I thought I'd lost, or perhaps a part I thought I couldn't revisit without pain. But here you were, drawing me back to memories. Beautiful, wonderful memories.

And I realized then that the Ashby still had a great deal of life left in it because people like you and my dear husband have passion, intelligence, and enough "magic" to keep it so. I'm writing you to invite you back to the beloved Ashby Theater. I have already enlisted your brother in renovations, and the previous board has started meeting again in order to reenlist the donors who have long supported this place. Peter must have hoped I'd come to this decision at some point, because he left substantial funds to make this happen.

All I need is someone with the energy and interest to help me bring Ashby back.

I believe that person is you.

Would you be interested, once your internship is complete, in becoming the executive director of the Ashby? I know your potential. Whatever your doubts about your age or inability, I believe I can provide sufficient answer to them.

I would love to discuss this further with you. Would you be open to a telephone call?

Sincerely,
JMC

· ·

From: Penelope Edgewood
To: Jacqueline Crenshaw, The Ashby Theater
Date: September 4
Subject: Re: A new adventure?

Mrs. Crenshaw,

It was so wonderful to receive your email! When I learned that the Ashby had closed its doors, my heart broke all over again for you. That place was as much a part of my childhood as *The Andy Griffith Show*, and I couldn't imagine the empty stage without the sounds of singing children and laughing actors.

I know you've heard me say this many times before, but you and your beloved husband really helped me become the person I am today. Your kindness, encouragement, and excellent advice on everything from shoes to the perfect lacrimator (though I never really needed one since I was so good at thinking of enough sad things to make me cry without assistance) to the best way to project my voice secured for me a love of the stage forever. In fact, your faith in me to teach classes and help with everything from direction to marketing at such a young age is what sparked my career choices, to be the one behind the lights instead of always in them. To help others shine. To bring to life other people's dreams through my knowledge of marketing and theater. I didn't realize that there is even more joy behind the scenes than in them. And the idea of celebrating the theater through encouragement, whether through marketing or teaching or having the perfect set of fake eyelashes at the ready, somehow fit me in a way I didn't even know! All of it just knitted together.

And even now, you are showering me with your wonderful encouragement! To offer me a job as an executive director? That's unheard of for someone as young as me! I am honored beyond what I have words to say—and you know that's quite a feat!

As Josephine told you, I'm currently interning at a theater in Fiacla of the Skymarian Islands. I won't be home until mid-December. I know your offer is remarkable, but I need some time to consider where I see myself next. I've always dreamed of traveling and seeing the world before—maybe—settling down back home.

Would this position offer a chance for traveling?

Thank you so much, Mrs. Crenshaw.

Sincerely,

Penelope

. . . .

From: Penelope Edgewood
To: Izzy Edgewood, Luke Edgewood, Josephine Martin
Date: September 4
Subject: I said no

Okay, I didn't. I said maybe. Because I just couldn't say no to Mrs. Jacqueline Morrow Crenshaw (again, three-word name)! She's the woman who inspired my love of the stage and appreciation for teeth whitener and excellent shoes. How could I immediately reject her when she asked if I'd like to become executive director of The Ashby Theater? It's Ashby! I wore my first fake eyelashes at Ashby! I sang my first solo at Ashby! I stage-kissed the Beast at Ashby! You just can't dismiss those sorts of life-altering moments, even if you feel certain you were born for world travel.

And if she and her wonderful husband hadn't taken me under their wings, I don't know if I'd have ever overcome my shyness and stutter. So how could I say no right away?

But I will. I have too many plans to see the world to think of settling now. (Do you realize it's almost unheard of for someone my age to become an executive director of a nonprofit theater????) I'm going to ignore the angst by plunging into research in the depths of The Darling House first thing tomorrow morning. When I mentioned this plan to the secretary, I couldn't tell whether she was waving away residual smoke from the man who walked by us with a pipe or she was making the sign of the cross. I'm going to choose to think the former.

Penelope

PS: I rode the bicycle almost by myself today. Despite what Matt says, the rip in his sleeve was already there, but I did offer to mend it for him.

PPS: Iris wore the silver shoes I bought her. I wasn't sure if Matt would let her have them, but evidently he gave them to her while I ran inside the cottage to change into bicycle-riding clothes.

His eyebrows did not approve of my riding today. He has very expressive eyebrows.

PPPS: Izzy, I'm going to call you when I investigate the storage rooms at the theater, so if you're awake at six in the morning, pick up your phone. What fun it will be!

· ·

From: Josephine Martin
To: Penelope Edgewood
Date: September 4
Subject: Re: I said no

Oh, Penelope,

Look at all that has happened to you already! Please do be careful with the whole bicycle riding experiment. It took so long for you to overcome the last incident and that was with your loving family supporting you. I don't want to imagine what it would be like if the accident happens all over again and you're this far away.

I know you enjoy traveling, but there really is no place like home. You own a pair of ruby-red slippers to remind you of that fact, too, as I recall.

Ember started saying "mama" yesterday. Patrick says it wasn't quite "mama" because babies cannot make the connection between their sounds and words yet, but she looked right at me when she said it. There's intelligence there. She knows who her mother is. So I promptly fed her to reward that connection all the more.

I told Jackie Crenshaw that you were only improving your skills in Skymar, so she's even more excited about the possibility of you joining her at her theater. Not only would you be in a position to choose all those productions and organize things, but you'd be near home and learn business from a woman who has effectively run one for decades. I really don't see how you could find something more suitable to your dreams, and I'd imagine she'd let you travel during the off-season all you like. Isn't there some travel in theater work?

Oh dear, I need to go. Patrick just walked in carrying two babies covered in something I refuse to describe. Poor man! He really has the most patience in all the world.

Love,
Josephine

• •

From: Penelope Edgewood
To: Josephine Martin, Luke Edgewood, Izzy Edgewood
Date: September 4
Subject: What????

The babies are talking??!!

And I'm missing it!!

This requires video footage, Josephine, as well as a live video chat very soon. I've always heard that the *p* sound is one of the earliest and easiest to say, so I can help them get an early start on my name! And of course, they can see me if we do a video call!! We simply can't have them forgetting me. I'm their aunt. Surely they'll remember. I'm the one who wears the bright-colored clothing!

Penelope

Text from Luke to Penelope: Babies can't talk at two months old, Penny-girl. No matter what Josephine or social media tells you. Don't forget that I dated a speech therapist four years ago. She tried to diagnose every kid we ever heard, even the ones in movies.

Penelope: I don't know if I would trust the judgment of a woman who felt compelled to match her lipstick, nail polish, and jewelry on a regular basis. I'm so glad that relationship didn't last long. What would she have done on her wedding day?

From: Penelope Edgewood
To: Izzy Edgewood, Luke Edgewood
Date: September 5
Subject: I am no longer confident in confidence alone

I'm writing a quick note before I get to work. Matt is walking Iris into school as I wait in his car, so I have only a few minutes, but I just had to share to prove that I AM trying to overcome my bicycle riding fear. However, I'm afraid I had a setback today.

I got ready early for Matt to "collect" me for the drive to work so I could test my skills before he came. You see, the driveway outside my cottage dips down a little hill as it leads to the main road. It didn't seem like a *big* hill, so I thought I'd use gravity to gain my momentum and help with balance. It worked yesterday, right? And THEN, Matt would pass me on his way to pick me up and witness my extraordinary bravery and skill firsthand. So . . . I placed my purse in the little basket, made sure to wear the most adorable Converse you could imagine (they're red), and proceeded to push off from the top of the hill. Just so you know, I also started singing "Journey to the Past" in high anticipation of overcoming my tragic bicycling backstory in one triumphant moment.

Unfortunately, Matt's car came into view just as I wobbled over the lip of the hill. Gravity really is quite dangerous and I think the hill must have grown, because when you look down it from the seat of a bicycle, it looked a lot different from when I was just standing in my red Converse on solid ground.

I suppose I was distracted. That's the only excuse I can make for what happened next.

I lost control of the pedals! I would blame the shoes, but they were Converse, so that makes no sense! But there I was, careening toward a little creek at the bottom of the hill, my legs out on either side of the bicycle, and I later found out I'd lost my hat. I'm not sure what would have happened if Matt hadn't stopped the car and run after me to catch the bike before I ran into a tree. It would have been almost romantic if he hadn't lectured me on bicycle safety for a good ten minutes afterward.

If only he could have seen how very brave I was trying to be, I think he would have been much nicer about everything.

At any rate, I felt encouraged because I kept my balance all the way down the hill. The only things I need to work on now are keeping my feet on the pedals and steering.

Penelope

PS: I do feel a little bad, though. After the bicycle fiasco, Matt asked to use the restroom in the cottage before we left for work. When he came out, it looked like he'd been crying. Or at least his eyes were red, and he'd developed a terrible cough. Every time I tried to justify my actions, he'd start coughing again. Wait! Do you think he was LAUGHING???? Why would he be laughing? I could have destroyed that bicycle!

PPS: Iris was exceedingly proud of me.

. . . .

From: Izzy Edgewood
To: Penelope Edgewood, Luke Edgewood
Date: September 5
Subject: ARE YOU OKAY????

If I don't hear back from you within two hours, I'm sending Brodie to The Darling House ASAP! I might even call the local police.

What happened to you?

One minute we're having a nice video chat and you're showing me the stairway that leads down into some creepy old basement in the theater, then the next minute all connection drops! In fact, things were made much worse by the fact that you'd just said something like "Oh, it's all vast and dark down here, like the Phantom's catacombs. What's that noise?" And then . . . nothing!

I'm all for imaginations and stories, but I'd rather things like this remain purely fiction, so tone down the drama and text me or email me back.

Izzy

Text from Luke to Izzy: You do realize that Penelope always bounces back from things, right? She's probably entered some fantasy realm in the basement of the theater. And made friends with the natives. Likely birds have started sewing her wedding dress at this point. I wouldn't worry too much. She'll bring souvenirs back with her.

Izzy: You're not worried at all, are you?

Luke: How many times has Penelope "disappeared" unexpectedly within relatively safe places?

Izzy: Point taken.

From: Luke Edgewood
To: Penelope Edgewood, Izzy Edgewood
Date: September 5
Subject: Re: ARE YOU OKAY????

Sorry I missed the video call, but some people prefer sleep.

If you find one of those half masks down there, I'll take one. I could wear it for Izzy's Book Parade and not have to worry about face painting.

PS: Of course Grumpy Gray was laughing. What a show! And you're not even onstage.

Text from Penelope to Izzy: I just got upstairs to take a late lunch and saw your five voice mails and ten text messages. I love your sweetness for checking on me. Seems that cell reception is nil in the storage rooms beneath the theater, but don't worry, I'll fill you in on everything via email when I get back to my computer. Soooo interesting!

. . . .

From: Penelope Edgewood
To: Izzy Edgewood, Luke Edgewood
Date: September 5
Subject: Babysitting and basements!

I don't have long to talk because I get to babysit IRIS tomorrow night!! Can you believe it? I think Matt must have been desperate to find someone because I heard him ask three other people before he got to me. I just happened to be standing near the reception desk trying to think of ways to brighten up and reorganize the area to make it more appealing. Rehearsals for the community theater group's first fall production start next week, but I think the folks in the community theater are people from all over Fiacla and maybe even the island of Ansling too! (I'm going to be working on the website a little over the weekend.)

Anyway, my phone reception cut off just as I made it to the bottom of the stairs and, to be honest, it was a little frightening. The light at the stairs didn't provide much illumination for such a vast space, so as I stepped forward and things got darker, I used my phone flashlight, but even it wasn't enough at times. I even tried to whistle a happy tune, but my mouth was so dry I couldn't get any sound to come out.

Then I saw silhouettes of people in the distance, standing there as if they were zombies in the dark—there was even a silhouette of a horse and something that looked suspiciously like the shape of a ghost—so I turned my silent whistling into singing. I must admit, my voice was too shaky to stay on pitch, but I had no problem being loud.

All of a sudden, I heard breathing nearby—a puff of it. Or a few puffs, and all I could see in my head was a giant Venus flytrap waiting to devour me. (I am never going to watch *Little Shop of Horrors* again!) Then I turned around and there were two figures moving closer to me from the stairway. Clearly, I was trapped, with the ghost behind me and the mysterious people in front, so I reached into my bag and pulled out my Swiss Army knife, a little teary-eyed at the thought that I was going to die in the cellar of an old theater in a country no one has heard of without ever having played Maria von Trapp or kissed a man in the rain! Can you believe it?! Then the light switched on, and before me stood Matt Gray and a young woman with the same stormy eyes and quizzical brow. But she smiled, which meant I automatically liked her. And she had a beautifully delicate appearance like Grace Kelly. Which meant I liked her even more.

There are so MANY things to discover down there. I only spent a few hours today attempting to orient myself, but in all honesty, there really was no organization about it. However, Matt's sister, Gwynn, told me that there were some old posters and letters from adoring patrons hidden somewhere, so I'm determined to find them . . . starting on Monday.

I took a late lunch with Gwynn and just adored her all the more. I think we're bound to be very good friends. She speaks in musicals too. Okay, I've gotta run. There's a staff meeting and I can't wait to see what everyone thinks of my berry pecan muffins!

Penelope

. . . .

From: Izzy Edgewood
To: Penelope Edgewood, Luke Edgewood
Date: September 5
Subject: Re: Babysitting and basements!

Luke was right. Again.

You are safe and even making new friends while I'm freaking out about your welfare. I'm glad to learn that you were not devoured by ghosts or a Venus flytrap, but next time you are in a live video chat with me and the reception goes off, please return to a place with reception and text me that you are not dead.

Love,
Izzy

PS: I woke up at five thirty for this, Penelope! Just remember that!

. . . .

From: Penelope Edgewood
To: Izzy Edgewood, Luke Edgewood
Date: September 5
Subject: Re: Babysitting and basements!

Luke isn't always right, Izzy. Saying so only encourages his sense of superiority. But I will try to remember to text you if we are disconnected in the future. It's not common, of course, for me to be swept away into a mysterious storage basement, but should something similar happen again, I'll make sure to set your heart at ease.

Gwynn and I got along so well and have similar hopes for The Darling House, but since she is still in college, she doesn't come into town except on random weekends. She wants to take a position at the theater once she graduates because it's her dream to support the place she's loved so much since childhood. I think she mentioned something about one day owning the theater. Hurrah for female business owners!

It did make me think of Ashby.

The muffins were a hit! I didn't have any left after the meeting and there were only five of us present. Mr. Lewis Gray, of course, didn't come and Alec is still out of town. Apart from them, there is Matt, Gwynn, me, Evelyn (the secretary), and Lars (the facilities manager). There's also a very sweet volunteer named Dani. It appears that Matt is highly involved in the productions (it seems like Alec used to be but hasn't been as available in the past few years), so . . . there's another possible reason for a financial slump. I'll know more once I see the productions in action.

Love,

Penelope

PS: Matt's asked me not to show Iris any princess movies so she won't get a fairy-tale idea about romance. I'm trying to decide between *Mary Poppins*, *Toy Story*, and *Tangled*. (Because *really*, *Tangled* is about a young woman trying to be free and eventually get back to her parents. Nothing too fairy-tale-ish about that.)

Text from Luke to Penelope: I'm not sure whether to be proud or not that you intended to massacre inanimate (or undead) objects with the Swiss Army knife I got you for your birthday. However, I've seen how you wield a toothbrush when scared, so I have no doubt it was one of the most entertaining roles you've ever played.

Penelope: You're supposed to be easier to ignore from across the world. Though I was thankful for the knife. It works great on apples.

· ·

From: Gwynn Gray
To: Penelope Edgewood
Date: September 6
Subject: Budding friendship?

It was such a pleasure to meet you today, though I wish it had been under different circumstances. I don't think I've ever seen a person's face turn so pale as yours when we found you in the storage room. Please don't mind my brother too much. He has one of the best hearts in the world, but since it's been terribly broken, he's not keen on showing it to strangers.

I think we are going to get along just fine. The Darling House is in desperate need of you, as you well know, and I only wish I could be around more often to brainstorm some creativity together, but now you have my email and I'll attach my cell phone number too. Already I can tell we have some similar views on how things should change around here if we're truly going to make a difference. Perhaps you'll have more influence than me, since both my brothers and my grandfather think I am too young to really handle the business side of things, despite the fact that

I graduate in December with a degree in business. (I've also told them that I got the degree for the sole purpose of making a difference in the family business. Men can be so infuriating sometimes, especially brothers.)

Anyway, I'd love to see some of your ideas. You mentioned making graphics and had some new website design ideas? Perhaps, as an insider to The Darling House, I could give you my perspective.

Also, I don't think I've ever seen my brother work so hard to control his laugh. His humor isn't usually overt, but he has a very keen sense of one. It's nice to know that someone can bring it out of him, even if you did so unintentionally. Unfortunately, the way his ex-wife left things has rather dampened his teasing nature. I'm positive he could do with a bit of your sunshine, whether he appears to appreciate it or not.

I'm glad you're accompanying us to church. Do you have plans for lunch after? Our family has lunch together after church every Sunday and I feel certain my grandfather would be happy to meet you.

Gwynn

PS: Plus, you simply must meet Scooby.

From: Penelope Edgewood
To: Gwynn Gray
Date: September 6
Subject: Re: Budding friendship?

Oh my goodness, Gwynn! You can't know how delighted I was to see your email in my inbox! I knew as soon as I met you that we were bound to become friends. Well, after Matt pulled the knife from my hand and my pulse returned to normal. You did catch me at an unusually terrified moment down there in the dungeon of the theater. However, at least it made our first meeting memorable, and I think there's a lot to be said for that.

I believe your brother thinks I'm ridiculous, and since you and I are close in age, I'm afraid that won't help your cause for being taken seriously. I've rarely been taken seriously my whole life because people just assume I'm ridiculous and an airhead because I'm so optimistic, but . . . I'm neither. Well, sometimes I am, but not as often as people think. I just prefer to see things on the rosy side of normal, which leads to all sorts of wrong assumptions about me from teachers, peers, MEN, occasionally food service individuals!

I had high marks in school and was a part of all sorts of fun AND serious clubs, and yet I have to fight to be taken seriously. But I don't think you have to be glum or intense or carry a briefcase to be seriously GOOD at what you do. I'm beginning to realize that it's okay just to be happy and try to spread that happiness around. People can think what they want, but I bet grumps rarely have as much fun as me doing . . . well, just about anything.

Besides, the world could do with a little more kindness and positivity and random acts of singing, don't you think?

Penelope

PS: I have lunch plans for Sunday, but could I take a rain check for the next one?

PPS: I get to keep your niece tonight! We're making cupcakes.

Maybe the extra sugar will sweeten up your brother a little too. Sunshine and sugar have to be one of the best happiness combos in the world.

PPPS: And tea. And chocolate.

Text from Penelope to Luke: Scooby is the name of Gwynn's dog! I thought you would like that. I plan to call him Scoobs for short.

Luke: Quality name. Quality cartoon. It shows Gwynn has smarts. If the dog talks, send me a recording.

CHAPTER 5

Text from Penelope to Matt: Iris left her shiny shoes here. She was so sweetly sleeping in your arms as you carried her out, I completely forgot to get them for you. Do you want me to bring them to you tomorrow? I could put them in the basket of the bike along with the princess hats we made and attempt to get them to you if you want.

Penelope: I mean, not that we made PRINCESS hats. They're more like pointy dress-up hats. Not princess.

Matt: Ah. Like a witch.

Penelope: Um . . . right. Pink witches with glitter. Not princesses, of course.

Matt: Like Glinda.

Penelope: Exactly.

Penelope: Did you know they make glow-in-the-dark glitter?? Can you imagine the possibilities? Glow-in-the-dark glitter!!

Matt: I can't say I ever have.

Penelope: Don't worry. If you ever want some ideas, I can provide them. And glow-in-the-dark glitter may come in handy in performances. I think I'll get some to keep in my bag.

Matt: Do you carry everything in your bag?

Penelope: Only absolute necessities.

Matt: You deem heart-print plasters, shoelaces, and red ribbons necessities?

Penelope: Clearly, you've never directed *Annie.*

Matt: I cannot say that I have. But I would like to thank you for taking such good care of Iris. When I tucked her in bed, she spoke of how you hoped to teach her to bake cookies that take a "spoonful of sugar." She insists tomorrow, but I feel you may be quite finished spending time with an energetic little girl for the weekend.

Penelope: I loved getting to spend time with her. She's such a sweetheart. You must have loved her so well for her to hug so sweetly and smile so readily. I'd happily volunteer to watch her anytime, and yes, I'd love to teach her to make those very delicious Mary Poppins cookies! And tomorrow—tomorrow is "only a day away."

Matt: I'll text you "tomorrow," then. Sleep well, Penelope.

Text from Penelope to Matt: BTW, I brought home a box I found in the storage room. It has playbills in it and this amazing photo of a woman wearing a magnificent dress and crown while riding a float in a parade. The float has "The Darling House" and "Community Theater" on the side. I feel this is important. What is it?

Matt: Do you realize what time it is?

Penelope: It's not even eleven yet! You really aren't old enough to go to bed this early, are you?

Matt: I'm a father. I feel much older than I look. But I also happen to be watching telly.

Penelope: Ooh, what are you watching? I found a classic-television channel and I have it on in the background while I do research on The Darling House. There's something so lovely and fun about tap dancing. And fake marriages.

Matt: Fred Astaire certainly has an elegant style.

Penelope: You're watching *Shall We Dance* too?

Matt: The photo is of my grandmother. She adored decorating a float every year for the Failte Feis and celebrating theater. The parade and festival happen in October to welcome autumn.

Penelope: What a wonderful idea! Are we decorating one this year?

Matt: We haven't since the year before she died. She was too sick to make it happen that year.

Penelope: Oh, I'm sorry. What a great way to celebrate small towns and theater, though. She sounds like the type of person who would like making Glinda hats too. Maybe even princess ones.

Penelope: And . . . there's nothing at all wrong with watching _Shall We Dance_, just in case you ARE watching it.

• •

From: Penelope Edgewood
To: Izzy Edgewood, Luke Edgewood, Josephine Martin
Date: September 8
Subject: Babies and secret plans

Josephine!! Thank you so much for the video call last night. Oh, it just made me miss those tiny babies all the more. I'm pretty sure they smiled at me, though, so I feel I'm still very much in their memories. I can't wait to dress them in vintage-style clothing. Can't you just see Noah in a derby and bow tie? Oh! Be still, my heart! Josephine!! Noah would be an amazing newsie! I can tell already. It's the crooked smile.

I'm up early this morning because I just couldn't get an idea out of my mind. A surprise for The Darling House. _I_ am going to create a float for Failte Feis. I've got time as the festival isn't until the third week of October. Failte Feis means "Welcome Festival" and it is a festival to welcome in the autumn. I've been watching a copious amount of YouTube videos about it and it's absolutely darling. People from all over come to Mountcaster dressed in COSTUME and listen to street music, buy tasty handmade treats, enjoy local arts and crafts, and celebrate theater. It's the perfect thing for me. I haven't decided what costume I'm wearing yet, but I do have ideas about the float. I just need to find some folks who will help me build it without giving away the surprise to the Grays (I have goose bumps of nostalgia). There is a long tradition of this float and it seems to be the main one that features performing arts in Mountcaster. I didn't see any floats by Emblem over the past few years, so no one has filled that particular marketing role yet. YAY!

BTW, did I tell you I get to keep Iris again tonight? We're going to make Mary Poppins cookies. Gwynn told me that Matt is going on a blind date that she's set up for him, and it's the first one he's been on since whatever happened with Iris's mom. That was THREE years ago! No dates in THREE years!

So Iris and I are going to read stories and bake cookies. We'll likely pull out the tiaras too. It's important for princesses to support one another.

Love,
Penelope

PS: I'm leaving for a walk to explore the lake nearby. Adventures await.

PPS: I've convinced Matt to let me show Iris the live-action version of *Cinderella*. Sort of. I told him it was about a young girl who works her way out of poverty by showing kindness to mean people, befriending animals, and showcasing excellent dance moves. I didn't mention magic . . . or shiny shoes.

PPPS: Mrs. Jacqueline Morrow Crenshaw responded to my email and said she planned to send me a proposal within the next few weeks, once her lawyer has a look at it. At some point, I will work up the courage to tell her I'm not interested, but for now . . . I'm just curious to see what's in that proposal.

· ·

From: Izzy Edgewood
To: Penelope Edgewood, Luke Edgewood, Josephine Martin
Date: September 8
Subject: Re: Babies and secret plans

Penelope,

Is this festival anything like the King and Queen Festival in Skern? If it is, you are going to have such fun! The people of Skymar LOVE their festivals, if the festival in Skern is any indication. It went on for DAYS and each day seemed a little more exciting than the last. Adding the arts to a festival? It sounds positively delightful.

And I remember the float you helped make for the Mt. Airy Christmas parade one year. I'm creative, but I had no idea you could make all those things out of cardboard, crepe paper, pipe cleaners, and shoelaces. Your Grinch looked perfect. Has Luke forgiven you yet for making the Grinch wear an apron that reads "My other name is Luke"? What ever happened to that apron?

BTW, have you decided when you're going to talk to Matt

about your idea to invite a touring theater group to The Darling House for a Christmas performance? Like you said on the phone yesterday, something new would really help with visibility and maybe reinspire interest in The Darling House. Especially with a centennial coming up.

And it might provide a little more competition against Emblem.

Can't wait to hear more! Enjoy your walk. Send pics.

Izzy

PS: Mrs. Crenshaw is a smart lady. And she knows you. Be prepared. You may be surprised.

· ·

From: Luke Edgewood
To: Penelope Edgewood, Izzy Edgewood, Josephine Martin
Date: September 8
Subject: Re: Babies and secret plans

Do you ever read what you write in the subject lines and wonder what the reader might think?

Anyway, there was more than cardboard involved in that Grinch's sleigh and house. Believe me. I still have scars to prove it.

Luke

PS: What apron?

Text from Izzy to Luke: Did you steal that apron after the parade?
Luke: No comment.

Text from Penelope to Izzy and Luke: I AM GETTING MARRIED! I found him! The man I'm going to marry. I'll email more later. Right now he's drying my clothes and just walked back into the room with tea. I bet it's excellent tea. Gotta go!

Luke: Penelope, you'd better finish your story very soon or there may be dire consequences that not even Rambo contemplated happening to your future husband. I don't care how good the tea is.

Izzy: He's serious, Penelope. I've already had to talk him out of purchasing a plane ticket to Skymar two times.

Izzy: Three times.

Penelope: What in the world is wrong with you, Luke? I am perfectly fine. In fact, I'm marvelous. I will email more later, but for now I'm trying to charm him with my devoted attention. It's very difficult to show devoted attention when my phone keeps buzzing against my leg.

Izzy: Four times.

Penelope: Oh! Wait! Now I know what you mean! Luke, nothing compromising has happened at all. I will explain it all in an email later, but right now . . . devoted attention.

Penelope: Also, I met him exactly the way I'd always dreamed of meeting my future husband. It was meant to be. I'm all aflutter.

Izzy: Oh! That makes sense now. You met him while scuba diving and he rescued you by sharing air with you when you got trapped beneath a sunken ship. I thought you were just going to see a lake. Do ships sink in lakes? And aren't you afraid of sea monsters?

Penelope: What? No! That was my dream when I was in tenth grade. Biology class was very influential.

Izzy: Or the biology teacher, as I recall. You couldn't have met Mr. Right at the Colosseum in Rome. You haven't had time to get there and back, so . . . did you meet him onstage? But why is he drying your clothes?

Penelope: No, no! Those dreams were from ninth grade and my senior year, respectively. I met him while out in a storm and he rescued me. Well, he didn't really rescue me, because I wasn't afraid. I was singing "Someday My Prince Will Come" and then . . . he rode up on a white stallion just like my very own prince. Ack! You have to stop distracting me. I'm losing focus on being devoted.

Text from Penelope to Luke: I didn't mean to worry you. I'm okay.

Luke: I'm just glad I don't have to kill anybody now. I have other people's houses to build.

. . . .

From: Josephine Martin
To: Penelope Edgewood, Luke Edgewood, Izzy Edgewood
Date: September 8
Subject: Re: Babies and secret plans

Penelope,

You already purchased Noah a derby, but it's a twelve-month size, which means you'll be back home in time to see him wear it. Though he does seem to have a large head for his age, but the doctor said he's not too concerned. Besides, I have high hopes Noah will take after his darling father. Patrick's head is large and look how smart he is.

I'll plan to call every Friday evening so you can see the babies. I can't imagine you having much to do on Friday evenings anyway. Building a romantic attachment in Skymar could only lead to heartache for too many people. I'm still adjusting to the idea of Izzy moving all the way across the world to most likely marry Brodie and work at a little bookshop in the middle of a country where people still have a tendency to wear kilts on occasion. There's something very unsettling about that thought.

You should certainly take photos of your float and send them to Jackie Crenshaw. It will keep you fresh in her mind.

Josephine

PS: Do keep your phone with you while you adventure, Penelope. And the pepper spray I sent. You never know who could be lurking in foreign places.

- -

From: Penelope Edgewood
To: Luke Edgewood, Izzy Edgewood, Josephine Martin
Date: September 8
Subject: Today my prince came!

The story! Oh, you will not believe it! It's too perfect.

As I told you, I went for my walk just beyond the forest near my cottage to find the lake I could see from my window. The forest was unlike any I'd ever seen before. So enchanted and beautiful, and even when the sun disappeared behind clouds, everything was so pretty. I'm attaching photos of the lake with the mountains behind it. Doesn't it remind you a little of home? And our Blue Ridge Mountains? I got a little homesick at the sight.

Anyway, it started raining. Not a hard rain like in that scene from

The Notebook. At one point I slipped on some moss and fell and am not too ashamed to say I started laughing at my own ridiculousness. But then I heard a sound like thunder, just as the sky was clearing a little . . . and looked beyond the forest to a lovely green field that was glistening from fresh rain. You will NEVER believe it!

Down the hill rode a beautiful man on a white horse. A. WHITE. HORSE!!

He came up to me, dismounted, and shot me this dazzling smile before saying, "I've always wanted to rescue a damsel in distress, but I never realized one would be so lovely in the rain."

Heaven HELP ME! Who says stuff like that? Only Skymarian men who ride on white horses in the rain????

I wasn't REALLY a damsel in distress, since I was just enjoying the rain. And he didn't start singing with me when he found me, but . . . he's absolutely perfect. When he took my hand to help me mount the horse, it was like . . . magic. Hmm . . . where have I heard that before? Was it from that old movie you like, Izzy, with Tom Hanks? The one where they never KISS! That was disappointing.

Anyway, my future husband was none other than Alec Gray, the other Gray brother! And he looks even more like Chris Pine in person! Except his hair is a bit lighter and his eyes are hazel-green instead of that piercing and somewhat distracting blue. But in all other particulars, mostly he's Chris Pine-y. (It's strange how both his brother, Matt, and sister, Gwynn, have the blue-gray eyes, though.)

Since I was soaked to the skin, Alec suggested I get out of the rain, so he took me to the very manor house I could see from my window!! AND! What else? It's the GRAY House! Grandpa Gray lives there with Matt and Iris. Alec sleeps there sometimes, when he's not staying in his townhouse in Mountcaster or traveling, and Gwynn lives there when she isn't at college. (Apparently Alec used to be heavily involved in the theater and has connections all over Europe! That's crazy.)

So I got to meet Grandpa Gray (which sounds so much more inviting than Lewis Clarkson Gray) *and* surprised Matt and Iris by being there having tea with Alec and Grandpa. Iris was much more excited to find me there than Matt. He sort of loomed in the shadows with his arms crossed, and his expressive eyebrows were equally unwelcoming. He made sure to get my clothes as soon as they were dry and offered to drive me home. I assured him I could walk. Alec didn't seem to be in a hurry for me to leave at all.

I'll send photos later. It's a beautiful old house. Iris will be here shortly and I need to turn on the new twinkle lights I added to the living room.

Penelope

PS: I'm ready to give Matt dating tips if he asks.

PPS: I don't think he'll ask, but just in case, I'm ready. As you know, I've watched ALL the right movies for it.

PPPS: Grandpa Gray was a DARLING! (Pun intended.) He was rather sad, but I feel certain he just needs some company. Now that I know where he lives, I can visit and bring cookies.

· ·

From: Luke Edgewood
To: Penelope Edgewood, Izzy Edgewood, Josephine Martin

Date: September 8
Subject: Re: Today my prince came!

Penny-girl,

Did you just turn Chris Pine into an adjective?

Stepping away from this conversation.

Luke

PS: Who goes horse riding in the rain? Weirdo.

PPS: You may be in more distress than you think.

Text from Luke to Penelope: Any guy with a first line like that
   isn't to be trusted.
Penelope: SOME people can be charming.
Luke: Some snakes can be too.
Penelope: Do you even have a romantic bone in your body?
Luke: It was the toe bone the nail went through. So no.

• •

From: Penelope Edgewood
To: Izzy Edgewood, Luke Edgewood
Date: September 8
Subject: Grumpy Gray weirdness & little princesses

What did Matt Gray mean? I need to know. I have my
assumptions, but the two of you will be honest with me. As you
recall, I kept Iris tonight so Matt could go on a date. Excellent
opportunity for him. Maybe the right woman will make him

less grumpy. It's definitely a trope I enjoy watching. Besides, I think sunshine characters should have more opportunities to be heroines. To be perfectly honest, the grumpy, sassy, or angsty heroines enjoy too much spotlight, and the sunshiny, optimistic, "spoonful of sugar" heroines rarely get as much attention. The world would be a very dismal place without sunshine. Think about that!

Anyway, Matt asked me not to go overboard with fairy-tale stuff, so instead Iris and I talked about the royal family of Skymar and watched *Cinderella*. I thought when Matt came in to find us halfway through the movie, he'd yell something atrocious about fairy tales and pull Iris from the cottage, but instead, he sent me an impressive glare, narrowed those eyebrows of his, and sat down on the couch on the other side of Iris. He even ate some of my special homemade Buncha Crunch mix. I think he liked the unique mix of chocolate, nuts, and popcorn, because he had several handfuls.

Iris fell asleep on the couch, so I took the opportunity to show him a few of my designs for the new website and some graphics I'd like to use on social media as well as for local advertising. (Did I mention their social media involvement is . . . not?) I've already started two social media accounts for them. (Nerdy theater people are GREAT at following new accounts and sharing the dramatic love. Also, the Skymarian Theater Troupe are devotees of The Darling House, so that's a definite plus. Oh, how I adore this community!)

Matt didn't say anything negative about the fact that I'd shown Iris *Cinderella*. He even made a comment about how poignant the forgiveness scene was at the end of the movie. When I mentioned how it reminds me of my part to play in the world and how kindness and courage are some of the most beautiful attributes a person can have, he stared at me a little longer than usual and I have to admit—his eyes are VERY Chris Pine blue, especially when he wears his black-framed glasses. *The Princess Diaries 2* vibes, y'all. Seriously. His date had to have been sufficiently distracted if he put on his glasses.

Then we had a brief discussion about faith and healing and what real love looks like. I liked him better then. Not that I didn't like him before, but I feel as though . . . well, I don't know. It was probably the glasses.

However, the next conversation cleared out whatever feeling I was feeling. Here's how it went:

Me: How was your date?
Matt: It went well enough.
Me: "Well enough"? Clearly, she's not the woman for you.
Him: Is she not?
(As if he didn't already know that!)
Me: Definitely not.
Matt: And why is that?
(Insert distracting quizzical eyebrow lift while wearing those glasses.)
Me: The right woman isn't going to leave a "well enough" vibe behind. She's going to make you want to linger and cause you to smile when you think of her. Like that feeling you get when you walk out on an empty stage after an excellent performance and you still FEEL the magic of it all whispering through the air. And you can't wait to perform again. Or see the performance again. Just to be there. It's like that.
Matt: *staring at me through those glasses and saying nothing until my cheeks grew hot*

Me: I hope no man ever says a date with me went "well enough."
Matt: (with an *almost* grin) I feel you would leave a very distinct impression one way or another on any date, Miss Edgewood.

Now, I ask you. What was that supposed to mean? Matt wouldn't elaborate even when I asked, and since I didn't want to wake Iris and Matt needed to get her home, I didn't push the subject. But really?

Penelope

PS: He seemed to like my designs. I sent them to Gwynn to get an honest answer.

PPS: He didn't mention his brother or the "daring rescue" incident, so I didn't either.

PPPS: He didn't ask for dating tips.

Text from Izzy to Luke: Don't you dare answer Penelope's newest email. I can only imagine what you would say in response to her question about Matt's reaction. Just don't.
Luke: Now where's the fun in that? Besides, after her whole "strange man drying my clothes" scare, I'm owed some fun.

Text from Luke to Penelope and Izzy: It's the hats and the shoes, Penny-girl. Not every man can handle such flagrant and color-coordinated self-expression.
Luke: Plus, you're kind of like Grandpa's "homemade" apple cider.

Text from Izzy to Luke: You're not helping.

Text from Izzy to Penelope and Luke: Penelope, he likely
means that you make a memorable first impression.
And it's true. You do. Even without the hats and shoes.
Your personality is very memorable. It packs a punch.
Luke: Thus the Grandpa's homemade cider reference.
Izzy: Luke!

Text from Luke to Izzy: Okay, okay, how's this? "You know
that whole popping into paintings and laughing on
the ceiling stuff, Penny-girl? Not everyone appreciates
Mary Poppins until they learn that her brand of stuff and
nonsense can be fun. And you have loads of stuff and
nonsense."
Izzy: Do you really want me to come over to your house and
hit you with my three-volume copy of The Lord of the
Rings?
Luke: It wouldn't be the first time.

Text from Luke to Penelope: Just like Mary Poppins, Penny-girl,
you thrive off of helping people. You've been doing it your
whole life. It's a God-given part of you. There are a lot of
George Banks folks in the world who need your brand of
sunshine to open their eyes to possibilities. That "spoonful
of sugar" nonsense.
Penelope: Izzy made you write that, didn't she?
Luke: No. She only gave me a Lord of the Rings–style nudge. I
can be nice when I'm forced.

Penelope: I think I just rolled my eyes so far back in my head I saw my own brain matter!

Luke: Well, at least you saw something in there.

Penelope: I totally set myself up for that one. Dork.

CHAPTER 6

Text from Matt to Penelope: Do you need a ride to church?

Penelope: Oh, how sweet of you! I thought Alec was going to pick me up, but he's not answering his phone.

Matt: He's still asleep. I'll be there in ten.

Penelope: Thanks so much! I forgot to ask Alec last night—is your church okay with women wearing hats?

Matt: I've never heard of any excommunications due to hat wearing.

Penelope: Was that a sense of humor peeking out from beneath the grumpy brows? I see the Lord is already answering my prayers!

• •

From: Brodie Sutherland
To: Izzy Edgewood, Luke Edgewood
Date: September 9
Subject: It's a jolly holiday with Penelope?

I feel fairly certain that neither of you have any reason to fret over Penelope Edgewood's welfare. In fact, she may be living out her best fairy-tale life now and not even realizing it. I ought to add that I've lived in Skymar my entire life, and I cannot boast the number of acquaintances Penelope has secured in her first couple of weeks. (Might I add, she even knew the names of people's pets.) I find myself simultaneously awed and terrified by her, but that seems to be a typical response, judging from the cursory view of those around us.

83

We were to meet in Mountcaster's Central Square. It's a lovely spot, surrounded by ancient sandstone and gray stone buildings with a fountain at the center. This time of year the rose trees are still in bloom around the fountain, so it makes for a particularly picturesque place at the heart of an already charming city. At any rate, I didn't immediately find Penelope, though it should have been easy enough with her unique hair color and proclivity for wearing brightly colored clothes. The town square was crowded because on Sunday afternoons people enjoy strolling the streets or picnicking in the park near the square. However, there was no need to fear, for Penelope found me as she rode up on a Vespa sporting a broad-brimmed hat, large sunshades, and a brilliant smile. She jumped from the scooter and embraced me, and though you warned me, Isabelle, I still wasn't quite prepared for her overt displays of . . . well, everything. Every emotion came extra-large-sized and, I'm thankful to say, they were all happy ones . . . for the most part.

I might also add that she was somewhat dismayed that I could not readily pinpoint the movie reference from her arrival and costume. I promised to watch *Roman Holiday* at my first opportunity.

Since the oceanfront is only a short Vespa ride away from town, Penelope convinced me to take the scooter and so off we went. I've attached a few photos, but I feel certain Penelope will have many more to share. I inquired after her job and she expounded with great animation about how much she's enjoying it, her adoration for the history of The Darling House, her certainty of some secrets hidden within the walls, her aspiration to discover true love, and her determination to find out what Matt Gray's laugh sounds like. There, I believe I've sufficiently summarized your sister's status.

I daresay she spoke about home enough to hint at missing it, so I take that as being very well aware of how much she's loved. (And a healthy dose of jealousy at having the twins love one of you more than her.)

I've invited her to Skern next Saturday and she agreed. She insisted on hiring her own car. For some reason, I felt a little concerned about that prospect, but she would not be deterred.

So there you have it. My accounting. I look forward to your responses.

Brodie

PS: I was only able to convince her to wade in the sea up to her ankles. She seemed absolutely terrified to go any farther. I didn't press the matter, but she did mention something about sea monsters.

• •

From: Penelope Edgewood
To: Izzy Edgewood, Luke Edgewood
Date: September 9
Subject: Brodie, Alec, and Grumpy Gray

First off, Izzy, you would have LOVED the church I attended this morning. The stone floors and the stained glass windows! I felt as if I'd stepped into a magical world, especially as the sunlight glowed through the windows and scattered rainbow-like colors across the room. I can see why you say that some places are more conducive to worship than others, even though I know we should be able to worship anywhere. I felt very much like this church would be a place Julie Andrews would have come as Maria von Trapp to worship, you know? Elegant and, well, like her. Just lovely.

And it made me realize a touring company would be an excellent idea. Something grand and glorious to grab everyone's attention. I just need to broach that subject with the men, who have NOT had a touring company perform at The Darling House in more than four years. But with my contacts, there may be a good chance of making it happen, even with such short notice!

Also, Brodie was wonderful. I can see why you love him so much, Izzy. He seemed to really understand my fear of sea monsters without one bit of sarcasm. Did you know he can drive a Vespa? I asked him to drive so I could ride on the back like Audrey Hepburn in *Roman Holiday*. I wore a red skirt just for the occasion. I'm so glad you were home so we could have a video call with you. It just seemed even better with you there. He's such a quiet fellow. I feel as though you probably have to carry the conversation most days, but I didn't have one bit of trouble with that. He invited me for dinner with his family next weekend and I can't wait to meet everyone.

Alec and I had dinner this evening, quite by accident, I think. I had walked up to the big house (after Brodie left) so I could visit with Grandpa Gray and ask him more about his "darling" wife. Oh, their love story is exquisite, complete with a rescue in the rain, a runaway sheep, and a little bit of a *Beauty and the Beast* vibe (with Lorianna overcoming Grandpa Gray's grumpiness). Maybe that's where Matt gets it from, because when I got ready to walk home in the dark, Matt sent a scathing look in my direction and told Alec to walk me home. I imagine Alec would have walked me home anyway, but being bossed around by his older brother probably didn't make him want to as much.

At any rate, Alec escorted me to my little cottage and we had a chance for a long conversation. He told me that The Darling House is such a family legacy, and they all want to see it grow, which is why he spends so much time traveling—in an attempt to build new relationships to bring more income, actors, and businesses our way. (Interestingly, he also has a second job as a business consultant. I don't know what that means, but he travels for it too.)

Since finances have been so bad for Darling, a few larger companies have made substantial offers to purchase it, but Grandpa Gray refuses to sell and Alec is concerned the business may end up bankrupt before it can turn around . . . if it CAN turn around at all. Alec made some comment about Matt not being as invested in the future of the theater as the rest of them, so I'm not sure whether that is a reference to the idea that Matt might be open to selling or that he wants to try something else for his future. Either way, it makes me wonder why he seems to work so hard for a place in which he isn't as invested. (I didn't end that sentence with a preposition like I wanted to, because I could feel eighth-grade teacher Mrs. Linder scowling over my shoulder as I wrote.)

The idea of the Grays losing The Darling House breaks my heart. There is such love and history and legacy in it, so obviously, I am determined to save it even more. I have confidence in me . . . and a lot of other people helping me, of course. I just have to find those people. From all I can tell, Matt seems to love the place, at least for his family's sake, if not for his own, but I don't sense a deep passion. (However, I'm not sure I've sensed a deep passion for much at all, except Iris, of course, and bicycles.) Alec shared some delightful memories of the place, nearly getting emotional about it a time or two, so he may have more of the passion.

But the most passionate one about it (besides Grandpa Gray) is Gwynn. I certainly have an ally in her. You know how I used to just walk through the hallways and stages of Ashby for fun? Well, I've found her in The Darling House several times, doing the same thing!

Anyway, when Alec walked me to my door, he took my hand and kissed it before leaving. He also told me that my hair looks beautiful in the moonlight. Good grief! I feel like I'm floating. (Do you think men in Skymar kiss ladies' hands in a totally platonic sort of way? Like a goodbye ritual or something? Because it didn't feel platonic.)

Penelope

PS: I know I've resolved not to date until someone (myself) in the relationship was mature enough to handle it, but if Alec Gray wanted to date me, I wouldn't object.

PPS: Am I allowed to date him since he's not my immediate supervisor? Oh dear, do you think Maria von Trapp felt this sort of dilemma when she started having romantic feelings for her boss? (But he's not my boss! Grandpa is the real one in charge.)

• •

From: Gwynn Gray
To: Penelope Edgewood
Date: September 10
Subject: Your ideas!

Penelope,

I'm still in school for marketing so my wisdom on this may not be expert, but these graphics and your marketing plan sound amazing to me. My graphic skills are not the strongest, but I know what looks nice. However, I DO know about business. I've not only been a part of The Darling House my whole life, but I've tried to learn as much as I can in school so our theater can have a second chance. Poor Matt is trying, but his skill set only goes as far as accounting (besides his artistic side), but he's no visionary, unless it's set to music. So the first steps of this marketing plan are great. Visibility and increasing (or creating) our online presence. I can't wait to hear more about some of the ideas you've hinted at.

In regard to historical information about The Darling House, I know there are plenty of things in storage, but you may also want to check the other stage (called Stage A . . . the smaller of the two stages). We haven't used it for several years, so it's been accumulating rubbish. I'm not certain what's there anymore. Did Matt really ask you to go through our mess, or what did he call it? *Inventory*? Or did you offer?

And I'll keep the float idea a secret, but I'd encourage you to try to get some help. Did you mention meeting with some of the theater troupe on Friday? Many of them have been a part of the festival for years and I would imagine they'd be happy to help. I haven't been highly involved in the group for a while, but they were a good lot for the most part. Of course, you have your Casanovas and divas, especially in theater troupes, but I imagine you'll find some kindred spirits too. I'd join you if I could, but I have a few meetings at university, which will keep me there this weekend. Talk to Dani (a.k.a. FA). He'll make sure you meet the right folks.

Gwynn

PS: Matt has a ridiculous fondness for chocolate éclairs. It's always good to know your enemy's weakness.

PPS: You understand that I don't believe Matt is your enemy. He's just rough around the edges because he has to guard himself from everything and everyone. But, as I'm sure you can tell, he's a great dad, so don't let his gruffness fool you.

PPPS: Grandfather loves you. I thought you ought to know. He hasn't had someone bring him freshly baked chocolate chip cookies in years. I think he might name his next pug after you.

• •

From: Izzy Edgewood
To: Penelope Edgewood, Luke Edgewood
Date: September 10
Subject: Re: Brodie, Alec, and Grumpy Gray

Brodie told me all sorts of fun things about your visit when we had a video chat last night. Oh goodness, Penelope, I can't believe you convinced Brodie to drive that scooter. He said he'd never driven one in all his life, but you had an uncanny ability to convince people of things they wouldn't normally do. I told him you got "the gift" from Grandma Edgewood, who always boasted that her long-ago ancestors from Scotland went all the way back to Merlin. I don't think she really knew who Merlin was (or is, as the case may be), but she boasted about it anyway. I really do think it has to do with your undying optimism. Your belief in people is just so unswerving, they can't help but believe in themselves too . . . and most of the time things turn out in amazing ways, except with trampolines or goats.

I love the video you sent of the sea. Oh, I'd forgotten how blue the water is there. I can't wait to get back and experience my own hand kisses (or any other kisses, as long as they're in person and from Brodie).

Maybe you could pick up on some of your *You've Got Mail* vibes and save the theater like Kathleen Kelly tries to do with her bookshop.

Izzy

PS: I think the hand kissing leans toward more romantic vibes. I'm sure this "type" of hand kiss may give off more romantic vibes than others, but it's still a strange thing for a ritual.

PPS: Sorry for the kissing talk, Luke.

⋅ ⋅

From: Luke Edgewood
To: Penelope Edgewood, Izzy Edgewood
Date: September 10
Subject: Re: Brodie, Alec, and Grumpy Gray

Your "hair looks beautiful in the moonlight"? (Do girls really want guys to say things like that?) How does your hair look the rest of the time?

Luke

PS: I've lived with you. I already know the morning look.

PPS: Anytime I see the word k__s, I skip the sentence because I don't want details. Neither of you realize the hazards of being the only male cousin in this family.

⋅ ⋅

From: Penelope Edgewood
To: Gwynn Gray
Date: September 11
Subject: Re: Your ideas!

I am so glad you like my ideas and graphics so far. It's wonderful to finally put some of the things I've been learning into practice. Despite Matt's grumpiness, he really does seem to take my ideas seriously. And no, *I* asked if I could inventory things in storage. I feel as if there's something within all those boxes and crates just waiting to be discovered. Your grandmother's photo was just one of many things. I found a glass slipper in pristine condition. That doesn't happen every day and few people truly appreciate such a find. (It fits me, BTW. In case you were wondering.) One should always take finding a glass slipper seriously.

Besides, if we're going to attempt to save this theater, we need to see what props, costumes, and things we already have so we'll know which productions we can perform with the least cost. I know you all consistently have done *Peter Pan*, of course, as well as *The Wizard of Oz*. (I found Elphaba's hat, Glinda's wand, and a replica of a flying monkey. In fact, that's what brought Matt and Evelyn running to the storage room. They heard my scream when I found it buried beneath a massive hat that looked like it came straight from the Ascot scene in *My Fair Lady*. Flying monkeys and Edwardian hats should never go together.)

The ONLY positive thing about that horrendous moment was the fact that your brother ALMOST laughed. I think. It sounded like he was strangling on something, but I'm pretty sure it was because he didn't want to laugh. Isn't that the most ridiculous thing? Not wanting to laugh! When I look back on it now, a flying monkey wearing an Edwardian hat could be very funny, especially when one is prepared by fluorescent lights. I love to laugh.

And thank you for the insights about the theater group. What a great idea!!

I look forward to seeing you again when you're back in town. I'd love to try that funky seafood place you talked about.

Penelope

PS: I'm getting ingredients for éclairs from the grocery tomorrow . . . so I will be armed.

Text from Penelope to Gwynn: Why does Matt feel like he needs to protect himself? Is it because he's concerned about someone wanting to buy the business? Because I'm not a dangerous person. Well, except one time, but that involved hot tongs and a tube of lipstick. And it wasn't my fault.

Gwynn: I think it's more related to protecting his and Iris's hearts than the theater. Though he does appreciate the theater. But his biggest love has always been his family. Despite his grumpiness, he's a closet romantic.

Penelope: Oh my goodness! Well, we need to help him find courage for his heart again, don't we? I think it's wise to carefully open your heart, for certain, but guarding it so tightly that you've stopped laughing? A closet romantic shouldn't live with such fear!

Gwynn: I think if we take a team approach, we could make great progress in helping him.

Penelope: Don't worry one bit. I'm on it like Maria on the Captain.

Penelope: Not in the dangerous sort of way, like an assault or anything.

Penelope: And not in the romantic way, of course.

Penelope: Just in a doggedly optimistic sort of way. Like an Audra McDonald singing "Make Someone Happy" kind of way.

From: Penelope Edgewood

To: Izzy Edgewood, Luke Edgewood

Date: September 11

Subject: Re: Brodie, Alec, and Grumpy Gray

Izzy!! But Kathleen Kelly DOESN'T save her bookshop!!

I'm going back to my Maria von Trapp reference. There is no bookshop or theater, but there is Julie Andrews and therefore everything will turn out all right in the end, even if I have to scale the mountains wearing three layers of clothing to make it happen.

Brodie is a doll!!! He's just so sweet and perfect for you! Perfect!! I think I need a man with more passion to really make me happy. And I don't mean *passion* in an R-rated sense of the word, but I mean it like emotion, even if I have to go in search of the passion at first. I like mysteries, so that could be fun too.

Alec has SO much personality! I think we're alike in that way. He's very gregarious and talkative. In fact, he talked most of the walk, sharing about his travels and his love for the perfect-fitting suit. And I must say, those suits look rather perfect on him. In fact, he's so put together that I don't even think he has a hair out of place. I might need to up my vintage-wearing game. Perfect is a little unnerving. I suppose that's why Mary Poppins is only "practically" perfect. More approachable for kids.

When I asked Alec more about The Darling House's finances and ideas on how to save it, he smiled and said that I didn't need to bother with things like that. I'm not really sure what he means. I can't be expected to come up with ALL the ideas myself, though I feel I am capable if I think about it a little longer, but being aware of the business helps me with my planning AND my idea making.

Anyway, I am working hard adding more history and photos to our new website, sifting through the storage rooms some more, and I think I'm going to investigate the stage that is being used for storage. There might be some things we can use for the float in there. Time to find my 1930s felt-tip hat and resurrect my glamorous red lipstick. Did you know red lipstick helps you at sleuthing?

Penelope

PS: I know that red lipstick doesn't really help at sleuthing, but I always seem to discover more treasures when I wear it.

· ·

From: Luke Edgewood
To: Penelope Edgewood, Izzy Edgewood
Date: September 11
Subject: Re: Brodie, Alec, and Grumpy Gray

I skip sentences about lipstick too.

Luke

PS: Two months ago you called off dating. Have you matured since then?

Text from Penelope to Luke: I can change my mind. I'm a grown-up.
Luke: You still wear a princess crown, break out in song without warning, and think Santa Claus is real.

Penelope: Your go-to clothing is flannel and you pick food out of your teeth with a knife. You can't judge me.
Luke: "Can't" is a strong word.

. . . .

From: Penelope Edgewood
To: Luke Edgewood, Izzy Edgewood, Josephine Martin
Date: September 12
Subject: Grandpa Gray and mysterious meetings

So Matt had to stay late for a meeting at work with some business associates and he asked me if I'd make sure Iris made it home to Grandpa Gray. We had the car drop us off at my house first, so we could make some chocolate éclairs (with sprinkles added by Iris) before taking them up the walking path (through a lovely little wood) to the big house. It will be a nice surprise for Matt when he gets home, AND I was a little in hope of seeing Alec. Iris and I had an in-depth discussion about excellent princess names, should we ever be asked the question, of course. I've had my answer for years, but I loved hearing her thoughts on the subject. Cordelia was one of her favorites and I immediately thought you'd like that, Izzy, because it reminded me of *Anne of Green Gables*. One of my favorite childhood memories was when you read that book to me while I was in bed recovering from the flu.

Grandpa Gray is a darling man. He has salt-and-pepper hair and grayish-blue eyes. Alec says he's a grumpy old sort, but I've not noticed much of his grumpiness. Of course, I brought baked goods and . . . well, you all know that they tend to soften people. Anyway, in a rather casual way I asked whether it was against decorum to date one of his grandsons, if one had happened to ask me on a date-ish activity. To which Grandpa Gray said that I could date either one of his "useless" grandsons since he's the one who holds the "purse straps." Anyway, we had a lovely talk about his wife and daughter. Oh, how he misses them, but he seemed to enjoy talking about them so much that he even brought out the picture book.

Alec was a bit ravenous when it came to the éclairs, but I ended up saving two of them so that Matt could at least try them. Iris placed them in his room to keep them safe. For a man who is built kind of like Chris Evans, Alec sure does eat a lot. Of course, he says he works out every day, so that's probably why. I've decided my favorite types of "working out" are long walks and bicycling.

BTW, have I mentioned my progress? I made it up the long drive and back yesterday without one mishap. If my next two days prove as successful, I'm hoping to bicycle to work this week. I've chosen the perfect skirt to celebrate the occasion.

I waited around for a little while to see if I could watch Matt try one of the éclairs, but when he didn't return by eight, I said my goodbyes. Alec didn't offer to walk me home, but it's still light here at eight. He did thank me for the éclairs and Iris gave me the best hug on the planet. She smells like flowers.

PS: Grandpa Gray liked the éclairs too. I saw it in his eyes.

PPS: I met Scooby. He's a Shetland sheepdog, so Scoobs fits him a little better than Scooby (in my mind).

PPPS: Alec smelled like the sea. I'm trying to decide whether I like that or not. I'm a big proponent of the sea and absolutely adore walking along the beach, but with my history with sea monsters, I can't fully commit to adoring the scent of the sea.

PPPPS: Do you think Matt really had a business meeting? Or do you think he was on another date?

Text from Matt to Penelope: Thank you for the éclairs. I appreciate the effort you made in saving them from Alec.

Penelope: Did you like the sprinkles? Iris chose yours very especially. With the green sprinkles. She said green is your favorite color, so I made sure to have those color sprinkles on hand.

Matt: I'm not certain what to think of you having green sprinkles on hand just for me.

Penelope: I can tell you're being sarcastic right now. I have a brother. But I can also tell you liked them, so I'm smiling even more.

Matt: I'm happy to know my sarcasm can bring a smile to your face. I'll be certain to enlist my sarcasm in the future with more dedication.

Penelope: Smiling bigger right now. BTW, my optimism always rises to the sarcasm as if it's going to battle. Some people view my optimism as silliness or lack of depth of character, but I assure you, my optimism is one of my best and surest weapons.

Matt: Optimism as a weapon? That's a rather original weapon you wield quite well. I'll come armed with my sarcasm to keep you amply engaged then.

Penelope: I knew the éclairs would help! See how much fun we're having through texts? Well-baked goods have magical qualities for curing grumpiness. You can be sure that I'm a devout consumer of delicious baked goods and look how happy I am!

Matt: Are you saying that I'm grumpy?

Penelope: **Your eyebrows don't lie, Matt. You could do with**
   a bit more optimism in your life. Lucky for you, I'm here
   until December!

Matt: Lucky me, indeed.

Penelope: **I'm sensing sarcasm again.**

Matt: It's a good thing you come armed then, isn't it?

· ·

From: Penelope Edgewood
To: Luke Edgewood, Izzy Edgewood, Josephine Martin
Date: September 13
Subject: Websites and bicycles

Lunch with Alec was delightful! He is so charming and curious.
He asked about my home and you all, and he wanted to know
about my education. Then he listened as I shared some of my
ideas for The Darling House, which proved providential because
it was like a dress rehearsal for the meeting I had after lunch. A
staff meeting consisting of Alec, Matt, Evelyn, and Dani, while
Grandpa Gray and Gwynn joined via video, occurred where
we discussed the upcoming performances, my initial ideas for
marketing (with examples of my graphics), and the website
draft (of which I gained unanimous approval to make live). It was
wonderful to feel a part of the team.

So I'm spending the rest of the afternoon working on the
website, which I also need to check AGAIN for grammar and
spelling. How is it that you can read something nine thousand
times and still find spelling errors? I think the computer does that
on purpose! Then tomorrow I hope to delve back into storage in
hopes of finding more things to use for the float!!

BTW, I am riding my bicycle to work tomorrow. It's supposed to be a lovely day!

Josephine, I ADORED seeing the twins in their swimsuits. Is there anything cuter than baby chub? Those legs!! I almost cried yesterday because I missed them so much, but then I rode my bicycle to the nearby lake and stared at the view. I felt better after that.

Plus, I made cookies.

Love,
Penelope

PS: Matt really did have a business meeting. But he has another date tonight so I offered to keep Iris again! I'm going to introduce her to *Alice in Wonderland*. No princesses at all. Just a crazy queen.

PPS: I think a tea party is in order for tonight too. I bet she'll choose my Edwardian Ascot hat. I'll send photos.

. . . .

From: Josephine Martin
To: Penelope Edgewood, Izzy Edgewood, Luke Edgewood
Date: September 13
Subject: Re: Websites and bicycles

Oh, Penelope, the twins are making the most delightful sounds. I'm attaching a photo of their smiles! Noah smiles a little more than Ember, but I believe it's because she's taking in everything with those intelligent eyes of hers. I can already tell that they're both brilliant. At the rate Noah is growing, he should be able to wear the derby you bought him by the time you're home for Christmas. Won't that be delightful! I can get a photo of the two of you in your hats.

Izzy and Luke have been wonderful! I can't imagine trying to manage taking care of the children without a little help. I really don't know how women actually get dressed and brush their teeth while managing newborns. Just getting to church without spit-up on me feels like a true miracle from heaven, but Patrick and I have gotten into a good routine, I think. Though at times I believe this fatherhood thing has rattled even his sanguine disposition. He arrived at church with two different shoes, and you know how much he appreciates shoes . . . and feet. What self-respecting podiatrist wouldn't?

Oh, Penelope! Randy Davis asked about you in church Sunday. It seems that he's never forgotten about that one date you two went on in high school. You remember? The one that involved a Ferris wheel ride and the ill-timed flight pattern of a bird? The scar on his forehead is barely noticeable. Anyway, I think you ought to look him up when you return to Mt. Airy, Penelope. He's opened his own restaurant and it's doing quite well.

Love,
Josephine

PS: I don't care that you watch *Call the Midwife*, I still don't think it's a good idea to ride a bicycle while wearing a skirt.

Text from Penelope to Josephine: Grace in the movie *Return to Me* wears a skirt when she rides her bicycle in Italy. I just thought you ought to be reminded that skirt-riding is not completely relegated to historical time periods, though that movie is moving into the "historical" category at this point.

Penelope: Randy Davis doesn't like Julie Andrews. The bird was a sign.

Josephine: Calling a movie that came out in 2000 "historical" is not helping your point. And perhaps Randy has grown out of his childish dislike. Some men do, you know?

• •

From: Penelope Edgewood
To: Luke Edgewood, Izzy Edgewood, Josephine Martin
Date: September 13
Subject: Strange coincidence or something . . . stranger?

Maybe it's nothing, but . . .

You know all those fun marketing ideas I've shared with the team at The Darling House? Well, today my first graphics came out in the local newspapers and on social media. They looked great and Gwynn sent me an email to say so. But then, this afternoon, I got a look at the paper and Emblem Studios featured their advertisements in the paper too. Same day. And their graphics look strangely similar to the ones I used. I know, I know . . . it could just be a coincidence. Likely it is. Their advertisements, of course, were twice the size of ours, so that wasn't helpful.

I plan to make some fun videos of the community theater group during rehearsals for their fall production, and I plan to make a few reels and posts for it. I didn't share that with the team because they don't appear to be social media folks, except Alec. He has a social media account, which consists of photos of him in various places around the world . . . and, might I add, he always looks fantastic. I'd LOVE to see him in some vintage suits. With those shoulders? Heaven help me!

Am I being paranoid about the graphics? The website goes live today and I'm delving into the depths of storage, but . . . well, the idea that someone on the team is sharing my ideas? Surely not! Who would sabotage their own beloved theater?

Never mind. I'm being ridiculous.

Paranoid,
Penelope

PS: But it is strange.

CHAPTER 7

* *

From: Penelope Edgewood
To: Izzy Edgewood, Luke Edgewood
Date: September 13
Subject: Curiouser and curiouser

Alice in Wonderland was a hit, of course. Well, I think the tea party was more of a hit than the movie, though Iris fell in love with the Cheshire cat more quickly than she ought. She's much weaker to the magic of pink than I am. But she also adores cats, so the combination of the two was like kryptonite to her heart.

We happened to have "The Unbirthday Song" on while dancing around the table when Matt showed up with his eyebrows at full furrow. Not to worry! His brows acquiesced to the adorableness of his daughter, and before I could even wrap my mind around it, he'd taken up his own teacup and joined us in the silliness. Sort of. His dancing consisted of giving Iris a few twirls, and then he twirled me once or twice. It took my breath away for a moment. I suppose it's been a while since I've had a good twirl. Clearly, I'm wearing the wrong skirts.

BTW, Matt is a very good twirler. Definitely a plus for Iris's twirling future. (As you all know, Dad never could get a twirl right. I'm so glad Luke learned how to twirl a girl much better than Dad.) I'm guessing Matt's date must have gone VERY well. I always felt like twirling after a good date. It was nice to see him look . . . happy. Have you ever noticed how eyebrows can change an entire expression?

Anyway, he didn't mention his date, though I made some very carefully placed statements like "Dinner must have been nice," and "You seem to be in a great mood. Good evening?" He didn't seem to catch my hints, but he did enjoy my cucumber sandwiches and chocolate éclairs. They're so easy to make, it seemed silly not to add a batch to our tea party.

Anyway, the community theater troupe rehearsals are getting off to a great start. Oh, I love a busy stage! Even if I'm not acting, it's a delight to watch a story come to life! But let me just say, they'd make much more money if they opened up the second stage. They could run two shows at once, or at least in close succession! Gwynn agrees with me. We had a video chat about it this morning, so I think I'm going to have to use my sweet talk to convince Alec and Matt what a brilliant idea it is. Though I imagine Alec would be all for it, since it will easily bring in more income.

Have I told you the first musical the theater is performing this season??!! You will never believe it! Are you ready for this?

MY FAIR LADY!!!!

I am having a Queen Esther moment! Do you see it? I just finished being Flower Girl #1 in our university's production of *My Fair Lady*, and now? NOW I get to help a community theater bring this production to life?!? The hats!!!

Penelope

PS: Thanks for the video call, Izzy. You helped assuage some of my concern related to the graphics-stealing debacle. You're probably right. Just coincidence.

PPS: I was so glad I had my Mary Poppins bag with me because no one was prepared with bandages. Did you know they're called *plasters* over here? Plasters instead of bandages. Isn't that the cutest thing ever?

PPPS: Do you realize who played the original role of Eliza Doolittle on Broadway? (I'll wait for your answer. No googling!)

- -

From: Luke Edgewood
To: Izzy Edgewood, Penelope Edgewood
Date: September 13
Subject: Re: Curiouser and curiouser

Please NEVER EVER type the words "Luke" and "twirl" in the same sentence ever again. Ever. Again.

PS: The doorknob is my favorite character in *Alice in Wonderland*.

- -

From: Izzy Edgewood
To: Penelope Edgewood, Luke Edgewood
Date: September 13
Subject: Re: Curiouser and curiouser

Penelope,

I'm so excited for you. I know you'll be such a great addition to the community theater and production. It's no wonder Mrs. Crenshaw wants you as a director for her theater. You really do have such a gift with people and visualizing things. It's always made me marvel. The idea of getting up on a stage to talk, let alone dance or sing, nearly makes me weak, but you really have a presence.

I think opening back up the smaller stage is a great idea and something that would be cost-effective. The stage is already

there, even if it needs to have all the storage removed. Throw
one of those theater-kid parties you used to have at home and
get them to help you prepare the stage. Teens and young adults
always come out for food. Who am I kidding? We live in the South.
There's NO age limit to people responding to food. That's why
all those paintings of the marriage supper of the Lamb from the
book of Revelation look like a giant potluck. Potlucks are eternal.

Izzy

PS: I loved brainstorming with you. I'm always available, except
when I'm not. Or asleep.

PPS: Julie Andrews, of course. And I didn't use Google. I used
to live with you. There was no escape from Julie Andrews. Or
Audrey Hepburn. I think you're the only person I know (or may
ever know) who actually had full-sized posters of Julie Andrews
and Audrey Hepburn in the same photo. Full sized.

• •

From: Penelope Edgewood
To: Izzy Edgewood, Luke Edgewood
Date: September 14
Subject: Re: Curiouser and curiouser

Ooh, Izzy! That's such a great idea!

There are lots of young people at the church the Grays attend,
but I haven't met very many of them yet, so I'm not certain
they are the theatrical sort. However, I'm meeting with some
of the folks from the online theater troupe tomorrow evening
and maybe I can get some pointers from them about who to
ask! I'll reach out to Gwynn too! She knows everything about

everything. Or at least, she knows things I want to know, so that's what matters to me.

BTW, Matt told me I had to convince Grandpa Gray to open up the other stage. He's the one who closed it because it was such a precious, intimate stage to his wife. Surprisingly, Matt didn't mind the idea; he just doubted my abilities to convince Grandpa Gray. I tried not to laugh. Clearly, he underestimates my charm . . . and baking abilities.

And Alec invited me to lunch. It wasn't my best look today for lunch with a man who is built like Chris Evans and looks like Chris Pine. I'd been in the storage room looking for any costumes and props to ensure *My Fair Lady* blooms with excellence, and I'll admit that it was kind of embarrassing when he pulled a cobweb out of my hair. But it was a wonderful lunch. He talked about his travels. Lots of travels. They sounded exhausting, and that's coming from me—someone who really likes the idea of traveling. He offered some marketing ideas, but . . . to be honest, they weren't very good ones, so I asked him if he'd be willing to do a promotional interview for the local television station. He seemed to like that idea. He also held my hand and complimented me on my shoes (I wore my white and black oxford heels and felt very much like . . . um . . . I won't mention her because Luke doesn't like that musical). Alec likes to hold hands in the braided fingers way. You know what I mean? It's not my favorite because I have bony knuckles. Bony knuckles against bony knuckles get uncomfortable after a while, especially if you're squeezing hard, but since he smelled like the sea and sandalwood, I didn't mind so much.

Anyway, I found a TREASURE today. The very first playbill for *Peter Pan* at The Darling House. It was in good shape, so I immediately placed it between two pieces of cardboard and took it to my office. I think there are more also. And letters! Letters from patrons who enjoyed the theater for years. Sweet notes! Somebody should do something with these things so that others can enjoy them too! The paraphernalia hidden away is remarkable and in surprisingly good condition.

Treasure-hunting damsel,
Penelope

PS: I would like to add that both Julie Andrews and Audrey Hepburn are/were positive people overall. I take great encouragement from them. Not only were they positive, but they were smart, talented, and kind. Just because someone is happy doesn't mean they can't care and think deeply.

PPS: A favorite quote from Audrey (I like to refer to her with just her first name): "Happy girls are the prettiest," and I believe that means at the heart. Not just superficially.

PPPS: For some reason, I can't refer to Julie Andrews as anything less than Julie Andrews, or the Queen of the Stage, or Empress of Musical Delights.

. . . .

From: Luke Edgewood
To: Penelope Edgewood, Izzy Edgewood
Date: September 14
Subject: Re: Curiouser and curiouser

"You are so weird."

By: Me

PS: The Empress of Musical Delights plays a mean tooth fairy.

Text from Matt to Penelope: The next time you wish to move large boxes from the storage cellar to abovestairs, would you please ask for help?

Penelope: I almost made it to the top of the stairs on my own!

Matt: If I hadn't caught you, I'm afraid our intern would have become another ghost of the theater.

Penelope: Fine. Thank you. I will ask for help next time . . . if the boxes are big.

Penelope: Do you mean there are ghosts in the theater????

Matt: Aren't there always?

Penelope: You're teasing me. That's a good sign. I knew the chocolate éclairs would work magic.

Penelope: BTW, Grandpa Gray and I went for a lovely walk in the gardens out back of your house. He told me about his and Granny Gray's wedding day. Oh! I'm so glad she had cherry blossoms at her wedding. They're one of my favorite blossoms.

Matt: Unfortunately, their blooming life span is very short.

Penelope: But they leave a lasting impression. That's the important part! Not only are they lovely and vibrant, but when the wind blows the petals loose, the world is covered with pink. Sigh. Lovely. It's an image that can last a long time.

Matt: I believe you may have stepped directly out of one of those movies you keep showing my daughter. It's a bit unnerving. I'm beginning to think you're not real.

Penelope: Um . . . the bruise I left on your forehead when you "rescued" me would suggest otherwise.

Matt: Ah, yes. That would help with proof.

Matt: By the way, thank you for helping with the actors this week. You have quite a gift for motivating people in a positive way.

Matt: And I don't want to know why you have marbles in your
bag, but they came in quite handy.

Penelope: I keep them for anyone who might have lost theirs.

Penelope: I saw that you read my last message and for some
reason I can almost feel you smiling. Don't correct me if
I'm wrong. I'd rather believe it's true.

Skymarian Theater Troupe •

From: JA
To: GK

The theater group was such fun! I stayed out much too late with
them last night, but they truly are so close-knit and encouraging.
I'd met two of them already because they're performing where I'm
working, so that made meeting the whole group a lot easier. But
most everyone was so welcoming, even if I had to ask some people
to repeat themselves too often. I'm still getting used to the accents,
and so many all at once was . . . new. Anyway, it was wonderful!
Theater people connect with other theater people.

Plus, by the end of the night, several of them volunteered to
come help me with a super-secret project! They were thrilled about
my idea and really believe that the arts have taken a hard hit over
the past few years. They want to find a way to resurrect that "vintage" love of the stage and dance and music and story!!

And what a mix of ages! Kinleigh couldn't have been more
than seventeen. I wonder if Fiacla has a children's theater group?
(Will google that after this email.) I think Kinleigh would be an
excellent mentor for younger thespians. I started teaching younger
kids about singing and acting when I was even younger than her. It
was one of the best experiences of my life!

Just googled. It seems that Emblem is the only real gig in town for children's theater, but they're producing obscure plays that are politically charged. Hmm . . . classics are classics for a reason. Do you think it's a bad idea to want to bring back the classics, even if we tweak them a little to fit our needs? So many of them spanned ages and socioeconomic differences because they told good stories. Good stories and great acting (plus a few excellent songs) really can go a long way!

Anyway, I'm planning to meet up with Rae, Oliver, and Marsh for lunch this week to talk about the secret project, so that's exciting. Hope to hear from you soon!

PS: Quick question. Sasha said that Liam always wears a kilt. Is that true, or was she teasing me?

Text from Luke to Penelope: Don't ever try to do a video call from a bicycle again. Though it was great comic relief from a brother standpoint and your fall was cushioned by grass, I'm now seasick.

Penelope: I had you hooked onto the basket, so I thought it would be a good setup to show you my progress without holding the phone at the same time. Did you notice my hat? It's new. I got it from a place called Alexandria's.

Luke: The hat that flew off like a Frisbee and nearly decapitated a man walking his dog? That one? And please tell me you are wearing tennis shoes to ride that bike!

Penelope: Of course I'm wearing tennis shoes. They have navy polka dots. To match the hat. And that man's name was Mr. Lawrence Carrington, who happens to be a banker in the area and adores theater. He liked my hat.

Luke: So you try to only de-CAP-itate people you know. That's an encouraging thought.

Penelope: Well, I didn't know him until just now, but since he walks in the park a few times a week, we're sure to get to know each other even better. Next time, he's going to bring his lovely wife who played Mother Superior in *The Sound of Music* about ten years ago at The Darling House! Isn't that wonderful! I feel as though we're bound to be friends.

Penelope: De-CAP-itate. You're such a dork!

Luke: You're bound to be friends with everyone you meet.

Penelope: Not everyone, but it certainly helps when you're far from home to at least try to find SOME people to hang out with, you know?

Luke: Penny-girl, you NEVER have trouble finding people to hang out with.

Penelope: There are people, and then there are the right people. Sometimes a girl needs people for her heart and sometimes she just needs people for company. It's easy to find people for company, but not always easy to find people for my heart.

The phone buzzed in Penelope's pocket as she pushed the bike inside the little storage shed beside her cottage. Her brother's number lit up on her phone screen and a sudden sting pricked at her eyes as she brought the phone to her ear.

"I'm really okay. I promise," she said as soon as she heard his deep "Hey." "It's got to be lunchtime for you."

"I have a few minutes. Can't hurt to check in every now and again."

His Appalachian drawl tickled her ears. Having been around Skymarians for a few weeks now, she found the familiar speech patterns of home to sound all warm and cozy, like she needed to wrap herself up in her pink robe and sip hot chocolate while watching old movies. She sandwiched the phone between her ear and shoulder, digging her keys from her purse. "Oh, Luke, I wish you were here. You'd love all the architecture and buildings. And the fact that people still do things like walk to work and own sheep."

There was a pause on the other side of the phone before he responded. "Penny-girl, I've never once wanted to own sheep. I don't need a reminder about why God used them as examples of His kids."

"It's not that!" She laughed and bumped the door closed behind her with her hip. The scent of oatmeal-raisin cookies still lingered in the air from her before-work baking, but everyone at work had seemed to like the treat. Even Matt smiled. A little.

Of course Alec raved like they were the most delicious things he'd eaten all week. Said they reminded him of his mum.

"The quieter way of life is similar to back home, it's just that over here everything seems a little fancier. Old stone buildings, cobblestone streets, church bells chiming the hour."

"We have a clock that chimes the hour on Main Street."

"Not the same thing." She shook her head and tossed her purse on the little table by the door, then she dropped down on the couch, pulling a nearby blanket up around her. She wasn't sure why, but talking to her brother with a blanket wrapped around her somehow made her feel as if it were a hug. How weird was that? "Maybe you could come for a visit?"

"What do you think of the theater folks that have come in this week? They keeping you busy?"

She sighed. Deflection meant no. But who could blame him? He'd just started a new business and was "busier than a squirrel in a windstorm," as he'd quaintly put it. So of course he didn't have time to drop everything and come see her. Besides, she hadn't even been away for a month yet. It was a rather ridiculous request. "I'm still doing my marketing research and making plans for the float, but I think they've been forced to ask me for help with some of the production logistics because they're so short-staffed here. Finances aren't great, and to be honest, Luke, some of the actors could really use coaching."

"Could you teach them? I mean, didn't you offer acting and singing classes during summers here?"

"Yes," she answered slowly, nibbling her bottom lip. "But that was with kids and teens. Most of these folks are adults. New to acting, but still adults. It's *My Fair Lady*. There are no kids."

"I thought classes were offered for adults too? As I recall, it brought lots of revenue for The Ashby Theater, didn't it?"

Luke's statement sank in. *Classes.* The Darling House used to offer classes years ago. Or at least that's what she thought Gwynn had said. If Penelope could discover some of the old brochures to find out what sort of classes were offered and who taught them, perhaps she could encourage the team to try again. With classes. Give Emblem a little wholesome competition.

"Luke, you're brilliant."

"You're just figuring this out?"

She rolled her eyes heavenward, but her lips burgeoned into a smile. "I try not to tell you too often because the rest of us can live with your arrogance only so long before we become overwhelmed with nausea."

"Mortals are prone to weakness."

She hugged the blanket closer. "I'm really glad you called, Luke."

"Anytime, sis."

From: Penelope Edgewood
To: Izzy Edgewood, Luke Edgewood
Date: September 16
Subject: Epiphanies and more epiphanies!

A museum!! That's what I could do! With all the theater paraphernalia and history! There is a lovely set of rooms on one end of the theater that no one uses anymore. They're not far from the main entrance and have gloriously large windows. It's a fantastic way to celebrate the centennial and also help newer folks grasp some of the theater's history. We appreciate things so much more when we know their histories. What do you think?

But . . . I spent the morning with Grandpa Gray (after bringing him some of my famous chocolate cheesecake) and he's agreed to consider opening the other stage, especially when I mentioned we could dedicate that stage to his wife. The Lorianna Gray Stage. Doesn't that sound wonderful? I mean, we'll end up calling it the Gray or the Lorianna, but officially it will be dubbed the Lorianna Gray. Being the smaller of the two, it would make a perfectly intimate spot for smaller plays and children's theater. And since Lorianna is the one who started the first children's theater in Skymar, it makes perfect sense! When I presented my argument in that light—celebrating his wife, renewing the children's theater, AND increasing business for the theater—Grandpa Gray began to have a little change of heart. I think. At any rate, he nodded more frequently, so I took that as a good sign.

Oh! And guess what?????

Matt's name is Matthias! MATTHIAS!! Can you even believe it? I thought it was short for Matthew but it's much cooler! I feel as though I've heard that name before, but I can't remember where. I did an online search for it in the Bible, but it wasn't there either. But I love it! Matthias Gray. Doesn't that seem to give even more character to him? I shall henceforth refer to him as Matthias because . . . why wouldn't I? (Izzy, did you like that use of "henceforth"?)

Gwynn thinks the museum is a great idea! We're going to keep it a secret and reveal it to Grandpa Gray when it's closer to being finished! She's coming in for a long weekend next week so we can brainstorm. She's also volunteered to help me with some of the social media stuff so I can focus on other things. I have a blog idea I want to try, so that will help.

Penelope

PS: Another weird coincidence? After I started putting up reels related to our current rehearsals AND began offering some "stories" of the cast, one of the actors sent me a link where Emblem started doing the same things on their social media platforms.

PPS: And their newest advertisement looks like a design I'd been working on but hadn't made public yet. I shared it with the Darling House team and Izzy, but no one else. Another coincidence? Please say yes; otherwise there's a real possibility that we have a mole in the theater.

CHAPTER 8

Text from Matt to Gwynn: Did you happen to express to Miss Edgewood that I appreciated her presence during rehearsals?

Gwynn: Why shouldn't I share with her something nice you said about her? It made her day. It would be even nicer if you said it to her. She's the sort of person who thrives on being helpful to others.

Matt: How do you know I haven't shared my appreciation for her? And yes, I see what sort she is. But she's also very young, believes in fairy tales, tends to sing an inordinate amount of the time, and carries that ridiculous bag around with her everywhere she goes.

Gwynn: I can actually FEEL you smiling right now, despite what you say. And as I recall, her "ridiculous bag" has come in handy. You know she calls it her Mary Poppins bag?

Matt: I don't know how she manages to have everything and anything within it. She's found tweezers, shoelaces, feathers, and a lollipop for when Iris had been waiting for me longer than planned. I'm starting to think it may very well be Mary Poppins's bag.

Gwynn: I knew you liked her. I was just wanting you to admit it.

Matt: I never admitted it.

Skymarian Theater Troupe •

From: FA
To: Skymarian Theater Troupe

It was great to see everyone on Friday. Welcome to our new members! I feel as though there's some new (and needed) energy to our group with former members returning and new members who bring such passion.

As a reminder, we have a team member who is looking for some creative help. You know who she is. Meet her at FS's garage Thursday evening after rehearsal if you have time to lend a hand. Remember, it's for a good cause and a great way to drum up some publicity for *My Fair Lady* (for those of you involved in that).

Let's join together for the cause of the "creatives."

Text from Penelope to Gwynn: Classes! Have we ever offered classes at The Darling House for things like acting lessons, dance, and voice? I feel as though I read something about it in papers I've uncovered, but I can't remember.

Penelope: Emblem does it, but the costs are astronomical and there are practically no classic dance classes. I've been around Mountcaster and a few of the existing villages enough to say . . . Skymar is a "classics" place.

Gwynn: We used to! In fact, Matt taught me dance, but after Granny and Mum died, things fell apart. And Matt stopped dancing after his ex-wife left.

Penelope read the text again and then dialed Gwynn's number. The phone rang just as the idea that Gwynn might be in class surfaced in Penelope's mind. She rushed to push the End button, but a hello greeted her from the other end.

"I'm sorry, Gwynn," Penelope said, hurrying forward before Gwynn could say anything else. "I forgot that you might be in class."

"Actually, I'm having a cup of tea and reviewing the website, so it's a perfect time to talk. Is all well?"

Gwynn's lovely accent always made Penelope smile—dulcet and clear like Emily Blunt or Emma Thompson, except with the special Skymarian curl.

"Not to seem overly curious, Gwynn, but is Matthias a dancer?"

"*Matthias*, is it?" Her laugh bubbled out. "Oh, he's going to love that."

"It's a wonderful name." Penelope stepped out onto the little porch of her cottage, orange and pink hues of sunset painting watercolors across the sapphire sky. She drew in a deep breath of the air, tinged with the scent of rain. Luke had taught her how to smell rain in the air. She wrapped an arm around herself in a hug. An Iris hug would come in handy right about now. "I can't understand why he'd be ashamed of it."

"Deirdre didn't like it." An edge entered Gwynn's voice, hinting at the identification of this Deirdre. Matthias and Deirdre. Oh, but those names would look lovely on wedding invitations. "One of the many things she decided she didn't like about Matt, especially not enough to give up her career."

"Is that what happened?" Penelope gasped. "She gave up her family for her career?"

"Matt and Deirdre taught dance lessons at Darling. He's been dancing since he was eight and it broke my heart when he stopped."

"He just stopped altogether?" Matthias Gray loved dance so much, he even taught it? And he stopped dancing because of . . . a broken heart? Penelope's breath squeezed in her chest. How on earth had he managed such pain? The death of his mother, then his dear grandmother, and then . . . the loss of his wife? A wife who, by all accounts, from what Penelope had learned so far, didn't know how to love her family very well.

"When Deirdre left with her agent—with whom she'd been

having an affair for almost a year—something inside Matt broke. He'd been through so much already and, well, I'd never seen him close himself off to the world before, but he did. He gave up dancing and even teaching it and pulled away from everyone except Iris. She became his whole focus for a while." Gwynn sighed. "He'd taken some accounting and business classes in college so resorted to hiding in his office and burying himself in the books. It's only been within the last year that he's started really showing signs of some healing. Attending counseling has helped, and joining a small group of men from church has given him better perspective, but he's still so . . . cautious."

Penelope stepped off the porch and looked up the road toward the Gray House as if she could see through the forest to where Matt was. Perhaps there was much more to his grumpiness than just a surly disposition. "*Cautious*?"

"To trust new people, especially women. It's a miracle he even agreed to go on the few dates I suggested."

"And have any of them worked?"

"No." She laughed. "I think he just went on those dates to get me to stop annoying him. Both ladies said he was very polite but rather dull."

"*Dull*?" The word popped out so loudly that a little squirrel scurried up a tree as if his life depended on it. "He's not dull. He's actually very funny in a sarcastic sort of way. And he's been so kind to help teach me how to ride a bicycle. And he has such thoughtful comments about things." She looked around to make sure no one was listening and then lowered her voice into the phone. "I even got him to watch a little bit of a princess movie when he came to pick up Iris from the cottage. I think that's definite healing progress, don't you?"

"He watched a princess movie?"

"Well, part of one. Oh, and . . . we twirled."

"You what?" A cough erupted from the other side of the phone.

"Iris and I were having a very unbirthday tea party and happened to be dancing in the kitchen when Matthias came to collect her, and after a rather disgruntled entry, when he saw how happy Iris was, he joined the dance. He gave her a few sweet twirls and then, well, he twirled me too." A little flutter erupted in her stomach at the memory. "No wonder he's such a good twirler! He's a dancer."

"Yes . . ." Her response sounded strange and slow. "He is . . . or was."

"Oh, I think the dancer is still in him. In fact, I've witnessed it. That's a sure sign his heart is healing, don't you think? And someone who loves his daughter so beautifully certainly has the potential to love romantically again."

"Family has always been his heart, which is why Deirdre's betrayal wounded all the more." Gwynn slowly measured her words, like she was . . . thinking? Perhaps it was just hard to talk about the whole thing. "He would have given up the theater without a second thought if he believed Deirdre would have stayed. He used to be quite the romantic."

"But see, that's what I mean! The romantic in a person may be wounded, but it won't die. Take it from a true romantic!" Penelope nodded to herself. Yes, she may not understand a great deal about the world, but she understood that. "He just needs to find the right person to prove to him that there are still faithful, loyal women out in the world looking for a smart, talented man just like him. We just need to nudge him in the right direction."

"We do?"

"Of course we do! He needs to know real love is still out there, Gwynn. We can't allow him to let it pass him by."

"You know, Penelope"—something in Gwynn's voice caused the flutter in Penelope's stomach to move into hyper speed—"I think you are exactly right."

From: GK
To: JA

I'm so glad you enjoyed the group. They are, mostly, a good lot. I'm glad they're going to help you with your secret project, but I'm curious as to what it is. Since I missed the meeting, I also missed the news and am desperately interested.

You're having lunch with a few of the best from the team. Dani, the self-declared team leader, is stellar. He and his wife are both involved in community theater as often as possible and he gives all of his free time to a local theater, from what I understand. He's played about every bombastic male role (and a few female ones) that our local theaters have offered. He's also a wealth of knowledge with a wide range of connections.

And the idea of Kinleigh as a mentor for children? That's a remarkable idea. Her friend Lucas would be another one I'd suggest. He comes to the group meetings sometimes, but mostly to see Kinleigh. However, he's an excellent kid and a stellar young thespian. If there were a way to pay them or provide some sort of stipend, it would also encourage other youth to become involved as interns.

And yes, Liam often wears a kilt. He grew up in the northern mountains of Ansling. There is a strong Scottish heritage in that part of Skymar. You should visit sometime, only be prepared for a much thicker accent than you might find in other parts of Skymar. In fact, some still speak Scottish Gaelic, which is delightful to hear but nearly impossible to learn. Well, at least it's been impossible for me.

Would you happen to be working in Mountcaster?

From: Penelope Edgewood
To: Izzy Edgewood, Luke Edgewood
Date: September 17
Subject: A mole?

I had Alec set up an interview with the local news station tomorrow and just got a call that they've rescheduled the interview for the less popular time slot because Emblem offered to pay for the top spot we had. Is that even possible? And how did they know we had an interview set up? The Darling team were the only ones I told, unless they shared it with other folks. Or someone at the news team did.

I'm starting to feel that my paranoia is grounded in some truth here, y'all.

The Skymarian Theater Troupe promised to remain silent about the float (and if a group of drama folks give their oath, it's nearly as binding as blood); however, if Emblem pops up with a float similar to mine, I'm going to KNOW something strange is going on. But why? Emblem is this huge, apparently thriving business. Why would they target The Darling House?

But I will say to you all, I've been researching them ever since I started getting worried that they have something against The Darling House, and I realized that The Darling House could have an edge against them in one important spot. The community. Emblem Studios only brings in outside musicals and offers overpriced, impersonal lessons. But The Darling House began out of a love for theater and for this community. And after a little snooping, of which I am NOT ashamed, I've discovered that Emblem's numbers have been in decline for about two years now. People have been traveling all the way to Limmick on the island of Ansling to take lessons because Emblem's reputation is of a cold and disconnected place. Darling used to fill that need here in Fiacla. Lorianna Gray, in particular, used her connections to cultivate an atmosphere of community for The Darling House. I think we need to find a way to bring that sense of belonging back. To help remind the people of Skymar what The Darling House has meant historically and how important it can be even today.

Oh, I'm so excited. Now I know exactly what I want to do with this float AND what my purpose for being here is all about!

I still want to see if I can bring in a larger production for the winter season so we can raise some funds, but the heart of this theater is the people of Skymar, and that's where the focus needs to be.

Penelope

PS: I wonder what helps a closet romantic come out of the closet? I've always been an out-in-the-open romantic, so I have no idea. Chocolate? Fuzzy socks?

• •

From: Luke Edgewood
To: Penelope Edgewood, Izzy Edgewood
Date: September 17
Subject: Re: A mole?

Penny-girl,

I just have one thing to say about this whole mole thing.

"To survive a war, you gotta become war."

Luke

PS: I can send you a red headband if you need one.

PPS: Some people want to stay in the closet. It's safer from all your Hallmark nonsense.

· ·

From: Izzy Edgewood
To: Penelope Edgewood, Luke Edgewood
Date: September 17
Subject: Re: A mole?

I'm glad you haven't included Josephine on these emails. There's a good chance she would have already called some police station in Skymar to suggest that Emblem Studios may have some sort of spy who will stop at nothing to destroy The Darling House, complete with *Mission: Impossible*–style explosions.

But I don't like the sound of it. As to "why," could it be as simple as it is in *You've Got Mail*? The Darling House is the competition? Maybe what you're doing for it is making a bigger impact than they anticipated? Or they're afraid it will? Was anyone at Darling trying to make changes before you came that could have started Emblem's concern?

Izzy

Text from Alec to Penelope: Good morning, princess, I'm sorry about the news interview. Since the time has been changed, I won't be able to be there. Perhaps Matt will stand in for me?

Penelope: Alec! The interview is today! In an hour! I sent you a reminder yesterday. Why didn't you let me know then?

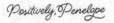

Matt is at a dentist appointment with Iris, so he can't be expected to prepare for it with such short notice.

<u>Alec:</u> Maybe check with Gwynn?

<u>Penelope:</u> She has classes this afternoon.

<u>Penelope:</u> I'll sort it out.

<u>Alec:</u> You're a doll.

- -

From: Penelope Edgewood
To: Izzy Edgewood, Luke Edgewood
Date: September 18
Subject: The knight just fell off his steed

I won't go into all the details, but Alec just told me he couldn't show up for a television interview I'd secured for him. If he'd just let me know sooner, it wouldn't be such a big deal, but it's in an HOUR. What was he thinking? He's supposed to believe this is even more important than I do! And if he doesn't, he should at least give his best for his family, if not for me! Argh!

I'm parked in front of the Gray House, and I have an idea. An impossible idea. But I'm going in with my very best smile, a whole host of promises, and some cookies. Please pray for a miracle or two. I'm losing confidence in confidence alone.

Penelope

<u>Text from Matt to Penelope:</u> How on earth did you convince my grandfather to join you for that television interview? I am certain, now more than ever, that you have some sort of magical power.

Penelope: I think he saw my desperation and felt sorry for me. I'm not sure I've ever felt so desperate, except maybe when I thought I was getting laryngitis before my debut as Belle in *Beauty and the Beast*. Didn't he do a fabulous job? I was so proud of him. We went out for ice cream afterward to celebrate. Some men just know how to wear a derby!

Penelope's phone went off in her hand to the ringtone "I Could Have Danced All Night." She'd changed Matthias's ringtone from "Don't Worry Be Happy" after she learned he was a dancer. Her smile spread so wide, it stretched across her face and she dropped back against the couch as she answered.

"An actual phone call? This must be my lucky day."

He huffed a response. "You say that as if we don't communicate almost daily."

"Not by phone calls." There was something different about hearing him over the phone. A focus on just his voice, his style of speaking. And she hadn't expected his voice to sound so . . . well, wonderfully delicious. Like he needed to break out in a rendition of "Some Enchanted Evening." She rolled her gaze heavenward. She was ridiculous! "But if taking Grandpa Gray out for ice cream will encourage spontaneous phone calls, then it's a huge win for me. Your grandpa's company, ice cream, and a fun conversation with you. How can that be bad?"

He sputtered for a second and then seemed to find his voice. "How did you convince him to go to the television station and engage in that interview? I can barely get him out of the house."

"Like I said, I must have looked pretty desperate, so when I offered to tag-team the interview with him, he agreed."

"Just like that?" His skepticism was not heartening at all.

"Well, I promised to make him carrot-cake cupcakes."

"And?"

She frowned. How did he guess so well? "Help him find some more of Granny Gray's photos that are packed away in the theater."

Silence followed for a few seconds and she twisted her finger through the little threads at the corners of the pillow in her lap. Should she tell him about her mole concerns? Could she trust him with her fears? What if he was the mole?

She shook her head. That didn't seem right at all! What would his motive be for The Darling House's fall?

"Thank you, Penelope." His quiet gratitude caught her off guard. Gentle. Sincere. Not that he wasn't usually sincere and, well, gentle with Iris. So gentle. And kind. But the way he said it left a sweet swell of warmth in her chest. "You were fantastic. Not just getting Grandfather on camera, which was a huge boon for the theater, but the way you added this positive energy to the entire conversation about The Darling House. Alec never could have done what you did today."

"I hope it helps." She squeezed the pillow close to her chest, his praise sinking deep. "I may never rescue a princess from a tower, or fight dragons, but I love showing people their potential, watching them . . . I don't know . . ."

"Believe in themselves, perhaps?"

She hugged the pillow tighter, a mist blurring her vision, so she closed her eyes. Men didn't usually see her that way. Not all the way to her heart. She often wished they did—former dates who took her for a silly, easy conquest, just a pretty face without a brain. But Matthias had just voiced a little piece of her heart that those men never took the time to figure out, and she realized that was exactly something that a friend was supposed to know. She drew in a quivering breath, not realizing how badly she'd wanted to hear a live person's voice until that moment. And he'd become a friend. "I'm really glad you called. I was feeling a little bit lonely for some reason, and your voice was exactly what I needed."

"You know that if you ever need personal contact, I could send Iris down for a massive princess fest, the likes of which we have never seen in Skymar."

A laugh burst out and Penelope sank back into the couch. "And I'm always happy to have her. Who knows? If you keep sending her, we might even convince *you* that fairy tales aren't all that bad."

"Humbug." But she heard the humor in his voice. Knew how to recognize it, and the knowledge spread her grin even wider.

"I suppose you'll receive plenty of warmth and attention from the Sutherlands this weekend." He cleared his throat. "And, I thought, if you needed it, you could borrow my car."

"Your car?"

"I can drive Grandfather's if I need one, unless your stunt today at getting him out of the house has awakened a sense of social prowess he's never had before."

She nearly spit out the tea she'd just sipped. "I'm not *that* magical."

"Ah, I'm not too certain about limiting your powers after today."

She stood and walked to the window, staring out at the forest in the direction of the big house. The faintest hint of light shone through the trees. "I don't want to impose, Matt." She caught herself before saying his full name, but it tingled the end of her tongue. A fabulous name like that ought to be said. Often. And rather sweetly, if she thought about it.

"No imposition at all." He sounded almost . . . chipper. "I'll drive it down in the morning."

"Thank you, Matthi—Matt. I'll see you in the morning."

A pause broke into the conversation. "Good night, Penelope."

CHAPTER 9

From: JA
To: GK

I'm going to speak to one of my supervisors about Kinleigh next week to see if we can get something in place very soon. The more we can do for the place I work to get the word out, the better!

And in answer to your question: I'm an intern at a lovely old theater called The Darling House. Its history is long and filled with all the ups and downs of most histories worth telling. I have a passion for vintage things and especially places like this, which have such love wrapped up in them. So I'm trying my very best to do all I can to make a difference.

I think of The Darling House kind of like Sleeping Beauty, slumbering beneath a curse of grief and uncertainty for so long that it's going to take a lot of fighting (hard work) and magic (imagination) to rescue it. I feel certain we have a good but small team for the challenge. I wouldn't mind a few millionaire fairies who might pop up to provide a little extra courage in the funding department, but at least there are the makings of a plan! Sort of. I have a lot of plans, but I'm not sure everyone else will want to jump on board.

And . . . I have some wonderful surprises.

I hope the team likes surprises. Only two of them know about some of the things I'm doing to help bring more visibility and clientele to The Darling House, but only ONE knows of my most delicious surprise. AND I have a whole bunch of other ideas that I plan to share with the team to see whether we can save this theater.

After meeting with the theater troupe in person, I've realized what a deep love the community actors have for the place, which is perfect for spreading the word. I know they've been trying as they can, but there's not been anyone to really pull them together for a unified purpose. Don't get me wrong. I'm NOT a leader.

But I am a . . . what's a good description? An encourager with an innate herding impulse? LOL.

Which doesn't mean I'm perfect by any stretch. If you met me, you would figure that out fairly quickly. I talk too much, come on too strong, give and expect honesty (and that honesty may come out with less finesse than it ought, usually because I'm talking faster than I'm thinking and, well, I think that's a part of my personality God is trying to work on), and have an unhealthy shoe fetish and a ridiculous fear of sea monsters. (Don't ask. The reason is equally ridiculous.)

I know the online group has sworn anonymity for all its members. And I totally get it! It's a very "theater kids" thing to do, so I won't share my name unless you want to know. But I would hope that if we figure out who each other are, we'd meet up for coffee and end up being long-lost forever friends.

Anyway, what would you do if you were tasked to save a historic landmark?

• •

From: Penelope Edgewood
To: Izzy Edgewood, Luke Edgewood
Date: September 20
Subject: A lovely turn of events

What a weekend! I love Brodie and his family. I can see why you adore the bookshop so much, Izzy. And the people at Sutherland's just love you. You're like some kind of legend.

Anyway, Brodie and his mom took me to tour one of the royal family's houses. I think the eldest prince lives there. He's the only one of the king and queen's five children who is married, so that means there are two princes around here somewhere still looking for their perfect princess. Brodie says the youngest prince and princess tend to stay out of the spotlight much more than the oldest three, so they're usually harder to find. How exciting, right? A prince could walk right into a restaurant at any time and, well, wow! Wouldn't that be amazing?

Oh, speaking of amazing . . . Alec texted me to apologize about the interview. He seemed genuinely upset about all I had to do and super surprised at me getting Grandpa Gray on the screen. So to "make up" for his "blunder," he invited me to dinner. Some restaurant that is in an old castle near here. Told me to dress up. DRESS UP! How am I supposed to say no to something like that? A dress-up dinner with a handsome man in a castle? It's like he reached inside my daydream and pulled out an invitation. I'm sorry to say that I didn't bring any of my evening gowns from home (not like I have a ton, of course, but that one pale-blue one? The one that makes me feel just a teensy bit like Cinderella? Well, I wish I'd brought it. I'm consoling myself with the fact that I'll have to go shopping.)

I got back to my cottage this afternoon, and since it is such a beautiful day, I decided to take a bicycle ride. Lucky for me that I did! As I was passing the park, I saw Mr. Carrington with his wife walking their dog. Mr. Carrington looks a great deal like Christopher Plummer in his older days, like his character in *National Treasure*, but surprisingly, Mrs. Carrington doesn't look anything like an older Julie Andrews. She gave off excellent Judi Dench vibes, like from James Bond. I only saw a James Bond film once because Luke tricked me into watching it by saying it was a classic. Just imagine my sad surprise when I discovered that "classic" for him and "classic" for me mean very different things. Though I got him back by letting out an appreciative whistle every time Daniel Craig showed up without his shirt.

Anyway, I've been invited for lunch with Mr. and Mrs. Carrington on Tuesday to talk about the theater and past stories and, well, I'm not sure what else, but they seemed excited too. And I got to hold their dog, Tootles. Isn't that wonderful, Izzy? Do you know who he was named after? Here's a hint: It's a character in a musical! In fact, Mrs. Carrington is a die-hard musical lover, which makes her one of my favorite people! She even likes hats! And Mr. Carrington has one of the best mustaches I've ever seen. I've asked them to adopt me as their temporary granddaughter while I'm away from home.

Izzy, in answer to your question about Emblem Studios and The Darling House—all I know is what Gwynn has told me. She said that Matthias has been doing a little research about how to improve things for the theater and Alec has been trying to build connections outside Skymar for financial support, which is what led to them hiring me, because Matthias's research had led him to learning about broadening their online presence and having a more consistent/active social media presence. And you guys know how much I adore social media. And graphics. And people!!! (Though I'm really glad that Gwynn is helping manage some of the social media, because this internship position has become LOTS bigger than any of us planned.)

Penelope

PS: I drove all the way to Skern and back without damaging Matthias's car at all, though at one point I got blocked in on both sides by cars when I stopped at one of the villages during market day to get a snack. I couldn't open my door at all so I crawled through the window. Let me just say, all those times I crawled out my bedroom window weren't in vain. I got my shoulder strap caught near the very end of my exit and a sweet little farmer and his wife caught me before I reached the ground.

PPS: They had the prettiest pig I'd ever seen. Her name was Esmeralda. I felt sorry for her because I'm afraid I knew her fate to be very much like her namesake's.

PPPS: Not that *The Hunchback of Notre Dame*'s Esmeralda ended up as a roast or something. I'm sure I wouldn't have liked the musical half as much if cannibalism was involved. I'm just saying both Esmeraldas didn't make it back alive, no matter how well they could sing . . . or squeal, as the case may be.

<u>**Text from Penelope to Josephine:**</u> **Did you get the link I sent you about pumpkin outfits for babies?? It was buy-one-get-one-free. Did you realize by having twins, you'd automatically get such amazing deals? I can't believe you had such foresight!**

<u>**Josephine:**</u> You've put too much stock in my planning abilities, Penelope. If you recall, the twins were a surprise. And these pumpkin costumes are for three-year-olds. Not three-month-olds.

<u>**Josephine:**</u> And, Penelope, please stop having gifts shipped here for the babies. I don't have room for them all. Tap shoes can wait! Ember and Noah can't even walk yet. I know you're homesick. I can tell from the daily video messages you leave while singing to the babies.

Penelope: It's never too early to fall in love with shoes. Can you tell whether the babies recognize my voice or not?

Josephine: If they're crying, they will quiet when they hear you sing.

Penelope: What? Oh my goodness! That just made me the happiest aunt ever. Just imagine what in-person singing would be like for them. It's very bonding, I hear.

Josephine: You can always end your internship early. I'm sure they'd understand if you want to come home.

Penelope: I am a little homesick, but I have a job to do here and I'm loving it! I just didn't realize how much I love home until now. Isn't that so strange? I'm not supposed to be the one who loves home so much. I'm the adventurer.

Josephine: There's nothing wrong with loving home, Penelope. And there's nothing wrong with wanting to go on adventures or even move away like Izzy is planning to do. But don't let all those big dreams in your head stop you from seeing that sometimes the best adventures can still be in the simplest things. Like home and family. And O'Dell's cheeseburgers.

Text from Izzy to Penelope: Brodie told me that you, him, and his little sister discussed The Lord of the Rings long into the night. You! The woman who feigns ignorance about who Gandalf and Bilbo and Frodo are ALL. OF. THE. TIME. Explain!

Penelope: Okay, Izzy. I confess. I've always known about LOTR. How could I not with you in the house? But it was incredibly fun to tease you about it. The fact you believed me was even funnier. And it seemed to make

you so happy to explain things as if I didn't know. So I
just went along with it.

Penelope: Besides, every time you'd talk about it, I always
learned more. I can't tell you how many times I won trivia
games at college just because of something you told me.

Izzy: You pretended? All that time?? I don't even know what
to say.

Penelope: Not ALL the time. At first, I really was pretty
clueless. But then when I would get something wrong,
you'd always get so excited to correct me. And after your
breakup, anything I could do to bring about your smile
seemed a good choice. Besides, most people think I'm a
ditz anyway. It's an easy part to play.

Izzy: First of all, I KNOW you are not a ditz. Second, your
intentions were good. Your means . . . skeptical. Third,
do you realize how much paraphernalia I bought for
you to help your memory? And fourth, WTG on the
trivia.

Penelope: All right, for the means, I'm sorry. For the trivia,
I did you proud. :) And for the paraphernalia, I have
digital and physical versions of the books and movies, a
mug that reads "I am no man," and an Andúril envelope
opener. I was holding out for a Gandalf hat, though. :)

Izzy: Well played, girl. And I demand you make it up to me by
having a LOTR trivia match, face-to-face, with Brodie as
the referee.

Penelope: You really want me to eat humble pie, don't
you? Well, I'll agree if I can wear a Gandalf hat while
competing.

Izzy: Deal.

Everything was quiet. Too quiet.

Matt pushed back from his desk and stepped to the doorway. It was much too early for the cast and crew to be making noise on the stage, even for some of the earliest arrivals. Dani's wife, Leigh, with Brooke toddling behind, usually arrived by ten to start laying out props and checking all the details for rehearsal. He didn't know how the performances would survive without the two of them. They'd basically taken over planning for the past few years, happily serving on what meager stipend Matt scrounged up for them. Mostly it was Dani's work, with Leigh helping as motherhood allowed, and Dani working around his plumbing schedule.

People made a great deal of sacrifices for what and who they loved. For their dreams.

An uncomfortable ache gnawed in his chest. He'd once thrived on dreams. Music, laughter, loyalty, family, love. But piece by piece his world had fallen apart and, well, he wasn't certain what to believe in anymore, except his slow-growing faith, Iris, and his family.

But love? The kind his icon, Gene Kelly, danced through the rain to celebrate?

He shook off the thought and turned his mind back to the theater and . . . the quiet.

With Dani's help and some small changes Matt had made over the last six months, the theater had started an upward financial trend. With Penelope's work, even more so. Maybe Matt could turn some of the revenue into a real salary for Dani or Leigh. Something to show his appreciation. The couple proved indispensable to rounding up actors every season and still pulling off as top-notch a performance as the Darling could offer in the moment. But things had started changing a little. For the good, he hoped. Not only the finances but the morale. A lightness of some sort had entered the place, bringing good memories back to light. And hope.

His gaze trailed down the hallway to the very last door. All that positivity usually came from the direction of a particular American. An oddly quiet American. He walked toward her office, passing Alec's, who rarely showed his face before noon. Then Gwynn's, who'd returned to university last night.

The scent of mangos floated toward him before he even reached Penelope's office door. Mangos and . . . he couldn't quite place it, but Iris called it "sunshine." Thankfully, it wasn't a potent fragrance but some sort of light scent dusting the air with a fresh mix of sweet and tangy. He rolled his gaze to the ceiling. *Sunshine?* His lips twitched at the thought. Very much like its wearer.

He'd never met anyone who wore sunshine quite like Penelope Edgewood. At first, it had been too much. Too overpowering and seemingly inauthentic, but then, over the weeks, her vibrancy melded into the spaces of this theater, shining in shadowy places no one had noticed for much too long. For a second, he wondered how they'd managed to make do without her. And how on earth they could go back to life without her ever-present . . . her-ness.

He shook off the thought and peeked around the doorframe. He hadn't been in her office for a week and she'd added more decorations. A bouquet of paper flowers, most likely from Wetherby's Magic Paper. She'd placed a bookshelf in the corner with a few books, all related to classic musicals or actors, except a set of children's books, which, upon closer inspection, were all written by Julie Andrews and her daughter.

A picture on the top shelf featured a quote in bright pink by Audrey Hepburn: "Happy girls are the prettiest." And above it on the wall hung a black-and-white painting of Audrey Hepburn with a list of beauty tips. But these tips weren't typical beauty suggestions. Matt's grin grew. They were much deeper. "For a slim figure, share your food with the hungry," said one. "For attractive lips, speak words of kindness." On and on, at least ten. One near the bottom read, "For lovely eyes, seek out the good in people."

And that fit her perfectly. From the bright-pink print to the sentiments in various decorative fonts. He'd been so certain Penelope's positivity and kindness were nothing more than pretense in the beginning. After all, most people didn't live with such generosity and optimism. Most individuals didn't run on boundless energy and unending joy. But each day, she kept proving her enthusiasm and goodness were a genuine portrayal of Penelope Edgewood's heart, and Matt wasn't sure what to do about it.

Which made the silence all the more noticeable. Usually he heard her come in every morning. She'd burst through the front doors, singing at full volume, with the scent of some sort of baked goods accompanying her entrance. But not this morning.

Her familiar teal laptop sat on her desk and her Mary Poppins bag waited nearby, which meant she must be in the theater *somewhere*. He spun around and marched to the front desk, where Evelyn sat behind her desk, her usual tight-bun hairstyle surprisingly replaced by a looser look. It gave the appearance of a younger, softer Evelyn Lennox.

"Good morning, Evelyn."

The woman looked up from her computer and offered him a small smile. "Good morning, Mr. Gray."

Despite his efforts, he could never get her to call him Matt. Even after five years.

"Did you happen to see Miss Edgewood this morning?"

"Yes, sir," she answered, patting a container on her desk. "She delivered her Monday breakfast muffins to"—she made air quotes—"'start our week off with a smile.'"

"Ah." Matt reached over and grabbed one of the muffins. "They certainly bring a smile to my face."

Her lips twitched a little wider. "If her enthusiasm in delivering them didn't, sir, her baking skills certainly would."

Matt gave a nod and gestured with the muffin before taking a bite. *Mmm*, this morning, banana.

"But if you're looking for her, Mr. Gray, she mentioned something about going to Stage A to treasure hunt. I believe those were her exact words."

"Treasure hunt?"

"Yes, sir." Evelyn's eyes brightened with her growing smile. "Because there are no ordinary hunts or mornings or, well, anything when it comes to Miss Edgewood."

"I do believe you're right. *Ordinary* is not a word to pair with Miss Edgewood at all." He patted the counter and took a few steps back. "Thank you, Evelyn."

"Mr. Gray." She waved a napkin at him and he smiled his gratitude. "If I may say so, I believe the muffins must be working, sir, because you've been a lot happier lately too."

Her statement caught him by surprise. Had he? Well, certainly Penelope's presence and skill set had relieved some of his worries, and having some positive numbers to bring to the business discussion lightened the burden of this place. Iris had been happier too. Singing around the house. Dancing. Even wearing tiaras on occasion and tapping his head with her "joyful wand" to inspire a tickle attack. He grinned as he moved in the opposite direction of the offices and the main stage. Yes, things had been better lately. Good, even.

Like he could take a breath and, perhaps, dream again.

It had been so long since he'd lifted his eyes above the everydayness of work and being a single parent. Beyond the wounds of a failed marriage and the insecurities and bitterness his ex-wife's choices left behind. Did he even know how to dream still?

He shook away the thought, the idea somehow constricting his chest.

As he neared the doors to the smaller stage, a bright-yellow sign to his left caught his attention. A large poster plastered to the front of a set of double doors leading into a space once used for various meetings held the words:

Secret Project
No Trespassing

Matt walked toward the poster and reread the notice. What on earth!

And yet, his grin widened. Those rooms hadn't been used in years. What was Penelope doing with them? And then he realized, a year ago he would have been suspicious.

But not now and certainly not with her.

What a strange sort of relief.

Surprisingly so.

With another look back at the sign, he turned and carefully opened one of the large double doors leading into the smaller theater. He drew in a deep breath as the scent of the space filled him. Though smaller and more intimate, this theater held so many memories, many of which were of his grandmother. This was the theater she'd overseen when her father started giving her responsibilities.

She'd nurtured a children's theater and then raised Mum to do the same, and they'd worked together as a team, until—

He paused, taking in the space.

Mum had been first. Unexpected. A car accident that left her in a coma for three weeks before she succumbed to her wounds.

And then Granny, but much different. Two years of battling cancer. Of fighting and failing. Of fading away—every part of her but her smile.

His eyes burned. He'd been hit with three blows in quick succession, with the betrayal of his wife after the loss of two of the other most important women in his life. The burden had felt too large, too heavy. But for Iris and the tattered faith still holding to his broken heart, perhaps he wouldn't have survived.

But he had. Like many people who had been through similar catastrophes before him. Somehow, on the other side, he finally started living again, instead of just breathing and putting one foot in front of the other.

A noise from ahead pulled him down the red-carpeted aisle and deeper into the theater. In the center of the stage, surrounded by boxes, sat Penelope. Her long ginger hair was pulled back in a ponytail and she stared down into a box of some sort. She'd worn more casual clothes today, if anything she ever wore could be considered "casual." Jeans and a pale-blue button-up with a multicolored sweater-vest over the top, making her look the part of a schoolgirl.

"Hard at work, are you?"

She looked up and a smile spread across her face, causing him to respond as if he didn't have any control over his face whatsoever.

"Oh yes. I have to clear this stage if we're going to use it in the future."

He rounded to the steps. "And where is all the rubbish going?"

"*Rubbish*?" She tilted her head back as he approached. "There are treasures to be found, Mr. Skeptical. Just you wait."

He pinched his lips tight and peeked down into a few of the boxes she'd scattered about. "Treasures, are they?"

"The treasures that are meant for the stage are going into the storage room." She waved toward the other boxes. "The other treasures are part of a very special—" Her green eyes popped wide, and she needled him with a stare. "You didn't go into the Secret Project room, did you?"

He stepped into the easy banter he'd grown to expect with her, narrowing his eyes before slipping down to sit across from her. "What would you say if I did?"

Her eyes narrowed right back. "Oh good. I'm so glad you didn't. Respecting a lady's request is a very important leading man trait, Mr. Gray." She looked back down at a paper in her hand. "And I'm planning a very special surprise for The Darling House, which I will reveal all in good time."

Leading man? He rolled his gaze heavenward. He was no leading man. Or hadn't been in a very long time, and he meant to keep it that way. Being a leading man meant the whole world found out about your heartaches, and there was nowhere to hide.

"You're quite keen on surprises, aren't you?"

She blinked. "Of course, especially when I know I've made a good guess."

"And this newest"—he waved a hand toward the door—"surprise of yours? Are you certain you shouldn't run it by someone in charge?"

"I have, oh ye of little faith." She looked up from her paper. "I got Grandpa Gray's approval."

"You little pixie!" Air burst from him. "What do you put in those cookies?"

"*Pixie?*" Her bottom lip dropped, but a very pixie-like twinkle lit her eyes. "I'm just a good baker." Her smile tipped. "And I've found that older people really appreciate someone who cares about listening to them. I love good stories and he likes to tell them, so it's a perfect match." She shrugged and returned to her papers. "He seems to like my enthusiasm too."

Matt had no doubt Grandfather enjoyed her attention. She was one of those people who listened with her whole face, as if you were the only person in the room. It reminded him so much of his grandmother. Likely for Grandfather too. "It's that enthusiasm, or lack thereof, which brought me here, in fact."

She tilted her head and her ponytail swished behind her. "What do you mean?"

"Your enthusiasm appeared to be lacking this morning."

"My enthusiasm?" Her nose wrinkled with her frown. "I don't understand."

"Well, you . . ." He cleared his throat, and for some reason he couldn't identify, his face became warm. "You weren't singing this morning, and I . . . I thought something might be wrong."

Her brow wrinkled to match her nose. "I wasn't singing?"

"Every morning you come into the office singing." He examined one of the nearby boxes. "And, well, this morning you didn't, and since you were away this weekend, I wanted to ensure everything went all right."

His attention rose back to hers, and she studied him with that direct focus she tended to have.

"Well, I have been distracted with theater things." Her smile didn't reach her eyes. "And I'm a little tired from my weekend, but it was a lovely time."

"But?"

Her entire expression softened in some kind of strange way that he felt in his stomach. Not necessarily a bad feeling, but, well, he wasn't certain.

"I *do* have theater stuff on my mind." She sighed. "And the other thing is just a ridiculous distraction."

"I came all the way to this stage to find out, so you might as well tell me."

She brought both her hands up to her forehead and then lowered her hands enough to peek over at him as if she were a sheepish little girl. "Tap dancing."

He laughed. "What?"

"I met with some community theater folks on Friday and a large group of them started doing a dance together." She sighed. "Tap dancing. They performed this wonderful routine they'd all learned together from somewhere and tried to teach me, but I just can't tap."

"You can't tap?"

"No. Well, not the right way." She rested her chin on her knees. "My tap teacher wasn't the best in the world. English wasn't her first language, so when she'd get frustrated, she'd yell in Serbian, which didn't help me understand at all."

His brows rose.

"I took French in school," she answered, as if that explained things. "Anyway, for some reason, tapping never came easily for me and I took the class twice." She held up two fingers. "Twice. Something never felt right. I can do simple routines, but never those really cool fast moves. There's a hitch in my step when I try. I just don't understand."

"Let's see it."

Her head popped up. "See what?"

"Your tapping."

"You want to see my tapping?" she repeated, her nose scrunched into her frown, which almost caused his grin to resurface.

His brain seemed to ask the same question. What was he doing? And yet he responded, "How will I know whether I can help you if I don't see what you're doing wrong?"

She stared at him for what seemed like twenty seconds, blinking a few times.

He'd committed to the lunacy at this point and decided to go all in. "You're not afraid, are you?"

"I . . . I . . . ," she started and then frowned. "I'm not sure where to start."

He drew in a deep breath to clear his head and gestured to the stage. "What about something basic? A shuffle ball-heel?"

Her face brightened. "Oh, I remember that one." And then she laughed as the color in her cheeks deepened. "Though it's been a while."

"No worries at all." His palms came up. "I'm only here to help, not be a critic."

She made to stand, and he offered her his hand. With a momentary look of confusion, she stared at his open palm and then awareness dawned, and her eyes brightened before she slipped her fingers into his. The contact was simple. Expected. Nothing out of the ordinary, yet it was completely out of the ordinary for him. The only person's hand he'd held in three years had been his daughter's, but the feel of her delicate, slender fingers sliding over his palm carried with it as odd a combination of familiar and new as longing and fear.

Was it odd, though? Or had he been living with the mixture for years now? Fighting hope for another chance. Another dream.

His hand tightened around hers, as hers did his, and with a little tug, he pulled her to standing. Something in the simple motion had him releasing her fingers as soon as he could. He brushed his palm against the side of his trousers.

"Thank you." She smiled up at him, evidently as unaffected as *he* ought to be.

He gestured toward her feet. "Your tapping, Miss Edgewood."

And after a moment's hesitation, off she went, her pink slip-ons moving in a pattern against the stage floor, their soft bottoms barely making a sound.

He squatted down to observe more closely, the problem apparent almost from the first shuffle. "Your ankles are too tight."

She came to a stop and burst out laughing. "Guys have said a lot of things to me, but that's a first."

He looked up at her, hoping his mock glare doused his waiting grin. "Very funny." But even as he said it, the glimmer in her eyes brought out his own smile. "I might add you should bend your knees a little more also."

"Do you say that to all the girls?" She winked. "Or just the inept ones?"

And he chuckled. "You are many things, Miss Edgewood, but inept is not one of them."

She stared at him a moment, as if gauging his sincerity. He paused on the notion. Was she often misrepresented as silly or stupid? He nearly groaned. Much like his initial thoughts of her. And in truth, he'd wondered at first how someone with so much enthusiasm and joy could also put a serious mind to task about the theater. But she'd proved him wrong about that and many other things.

"Okay, so . . . bent knees and loose ankles," she repeated, looking down at her feet, though her smile remained in full bloom. "I should be used to weird-sounding commands by now. I've been in theater most of my life, but there are still times when I lose it like a junior high girl." She looked back at him. "What do you mean by *loose ankles*?"

He stood and bent his knee so that his foot rose off the ground. Giving his knee a shake, his foot wobbled back and forth like one of those bobblehead dolls. "The control is in your feet and posture, not your ankles. A loose ankle allows your foot to move more quickly through the steps. Watch." He went into a routine of shuffle ball-heel and then time step, repeating the movements a few times in order to demonstrate what he meant.

"That was wonderful," she said, laughing, mouth wide in surprise. "Oh, Matt, and the way you grinned when you did it." She waved a palm in front of her face. "Swoon alert. I could just picture you in pinstripes and a fedora doffed to the perfect tilt." She released another sigh. "Oh, how I wish I could have seen you dance back in the days when you loved it so much."

Her comment shook him. When he *loved* it so much? Past tense? But had he lost it? That love and thrill of dancing? His body nearly quaked to take another slide or touch of heel to toe.

She didn't seem to realize his internal conflict.

"I'm determined to practice this now and show you my improvement later." Her chin tilted up in challenge as a glint lit her eyes. "And just so you know, though my tapping is not up to par, you should see me waltz and quickstep. I got the highest marks in my class on the waltz and the instructor loved my shoes. The right pair of shoes can totally save your day, it just so happens."

"Highest marks on the waltz, is it?" Her easy playfulness seemed to inspire his continued lunacy, especially with her face upturned and her smile beaming. "Show me then."

CHAPTER 10

Show him? Penelope looked from the top of his head to the bottom of his feet, pausing only a moment to grin at the fact she'd seen him dance, and then back to his face. "Show you my waltz?"

He raised one of those infernally expressive eyebrows of his and she braced her hands on her hips. "Fine. I will. But it's a two-person dance, so that means you're going to have to dance too."

The statement seemed to shock him, including his eyebrows, because they shot skyward with great speed. There was something extremely endearing about a befuddled Matthias Gray. She wasn't exactly sure how she befuddled him, but there was no use in wasting the moment.

"*You're* not afraid, are you, Mr. Gray?" She bent forward and offered him an exaggerated grin, playing his own words back to him.

His eyes narrowed as he examined her, and then he drew up to his full height, which was quite a bit taller than Penelope, and she wondered a bit how the whole waltz thing would work when the top of her head made it just under his chin. However, she'd witnessed a wild variety of dance pairings.

"I think I can manage it."

"Good." She wiggled her own brows and pulled her phone out of her pocket. "Now, which song?" Her finger slid over the screen. "Aha, I already have my Gene Kelly playlist up." She skimmed through the selections.

"Your Gene Kelly playlist?"

Her gaze shot to his, but she had to tilt her head back a little at his closeness. Surely he couldn't object to Gene Kelly, regardless of his past heartbreak. After all, it was Gene Kelly! "You say that like it's weird. Don't you like Gene Kelly?"

149

"Of course—he's one of the most creative and athletic classic dancers in history."

"And he's swoony."

Matthias's lips twitched. "I can't say a man has ever made me swoon, but if I were ever tempted, I should think Gene Kelly would do the trick."

Her laugh burst out and she squelched the urge to just reach over and hug him. It was so strange to keep feeling tempted in such a way. He had this cute humor and subtle teasing that spurred a hugging desire, as if her heart knew he really wanted one but his behavior shouted, "Whoa there, crazy southern American." Even if he didn't want to show it, she guessed he was a good hugger.

"You don't strike me as a regular swooner, but at least if you did decide to swoon, you have great taste in the object of your swoon."

"I can safely say I've never heard the word *swoon* used so frequently in one sentence in my life."

"Well," she said, shrugging. "I bet you've never met anyone like me before either."

His gaze softened with a whisper of a smile. "Without a doubt."

Her attention held in his for a second longer before she turned back to her phone, her cheeks oddly warm. "Well, none of these songs are in three-quarter time, so—" Her head popped up. "Wait, my friend recently had a wedding where they danced to a more modern song." She skimmed over the options, typing in the title. "But it's from a princess movie." She winked. "Do you think you can handle it?"

His eyes narrowed for the briefest moment. "I'll do my best."

Her grin split wide. "Don't worry, it's about an unconventional princess and an ogre."

"'Unconventional princess'?" His lips quirked just a teensy bit, with an added glint in his stormy eyes. "That seems fairly appropriate."

"Maybe I should stop praying for your sense of humor so much." She waved the phone at him before setting it on a nearby box. "If I'm the princess, does that leave you as the ogre?" She shrugged a shoulder and offered a syrupy grin, attempting his accent. "Fairly appropriate."

His chuckle took on more volume this time and her smile responded to the warm sound. "Very funny, Miss Edgewood."

"My sense of humor is one of my most undervalued qualities." She pushed the song's icon and the flute introduction started, followed quickly by a lovely violin addition.

She turned to face him, and he'd already taken position, poised with hand outstretched. A wonderful trill of anticipation trembled through her as she stepped forward. Oh, how long had it been since she'd waltzed? And with such a delightful friend as Matthias Gray!

Her body relaxed. Yes, he was becoming her friend, and perhaps he needed this waltz even more than he realized.

As she placed her left hand against his shoulder, his right palm slipped to her waist and then up to stop just beneath her left shoulder blade. He faced in the direction of what would have been her right shoulder, if she'd stood a few inches taller, but she refused to stare directly ahead . . . into his left shoulder. Instead, she tilted her chin up a bit higher and focused on the wave of hair swirling just over his left ear. What a fun little piece of knowledge about him! An unruly piece of hair to contradict his pristine persona! Kind of like the sneak peeks of his humor.

With a deep breath that raised his shoulders, he led in the first step.

It had been much too long since she'd danced. At least, since she'd danced with another person, and that must have been the reason it felt so right and magical and perfect. Dancing around the kitchen with a spatula in hand or with a pillow as a partner really didn't compare to the rhythm and shared pleasure in dancing with someone else. Especially when the someone knew how to dance.

And he did. The ease and confidence as he led them into their first beat with a strong body swing, the rising on his toes during the second and third beats. The way his sway sizzled with conserved energy for the next "first beat." It was practically perfect. Beautiful.

Oh, how she wished she'd worn a skirt. A skirt swishing and swaying with the changes in the waltz would have added a bit of earthly magic to it all.

And then she noticed it. Though Matthias glided with ease as the music swelled through the space, his neck and chin strained with tension. Why? Her heart squeezed. Was it because dancing brought back painful memories? Did he miss it? Oh dear, she wanted to hug him even more now. Perhaps a distraction would help?

"I've been thinking about another way to create visibility for the theater."

His gaze lowered to hers. "Does your brain ever grow tired?"

"Well, I never have trouble falling asleep because I'm usually exhausted by the time I stop for the night."

"No wonder." His chin relaxed with his subtle smile. Distraction had been a good choice. "If I had half your energy, I could likely save the theater all by myself."

"I'm glad you don't then." She squeezed his hand as a little reprimand. "Because I get to help, and I love helping. It's a wonderful thing to know that our creativity and hard work and . . . TLC can bring something out of the shadows that never should have been in the shadows at all. The Darling House, your grandparents, and you deserve that chance. Don't you think?"

His gaze held hers for a few seconds and then he nodded. "I like the way you think, Miss Edgewood."

"Well, at least on this point. I can list a few dozen other times when my brand of thinking wasn't your favorite."

His lips split into a grin, and she embraced the warmth pouring through her at the sight. He'd smiled a lot more lately. She took it as a clear sign that her work had helped relieve some of his burden.

"So what is this idea of yours?"

She steadied her shoulders and he chuckled. "Oh dear, am I ready for this?"

"Probably not, but it's a very good idea."

His chuckle almost increased to a laugh. Almost. "Let's hear it."

"Well, Grandpa Gray has approved of us reopening this stage, which is why I'm getting it cleared off, so that Mark—the carpenter from the community theater troupe—can get in here and make repairs."

"Mark has offered to do that?"

"Of course he did, though Grandpa is going to give him a stipend for his trouble. Your community theater peeps are die-hard fans of The Darling House and all it stands for. They want to see it succeed, too, because they care about its history and story." She sobered. "I think you should really tap into their passion and creativity. And let them know you are grateful for them."

"You're right." His shoulders gave a momentary droop. "I've been so distracted by my own life and trying to make it from one season to the next, I've lost sight of the good in it all. About a lot of things."

"Like dancing?"

He squeezed her hand back, his lips crooking ever so slightly. "Perhaps."

They took another quarter turn, allowing the music to fill the silence for a moment. He'd said "perhaps," which meant reviving his love for dance might still be a possibility. The thought settled deep, and almost painfully. Maybe Matthias Gray was as overshadowed and forgotten as this theater. Maybe he needed as much of the right loving touches and faith to bring him back into the spotlight of who he was meant to be too. Her smile spread. It was a good thing she was here! Bringing people into the spotlight was her specialty.

"Your idea, Penelope?"

Gee whiz, she loved hearing her name in his accent.

"Since this theater is more intimate and carries such a wealth of historical significance from your grandmother and mother, I think we should use this stage for the children's theater and the small productions, like some of the plays."

"And the larger stage?"

"Well, we'd still have our adult community theater productions there, but . . ." She bit down on her bottom lip to attempt to rein in her excitement. "It's been over four years since The Darling House hosted a touring company, and I think it's time to try it again."

"A touring company?" He shook his head. "We're not the theater we once were. What company would come to perform here?"

"There used to be plenty of companies who came in the past. And I have some connections through my university contacts. I think we have a good chance of hosting a group this December as they travel from the UK to the Netherlands, with Skymar as a stop-off point."

"That's barely months away. It's impossible to schedule a touring company on such short notice."

"'Impossible'?" She shrugged a shoulder. "To quote Cinderella, 'impossible things are happening every day.' And we won't know unless we try."

"Well, you've certainly proved that point where Grandfather is concerned. In fact, you seem very much like a veritable Cinderella."

"Oh my goodness, that's one of the best compliments anyone has ever given me." She sighed. "But I believe this is very possible. Shows get canceled all the time and need a new venue. We could very well be that venue. But we need to make sure the production is something really popular and makes people think of Christmas, because not only do I hope to have them come near Christmas, but"—she shrugged—"everyone loves Christmas."

Matthias's facial expression remained unreadable, so she nibbled her bottom lip a moment as she studied him. "You *do* like Christmas, don't you?"

His brows crashed together. "Of course I like Christmas."

"Oh good." She sighed. "Because I figured Christmas would be right up there with your rather gloomy views of fairy tales and romance."

His expression softened as he gently tugged her the tiniest bit closer. "Between you and Iris, I find fairy tales growing on me."

"You say that like they're a fungus."

He pinched his lips tight as if going for a frown, but she caught the twinkle in his eyes. Why, yes, Matthias Gray's sense of humor was making a fantastic debut.

"Well, fungus or not, I'm glad they're growing on you." She gave a curt nod. "Everyone could use a bit of fairy tales, especially grumpy pants like some people I know."

"'Grumpy pants'?"

"I call it like I see it." But her giggle bubbled out in contrast. "Well, you're not as grumpy as you were when we first met, so perhaps those fairy tales are working their magic on you."

Perhaps she'd grown on him a little, too, with all her positivity and weirdness. She frowned. Maybe she *was* kind of like a fungus. She shrugged a shoulder. At least some fungi were pretty.

He narrowed his eyes as if he were going to make some sort of grumpy retort, so she pushed ahead with her idea. "*The Sound of Music.*"

He stumbled a moment in the turn but regained his footing for the second beat. "What?"

"*The Sound of Music* would be a wonderful musical to perform during Christmastime."

One of those indicative brows jutted skyward. "*The Sound of Music* is not a Christmas musical."

"Neither is *Peter Pan* and you guys always perform it near Christmas."

His frown returned.

"And *The Sound of Music* is a perfect Christmassy musical." She rushed ahead with her defense. "In fact, it has been a family tradition. My entire life I've counted on *The Sound of Music* playing on television during the Christmas season every year." She squeezed his hand. "Every year. It's definitely a Christmas musical."

"And what makes it so . . . *Christmassy*?" He repeated the last word with as much exaggeration as the best thespian. Aha, she was bringing out his dramatic side. Surely that would come in handy.

Penelope opened her mouth to respond but stopped. What *did* make it Christmassy? A myriad of images passed through her mind. "Brown paper packages tied up with strings"? No, that could be any type of present. Sleigh bells? Nearer the mark. Her bottom lip dropped into a smile and her gaze zeroed back in on her friendly adversary. "Well, doesn't Julie Andrews make you immediately think of Christmas?"

Any tension around his pale eyes softened, gentling his gaze in such a way that she'd never realized how very stormy gray-blue they were. She'd never really been a fan of storms, unless it meant getting rescued in one by a charming hero, but stormy looked rather nice on him. She supposed if someone was going to have expressive eyebrows, they ought to have equally expressive eyes to go along with them.

"How can I argue with logic like that?"

"So I have your support?" She stopped moving and grabbed his other hand while still keeping hold of his left one. "About this stage and the touring group?"

His smile crooked and he tugged his hand from hers. "Well, I assume you've already gotten Grandfather's blessing?"

She braced her hands behind her back and rocked forward, smile wide.

"Ah, I see you have." He grinned and stepped forward, his fingers sweeping against the hair on her shoulder. "You still have dust in your hair from your adventures with the boxes."

She looked down at her shoulder, a tingle running across the cloth of her blouse at his touch. Her gaze met his. "Thanks."

His attention shifted over her face and hair, likely looking for more dust. But for some reason, she didn't mind the dust so much.

"Let me know how I can help with all your grand plans. I don't think The Darling House could have asked for a more enthusiastic savior."

Enthusiastic savior? Her breath caught at the sweetness of his sentiment. And if he hadn't said it with such tenderness right after waltzing with her, she probably could have refrained from hugging him. But she didn't. And promptly wrapped her arms around his neck. "Thank you, Matt!"

His body stiffened and she pushed back, offering an apologetic shrug. "Sorry about that. Just a little excited about the possibilities, that's all."

He stepped away from her and shoved his hands in his pockets. "I'm going to return to work now and let you finish your treasure hunting."

The sweet glow left behind from the teasing conversation and lovely waltz dissipated, and she took a few steps toward his retreating frame. What had she done wrong? The fairy-tale talk? The touring company? "Matt."

He paused on the first step off the stage and turned.

"You're a fantastic dancer. I've seen a few videos in the archives of some of your classes." She gestured toward the boxes. "I hope . . . well, I hope you can rediscover your joy. From all I've heard, it was a contagious sort of gift you had. The very best kind."

He bent his head in acknowledgment but didn't say anything else as he made the long walk up the carpeted aisle and out the door. She supposed dancing quite unexpectedly after such a long hiatus may have rattled him?

Penelope stared at the place from which he'd disappeared, offering up a little prayer for Matthias's heart, and then scanned the rows and rows of vacant seats. Four box seats, specially designed with carvings on either side of the stage for the "best" spots in the house, seemed to stare back at her. Four box seats in the Lorianna Gray Theater. Hmm . . .

She glanced back at her boxes, so many of them filled with nostalgic delights from ages past. Skymar may have a few folks who'd be willing to pitch in their resources and passions to make this stage come to life again.

Impossible? Her grin widened. Not while she wielded the magic.

From: Izzy Edgewood
To: Penelope Edgewood, Luke Edgewood
Date: September 22
Subject: The Sound of Music

Penelope,

I am so excited for you that your ideas for the stage and the touring theater group got the go-ahead! It really sounds like a great idea to help The Darling House.

Brodie said you guys had such a great time and his mom adored you, but your BIGGEST fan was Fiona, I think. Brodie said she adored the fact that you would sing show tunes with her, even while you walked down the street.

But now to the serious matter of your last email: You danced with Matt Gray?? Legitimate dancing, even. Not the kind I do while blow-drying my hair, alone, where no one can see. A waltz!! On a stage!!

You know what Jane Austen says about dancing? "To be fond of dancing was a certain step towards falling in love."

Izzy

PS: Tootles is a Lost Boy from the classic *Peter Pan*! Do not doubt my literary prowess.

. . . .

From: Luke Edgewood
To: Penelope Edgewood, Izzy Edgewood
Date: September 22
Subject: Re: The Sound of Music

If you stop reading the quote after the word "falling," then I agree. Otherwise, bah humbug.

Luke

PS: I thought *tootles* was a word Aunt Jane said while wearing her bright-red lipstick and terrifying sunglasses when she exited a place.

PPS: Weird stuff happens on stages. I wouldn't put a lot of stock in it.

. . . .

From: Izzy Edgewood
To: Penelope Edgewood, Luke Edgewood
Date: September 22
Subject: Re: The Sound of Music

Luke, you just resorted to your seven-year-old self.

And it's a stage! Of course weird stuff happens. Have you ever watched the stage production of *Charlie and the Chocolate Factory*? There are things you can't unsee.

From: Luke Edgewood
To: Penelope Edgewood, Izzy Edgewood
Date: September 22
Subject: Re: The Sound of Music

There are times when I'm not my seven-year-old self?

And why would I EVER watch the stage production of *Charlie and the Chocolate Factory*? There's singing involved.

Luke

From: Penelope Edgewood
To: Izzy Edgewood, Luke Edgewood
Date: September 22
Subject: Re: The Sound of Music

As soon as I got back to my office, I started sending out loads of emails to folks to see what I could discover! I already know of one touring group who are performing *The Sound of Music* through Europe, but I'm not sure if we can snag them. Oh, I hope! They have one of my favorite actresses playing Maria! She's no Julie Andrews, but who is? However, she breathes sunshine and joy and all things lovely. And her voice is sublime!

As far as the dancing incident: I am fond of dancing, but I'm not sure he is anymore, though he's very good at it. Graceful, elegant, strong. Oh, my face is getting warm at the very thought. I ADORE watching men dance!! Well, classic dancing, anyway. I don't think Matthias has done a lot of dancing since his wife left him (long, sad, horrible story that makes me think very bad thoughts about his wife and her agent), but he danced an excellent waltz. And taught me some tap moves. Nothing big like Fred Astaire or Gene Kelly but basic technique that truly helped. However, none of this has anything to do with romance. And especially not with Matthias. Besides, I'm going on a date, sort of, with Alec on Friday night and it would be very weird to like two brothers in a romantic sort of way at the same time. Very Sabrina-ish. And no one wants that sort of drama! Not even a thespian like me!

Besides, Matthias is the oldest brother. He's almost thirty. Or at least close to thirty. I'm not sure how I feel about dating a man who is almost thirty and has a daughter. Though I adore his daughter, but that's beside the point. Anyone would adore his daughter! I would make a wonderful mother to a daughter.

But Matthias is almost thirty.

And there is no war.

Penelope

. . . .

From: Izzy Edgewood
To: Penelope Edgewood, Luke Edgewood
Date: September 22
Subject: Re: The Sound of Music

Penelope,

So let's say Matt's twenty-nine. That's a grand total of six years. That type of age difference is not what we're talking about when war is involved. Think of Jane Austen's *Emma*! We're talking about *that* type of age difference. Double digits!

Izzy

PS: Captain von Trapp and Maria had a considerable age gap, I bet.

From: Luke Edgewood
To: Penelope Edgewood, Izzy Edgewood
Date: September 22
Subject: Re: The Sound of Music

Remind me of the war reference and thirty-year-olds again? I feel like I'm missing something. You're closing in on my age with your references, and the only war I want to see is the one Rambo starts.

Luke

From: Penelope Edgewood
To: Izzy Edgewood, Luke Edgewood
Date: September 22
Subject: Re: The Sound of Music

It's about the old-fashioned relationships of older men and younger ladies, Luke. Regency-ish. Like all of Izzy's favorite Jane Austen books. Back then it was common to have age gaps in marriages. And there's usually a war when the romance happens.

Penelope

PS: Oh, Izzy! How dare you bring up my precious Maria as a weapon!

PPS: But there was also a war.

PPPS: I suppose six years isn't *so* bad.

From: Luke Edgewood
To: Penelope Edgewood, Izzy Edgewood
Date: September 22
Subject: Re: The Sound of Music

Isn't there always a war when the romance happens? Regardless of ages?

Luke

Text from Izzy to Luke: I think we really need to get you a different dating experience.

Matt checked his watch. He had fifteen minutes to make his lunch meeting with Dani Lawrence, Darling volunteer who also headed up the Skymarian community theater troupe, and only one block left to walk. The sky promised a bit of afternoon rain, so driving the car this morning instead of riding his bicycle had proven providential.

And, of course, Penelope came to mind. She was now eternally linked to any thought of bicycles. He pinched his lips tight to battle against his smile. Whatever happened yesterday had to stop—the waltz and the hug and the way her joy wiggled its way into his pulse. He may not be her employer, but he wasn't interested in an inexperienced, lighthearted, fairy-tale-dreaming partner who wasn't prepared for the real-world work of a ready-made family.

That was just the truth of the matter.

She was young. Perhaps not *as* young as others, but in her . . . personality.

And she lived on the other side of the world. A very *real* difficulty.

And he had the heart of his little girl to consider. Iris didn't deserve another disappointment from a woman in her life.

He growled and pushed the thoughts away. Why was he even having this argument with himself? It was ridiculous. All of it. Utterly ridiculous. Penelope Edgewood was not in his future.

His phone buzzed in his pocket and he noted Gwynn's name on the screen.

"I'm on my way to a meeting," he said as he put the phone to his ear. "So I only have a few minutes."

"You danced with her?"

Matt ground to a halt. "What?"

"You danced with Penelope?"

Heat drained from his face. "She told you?"

"No, Evelyn did. You haven't danced with anyone except Iris since—"

"She told Evelyn?" How had his voice become so high-pitched?

"No, Evelyn saw the two of you. Someone had phoned for you and she went to find you, walked into the theater, and there you were, center stage, spotlight shining, arm in arm—"

"I get the point," he growled and resumed his walk, at a much more agitated pace than before.

"Do you . . . do you fancy her?"

"Fancy her?" The words burst out loud enough to garner a look from a passerby. He quickly lowered his voice. "Of course not. I like her well enough. She's . . . certainly a benefit to us at the theater and a . . . pleasant personality, for the most part."

"Pleasant enough to dance with, it seems."

"I don't know what happened." He shook his head. "One minute I was giving her tips on tap dancing, and the next minute I asked her to waltz."

"A perfectly reasonable segue, of course."

The sarcastic response did nothing to clear his head. "It was like I had no control over my brain any longer. The pixie!"

A snort came from the other end of the phone, only rallying his defenses even more. "I tell you, it was magic. She put a spell on me with that smile and those eyes and her ever-present ability to convince people of things. It's probably what she's done to Grandfather. She would be the sort."

A series of halted breaths greeted him from the other end of the phone.

"Stop laughing. You haven't been around her enough to have a full understanding." His feet slowed to another stop. Even trying to explain it sounded preposterous. "She's . . . she's not like anyone I've ever met before. She sort of attaches herself to people and then convinces them of things they don't realize they're going to agree to until it's too late. You saw what happened with Grandfather. He was on the news!"

"And it was amazing and exactly what he needed." Gwynn's voice still held tinges of humor. "It seemed to open up some sort of door for him to enter back into life. As if he didn't even know what he was capable of until he tried something completely new. He's even planning to come to the festival. Do you realize how long it's been since he's done that?"

"That's what I mean!" He huffed, remembering the way they glided across the stage, the steps in perfect synchrony, her sweet scent wrapping round him. He blinked. He still couldn't understand his own behavior. "It's like she bewitched me, perhaps without even meaning to."

"Has she bewitched you, body and soul?" came the strained question.

"What?"

"Never mind." A choking sound ensued. "And bewitching people for the good seems like a rather benevolent undertaking, if you ask me."

"Dancing is for my good, is it?" But even as he spoke, he knew the answer. Somehow pinning a better memory with dancing—with

Penelope instead of Deirdre—lessened the ache of dancing altogether. In fact, he *almost* wanted to do it again.

"You know the answer to that question." Truth sobered her tone.

His heart wrestled against the desire for—well, he wasn't even certain, and he cleared his throat. "Listen, I need to run. I'm meeting Dani Lawrence for lunch."

"Dani? The volunteer-liaison-with-the-community-theater Dani?" Praise be, he'd gotten her distracted from the dancing topic.

"Yes, the same. I'm going to speak to him about coming on staff as a liaison for the community theater actors. A salaried position."

"That's a brilliant idea, Matt."

"I got it from the pixie." His frown deepened. "Heaven help me, she's everywhere."

"And she's very smart. Just because she's . . . unusual, sometimes, doesn't mean she isn't quite capable. We've seen that."

"Which is why I can even broach the subject of hiring Dani. Our sales numbers for this production are double what they were for last season. And I've been able to secure two additional donors who weren't as interested in giving, but after reviewing our new website and the history section, they've changed their minds. It's almost as if she bewitched the website too!"

Gwynn's laugh burst out just as the restaurant came into view. Perfect timing.

"I've got to go."

"The conversation's getting too poignant for you, is it, brother?"

"Or too ridiculous."

"Let me just say"—her voice gentled—"a little bit of ridiculous sweetness and enthusiasm may be exactly what you and Iris need most of all. Deep hurt needs great love, I think."

"Gwynn, don't even imply—"

"After all, you wouldn't have taken the initiative to reach out to Dani or contact those donors six months ago or dance on the stage, but now?" Her chuckle returned with added barbs to the stinging in his chest. "It's all very bewitching, indeed."

He hung up the phone on her laugh. Just as he shoved the phone back in his pocket, he glanced left into the window of Neeps and Tatties to find Penelope sitting across the table from the very last person with whom he'd have expected to see her. Niles Westing?

He drew to a complete stop in the middle of the sidewalk.

Why was Penelope meeting with the owner of Emblem Studios?

CHAPTER 11

Penelope sat by the window of Neeps and Tatties, sipping her tea and attempting to work up enough bravery to taste the haggis sandwich she'd purchased. Luckily for her, the lunch order included a sandwich sampling of two halves, so she'd chosen the BLT and . . . the haggis, because she'd promised Grandpa Gray that she'd try it. It wasn't so much that the "meat" within the sandwich looked unappealing. Strange with its blackish, speckled coloring and spongy consistency, but not as gross as she thought it might look. But the idea of its contents proved the real deterrent. She gave it a few pokes with her fork and took a bite of her BLT.

Mr. and Mrs. Carrington were due to arrive within the next fifteen minutes, so if Penelope wasn't brave enough to eat the haggis sandwich, one of the Carringtons may want it. After all, they were Skymarian.

And there was always Tootles. He probably loved haggis.

"Ah, Miss Edgewood, isn't it?"

Penelope looked up from her seat to find a rather disturbing person standing over her. She knew his face and rather fierce-looking mustache. The Emblem Studios man! She pushed up a smile. "Mr.—" She floundered, then shrugged. "I'm sorry, but I can only remember Niles."

"Westing." His smile curled with as much animated proportion as any cartoon. "Owner of Emblem Studios."

"It's nice to see you again, Mr. Westing."

And he proceeded to sit down across from her without an invitation. "I'm surprised we haven't run into one another since your arrival, but I hope you've enjoyed your time in Skymar so far."

Apart from the mustache, Mr. Westing didn't look unnerving, but there was something about him that put Penelope on edge. Was it because she suspected he'd planted a mole to sabotage her and The Darling House? Perhaps and, well, that was enough. She sighed out her frustration. But everyone deserved a chance to prove her first impression wrong, didn't they? Just like the Beast from *Beauty and the Beast*, or Dimitri from *Anastasia*, or Captain von Trapp!

"It's been a lovely stay so far. Are you a native of Skymar?" Maybe learning more about the man would give some clues to what he really wanted. Oh, how she wished she'd worn her red fedora.

"I'm originally from England," he said with a wave of his hand. "But I consider this my home now."

"I can see why you'd want to stay." She glanced around the restaurant, praying Mr. and Mrs. Carrington arrived soon. "I'm sorry, Mr. Westing, but I'm meeting some people here for lunch today. So I don't have a long time to talk. Is there something you needed?"

He leaned back in the chair, making himself way too comfortable for her own comfort. "I've followed some of the things you've been doing for The Darling House. You have a gift for seeing what is needed and making it happen. I . . . appreciate people like you."

"That's very kind of you to say." Pinstriped suits looked so much better on Cary Grant—it must be the broad shoulders. "I've had such a marvelous time doing it."

"Clearly, you have talent." His dark gaze roamed her face, one brow curving upward. "A talent, I fear, which will be wasted on a dying theater like The Darling House."

"I don't think it's dead just yet, Mr. Westing." Penelope trained her expression, but her top lip tempted to snarl just a bit. "There's still a lot of life left in that theater, if hope and hard work can make it happen."

"*Hope and hard work*," he muttered and then leaned forward, braiding his fingers together in front of him on the table. "It comes to this, Miss Edgewood. I want to hire you. I could pay you very well and give you everything you could want in a position at my theater. Top-floor office with a view of the coast. Massive performance halls. Staff to work for you. A dream job for someone so young."

Her heart twinged just a teensy bit when he mentioned the salary, and the flash of a shoe closet blared to mind. But then Iris's smile overshadowed it. Followed by Grandpa Gray's gentle hand to her shoulder. And then Alec's look of admiration, and Matthias's . . . well, just Matthias.

She wasn't tempted, really. Just a momentary daydream. It really was the shoes' fault.

"Thank you for that most generous offer, Mr. Westing, but I must decline."

"Decline?" Both his brows rose. "You cannot be serious! I can offer you twice what that little theater pays you, and a penthouse office instead of the tiny hole you have now."

How did he know about her salary or her office? "Mr. Westing, as I said, I appreciate your generous offer, but I've made a commitment to The Darling House and I am true to my commitments. A trait which any quality employer should value in an employee, don't you think?"

His frown deepened to such an extent that his chin quivered.

"And I think the very best businessmen can learn how to appreciate healthy competition, don't you?"

"Healthy competition." He released a humorless laugh. "Bah! Darling is a relic. It doesn't stand a chance against Emblem."

"Your attempt to hire me away from it would suggest otherwise." She smiled much more sweetly than she felt and took a sip of her tea.

"Time will tell, won't it, Miss Edgewood." With that, he pushed back from his chair, offering her a scowl before, with a dramatic wave of his hand, he disappeared out the door.

From: Penelope Edgewood
To: Izzy Edgewood, Luke Edgewood
Date: September 24
Subject: The good, the unexpected, and the unexpectedly weird

Something weird just happened. Well, I mean weirder than my usual weird.

I'm sending a quick note before riding my bike to talk to Grandpa Gray about my visit with the Carringtons.

Anyway, the owner of Emblem Studios (the larger, newer theater here) approached me about an hour ago and tried to buy me away from The Darling House. I mean, movie stuff. Offering me twice the salary and a big office and, well, all the fancy bells and whistles. I turned him down, of course, but he knew things about my salary and my office that he couldn't have known unless one of the Darling staff told him. It's all very strange.

But the good news is, the Carringtons were just as lovely as I thought they'd be. I'll tell more later, but they ADORE The Darling House, and Mrs. Carrington was particularly close to Lorianna Gray, which means she's even more invested in bringing the theater back to the forefront of people's minds. But the Carringtons are rather rich. And since their children were so fond of performing in the community theater, they are even more invested in seeing their grandchildren experience the same atmosphere and intimacy that The Darling House offers. What does this mean? They want to give to the theater. And I think we should do something grand for them to ensure they feel appreciated for their generosity. Like name the other stage after them (seriously, big money). I'm going to talk to Grandpa

Gray right now. And Mrs. Carrington mentioned something else, which I think may be another brilliant idea for visibility and fundraising. They also want to sponsor Kinleigh!!!

I'll share more later!

. . . .

From: Penelope Edgewood
To: Izzy Edgewood, Luke Edgewood
Date: September 24
Subject: Re: The good, the unexpected, and the unexpectedly weird

Grandpa Gray was overcome by the generosity of his wife's friends, the Carringtons, and is in full support of naming the larger stage after them. He also suggested we offer to some of the other rich theater-loving folks in town the opportunity to purchase a "theater box" to have named after them. We have four. Well, three if you count the fact that Grandpa Gray already said the Carringtons get one by default.

Then (are you ready for this?) we talked about renewing the Darling ball. You read that right!

A BALL!!!! Cinderella-style! (Which, BTW, is one of our spring productions!! AHHH!!!) It's the year of Julie Andrews!

Oh, that just reminded me of something to add to the float.

Anyway, the ball used to happen in November, the weekend before the annual *Peter Pan* performance, as a thank-you from the Grays to the community.

I rode my bicycle all the way back to the theater so I could help with rehearsal tonight. What. A. DAY! What started out as a possible creepy conversation has ended in a magical opportunity sprinkled with my very own Cinderella moment.

AHHH!

Alec caught me while I was leaving Grandpa Gray's study and asked what I was doing at the house in the middle of the day (I could have asked him the same thing, but I didn't think about it until just now). Anyway, I told him about my meeting with the Carringtons and about Mr. Westing's offer. He was genuinely astonished. I would be, too, at the audacity of the eerie man.

I hoped he would offer to drive me back to the theater, but he didn't. He seemed preoccupied and I'm sure there are lots of things to think about when a production is being rehearsed.

AND (thanks to some guidance by the community theater group and approved by Grandpa Gray) we're going to run another production. *My Fair Lady* is performing in two weeks, but tryouts for—are you ready?—*The Lion, the Witch and the Wardrobe* can go ahead and start so we can have *My Fair Lady* performing on the larger stage (the Carrington?).

Rehearsals for Narnia (the other title is too long to type) will be overlapping in the smaller theater, so when the *My Fair Lady* performance ends, we can begin tryouts (and possibly rehearsals) for *Peter Pan* (which they do EVERY year in November and will transfer over to the smaller theater once Narnia is finished). That will lead into the big theater being used for *The Sound of Music* with our touring company (hopefully). It's going to be the fullest two seasons Darling has had in four years!

If the team agrees.

But Grandpa Gray said yes.

Penelope

PS: Can you imagine Iris dressed for the ball? Oh, I hope Matthias will let me curl her hair.

PPS: I have no ball gown, but I was able to find a dress for my date with Alec (in the castle, in case you forgot).

Dani took the position with a nod and handshake, appreciation clear in his eyes. He'd deserved to be on salary a long time ago for all the work he did bringing actors to The Darling.

It was one of the best feelings Matt had experienced in a long time. Right and good.

Matt hadn't realized the full extent of work Dani did for The Darling House in his spare time. Somehow, he and his wife kept recruiting actors from the community and steering them toward The Darling House despite Emblem's intention to steal away as many as possible. And Dani had done all of that work on a meager stipend. Imagine what the man could do full-time! Why had it taken Matt so long to step back into his relationships with these people he'd grown up knowing? Had he truly allowed the grief of his loss and humiliation to steal his time with these people?

He'd slowly been stepping back into relationships for months, but Penelope's presence spurred him into relationships, dance, joy . . . dreams.

He frowned. And he had been avoiding her for two days. Admitting it would make him sound immature and ridiculous, but the truth of the matter was, he hadn't realized two very unexpected things:

One, how much he missed dancing.

And two, when she'd hugged him, something inside him broke,

then came back together. That singular moment reawakened something in him for . . . He closed his eyes and shook away the thought. No, he wouldn't entertain that particular thought, and certainly not with a woman who was moving back to America in two months' time.

But he'd held his love of dance and family close for years—trusted in their beauty and consistency—until Deirdre shattered them. His sweetest dreams. She'd distorted both of them in one fell swoop, leaving his grieving heart to sift through the pieces for some semblance of hope. He'd never cared for spotlights or riches. His heart turned toward simpler dreams. Simpler didn't mean less costly; in fact, the dearest dreams came with the highest price.

Yes, he'd begun to heal, to make it to the other side of suspicion. To live above the wisps of grief stitched into unexpected moments and memories. To trust again.

And then he'd seen Penelope with Mr. Westing.

All the feelings of betrayal resurrected, reminding him of the risk and cost of fairy tales and daydreams. Penelope had seemed so different. Honest. Authentic. Generous with her heart and her time. Had it all been a ploy, much like a six-year marriage where he'd been the one to sacrifice his time and desires for his ex-wife's dreams, moods, and whims?

Or had Penelope fallen prey to the temptation of something better?

He shouldn't take it personally. After all, Emblem Studios could offer much more than Darling, but the wound knifed deep. With a growl, he steeled his emotions against the hurt.

He steered his car out of Mountcaster, thankful Gwynn had been willing to take Iris home since he stayed late to meet with some of the board members about ways to reach possible new donors.

A light rain misted the front of his car and caused the streetlamps' glow to reflect against the dark street.

Suddenly, a flash of something on the side of the road caught his attention. A cyclist? In this weather? He slowed. Who on earth would ride their bicycle at dusk through the—

A flash of a red skirt flapped into the glow of his headlamps, and he slowed even more, pulling nearer the cyclist. Penelope glanced toward him and, upon recognition, her smile flashed wide. After being so crowded only a moment earlier, his mind drew completely blank. How did one respond to the simple fact that the woman was crazy?

He blinked. Well, that explained a great deal, didn't it?

He passed her and then pulled over on the side of the road, snatching his umbrella from the passenger seat before exiting the car.

"What are you doing?" He opened his umbrella and marched toward her.

She skidded to a stop just behind his car and looked up at him with those wide eyes of hers. "What do you mean?"

"It's raining." He held the umbrella over her head as if to prove his point. "You should have let me know you were biking home and I would have given you a ride."

"But it's not raining all that much." She looked upward and then back at him, her smile so inviting he just couldn't place her as a betrayer at all. "And I decided I could not only sing in the rain, I could cycle in the rain too."

Her light laugh bounced through the space between them.

He stared for a long moment. "You're impenetrable."

Another laugh bubbled from her. "I'm sure you mean that much kindlier than the way it sounds."

He pushed the umbrella into her hand and took control of the bicycle, his head shaking. If he could have thought of a response, he would have spoken it, but at the moment, he could barely get words into a sentence. Who was this woman?

"Let's place the bike in the boot and then I'll drive you home."

"I love it when you call the trunk of the car the boot." She sidled up next to him, holding the umbrella more over him than herself. "And I don't mind the rain."

176

"Well, I do, and this way you can spend the next ten minutes in the dry of the car."

He worked the bike into the boot, with a little of it still protruding a bit, and when he looked back over at Penelope, who still held the umbrella over him, her smile took a softer turn. "Thank you, Matt."

His gaze paused in hers a moment. "Of course."

He wrapped his hand around the umbrella handle, his fingers brushing hers for a second, and the dance came back to mind, so he tugged the umbrella free from her grasp and gestured with his chin for her to get in the car. She'd almost made it to the passenger door when she spun around to face him, her navy hat crooked on her ginger head. "Do you mind if I call you Matthias?"

And, as if struck by lightning, he finally realized why a word like supercalifragilisticexpialidocious could come in handy. In fact, Penelope should wear a disclaimer as a caution for the people she met. Warning: This word may be helpful when in a friendship with me. *Supercalifragilisticexpialidocious.*

His bottom lip loosed, but he collected himself. "Get in the car, Penelope."

Her smile dropped but she obeyed. He rounded to the driver side to join her in the car.

He put the car back in Drive and started forward.

"Don't you like the name Matthias? It's a very heroic sort of name, I think."

His eyes winced closed even as his lips curled into a smile. "*Heroic?*"

"There's something about it." She tilted her chin up. "Matthias Gray." She swept a broad gesture with her hand as if making a regal entrance. "Yes, like a knight or something. Sir Matthias. Ooh." Her shoulders trembled. "Oh yes, very nice. It's certainly the type of name for someone who would rescue a lady in the rain."

Supercalifragilisticexpialidocious. Yes, that word came in very handy.

177

"Names have power, you know?" she continued, nonplussed. "Matt is a fine name, of course, but Matthias has a certain something special about it."

He cleared a laugh from his throat. How on earth did the woman live with so much . . . whatever it was, all the time? "My mother used to call me Matthias. Grandmother also." He focused ahead, the admission stirring up a strange tenderness. Grief, he supposed, but something else. A sweet memory. Like an endearment almost.

"Then if two of the most important women in your life called you Matthias, you have to like the name a little." She patted her knees and relaxed back in the seat, her damp hair curling around her face.

The quiet sobered the moment.

"I hate the word *cancer.*"

He glanced toward her, attempting to follow her logic but without success.

"It's such a painful word. I know your mom didn't die of cancer, but your grandmother did. So much loss for your tender heart." She placed her palm on his arm, her touch as comforting as the tone of her voice. "I think it might be sweet for someone to call you Matthias again. And the name suits you."

A strange mix of humor and tenderness swelled through him, fighting for a victor. Clearly, her type of crazy was rubbing off on him.

He refused to glance in her direction.

"My best friend in high school—she fought cancer for as long as she could." Her voice trembled a little but then steadied. "*Inoperable* is an ugly word too."

He turned then, and she looked up at him, her eyes glossing in the pale light, but a small smile still played across her expression. "I got a secret tattoo in her honor. A butterfly on my shoulder." Her finger rubbed at the spot between her neck and edge of her shoulder. "Dad would have killed me if he'd found out, but for some reason—" She sighed. "I know I have memories, but, well, memories didn't seem permanent enough for someone who'd been such a big part of my life."

The road blurred. Heaven help him, the blasted woman had him nearly in tears.

"Is your dad still alive?"

He drew in a breath, grateful for a diversion from the current topic. "He remarried a year ago and moved to Ansling to be with my stepmother and her children. They're younger and needed more stability, and Dad had never been as connected to the theater as Mum."

More silence. "I can understand why laughing would be difficult for you, though. Your mom, grandma, and then your wife all within such a short time. It's a miracle you've retained your smile."

The rain pattered in the silence. Whether from its calming rhythm or Penelope's gentle care, he continued the conversation. "Who told you about Deirdre?"

"Gwynn," she answered. "Grandpa Gray too."

More silence. What was there to say?

"I can't imagine what selfish desire could lead a woman to leave something as sweet as you and Iris. I just can't."

The bewilderment in her voice softened his discomfort a little. "I don't believe 'sweet' has ever been a word used to describe me."

Her face turned in his direction and he raised a brow, watching as her ready smile spread at the awareness of his teasing. "True, I was probably talking more about Iris with the 'sweet' part. But I must defend the heroic name of Matthias now, and add that you are a very good man."

"Good?"

"Of course you're good. And kind, smart, creative, funny in your own way when you actually let funny happen." She waved toward the back of the car. "You *did* just pick me up from riding my bicycle home in the rain, so that shows a definite heroic streak. And you taught me to ride the bike, which certainly speaks to your perseverance and patience. Luke gave up lessons after only two days."

And then he laughed. Not a huge belly laugh, but something louder and less used than a chuckle. Supercalifragilisticexpialidocious. For certain.

"Well, in the future, please find me when it's raining and you're leaving the theater." He turned toward the drive leading up to the cottage, then the house. "I might enjoy a chance to be heroic now and again." He shot her a look. "But only in the rain."

She stared at him a moment. Then her expression softened in such a way, his broken heart pulsed in response. Lamplight flickered across her face and hair, bringing out the deeper reds among those lighter hues.

Attraction? He steadied himself, forcing his senses to dull.

"I'll keep my expectations duly aligned then, Matthias."

Her use of his full name slammed directly into his thoughts with the force of fairy dust on a laughing child.

He pulled the car to a stop in front of the cottage and handed her the umbrella. "I'll collect the bike."

She met him around the back, umbrella open, but of course, she held it over him instead of herself as he walked the bike to the cottage porch.

"Do you know Mr. Westing?"

His stomach dropped at her question. "Emblem Studios' owner?"

"Yes, him." They stepped up on the porch and she handed him back his umbrella, her brows creased. "He gives me the creeps. Especially that mustache. Definite villain vibes." She shivered. "He had the audacity to join me at my table I was saving for the Carringtons and then proceeded to offer me a job."

"Offer you a job?" Something much better than anything he could offer.

"Yes." Her frown deepened. "A ridiculous offer. Double my salary. Top-floor office space. Even a staff of my own for marketing and promotion."

"And . . ." He leaned closer, studying her face, and the realization dawned like another blow to his assumptions. "You turned it down?"

Her gaze flew to his. "Of course I turned it down. I made a commitment to The Darling House, and I keep my commitments. Plus, I think what we're doing is a worthwhile endeavor much deeper than money; it's for the heart of the community and the love of real theater." She shot him a wink. "Besides, who wants to work for a man who tries to intimidate people with the size of his mustache?"

Whether from relief or her ridiculous comment, another laugh burst out. This time, much more than a chuckle.

"Well, well, look at that, Mr. Gray." She touched his arm again, a trait she'd shown since their first meeting. Touchiness. It was her way of connecting. Of showing her care. "We found your laugh."

He looked up at her, shaking his head and blinking like a man who'd stepped into the light after a long time in the dark. "I suppose we did."

"It's a good sound. Soft and warm." She stepped back toward the cottage door. "Your brother's is so loud and easy. I suppose he hasn't had the same kind of heartaches as you." She pulled her key from her purse. "I think that's what makes hearing your laugh all the sweeter."

His brother. Alec. Weren't they going to dinner on Friday? He pushed a hand through his hair and stifled a growl. What was he thinking? He didn't even know, but whatever it was that made him want to keep close to her and breathe in her joy and bring out her smile . . . well, there was no way he could continue any part of that . . . fairy tale. Every possible ending involved hurt, not just for him but for Iris. And he wouldn't risk anything to wound his darling girl. She'd been hurt enough in her young life.

Penelope lived for the fairy tale. And he couldn't give it to her.

He could only offer her his heart, and a broken, fumbling one it was. Even if he could afford to be interested in her.

And when it came to any comparison to Alec, he fell short. He'd never been the extravagant or spotlight sort. No, even if he were interested in winning Penelope's heart, she would never choose him over Alec. Even the best fairy tales didn't work that way.

"He's borne his troubles differently, I suppose." Matt moved to the porch steps, opening the umbrella as he reached the breach between the porch roof and the open sky.

"I suppose." She tossed a look over her shoulder as she pushed the cottage door open. "Would you like to come in for some tea?"

He looked away and gestured toward the car. "I'd better get home in time to put Iris to bed."

His gaze caught in hers as she studied him. "Thank you, Matthias, for rescuing me."

His pulse responded to the name again, to the tender look in her eyes, and an ache branched out through his chest. One thing was certain. He wouldn't dance with her again. He couldn't. As the song said, "Music leads the way to romance," and especially dancing for him.

So he had to end any possibility before it even began.

"Good night, Penelope."

He returned to his car and sat for a moment, staring at the cottage door. The warm lights from the windows beamed with an invitation to the wet world outside. Home. Warmth. A second chance.

He wanted them all.

But not with Penelope Edgewood. The risk proved too great.

CHAPTER 12

Text from Matt to Penelope: You tell me about Mr. Westing but don't share the most important details!

Penelope: What do you mean? I told you he was going to give me a top-floor office.

Matt: The Carringtons, luv. You didn't mention the simple fact that the Carringtons are going to donate a massive amount of money to the theater AND support a position for Kinleigh as an intern to grow the youth theater. Just those two minor details.

Penelope: I'm confused. You sound angry but you called me luv, so I'm not sure how to respond.

Matt: I'm not angry. I'm over the moon. Impressed. Astounded. You truly are a gift to us, Penelope, and I'm extremely grateful for you.

She stared down at the text. It wasn't like Matt had made any grand gesture or sweeping soliloquy, but the tenderness in his sentiment hit her. Being helpful and creative and reaching out to people came so naturally to her, she didn't really do it for gratitude, but his message meant something special for some reason. Maybe it was because it came from him. Or because it seemed so deliberate and heartfelt?

She walked to the window and stared out across the woods, barely making out the roof of the Gray House. Her finger hovered over his name, which she realized she needed to change to Matthias in her contacts instead of Matt. She shook her head. She didn't need to call him. Why would she even think that? They'd talked only an hour ago in person. Talking in person could wait until tomorrow, of course. She could respond now by text. With a turn away from the window, she sat down on her bed.

"*Your message was so sweet*"? No, that didn't quite convey the right feeling.

"*I really appreciate your kind words*"? She wrinkled her nose at the text and then deleted it. Though she *did* appreciate his words and they *were* kind, that particular response didn't seem to hit the mark either.

"*Would you mind repeating your message in person so I can hear what 'luv' sounds like from your voice*"? She grinned and promptly deleted that one too. Silly. She nodded toward the blinking cursor. Though a very legitimate desire.

> **Text from Penelope to Matthias:** It's such a joy to be a part of the magic of bringing The Darling House back to life. I feel kind of like a fairy godmother (though I'm much too young to be one, you know).
>
> **Penelope:** And thank you, Matthias. For your text. It really mattered to me.

Skymarian Theater Troupe •

From: GK
To: JA

You're an "encourager with an innate herding impulse"? I actually laughed out loud when I read that. The Darling House is a lovely theater with so much character and, I hope, many years still left in its bones. And getting a youth theater intern involved is a splendid idea. You're just overflowing with ideas, aren't you? I'm sure the people at Darling are pleased to have you on their team.

Well, sea monsters and a shoe fetish? I have to say I've never read those words in the same sentence before. I understand the shoe fetish, though. A great pair of shoes can change the trajectory of your day.

I hear the two brothers who are running The Darling House can be a little frustrating at times. Have you found that to be true? Is the grandfather really a recluse? What about the little sister? I hear she's barmy.

Text from Alec to Penelope: Are we still on for Friday, princess?
Penelope: I hope so. I bought a special dress for the occasion.
Alec: Excellent. I should be there around seven. Give or take.
Penelope: Are you not going to be at the office this week?
Alec: I have a few meetings, so hopefully my absence will
        make your heart grow fonder.

. . . .

From: Izzy Edgewood
To: Penelope Edgewood, Luke Edgewood
Date: September 26
Subject: Re: The good, the unexpected, and the unexpectedly weird

A ball? Dinner in a castle? Good grief, Penelope, it's like God just looked right into your head and made all your fairy-tale dreams come true. How crazy is that? And you're going to be so busy! What part do you play in getting the performance ready? What do Alec and Matt do? Does Gwynn get involved with performances too?

Okay, I'm glad you got away from Mr. Westing. He gave me the creeps just hearing you describe him, but what great news for the theater. Donors and all your team's hard work!! It's all about the team. I can't wait to be at Sutherland's in person again. Don't get me wrong, I'm grateful I can pick up the phone and see Brodie on video chat, but working with the whole team at Sutherland's was fantastic. I'm sure you feel that way, kind of like when you did summer theater camp at Ashby.

BTW, I'm sending photos from last week's Mayberry Days. Luke and I helped with the library booth and, as per usual, Luke dressed up as Tom Sawyer, sort of, though I seriously doubt Tom Sawyer wore tennis shoes and flannel. Before Josephine emails you, I thought I ought to warn you that we saw Jacqueline Morrow Crenshaw (can we please refer to her as JMC?) and she asked if we had any idea of your interest in her offer. Evidently, she looked up The Darling House online and saw all your work. She's even more interested in having you as the director and, Penelope, it's quite an amazing offer. At your age, to be an executive director of such a historic theater! And with your work in Skymar, you'll have so much more experience. Had she mentioned anything to you about wanting an answer by December? It seems that if you don't join her, she's considering selling the place. (No pressure, BTW, I just thought that was an interesting bit of info.)

Gotta run. I'm babysitting the twins so Josephine and Patrick can have a date night. You'd love it, Penelope. The twins have just started laughing!

Izzy

. . . .

From: Luke Edgewood
To: Penelope Edgewood, Izzy Edgewood
Date: September 26

Subject: Re: The good, the unexpected, and the unexpectedly weird

The same man won the pie eating contest as last year. No news there.

But you missed the dog parade and the whistling competition. I remember that you almost won that competition when you were thirteen. One of the proudest brother moments of my life.

Luke

PS: I ate a pork chop sandwich in your honor.

PPS: Both of them were equally delicious.

<u>Text from Penelope to Luke:</u> **"Both of them were equally delicious"? I hate you.**

<u>Penelope:</u> **And I miss home. And you, surprisingly. And lots of other things, but mostly just knowing my family is around the corner. I never thought I'd feel that way. I'm supposed to be the adventurous one.**

<u>Luke:</u> Penny-girl, you ARE the adventurous one! In your head, you've always had a tendency to "boldly go where no man has gone before." And usually where no man really WANTS to go: romance.

<u>Penelope:</u> **I can actually imagine your expression right now. Like you stepped in dog poo. And thanks for that encouragement, even though you had to evoke a quote from *Star Wars* to make it happen.**

<u>Luke:</u> *Star Trek.* TREK. As I recall, you sat through watching most of the episodes with me and Dad. You should remember.

Penelope: Oh, right. The one with the flying blue phone booth that travels through time.

Luke: I disown you. And I know you're joking now. You didn't even like *Doctor Who*.

Penelope: The robot things made me have nightmares. Besides, Captain Kirk was a cutie.

Luke: I refuse to respond to the last half of that text.

Penelope: Promise me you'll call me on my birthday. You do remember when it is, right? I'm trying not to make a big deal out of it around here, but I feel as though twenty-four is a pretty big deal. And I have no family here. So I've decided that I'm going to take the day off work and go to the beach and . . . maybe enter the sea up to my knees. As an act of bravery.

Luke: Excellent. It's common knowledge that sea monsters don't like kneecaps.

Luke: And, yes, I remember when it is. It's a life-altering event when you realize you are the lone boy born between two girls.

Text from Matt to Gwynn: Grandfather showed up to work this morning. It took a full ten seconds for me to comprehend what was happening and then another five to remember where his office is.

Matt's phone buzzed to life, and he raised it to his ear.

"What is going on?" Gwynn nearly shouted. Perhaps living with Gwynn helped prepare him for Penelope's oddities a little. Drama ran deep in the women of his family.

"Is Grandfather all right? He hasn't been to the office in . . . what? Three years?"

"Longer, if I recall." Matt leaned to the right to peer through his open office door where he could see into Grandfather's office across the hall. His grandfather leaned forward at his desk, tapping at the keyboard of his computer with his index fingers. "Bless Evelyn for keeping his office in order and not letting Alec use it for storage, because Grandfather started right back into running things as if he'd never left."

"I don't even know what to say." She paused as if to emphasize her bewilderment. "What do you think caused this change?"

Matt's lips edged wide. "I think it may be more of a who than a what."

"Penelope?" Gwynn laughed. "You think she inspired this?"

"I think her enthusiasm is contagious." Matt leaned back in his office chair and studied a half-eaten croissant Penelope had dropped by that very morning. "And she took a special interest in Grandfather, listening to him reminisce and unravel every story about Grandmother he could remember. Perhaps he needed to do that all along. To be able to move forward?"

"If he really comes back, Matt, maybe you can stop working so hard on the business side and return to dancing." She softened her tone, almost in entreaty. "I know you miss it."

He did and he hadn't realized how much until he'd danced with Penelope.

"I know you've been hurt so badly, but I think it's time for you to dream again, brother." She chuckled. "I'll start sending Gene Kelly memes to encourage you. Who knows? Penelope might be the inspiration you need too. Bewitching and all."

"Very funny." But his neck grew warm anyway.

"You're right," she added. "She's only here until December and is probably too young for a *bodach* like you."

"I'm not an old man!"

"We've had a lot of wounds lately, Matt." Gwynn sighed. "You more than the rest of us. And you've borne it all with such strength, but you also buried parts of the brother I once knew beneath the hurt. I can't remember the last time I heard you laugh."

His thoughts went immediately to his recent car ride with Penelope. He'd laughed with her.

"I think . . . well, I think I'm beginning to try. I mean, I did dance this week."

"You did." She chuckled. "And that's a great sign of things to come. Despite the way you hide all your feelings, I know you. You love with such fierce passion, Matt. I don't want you to give up on finding someone who will love you with as much devotion as you will love her. I know she's out there."

"Clearly, since you keep setting me up on all these blind dates to help me find her."

"Well, I've decided to stop with the whole blind date thing."

He shook his head. "Don't say things you don't mean, *suz*."

"I'm serious. I believe, since you are starting to step back into your life on your own, I'm going to let nature take its course."

Warning bells went off in his mind. Gwynn Gray rarely backed away from matchmaking opportunities, whether they were welcome or not. In fact, she seemed fueled even more by the unwelcome ones.

"What are you up to?"

"*Up to?*" Her pitch rose in overdramatic offense. "Merely doing as you've asked me to do all along. Leaving your romantic life to you and . . . whomever *you* fancy. But let me just say, dear brother, I don't think you need look too far for the right match. If you're willing to see, that is."

"Willing to—"

"And if you're brave enough, of course."

A knot started forming in his throat and he almost asked Gwynn to find another date for him. Anyone. Just so his mind would not return to the ginger-headed pixie waiting in the wings to bewitch his heart.

From: Penelope Edgewood
To: Luke Edgewood, Izzy Edgewood, Josephine Martin
Date: September 29
Subject: Jacqueline Morrow Crenshaw (JMC) & floats

I just wanted you all to know that I had a video call with JMC during my lunch break today. I think the video of the twins laughing is what spurred my courage. JMC took me on a virtual tour of the theater while she asked questions about what I'd add or change or improve. It was like giving me an empty stage to create whatever masterpiece I wanted. Just from my time here, I can already imagine how we can incorporate the community and donors and social media.

I mean, I'm going to need a job when I get back home anyway, aren't I? And to be executive director automatically gives me a chance to use my gifts and training in ways I'd never expected to in my first year postgraduation.

Just so you know, I've already decided that it would be worth the thirty-minute drive, though, to live in the mountains outside Mt. Airy so I can have a view in the mornings. After being here, there's just something energizing about waking up with a view of nature to start your day. And since I inherited that little piece of land from Grandma Edgewood, I thought I could build a little cottage there, just for me and my future family. Hiking trails are nearby. A biking path too!

I didn't give JMC an answer yet. We just discussed more specifically the nature of my role and the plan to expand, so I'd manage a small staff. She wanted to make sure I knew her desire is for me to be the one to travel for further training and marketing, and she wanted to assure me that she fully supports my desire to have a family someday.

I mean, it really does sound perfect.

The longer I'm away from home, the more perfect it sounds.

But am I just speaking from homesickness? If I make this decision right out of school, will I regret not becoming a world-famous Broadway star or West End actress? (Stop laughing, Luke. I can practically hear you. Besides, we already know I don't really want to follow the spotlight.)

Just a reminder: *My Fair Lady* plays next weekend (Th–Sun). I've been able to help out in some of the rehearsals and the theater group is AMAZING. I'm so proud to be involved, even if on the periphery.

AND . . . some folks from the theater group met with me last night to help with the float. Gwynn showed up, too, which was an added bonus. BUT the biggest thing was that Mark, a carpenter who is part of the online theater troupe, had already taken some of my ideas and partially finished the float. Y'all!! It's on two trailers. TWO. One features the upcoming musical and the next gives a teaser for upcoming productions—with lots of fun characters they may see in the future—with an added invitation to folks to join the theater. Gwynn has promised to take photos so I can show you because, as you can imagine, I MUST be a part of it. I'm handing out goody bags . . . while in costume, of course.

Penelope

PS: I know that I haven't the extreme talent for Broadway or West End, despite what my high school drama teacher said. I have the voice, but my acting could use a little polish.

PPS: And both would take me away from home for a long time, so . . .

PPPS: There is something special about belonging somewhere. It's an indefinable sort of something, but when you are away from it for a little while, you know.

Text from Izzy to Penelope: You're still young, Penelope, and this is your first really big adventure. You'll find where you belong. I promise.

Penelope: I love it here, Iz, but I have this longing for the familiar that I didn't really understand until now. I feel like a failure somehow.

The song "Concerning Hobbits" started playing from Penelope's phone. She smiled and placed the phone to her ear. "Hi, Izzy."

"You're not a failure, Penn." Izzy's voice slid over Penelope with a sweet sense of home. "Believe me, I know what it feels like to second-guess and waffle around like a one-flippered seal."

"A one-flippered seal?" Penelope laughed, closing her eyes to enjoy Izzy's familiar voice.

"Okay, not the best analogy, but I understand trying to find where you belong. To be honest, if Brodie had come into my life when I was twenty-three—"

"Almost twenty-four," Penelope amended.

"Almost twenty-four," Izzy repeated with added emphasis, "and asked me to move to Skymar, there's no way I could have done it. I wasn't ready. Just because your heart loves home doesn't mean you're a failure. Home may be exactly where you're supposed to be for now, and then somewhere else may turn into home in the future. And even if the rest of your life is spent in these Blue Ridge Mountains with the joys of family and theater and the familiar all wrapped around you, then I'd consider that a pretty wonderful life too. Like Samwise."

"Your dog?" Penelope could almost feel Izzy's smile. "Okay, I know. The hobbit." Penelope settled into the thought. She'd never pictured being a hobbit. The elven ladies with their lovely gowns always appealed to her more, but how could she argue against the virtues of a hobbit who carried the love and hope of home with him through the greatest perils, only to find his greatest contentment and joy in returning home at the end of the story? "Who are you to talk, anyway? You're the woman who is moving across the world to be with her Bookish Charming."

Penelope could almost feel Izzy's dreamy smile. "I am. And I'm going to miss this place and especially my family, but I know in my heart that I belong there with Brodie. And I'm ready to belong there, Penn. But don't discount the good of staying near what you've always known. There's no shame in that."

Penelope ran her finger over the edge of the plate in front of her where half the quiche she'd cut for herself still waited uneaten. No, there wasn't. And to live her dream of running her own theater? While near her beloved mountains and family? Something in her embraced the idea with full heart and hands.

"I think you've convinced yourself of an idea that isn't necessarily true." Izzy chuckled. "You do that sometimes."

"I know." She dropped back in the chair, digesting Izzy's words. "And you're right. I think I may have gotten lost in those fairy tales and famous-people stories a bit too much. Imagine that."

"Hey, you may talk the fairy-tale-musical talk, but you have a very good head on your shoulders. When you *must* return to the real world, you know how to handle it."

"Thanks, Iz."

"And it sounds like the job with JMC will allow you to travel a little, so you could possibly get home and a little fairy tale too."

"That's true." She nodded as if Izzy were in the room to see her. "There's a lot to be said for living the life of my favoritest of hobbits."

"Exactly." Her voice warmed with her ardent devotion. "And don't let your love of home stop you from loving the right now, too, Penelope. You have so much love to give people, and you may even be surprised at how much love can come back to you in the process. From Grandpa Gray or the theater group or Iris, or even the Gray boys. I'm a living example of the unexpected becoming the best decision of my life."

Penelope dipped her chin with determination. "Then that's who I'm going to be. A hero at home or abroad."

"Perfect. Seize the day and pump your sunshine all over the place."

They exchanged a few other updates and then ended the call, only to have Penelope's phone buzz with a message.

Text from Izzy to Penelope: Just a quick reminder of a quote from one of your favorite childhood storybooks, *Winnie-the-Pooh*: "How lucky I am to have something that makes saying goodbye so hard."

Penelope smiled down at the message and then looked out the window into the deep blue-purple of "gloaming," as the natives called the dusk. It was a perfect word for the dying glow of sunset into the twinkling glow of stars. There was a sweetness in loving home, but—her smile grew—a sweetness in the new too. She closed her eyes and drew in a long, deep breath, gratitude pressing into her chest. Yes, she'd take all the strength and joy she'd learned at home and sprinkle it through her last weeks in Skymar. Love big, celebrate authentically, and embrace the relationships God had brought to her along the way.

And she'd learned so much already. About herself and her work. About people she'd grown to care about.

She opened her eyes and walked to the window, staring up at the stars. And surprisingly, just talking through her heart struggles brought about a wonderful sense of contentment. An acceptance of the now, wherever the now might take her.

It was impossible to think of the present without her thoughts moving in the direction of Matthias, which made her realize she'd never sent him a message earlier about a certain rumor she'd heard.

Text from Penelope to Matthias: You hired Dani???? That's an amazing decision.

Matthias: I think your encouragement along the lines of getting more involved with the community theater has truly made me reassess a lot. I've even found a few of Grandmother's old contacts and have been making calls most of the afternoon.

Penelope: That's wonderful, Matt. I know you want to do more than work on the budget and I know you love these people. I'm so glad you've found your joy for it again!

Penelope: And Grandpa Gray was in the office again today!! (He looked ten years younger too.)

Penelope: I adore bow ties. He looks incredibly dapper in them. I told him so and promptly kissed his cheek. He hugged me! I feel as though I'm deficient in hugs since leaving home and that one just made my day.

Matthias: It sounds as though a visit with Iris is long overdue. And she will fill your hug quota to overflowing.

Penelope: Oh yes! Maybe this weekend? I have a super-secret
    project we can do together.

Matthias: Oh dear.

Penelope: Don't worry. You'll like it.

Penelope: I think.

A knock from the cottage door brought Penelope's attention away from the open oven and toward the front of the house. She glanced at the clock. Only six thirty. She still had half an hour before Alec was due to arrive. Was he early?

She frowned. He didn't seem like the type who'd be early. In fact, he'd been late to about every meeting she'd been in with him. Unless he was just eager for their dinner? She tapped her smile and closed the oven door. Wouldn't that be a pleasant surprise! A girl never minded being the center of attention in a man's mind. Well, as long as it was good attention.

With a quick pause to set the oven timer, she tossed her oven mitt on the counter and walked to the door.

Matthias stood on the threshold, navy jacket open with a paler blue button-up underneath and his hair tousled by the chilly wind. She paused to take in the very pleasant view. Blue was a very good color on him.

"What a wonderful surprise!"

His smile responded by slow degrees, even lighting his eyes. He had a very nice smile. She was so glad he'd decided to use it more often.

"I can send the cookies up to the house with you."

"Cookies?" He glanced down to her sunflower apron as she gestured him inside. "Oh, they smell fantastic."

"I promised Iris I'd make her star cookies if she finished her first book report, and she called me from the house an hour ago to tell me she had. Even read it to me. We switched to a video call so she could show me her illustrations. I wish I could have drawn fairy wings that well at seven." Penelope walked back toward the kitchen. "And since I'm a woman of my word, I got to work on those cookies."

"You've certainly helped make those types of homework projects easier." He removed his jacket as he stepped up to the little island in the kitchen. Rolled-up shirtsleeves and khaki trousers. Hmm . . . who did he remind her of? Someone famous. And a dancer. "I think your enthusiasm makes everything a little more exciting."

"Are you being sarcastic?" She shot him a narrow-eyed look over her shoulder as she placed the first batch of cookies in a plastic container. "You didn't sound super excited about my secret projects. Not the one at the theater or the one with Iris."

His palms came up in defense. "With my history, I've become a little leery of surprises."

"Oh." She stared at him for a moment and then returned a few steps to stand in front of him, offering a cookie almost like a peace offering. "I wouldn't do anything to hurt you or Iris, as long as I could help it." She leaned closer and lowered her voice as if someone were nearby listening. "And I only pick very good surprises."

Something in his face shifted, softened, and his gaze held hers in such a way that her breath hitched just the slightest bit. Yes, stormy-blue eyes suited him very well. So did smiles. Gentle or wide. She liked them all.

He took the cookie from her hand, never breaking eye contact. "Thank you."

"Of course." She drew in a shaky breath and dusted her hands against the apron. "I didn't think I'd see you today."

"Oh yes." His eyes grew wide. "Right. I popped in to share some news."

"Good news, I'd say, from the glint in your eyes."

"Very good news." His wider grin resurfaced. "I've sold two of the other box seats and recruited another large donor for the theater. The Marshalls."

He mentioned the amount and Penelope staggered back.

"That's amazing, Matt!" And before she realized it, she jumped forward—as if it were the most natural thing—right into a hug. As his arms wrapped around her, she burrowed deep, basking in the feel of his strength. He smelled of cedar and . . . what else? The sea? Vanilla? She breathed it in, resting her chin against his shoulder as she did. She hadn't really thought about what Matthias's hugs would be like, but he was a good hugger. Wonderful even.

The timer buzzed and Penelope jumped back, laughing. "Sorry, I was a little mesmerized by your hug and cologne." Her cheeks flamed and she sighed as she turned toward the oven. "I think that hug could do me for at least three days. Whew."

"My hugs are at your disposal anytime."

She turned back to gauge whether he was teasing, but his expression was serious. So serious, in fact, that her cheeks warmed and she didn't know why. But it wasn't a bad reason, because she had the overwhelming desire to run right back into his arms again.

"So you just stopped in to share your news with me?"

"You were the first person I thought of." He shrugged as if helpless against the idea. "After all your hard work."

She was the first person he thought of? Was that the sweetest thing ever? "*Our* hard work."

"Our hard work." His voice gentled and somehow reached out and touched her pulse.

She drew in a quick breath and turned to remove the cookies. What was that all about? Had she been away from home so long she didn't even know how to have a conversation with a friend anymore? She paused on the thought and smiled. And he was her friend. Her closest friend in Skymar except, maybe, for Gwynn? No, she knew him even better than she knew Gwynn. And she would have wanted to tell him her good news first too. Her smile spread wider as she started placing the last batch on the additional cookie sheet.

"Is there anything I can do to help?"

She set the timer and then turned. "Would you pull those cookies out of the oven for me if I'm not back down here in ten minutes?"

He looked from her to the oven and back. "I can do that."

"Thank you!" She untied the apron." Your brother is supposed to be here at seven and I need to get dressed." She gestured toward her face. "I did my makeup already and just need to pin up my hair."

"Right." The smile left his eyes. "Your date with Alec is tonight."

"Well, *date* might be a strong word to use." She pulled the apron over her head and placed it on the island. "He says it's an apology dinner, so I'm not sure if that counts as a date. Besides, I'm not sure I would want any possible relationship to start with an apology dinner, you know? I'd prefer a sort of mesmerized 'you're the one for me' type dinner for a real date." She shrugged. "But it is in a castle, so maybe it does count as a date." She grinned as she slipped past him toward the stairs. "Regardless, I plan to take copious amounts of photos to show to generations of my posterity."

She rushed up the stairs, pondering Matthias's reaction. Was he upset about her dinner with Alec? Did he think she was being unprofessional to go out with him? Or maybe he disapproved because he didn't want his brother forming an emotional attachment with someone who was leaving in a couple of months.

Her eyes popped wide. Or maybe the cookie didn't taste so great.

She shook her head as she slipped off her T-shirt and jeans. No, she'd tasted three already, and they were delicious.

With quick work, she twisted up her hair so that a few curls spilled over the top of the clip. Then she slipped into the dress with a happy shudder. As soon as she'd seen it on the rack at the "charity shop," as they called consignment shops here, she'd fallen in love. Pale pink, strapless, with a layered skirt cut in a pixie style to just below the knees.

She paired it with some silver strappy heels and a thin, faux-diamond headband.

With a glance at herself in the mirror, she gave a little twirl. "A princess for a night."

The buzzing timer echoed up the stairway, so she snatched her silvery sheer scarf from her bed and draped it over her shoulders, then made her way to the kitchen.

Matt had just set the cookie sheet on top of the stove and turned at the sound of her heeled-shoe entrance. She froze in the doorway at the look on his face. His gaze started at her head, trailed slowly down, and then settled back on her face.

It was a moment every girl savored. To recognize that someone thought she looked beautiful, and she felt his appreciation all the way down to her secondhand Jimmy Choos.

He shook his head as if entranced. "You . . . you look stunning."

Penelope tugged at the scarf, warmth climbing up her neck to settle in her cheeks, and then she spun in a circle. "It has an excellent twirl." Her gaze caught back in his. "It's the true measure of a dress. Especially for dancing."

His smile brimmed again, lighting his eyes. "Then I believe you've found the perfect one."

"Iris would love it, wouldn't she?" Penelope pulled her attention from his. "It's pink."

"Without a doubt."

She stepped up beside him and started moving the cookies into the container.

"And this?" His finger brushed against her shoulder where the small butterfly tattoo peeked just above the top of her dress. "For your friend?"

Her thoughts evaporated completely at the effect his touch had on her skin, paired with the sweet, intimate knowledge he had of her. And maybe her voice was gone, too, because she couldn't offer up a response at first. A tingle of awareness traveled from his touch over her shoulder blades, and she blinked a few times to try to remember any words at all. Or syllables. Maybe just vowels?

Her gaze searched his as if he knew the answers to what was happening, those familiar eyes somehow becoming a little dearer to her in the process. He kept growing more important in her thoughts, like some of the best of friends, but this? Well, she didn't know quite where to place the feeling.

Then he raised a brow as if waiting for her, and she quickly collected all the thoughts from wherever they'd scattered. "Yes."

Excellent response. Actually spoken. On topic. And to the point.

His lips softened into a gentle smile and she tried very hard to sort out why it was so hard to look away from him.

A knock at the door pulled her attention away. What was wrong with her? You'd think she'd never been hugged, complimented, or touched before.

She drew in a deep breath, shook her head, and rounded Matthias to go to the door. "That's . . . that's probably Alec."

Before she even reached the door, Alec burst in. Wearing a sleek black suit and silver tie, his goldish-brown waves set to perfection, he looked like something out of a magazine. Broad shoulders, perfect tan, soft hazel eyes.

His white grin flashed wide as he glanced over her. "My, my, aren't you lovely."

"Thank you," she said, basking in the appreciation. "You look very—"

"Do I smell cookies?" Alec swept past her and walked toward the kitchen. "Matt, did you bake cookies here?"

Penelope turned to find Matthias with the cookie container in hand, attempting to fasten the lid. "Penelope made some for Iris."

"Isn't Penelope the most wonderful girl? Bakes, sings, creates beautiful websites." Alec reached into the container and snagged two cookies, sending a wink to Penelope over his shoulder. "To tide me over until dinner."

The change was so abrupt, she stood in the doorway trying to catch up with the sudden shift from adoring dinner date to cookie thief. And something about the way he listed her "attributes" fell flat. There was quite a bit more to her than baking, singing, and creating websites.

Her attention moved from Alec to Matthias, whose eyebrows had taken a massive downturn. "I need to get home." Matthias pushed the lid down on the container, sending Alec a warning look as he reached for another cookie. "Thank you for this, Penelope." He gestured toward the container as he passed, looking between her and his brother. She wanted to reach out and touch his arm, reconnect to whatever she'd felt with him only a few moments ago, but he slipped to the door. "Enjoy your evening." His gaze roamed her face for a brief moment and then something in his expression hardened. "Good night."

Was Matthias so upset with the cookie thievery? No, that reason didn't seem right.

"Don't wait up, Matt." Alec slipped his arm around Penelope's waist, sending a little wink in her direction. "I have a magical night planned for our best darling of The Darling House."

Alec laughed at his phrasing, but Matt didn't reciprocate the humor. Was Alec baiting Matthias? But why? With a small step to the side, Penelope slid from Alec's touch. She wasn't a temptation for Matthias Gray at all. Too young. Probably too fairy-tale-ish. Definitely too emotional. And without a doubt, she sang too much for his taste.

But the self-admission didn't sit too well with her.

"I'm certain she'll enjoy anything magical." Matthias's gaze moved back to her and then, with a dip of his head, he stepped over the threshold to the porch and left.

Alec kept speaking about the cookies, but Penelope's attention followed Matthias's retreat until he disappeared up the drive, wondering the whole time why she felt like she'd done something wrong without even knowing it.

As Alec opened the car door for her, she blinked out of her thoughts. Date or not, she was living a dream come true and planned to enjoy every moment. A dashing companion. A castle. Possibly a walk along a moonlit beach a good distance from the actual water?

A fairy-tale evening.

Her attention flitted back to the direction in which Matthias had disappeared.

Then why did it feel like she'd just stepped into the wrong scene of her own story?

CHAPTER 13

In preparation for the upcoming festival, twinkle lights hung along Mountcaster's streets, adding a sprinkle of extra magic to the historic town's usual ambience. Penelope adored this city, yet she still longed for home. What a strange dichotomy of feelings, to truly appreciate and find joy in one place but ache for the other. Could the time come when she'd long for another place more than the home she'd always known? Where the love of the "other" became larger and more necessary?

Alec steered through the city, pointing out a few sites and restaurants along the way. He wore handsome effortlessly, like some of her favorite fairy-tale heroes, and his profile? Well, if anyone could possess a perfect nose, it was him. Strong, straight, but not too large. She'd never heard him sing, but as a theater kid, he probably had the perfect voice too.

He must have caught her staring and sent a crooked grin her way. "Like what you see, princess?"

Heat flooded into her face and she looked away. "I was just thinking about how your nose is perfect."

His laugh burst out. "My nose? You are a curious one, aren't you?" He spoke more to himself than her, then his attention came back, one eyebrow raised. "There's much more to come than just my perfect nose, my dear," he crooned. "I'll show you a night that your little fairy-tale heart will not soon forget."

His words should be music to her ears. But her heart didn't seem to agree. Maybe it was just because his aftershave took up more room in the car than . . . the car itself. And the scent was nice, of course. All ocean breeze and spice. And it would wear off in a while. She just needed to take shallower breaths until then.

"Do you dine at the castle often?" What a remarkable question to actually voice!

"Often enough to get us good seats." He shrugged one of his very impressive shoulders. "It's a great place for entertaining and impressing clients."

"What sort of clients? Donors, you mean?"

"Sure." He focused ahead, the road taking a sharp turn to the right. "And I have some private clients who I help with business planning." He shot her a grin. "Not a lot of money in resuscitating a dying theater."

"No, I'd say not." She played with the ends of her scarf. "But hopefully it won't stay that way. There are lots of good indicators that our hard work is moving The Darling House in the right direction."

His shoulders slumped with his sigh. "Listen, Penelope, I don't know what my brother or sister have told you, but apart from its heyday for a few decades nearly a century ago, it's not been the most profitable endeavor from the start. Small theaters rarely are."

JMC's call yesterday confirmed some of those concerns, but not entirely. Penelope had grown up in the Ashby. She knew the business worked with the right place and the right people . . . and a whole lot of passion and snacks. Some theaters went under, it was true, but with hard work, creativity, the proper productions, and community support, a theater could thrive. Most of the theater owners she knew didn't end up filthy rich in the venture, but they lived well enough. And loved what they did.

And she'd still heard that love in JMC's voice yesterday. The passion and hope of providing the beauty, escape, talent, and creativity of the stage to the community.

"But we've made good progress."

"For how long, princess?" His sad smile bordered on condescending. "You've not been in this business long enough to recognize a sinking ship when you see one. In fact, you're barely out of the crib as far as business is concerned. We may win this battle for the moment, but we can't win the war, no matter how much we may wish it."

"Some of us have ideas that will make a long-term difference." She stiffened. "Even for someone 'barely out of the crib,'" she added with air quotes. "Besides, I don't think you're *that* much older than me. What? Three years? Four?"

"Life experience can't always be measured by years."

She rarely wanted to punch anyone in the nose, but he was getting pretty close to forcing the desire to the front of her mind. And it would be a shame to damage such a fine nose. "I've been working in theater since I was thirteen. From volunteering to designing the summer camps by seventeen and teaching classes by nineteen. So I can boast some life experience too."

His expression sobered and she continued. "We may not end up rich in money, but we can stay afloat, so I'm all for folks who have a real desire to fight hard enough to win the war."

"I'm sorry I not only offended you but underestimated you." His expression gentled and she relaxed the death grip on her scarf. "You have made excellent changes, ones that prove you are not as naive as I inadvertently made you out to be. Forgive me?"

She gave a slow nod, allowing his admission and compliment to sink in. Alec didn't know her as well as Matthias did, so of course he'd misjudged her like most everyone did.

"I hope our dinner will make up for my blunder." He flicked her his grin, a dimple flashing to life. A dimple. She softened even more. She'd always loved dimples. "I look forward to hearing about all your lovely ideas, princess." His accent curled over the *r* in his words. "I feel certain your passion will inspire mine and together we can make those ideas a reality."

"The more people we have in the battle, the better," she added, her comment bringing out his chuckle.

"I'd better join the fray, then. I certainly don't want to be left out of watching you work your magic."

She settled back into the seat and breathed out her frustration. Here she sat, ready for her fairy-tale moment in a castle, and a little tiff wasn't going to dampen her experience. Honestly, how often did a girl dress up for a very handsome man to have dinner in a castle on a quaint island to talk about theater? She was living her best dream.

The road narrowed and began a twisty climb through evening-soaked countryside. And then, on Penelope's side of the car, the road fell away to reveal a view of the sea. Bright moonlight bathed the water in pale silver and summoned thoughts of fairies, mermaids, lost boys, and pirate ships rather than sea monsters. Just around a bend in the road, the dark-gray castle came into view, towers jutting up into the night. Cradled by the hillside, its lights glowed welcomingly at their approach.

The inside proved as dramatic as its exterior. Stone walls rose on all sides, some covered with tapestries. Despite the fires in the massive fireplaces, a chill cloaked the air and she drew her scarf more tightly around her shoulders.

Their server, a young woman with absolutely movie-worthy blonde hair trailing down the back of her little black dress, welcomed them with an equally movie-worthy smile. Alec must have known her, because he engaged in some light small talk and some definite glances of appreciation at the way God had made her. Penelope stilled herself against the sudden rise of annoyance. What did she expect? Didn't most guys in the real world have a wayward eye or two? She looked away and steadied her expectations. No wonder she preferred fairy tales and classic musicals.

In the real world, girls had to settle.

She shook her head. No, they shouldn't. When she loved someone, she was all in, eyes included (well, except for an occasional movie crush here and there), but nothing serious or distracting.

And she and Alec hardly knew each other, so if anything were to develop into a relationship, it would take time. Besides, this wasn't even a date, so why should she expect undivided attention—though he did owe her for the interview debacle.

She nodded at her internal dialogue and followed the server into a large room, which must have been a ballroom at one time. Tables dressed in white dotted the space and windows lined the wall facing the sea. With a flourish of her gloved hand, the server placed them at a table with a breathtaking view of the cliff-lined coast until the sea disappeared into the dark horizon.

After they'd settled into their places and ordered, Alec stared at her from across the table, his hazel-green eyes glittering in the candlelight.

"You really do look amazing."

"Thank you." She smiled and turned her gaze to the room. "This isn't a place you show up to in jeans and a T-shirt."

"Most certainly not." He chuckled, taking a drink. "But I daresay, you rarely go anywhere in a T-shirt and jeans."

Her smile stilled on her lips. Actually, she'd spent two days out of this week working backstage in the dusty boxes and dilapidated theater props. Jeans and a ratty T-shirt proved indispensable, though the T-shirt boasted some very well-loved sunflowers. But again, Alec rarely made an appearance at the theater, so how would he know?

"What do you love most about The Darling House?"

His eyes widened for a moment and then he relaxed back into his chair. "The memories, I suppose." His focus turned to the view. "Mum loved it and she seemed to make everything a bit brighter wherever she went. Granny too." He grew quiet, as if he'd stepped into one of his memories. He wore pensive very well, especially with such a nose. And her heart went out to him. What grief! Matthias had been right in saying Alec wore his grief differently. In fact, she wondered if he tried to hide it.

He drew in a breath like he'd returned from wherever he'd gone. "Like I said, it had its day in the sun, and it was glorious."

She studied him. Did he stay away from the theater because the memories hurt so much? "They both sound like remarkable women." She smiled, hoping her expression offered some sense of her compassion. "Your grandpa has shared so many stories about your mom and grandma and their love for The Darling House."

"I'm sure he has." He leaned forward, fingers braided in front of him. "I just hope these reminiscences don't set him up for another heartache, Penelope."

"From his response so far, I think whatever happens, he's on the road to stepping back into his life." Penelope sat straighter. "To be honest, he's been one of my very best brainstormers. He's really been the mastermind, inspiring so many ideas Matt and I are currently putting into practice."

"Really? I'm glad to hear it." One brow rose in a perfect slant. "But be careful with Matt and Gwynn. They don't always have a clear business head on their shoulders. Idealists, you know?" He nodded toward her. "And you would know. They all need a bit of reality to get a clear picture of things."

"'Clear picture of things'?"

His attention trailed to the right, as it had done a few times already, so Penelope took a sip of her drink and sent a quick glance in that direction. A table filled with young women, all model worthy with enough skin showing to shame a beach scene. It was pretty distracting, especially with all the loud laughing.

But she didn't think Alec was particularly distracted by the laughing.

"The real numbers on the theater. Matt's a stubborn idealist, I'm afraid, which is likely why what happened with Deirdre hit him so hard. The business and Iris became his life."

"I think having your wife leave you and your child for a dance routine would hit anyone really hard."

He dipped his head in half-hearted agreement. "But three years? I'd say that's a bit too long, wouldn't you?"

Not if you really loved someone.

"When he was younger, he could have taken on the world with his dancing and his ability to teach it. People swarmed into his classes. And he'd poured his heart into those children and choreography." He gestured with his glass toward her. "He even taught classes at the university. Did you know that? And he just let it all disappear into his grief and a dying theater."

Matthias teaching college classes on dance? She could see it, now that she knew him better. He'd be a calm sort of teacher, a gentle guide, she guessed. An encourager.

"And Gwynn's getting degrees in marketing and business with the sole purpose of saving the theater." He shook his head. "Stubborn girl. I tried to convince her to put her education in a profitable direction, but she is annoyingly determined."

"She has great ideas, too, and a deep love for The Darling House." Penelope rallied to their defense. "Passion, ingenuity, and hard work can go a long way. I worked for a couple who took a desolate little theater in our small town and turned it into a thriving business, against all odds. The owners taught me a great deal about the power of heart in a business, and I think Gwynn has that in spades. So does your grandfather. Matt too. Why don't you?"

"Reality, I'm afraid." He offered a sad smile. "As a career planner, I see the writing on the wall. Have for years. If we're going to save this place, we need something to shock the theater back to life or give up altoge—"

"A touring company." The words popped out before she could stop them. "I'm trying to get *The Sound of Music* here for December."

A laugh burst out of him, but her expression must have sobered him. "You're serious."

"It's possible."

"Not really," he said, patting her hand on the table. "And *The Sound of Music*? There's no way you can get that. Touring companies, or those worth seeing, are scheduled years in advance."

"But sometimes there are cancellations." She pulled her hand from beneath his. "That's what I'm banking on."

"I'm sorry, princess, but it's much too far-fetched to become a reality." He shook his head and took another drink from his glass. "No, you'll have to think of something else."

"Can't you just be a little hopeful with me?" She leaned forward, curbing the desire to slam a fist against the table. "We should pull out all the stops, especially the far-fetched ones. That's what you do when you care about something or someone." She lifted her chin, staring him down. "Some of the best stories and movies are about overcoming unimaginable odds. *Cinderella* is a grand example. *Annie*, *Brigadoon*—"

"All fictional."

"I could give you some good old family history stories that are not fictional at all, but it sounds like you don't care." She started to rise and he caught her arm.

"Please, I'm sorry." He sighed. "Sit, please. I suppose I become pessimistic because I want it so badly."

She crossed her arms over her chest. "Do you?"

"How could I not?" His gaze trailed away and back. "It's family history. Memories saturate nearly every brick of the place."

Something in the way he spoke, the edge in his voice, caught her attention. Pain. She studied him more closely. Sometimes grief had a way of haunting places and either drawing you to the spot or causing you to recoil. She had embraced her own memories, but not everyone grieved in the same way.

"You must understand, princess." His gaze held hers. "False hope leads to monstrous and unnecessary heartache when everything falls apart."

"What if it's not false?" She gentled her approach. "Have you actually seen the numbers lately? Between selling the box seats and restoring the smaller theater, I think we really have a chance."

"You're opening the smaller theater?"

"If you'd been in on the last meeting, you'd know a lot more and maybe feel encouraged." She patted *his* hand now. "And Matt's worked so hard to draw in donors. Your grandfather's interview really stirred up sentiment like nothing else. I think people just needed to see that Lorianna Gray's husband still held a passion for the place and was willing to be a voice for the theater."

"Well, that is good news." His smile returned after a moment of working through a few other emotions, as if he wasn't quite sure which one to land on. "Very good." He leaned forward, staring at her across the table. "You really do bring your own magic, don't you?"

"I'm afraid, despite my love of fairy tales, magic has very little to do with it, but I do care about The Darling House and the people who love it."

He wrapped his hand around hers, drawing it up to place a kiss against it. "I think, Miss Edgewood, you've helped me find a reason to fight for the theater too."

She warmed a little at his subtle compliment combined with the touch of his warm lips on her skin. The candlelight and overall ambience probably helped a little too.

She stared at Alec's car until it disappeared behind the blind of trees separating her cottage from the main house. Rain began a gentle sprinkle, adding a natural rhythm to a few of the other night sounds. An owl made his addition to the symphony, calling her to linger a little longer in the night air.

She wiped a hand across her lips as if to remove the memory of Alec's good-night kiss. She probably should have told him she wasn't interested in another dinner date before the kiss, but he swooped in without any warning, and then she'd had to gently say "thanks, but no thanks" to any more of those rather . . . desperate kisses. He didn't seem to know how to respond, except he looked a little offended, returned to his car, and then drove off.

Yet again, a hopeful Prince Charming had proven he was not the man for her. Why did she always seem to guess wrong? She searched the sky as the rain misted her face. Surely she'd grown out of the knight-in-shining-armor idea. She shrugged. *Mostly.*

If she had been playing the lead in a musical, this would be the perfect moment for a song about longing for love. She chuckled to herself and gave a little twirl as she neared the porch. What she wanted was someone who would take her seriously.

Yes. That's what she wanted. Someone who would take her seriously and love her wildly. Someone to laugh and cry with. And she didn't mind the idea of him thinking she was deliriously beautiful. She knew she wasn't deliriously beautiful, but the idea of her one true love seeing her that way certainly seemed a wonderful idea.

She tugged the silver headband from its place within her curls. And she was pretty sure she never wanted to be called *princess* again.

Alec hadn't been mean, but so many pieces of the evening confirmed she'd jumped to conclusions yet again. After their dinner, they'd gone for a walk on the beach by moonlight and he'd invited her on his boat, which she politely refused. Though she couldn't deny that the family boathouse reminded her of an adorable cottage from *Into the Woods.* When she'd refused a moonlit boat ride, Alec had attempted to talk her out of her "childish" fear of sea monsters, the condescension showing back up with a curled lip in tow. He hadn't even been willing to listen to her irrational reasons, and she had a great deal of irrational reasons.

No, Alec Gray still had some growing up to do, especially about the things that mattered most. Maybe some more healing to do too.

Besides, it never impressed her to hear someone speak badly about their own family. And even without the additional vulture looks to lovely ladies they'd passed, something just didn't fit.

Oh well, it wasn't like her heart was invested or anything yet. Just her silly hopes.

She took the steps up the porch and came to a stop. Resting at the foot of the door sat a little silver box, wrapped rather . . . adventurously, and topped with a pink bow much too large for the container. An envelope was taped to the bottom, so she pulled it off and removed the card.

A child's handwriting scrawled across the page.

Thank you for the cookies.

I wanted to make you some thank you cookies.

Daddy helped me make them. He let me use the pink sprinkles.

Daddy said you would like the heart cookies best. I ate the others.

Daddy said you'd even like the silly shaped ones because they were from me.

Love,

Iris Gray

Penelope opened up the box and inside waited about a half dozen heart-shaped sugar cookies, some more recognizable than others, and all with an abundance of pink sprinkles. A drop landed on the paper and Penelope looked up. She was still standing under the protection of the porch. And then she reached up to touch her cheek. Damp. A sniffle shook her shoulders as she took a bite of one of the silliest-shaped heart cookies. Sprinkles crumbled from the cookie and fell to the porch. Penelope followed their direction and slipped onto a nearby chair.

Why was she crying? She'd just had dinner in a castle with a handsome man while overlooking a moonlit sea. She looked down at her dress. In a really cute dress. She sniffled again and took another bite of the cookie. A smile pulled at her lips. The cookies tasted great. Maybe

Iris was destined to become a magnificent baker, and as everyone knew, baked goods could solve almost every first-world problem. Almost.

Text from Penelope to Izzy: Alec kissed me tonight. One kiss. A good-night kiss.

Izzy: And . . . ???

Penelope: Well, I've been kissed before, of course, but I don't think I have ever been kissed quite so ferociously.

Izzy: Ferociously? Please explain.

Penelope: You know all those movie kisses you used to make fun of, the ones where people looked like they were eating each other's faces? I understand it now.

Izzy: Um . . .

Penelope: Perhaps it had just been a long time since he'd kissed someone. Maybe with more practice he will become less . . . hungry?

Izzy: Is more practice in his future?

Penelope: Oh, I'm sure, but not with me. Besides, I think he has a much broader interest than happily ever after right now. There were way too many cute distractions for him to stay interested in me for very long. Not everyone can find a Brodie, I guess, Iz.

Izzy: Don't give up altogether, Penn. If you recall, I didn't find my knight in cozy sweater vests until I was thirty. And he was worth all the heartache and long wait.

Penelope: It's probably best if I wait to get home before trying to find my knight. Besides, if the girl can't get the dream guy, then at least she can get the dream job.

Izzy: Have you decided about JMC then?

Penelope: Yeah, I think so. I love what I do. I've realized that from being here. And I love home. Getting to put them

both together, well, it's the right thing for me. I'm still going to wait until later in October to give her a definite answer, but I think I know what I should do.

Skymarian Theater Troupe •

From: JA
To: GK

Okay, anonymous GK, I have a deep question.

Why is it that good girls have such a hard time finding good guys? What is so attractive about women who wear *Moulin Rouge!* outfits but can't have a thoughtful conversation? Or have legs longer than a tree but can't show care to others? And why can't happy girls get the good guys? Why are we overlooked or underappreciated? Don't men want a wife who is happy? Solemn and repressed can't be that attractive, can it? No matter what the movies say?

(I suppose that was more than one question, but all basically originating in one place.)

Why is it that you can only be taken seriously as the main character of your own life if you have either some tragic backstory or a subdued, mysterious personality? Or are incredibly sexy and alluring. Sexy, alluring, and tragic?

Why can't sweet, happy, and loyal help a girl find a lifelong romance? I'm sure the future children would appreciate it, not to mention the future husband!

There was a time when I thought about creating a tragic backstory for myself to see whether it made a difference, but then I broke out in hives because I would have to lie.

There's a lot to be said for a stable, nice backstory. And women who like to wear vintage clothes. Are hats the ultimate deal breaker?

I'm sure you've figured out by now that I'm all about fairy tales and sweep-you-off-your-feet kinds of things, but deep down I've been realizing what is even better than having a man walk into a forest and finish your dream song. It's having a man who listens to me. Who wants to KNOW me and cares about what I have to say. Who sees beyond my age or my clothes or my random silliness and knows that deeper than all those things is a heart that cares and a mind that thinks. I mean, I wouldn't mind him counting down the minutes to see me each day or running through rain to rescue me either. But at the end of the performance, there's the ever after. And I want someone for the ever-after part, when the audience is gone and the stage is empty, and the only crowd we're in front of is each other.

Thanks for being my void in which to send out my thoughts. That makes me think of *You've Got Mail*! LOL. So "good night, dear void."

Text from Luke to Penelope: I just had dinner with Izzy. Listen to me, Penny-girl. The right man will see only you and he will want only you. I promise.

CHAPTER 14

From: Josephine Martin
To: Penelope Edgewood
Date: October 1
Subject: The munchkin onesies

Penelope,

The munchkin onesies finally fit the twins! I didn't think I'd like them at all because of the pointy hats, but the adorableness is beyond words. If they don't grow out of them by the church's fall festival time (or stain them with spit-up to the point of disgust), they can wear them to the costume party. Patrick was able to find shoes small enough to fit the twins that go with the onesies perfectly. I'm sending photos.

Do remember, when we have our video calls, the little ones cannot maintain attention to the screen as much as you want, Penelope dear. They're barely three months old. Things like ceiling fans, barking dogs, and dangling elephants are a bit more entertaining to them than a face on the screen, no matter how lovely or animated the face. And speaking louder doesn't change that fact.

Jackie called me yesterday and mentioned what a good conversation she had with you last week. She felt very positive about it. I'm trying hard not to be pushy or controlling (as Izzy and Luke made it VERY clear from the Brodie experience that I have a problem with those two things), but I do think it's an excellent opportunity. Just think! Director of a theater at twenty-four years old!

How exciting!!

Josephine

PS: If lung capacity is a hint to singing voices, I think the twins are destined to be very successful future singers.

Skymarian Theater Troupe •

From: JA
To: GK

I'm sorry! You asked me a question in our last message and I completely forgot to answer it last night during my emotional meltdown.

First of all, I had to look up *barmy*, and then I laughed. As far as I can tell, Gwynn is probably the most normal of the entire family. I haven't gotten to spend as much time with her as I would like, but I am certain we are on track to becoming great friends. My grandfather would call her a *spitfire*. Do you all use that word here in Skymar?

No, their grandfather is not a recluse at all. He's one of the loveliest men and has the most interesting collection of historic shoes that you could ever imagine. Talk about a fetish! But it's a stylish fetish, so I can only admire him all the more. He also has one of the best speaking voices. Think Bing Crosby with a Skymarian accent. Does that melt your heart too? Sigh.

As far as Matt and Alec? Hmm . . . well, the younger of the two definitely lives his life as if he were born for the spotlight, though he doesn't seem as invested in the theater as his elder brother. He's charming and handsome and, well, I've only recently realized, much to my surprise, not my type.

I consider Matt my friend. He's more reserved and harder to get to know, but there's a kindness and warmth beneath his stand-offish exterior. And once you do start to really know him, he's . . . well, worth knowing. I'm not sure why describing him took such hard work. I think I typed six different words before committing to "worth knowing," but he is. And I'm so glad I do.

Anyway, I don't know if you're interested in joining some of the others in the theater group, but we have a huge surprise planned for the festival this week. PLUS, it's opening week for *My Fair Lady*. AND . . . right after, it's my birthday week! I'm so excited about what's in store. If you're going to be at the festival, you'll have a front-row seat to a very special Darling surprise.

PS: You know how I was talking to you yesterday about needing a tragic backstory or a more subdued and mysterious personality to get the man of my dreams? Well, fiction reminded me of something very important (my cousin Izzy would be so proud of that fact). Julie Andrews's character in *The Sound of Music*. She was happy, and clever, and positive, and she didn't just get the guy, she got the whole family. I realize *The Sound of Music* is a one-in-a-million kind of story, but I guess I just have to wait for my one in a million. For that somebody who wants me in all my ridiculousness and positivity, and it fits them in all the right ways.

PPS: I would also add that Cinderella's story works in this particular example too. But she gets the guy AND the castle! I'm not aiming for a castle anymore. I take that as real character growth.

How Deirdre had the audacity to expect Matt to drop everything and bend to her whim was beyond him. She hadn't changed at all!

Matt tossed the letter down on the desk in his home office and shoved a hand through his hair as he leaned back in the chair. Nothing. Not a word for three years and then, out of the blue, she writes to ask for Iris's baby clothes?

Heirlooms, she called them. Clothes she'd worn as an infant.

He propped his elbows on the desk and pressed his head into his hands. Pregnant with her new husband's baby and *now* she wanted to focus on her family? His fingers curled into his scalp. No interest in contacting Iris. Not even a question about how her daughter was doing.

His palms raked over his face to slam against his desk. What sort of imbecile had he been to marry her? He'd dismissed any warning signs of her selfishness. Convinced himself her emotional whirlwinds were the typical characteristics of a performer. And he'd tried to "save" her, to be the stability he thought she needed, but deep down he knew, when he looked back on it later, he'd been temporary. Not permanent for her. Not enough.

But worse, neither had Iris.

"Hey there."

He looked up as the quiet voice invaded his fury to find Penelope peeking around the doorframe, her vibrant hair spilling over one shoulder as she peered in. Almost at once, her expression transformed from a smile to one of concern. She moved toward him.

"Oh, Matthias! Are you all right?"

He stood, rounding the desk to keep it as a barrier between them. He'd already had to come to terms with her dating his brother; the last thing he needed was to feel her in his arms again to make matters ten times worse.

"Yes, I'm fine." He waved toward the desk. "Just finishing up a few things."

She studied him, her attention so intent on his face, he wondered if she read his thoughts. He looked away.

"I . . . I just wanted to check in with you." Instead of stepping back, she moved closer. Why didn't she take the hint that her nearness only made things harder on him? Not easier. "I thought you were going to bring Iris by yesterday, and when I didn't see you in church this morning, I thought something must be wrong." She raised the silver container Iris had insisted they use for Penelope's cookies. "And I'm returning this." She wiggled her brows. "With a few strawberry tarts inside."

His heart was tempted to soften a little to her presence. That dance, her hug . . . it all initiated an unraveling he hadn't expected. But his emotions were already frayed from his own frustration over seeing her and Alec together. Now this letter, from out of the blue, tossed his insufficiency and failures back in his face with a greater sting. It would be much too easy to care for Penelope Edgewood. Her passion and generosity made it as easy as breathing. But then she'd break his heart because, in the end, she wouldn't choose him. She'd leave too.

And he was full up with getting his heart broken by women who chose someone or something else in the end. He wouldn't put himself or Iris through that.

"Thank you. Just a lot going on with the theater."

Penelope scanned the room, her teeth skimming over her bottom lip as she tapped her index fingers together in a failed attempt at disinterest. She wasn't taking the hint. At all. And he needed her to. His heart needed her to.

"And your ex-wife?"

His gaze shot to hers. "How did you—" His shoulders sank. "Gwynn."

"She let me in. Said you'd gotten a pretty disheartening letter."

"Infuriating, more like. Deirdre hasn't contacted us in three years, and she sends a letter now without even asking about Iris. No mention. It's unfathomable."

With incomprehensible speed, she slipped around the desk, near enough that her scent wafted through the distance between them, teasing him with impossibilities. He stiffened against the hope, the desire. Why couldn't she just leave him be?

"I'm so sorry, Matthias." She rested a palm against his arm. "So sorry for your broken heart. I can't understand how any woman would ever choose to leave a life as wonderful as one filled with you and Iris. It doesn't make any sense."

Old insecurities resurfaced, nearly choking him. Her compassion burned like salt in his reopened wounds, teasing something he couldn't have . . . couldn't risk.

"Life isn't all fairy tales and show tunes for everyone, is it?"

Her brow pinched as she looked up at him, clearly unintimidated by the ire in his voice. "Actually, I've always drawn strength from fairy tales and show tunes because even after the broken hearts, there's always something else that brings a happily ever after most times. The 'Climb Every Mountain' moment. The chance to dream again, if we're willing." She squeezed his arm. "I know that dreamer still lives in you. I've seen him a few times, even. Still hoping for a fairy tale, despite what you say."

"You don't understand. How can you?" A harsh laugh rose from his throat. "In your happy little world, people choose to stay and grow old together. But this isn't a Broadway finale with magic and lights and dancing off into the sunset. This is the dirty, hard, painful actual life of things. The guy doesn't always get the girl. People walk off the stage, remove their makeup, and step back into the shadows and heartaches of the real world. If someone wants to leave, they leave, and there's nothing I can do about it."

"But people also stay." She held his gaze. "One experience doesn't dictate every other relationship. The right people choose to stay, even off the stage."

"And your wealth of experiences makes you an expert on relationships, does it?" Was that his voice? The harsh, hateful sound?

"This again?" A light flashed in her eyes and her jaw tightened. "Just because I've not experienced your exact type of pain doesn't mean I can't feel for you and pray you find hope again. I see your potential, Matthias." Her smile flickered to life, despite the steely look in her eyes. "Such amazing potential. There's a hero tucked away in there, fighting to get out."

He pulled back from her touch. "You can't understand."

"You're letting her win, you know. Still. When you have the power to change things." She followed him, not allowing him to retreat. Those eyes intent, focused. All her energy, her hope, battering his wounded heart. "You've let your villainous ex-wife keep stealing things from you for years, long after she actually left."

"What do you mean?"

"Your hope. Your joy. Your belief in love and even—" She shook her head. "She stole your dancing. But I think"—she stood a little taller—"your present difficulty isn't so much a broken heart as a gratitude problem. You're focusing on what you don't have instead of what you do. And you have so much! And you're *good* at so much."

Her words hit so hard that he flinched. She was right. Painfully right. And he didn't want to admit it. Another failing. "What . . . what do you know about it? Nothing. There's no salvaging what's happened here, so don't pretend you understand anything at all, and don't lecture me from your pious position of wisdom. You can't write a fairy tale into this situation no matter how hard you try."

"You're stronger than this." She backed away, a glossy sheen filling her eyes. "I know you are. And I've seen the flickers of the wonderful, hopeful man you are peeking out from behind the pain. He's still in there, trying to get out and dance again. Laugh again. What would happen if you actually took hold of a little bit of that fairy tale? The hope, the fight for what is light and beautiful and possible." Her grin flickered, but the joy had left it. "Maybe even the impossible. I know it would do you good. For you and Iris. Fear rarely leads to a better ending."

He growled and turned away from her, the truth knifing into all his insecurities and peeling back the pain layer by layer.

"Right," came her sad response, more distant. "But what would I know?"

Silence followed her words—an empty silence. He drew in a deep breath and turned, but Penelope had gone. His chest deflated with a burst of air and he collapsed back into his chair. What had he done? She, of all people, wasn't his enemy. Even if she'd chosen Alec, her intentions were good, and—God help him—she was right.

"Well, that was nicely handled." He looked up to find Gwynn, arms crossed, leaning against the doorframe.

He buried his face in his hands. "Why did she have to show up at such a wrong time?"

"Maybe it was the exact right time and you manhandled it." She waved a hand toward him. "Clearly."

He glared over at her and then groaned as he replayed his words to Penelope.

"Exactly," Gwynn said, as if reading his thoughts. "You can't move forward if you're always looking back, Matt." She sighed. "And I think the woman who was standing right in front of you a few minutes ago is worth seeing . . . and believing."

"She's chosen Alec."

"So you do think she's as ridiculous and unintelligent as you just implied?" Gwynn shook her head.

He winced.

"You needed to feel that." She sighed and stepped forward. "Don't underestimate her. She's proven she's worth much more, and on most days, you're much smarter."

He shot Gwynn a glare and then stared down at Deirdre's letter still lying before him.

She was his past, and he had learned from his past. He wanted joy and love and hope. He wanted to take back his future. For himself and Iris. Three years ago, he fought. Chasing Deirdre to the airport, begging her to stay. Even getting into some fisticuffs with her lover. But Deirdre had chosen someone else instead.

Matt's mind raced through scenes with Penelope. She had shone light into his heart even when he hadn't been looking. She drew things out of him that he thought were dormant or destroyed. She *saw* him.

And—he pushed up from the desk—she hadn't deserved his wrath. Not when all she wanted to do was bring tenderness and hope. Perhaps he couldn't spend a future with her, but he could make the present count.

"Oh good, your smart side is coming out." Gwynn stepped out of the way as he passed and he shot her another glare, which merely bounced off her smile. "Good luck, Sir Matthias."

He rolled his gaze heavenward, regretting, yet again, that he'd ever mentioned that conversation to his sister. With a snag of his jacket from the hook by the door, he dashed out into the night. The cool October air hit him as he took the stone path toward the forest trail. Moonlight bathed the world in a pale light, haloing the pines against the starry sky.

Rounding a group of trees, he spotted Penelope's pale-blue blouse as she marched through the night. She nearly ran, she walked so fast.

"Penelope," he called.

A hitch in her step proved she'd heard him, but instead of turning, she increased her pace. He followed suit, closing in.

"Penelope, please."

Before he even reached her, she turned on him.

"You're wrong. So wrong." She pointed a shaking finger at him, which shook even harder when she prolonged the word "so." "Don't think that just because I'm young and happy most of the time, I don't understand hurt and grief."

"I know I was wrong. And I don't think—"

"I've *chosen* joy, but that doesn't mean I didn't have to fight for it.

227

And sometimes that fight starts as soon as I wake up in the morning." Her voice broke on the last word, drawing him nearer, flipping his heart over.

"Penelope." He barely whispered her name, near enough to touch her if he wanted. And he wanted. He wanted to wrap her in a hug. To cup her face in his hands. To bring back her smile. He fisted his palms at his sides.

She looked up at him, her eyes glossy, pooling. "Your hurt may be different than mine, but you still have a choice. Just like me."

Those tears unraveled whatever fragile hold he still had on his past pain, and with one long sigh, he let go.

"You're right. I do." He placed a gentle palm against her shoulder, as she'd done with him in the house, but she didn't pull away. "I'd gotten so lost in what I didn't have, I'd forgotten to find joy in what I did."

"Not every woman is like your ex-wife, Matthias." A single tear slipped down her cheek.

"No," he whispered. Before he caught himself, he reached up to catch the tear, the touch and her words proving his heart more than ready for this risk. She made it so easy to fall. So terrifyingly easy. "You've helped remind me of that fact."

His finger lingered on her cheek for a second longer, the moon's glow like their own private spotlight on the stage of this forest meeting.

She searched his face as his hand slipped away, those large eyes measuring him. And then, as if she'd come to some conclusion, she sighed.

"I can't imagine how much she hurt you. And you're right, there are things I can't understand." The previous hurt and anger dissipated from her expression, replaced by the gentlest look. "I can't understand how any mother would ever wish to leave a sweetheart like Iris or such a good man like you." She folded her arms across her chest, her shoulders giving a little shiver. "But I believe in you. Your sister and grandfather believe in you." Her smile tipped a little, nearly causing him to pull her close enough to taste those lips. "You're the only one lagging behind."

How could her hurt slip away so quickly?

The little pixie tempted him to fall so hard without even trying. She just loved and cared with such utter abandon. It drew his limping heart toward her light despite all attempts to stay away from the certain burn.

"I'm glad you're here, then, to catch me up. Someone's needed to for a long time." He slid his jacket off and wrapped it around her shoulders. "Do forgive me, luv?"

"Well." She pinched his jacket around her. "Since you said *luv*." Then she studied him a moment longer before turning toward the cottage, her pace slower, easier, beckoning him to follow.

She'd worn some sort of trousers, or . . . were they jeans? With sunflowers all over them, and a pair of yellow shoes peeked out from beneath the wide legs. Her pale-blue blouse was much too thin for a walk through the forest at dusk in October, which only proved how concerned she'd been about him.

He followed along in silence until they made it to the cottage. The porch lights glowed into the growing dark. Instead of taking the steps inside, Penelope glanced skyward and then lowered herself on the front porch step. With a look up at him, she slid over in invitation.

He smiled as he lowered his head. What had he expected? Not her. For certain. And not such a swift forgiveness. No, Penelope Edgewood was certainly not like his ex-wife at all.

"Unless you're too cold?"

In answer, he settled down beside her, their shoulders touching.

"Your relationship with your ex-wife couldn't have been all bad." And of course she'd try to find some sunshine in it all, wouldn't she?

"She brought you Iris. And maybe she helped you realize what you really wanted instead of what you thought you wanted." She stared up at the sky, her long hair falling down her back. "I've been learning that myself too."

"Have you?" He leaned back on his palms, embracing the moment. The quiet. The ease of being with her.

His throat tightened. He wanted this so badly. This . . . tenderness.

"Some of what you said about me was right." She pulled the little silver container she'd evidently carried with her from the house into her lap and opened the lid.

"Only some?" He glanced at her in his periphery and noted her growing smile.

"I think I have gotten the stage and real life confused sometimes. I expect the glitter and magic of make believe so much that, maybe, I don't always focus where I should."

"If changing that means you'll lose the overall pleasure that is you, then I would urge you to keep your head in the clouds."

"Nice way to slide that compliment in there, Mr. Dashing." She laughed a quiet, contented sort of laugh and then handed him a tart. "But it's true. I've filled my world with so much drama and consumed so many fairy tales that I'm beginning to realize how it may have warped my expectations a little. That sometimes the simplest things are the sweetest."

Perhaps Matt hadn't underestimated Penelope so much as he disbelieved in something so . . . beautifully authentic. Someone with such a big heart, big enough for him and his little girl? He closed his eyes and refused to contemplate anything more than right here and now.

They ate her rather delicious tarts as the night noises bled into the quiet.

"What a weekend! An argument with each of the Gray boys. I feel like I should receive an award." She gave a slow shake of her head and took another tart from the container. "Is that some sort of Darling rite of passage or something?"

"You had an argument with Alec?"

"Kind of the same one." She waved the half-eaten tart as she spoke. "Too young. Know nothing. Et cetera."

He cringed and took a bite of the tart—strawberry, sugar, and butter melting over his tongue. The arguments against falling in love with her kept shrinking.

"Yours hurt worse, by the way. Just so you know."

He pressed his fingers into his chest. "Ouch."

"Good." She narrowed her eyes in mock pleasure and then took a bite of her tart. "Maybe you'll learn your lesson a little."

To be the younger of the two of them, she certainly taught him a thing or two about forgiveness and moving on. "I feel the sting to my heart." He stared at her upturned profile, hoping the intention in his words came through. "I . . . don't want to hurt you."

She glanced back at him, holding his gaze for a moment. Her expression softened before she turned to look back up at the sky. Silence followed as they enjoyed another taste of tart.

"It hurt worse only because I know you don't really believe those things about me." She shrugged. "You've been one of the few men I've met who actually took me and my ideas seriously from the start. And I guess it just hurt worse because we're closer friends than anything Alec and I will ever be, so your words mattered more."

More than Alec's words? How could he feel utter shame and pure delight at the same time?

"So it means all the more that you came after me. Because it only proves you are who *I* already know you are." She took another bite of tart as if this were a simple, everyday conversation, instead of the world-breaking and hope-building one he felt it to be.

The trill of the robin, likely one of the last bird sounds of the fall evening, permeated the quiet, followed by the hoot of a tawny owl. The scent of rain drifted on the light breeze, tinted with a hint of mango, and his heart stumbled forward into feelings he shouldn't have for this woman.

"Autumn is my second favorite season." She sighed. "I love the briskness of the air and the rainbow colors growing over the trees. They're so vibrant here."

Second favorite? His smile brimmed. "I'm afraid autumn is rather short in Skymar."

"It's longer where I live and just as lovely." There was a wistfulness in her tone.

Which meant she'd surely leave. And he'd known that from the start when he'd brought her on, but now things were different. The risk greater. The wounds more imminent. And yet he couldn't stop wanting what he wanted. Not now. "You miss home."

"More than I thought I would. The place and people are such a part of me. You would like it there, I think. It's a nice, quiet life, except, well, for me." She looked over at him, her eyes lighting with her smile. "And I'm an aunt now."

His smile responded to hers despite the sudden pain in his chest. "I've seen the photos."

She laughed. "A few *dozen* times, I'm sure."

Quiet blanketed the moment again and his chest constricted a little more. Was this what his future could be? Was his heart strong enough to manage the consequences if . . . if it didn't work out? How could he even contemplate risking his daughter's heart too?

"So what is your *first* favorite season then? Christmas?" Evidently, his heart thought so.

"Christmas is my favorite *holiday*." She raised her finger to make her point. "My favorite season is spring because everything that has been waiting for months beneath the sleep of winter comes back to life. The world is suddenly filled with color and scents and this kind of happy awakening again." And then, with a little sigh, she rested her head against his shoulder as if it were the most natural thing to do. "But I do so love Christmas."

And he fell, completely and utterly. An ache branched out through his chest.

But he couldn't have her. Not when she longed for home and his home was here. Not when the good of Iris's heart had to come above the needs of his own.

Then he realized what was worse than having someone else break his heart.

Choosing to break his own.

CHAPTER 15

From: Penelope Edgewood
To: Luke Edgewood, Izzy Edgewood, Josephine Martin
Date: October 2
Subject: Parades and plays and stuff

This week is going to be so full, y'all!! The festival is this week, and when I rode my bike into town this morning, things were looking just wonderful. Autumn colors everywhere! Some of the fall flowers they have here, along with some of the same ones we have back home, are scattered throughout the place, and as any good festival should, this one has twinkle lights. It feels very much like home except with a special bit of "magical foreign island" sprinkled in. I'm attaching pics.

The parade is Wednesday, and I have another float-building meeting with folks from the theater group tonight to finish everything. It is going to be SUCH FUN!!! Gwynn and I have been sneaky and have Iris involved. She's so excited. I think Matthias is going to be so wonderfully surprised. Grandpa Gray too (although he knows about it but doesn't know what it looks like).

Grandpa Gray put in enough money to get our float closer to the royal carriage because, evidently from what Grandpa Gray says, the closer you are to royalty, the more people will notice you. (No surprise there.) Plus, maybe, just maybe, I'll get to MEET THEM!!! And I imagine with the costume I'm planning to wear, the queen would find me very impressive.

As far as the production schedule: Narnia is next, then the ball, then *Peter Pan*, and then (fingers and toes crossed) *The Sound of Music*. I've sent emails out to every possible person I know and a few I don't.

My Fair Lady opens on Friday night and the set is stunning. I've already enlisted Mark, with Grandpa Gray's approval, to start making repairs (and updates) to the smaller theater. (I'm sending a pic, Luke, because I think you'd appreciate the craftsmanship of the proscenium arch). But I've made a list of a few other things throughout the theater that could use some extra love too. The foyer is the most extravagant two-story entrance of loveliness, but it's showing its age. Updated carpet would be wonderful, but since that's not in the budget just yet, Evelyn has arranged for a deep clean of the entire front area. I *have* gotten approval for the bathrooms and the concessions updates. Did you know they haven't been running concessions at all? You make loads of money on concessions, and if they put some of the local drinks on the list for purchase, they'd do even better (I learned that from you at Sutherland's, Izzy). Mountcaster has a fun specialty snack called a *Kaas Spiral* (cheese twist) and a little dessert called *chocotuit* (chocolate drops) that would make great additions to the concessions.

Evelyn said the renovation guys think they can have the bathrooms completed by the time we open for *Peter Pan* in November!! YAY!!! Which means they'll be ready if we get *The Sound of Music* so that the changes can be on display for any new guests.

All right, gotta go. Love you!

Penelope

PS: Matthias likes strawberry tarts almost as much as chocolate éclairs.

From: Luke Edgewood
To: Penelope Edgewood, Izzy Edgewood, Josephine Martin
Date: October 2
Subject: Re: Parades and plays and stuff

I'm exhausted just reading your emails. It's like someone took my head and squeezed it between both of their hands. Which means you must be happy.

I have to say, I do miss your baking. Do you realize how long it's been since I've had a strawberry tart worth eating?

The craftsmanship in that theater is great. You just don't see woodwork like that anymore. Looks like the stage floor could do with a good polish, though. Did they use ash wood on the floor?

Luke

PS: Make sure you wear the right T-shirt to meet the queen.

Text from Matt to Gwynn: Grandfather is coming to the parade! He also texted me using his phone.

Matt: I feel as though the world may be coming to an end very shortly, so you'd better purchase that dress from Danique's you've been eyeing for four months.

Gwynn: Grandfather texted you??!! I'm more jealous than surprised.

Gwynn: Okay, I'm surprised too.

Text from Alec to Matt and Gwynn: Grandfather just texted me and asked if I was coming to the parade.

Alec: Which one of you is using his phone? I already told you
I'd be there this time.

Matt settled into his camping chair by the large cherry tree on the green in downtown Mountcaster, right beside Grandfather. He had attended the parade the last few years only for Iris's sake, but life had changed rather dramatically in the past couple of months, which brought a whole new anticipation to Failte Feis. Iris had been whisked away by Gwynn early that morning so the "girls" could prepare for the parade, but whatever that meant, Matt had no idea.

The glint in Grandfather's eye suggested he may know, though.

How he'd missed his grandfather's subtle humor! He grinned. They both seemed to be finding their paths again after a long time of wandering. The process may have begun a bit before Penelope arrived, but there was no doubt she'd helped speed the progress.

And Matt couldn't get her out of his mind no matter how much he tried. A part of him liked her there.

"An excellent turnout."

Grandfather's comment pulled Matt's attention toward Main Street Mountcaster. People crowded down each side of the street, many arrayed in festive hats decorated with autumn finery. Music sounded from a band near the city fountain, waiting to begin the parade. This was the starting point—Main Square—and from here the parade took a long trek down Main Street and circled back around. People from all over Skymar came to enjoy street vendors, live music, handmade crafts, and every apple or cherry dessert that could possibly be designed by human hands. An apple or cherry *zak* was possibly his favorite. Soft, sugary pastry surrounding a wealth of fruit and topped with a special cream that blended it all together rather perfectly.

"Were you speaking with Jansen earlier?" Matt asked as he took a drink of the *seidear heet*, the warm apple flavor ushering in everything autumn.

Grandfather turned his pale gaze from the band, a smile creasing his face.

"I'd forgotten how much I appreciate the people in this city, lad." He looked back toward the street. "How much your grandmother and mother would have wanted me to keep on appreciating them."

"They would." Matt followed his gaze, the excitement as tangible as the laughter all around. "For all of us and for our Darling."

Grandfather's smile softened at the pet name Grandmother had always called the theater. "I'm keen to take back some of the work you've overseen as well. I fear you've gotten lost in balancing the books, the board, and the business for much too long."

"I'll gladly go over things with you first of next week and we can decide what would suit you to take in hand." Matt drew in a deep breath, his smile spreading with the pride in his chest. "It will be good to have you full in, Grandfather."

"Aye. 'Tis good and too long." He nodded. "Jansen's an artisan if ever there was one still left in the world, and I'm meeting with him next week to secure his services."

"His services? For the house?"

"The house is well enough." Grandfather huffed. "For the theater. If we're to celebrate a centennial, we need to fix a few things about the place, and I'd trust no one to refurbish the historical moldings, window frames, and ceiling fixtures as I would him." He dipped his chin to add confidence to his words. "One hundred years is a long time, and I'm determined to make up for what I've lost."

Matt started to inquire further, but a burst of trumpet and a shout from the crowd alerted onlookers of the start of the parade. A lightness rested on Grandfather's shoulders, as if, like Matt, he had unshackled some of the shadows of the past. A new start sounded like a wonderful way to celebrate a centennial.

Matt stood alongside his grandfather in preparation for the royal entourage, as their carriages led the way for the rest of the train, a festive collection of floats, bands, vintage automobiles, and a few surprises.

"I see you all found a good spot." Alec pushed in between them, his hair giving off a styled look of disarray. "It looks like I just made it."

"We're all surprised, lad," Grandfather said, his brows taking flight. "I hadn't expected you for a half hour yet."

"Yes, Grandfather." Alec nudged Grandfather with his shoulder. "But I hear great surprises are in store for us today."

Grandfather gave a grunt but slid a glance to Matt, showcasing a twinkle in his eyes.

Oh yes, his grandfather's personality had come back in full mischief. Perfect. Matt paused on the thought. Well, he hoped. His grandfather's mischief ran in the same direction as Gwynn's.

"I've heard the same," Matt said, keeping his attention fixed on the older man.

"With Miss Edgewood at the helm, I had to pop in to show her my support."

Matt looked over at his brother. "You see it, too, then? All she's doing for the theater?"

"It's difficult not to notice." Alec waved a hand toward Matt. "Of course, you had started making some changes before she came, but she rushed in like a—"

"A pixie on a mission?"

Alec looked over at him with a grimace. "You say the strangest things. She's certainly more princess than pixie, if we must use your analogy." Alec patted his chest. "Just my style, though she'll take a bit more time and attention to convince."

Matt trained his expression, though he had the sudden urge to muss his brother's perfect hair. "The usual dining at the castle didn't work for you?"

"She only wants a bit more wooing." Alec winked. Matt's fist tightened just a bit. "The smart ones always do."

Matt readied a response but Grandfather's movements caught his attention. The man, who despised the idea of using his phone for anything other than voice calls, held the device up and proceeded to record the parade.

Matt looked over at Alec, who stared back wide-eyed.

"Just because I'm old doesn't mean I can't learn, lads," Grandfather said without turning their way. "Iris is a *braw* teacher."

Matt's smile broke free and he looked ahead as the royal band led the procession wearing the patriotic colors of cobalt blue and white, with a small band of gold crossing their chests and a small rosette in the center of their hats. The triumphant opening of the Skymarian national anthem blasted through the air, prompting cheers from the throng.

The royal guard followed both before and behind the royal carriages. For a few years, the royal family had used automobiles in the parade, but after the current king took the throne, he brought back the horse-drawn open carriages.

King Aleksander and Queen Gabriella rode in the first carriage, both as poised and as elegant as ever. Crown Prince Stellan Caliean and his wife and eldest son were followed by the two princesses, with their two unmarried brothers riding their own steeds alongside the carriage. Several of the younger women called out the princes' names as they passed, but the men merely waved their greeting and moved on, likely used to the attention from the royal-watching populace.

A few floats followed the royal entourage, one for Darrows, a large business in Fiacla known for its textile production, and another for Eller Keen, an energy company. Both boasted simple vehicles displaying heads of the company and their families. Then followed a float from one of the largest tourism companies, Avontur, complete with a miniature map of the islands and small representations of reasons to visit, such as the castles, mountains, cliffs, and ruins.

After such a coterie, a vintage black convertible came into view, two small red flags flying from its back, and on the side a simple sign that read "Emblem Studios." For such a large company, the unpretentious and somewhat bland presentation seemed out of place among the pageantry. And why were they so near the front of the parade? Had they paid for the spot?

A woman and a man dressed in gothic attire sat on the back of the convertible, waving to the crowd, as Mr. Niles Westing rode up front with his chauffeur driving the car. The couple must have been the stars in Emblem's new production of a dark comedy entitled *The Shadows*.

"They look like they tossed something together at the last minute," Grandfather said, waving his phone in the direction of his attention. "And collected a few vampire mannequins from the wax museum in Port Quinnick."

"Grandfather!" Matt attempted to reprimand through a laugh.

"Whatever they've done, they've got a good spot for visibility, haven't they?" Alec offered, shaking his head. "Only a few places behind the royals."

"And sandwiched between Avontur's overcrowded but eye-catching display and—" Grandfather clicked his tongue. "Well, well, what do we have here?"

Matt turned his attention back to the parade and his jaw slowly and quite impressively dropped. A massive float, easily the best in Darling's history, followed a distance behind Emblem Studios'. Pulled by a lorry that was driven by Dani, dressed in top hat and suit, came a display made up of two trailers fitted tightly together to encompass the whole ensemble. The lead actors for *My Fair Lady*—Professor Higgins, Colonel Pickering, and Eliza Doolittle—danced about a smaller version of Professor Higgins's study with the song "I Could Have Danced All Night" sounding from the speakers. Interestingly, a wardrobe had been placed within Professor Higgins's study and stood, doors open, to reveal the next part of the presentation. A step into Narnia, complete with a small spot for a lamppost and the four children already chosen to play the main roles. And just behind, on a raised section, taken from the Darling's set, stood the front third of a pirate ship with a clashing sword fight happening between Captain Hook, currently played by Mark, and—a laugh burst from him—Gwynn as Peter Pan.

The float displayed the three upcoming productions. *My Fair Lady*; *The Lion, the Witch and the Wardrobe*; and *Peter Pan*. Brilliant. And easily one of the largest floats of any he'd ever seen at the parade, which wasn't saying a great deal when compared to much bigger parades, but for Mountcaster it certainly stood out.

There was no mistaking whose handiwork was behind this creation. This style of float must reflect some of her American grandiosity.

But where was Penelope?

Grandfather laughed and gestured with his phone toward the float. "She really outdid herself, didn't she?"

"I've never met anyone who enjoys 'outdoing herself' more," Matt replied, chuckling and meeting Alec's astonished expression before turning back to the parade. "Grandfather, is that the wardrobe from your study?"

His grandfather's smile grew so large that it stretched his graying mustache.

"You used the wardrobe from your study and let them cut out the back of it?" Alec gaped.

"Nothing a few nails won't fix afterward." He turned back to his videoing. "Besides, Lorianna would have loved it."

She certainly would have. Matt drew in a deep breath, his chest expanding with waiting laughter.

On either side of the float walked various people dressed in costume. A few Lost Boys. The White Witch. Two or three couples dressed in Edwardian finery fit for the races in *My Fair Lady*. And then a little pixie in green caught his attention. She carried a basket and tossed something that looked like sparkling confetti toward the crowd. His eyes stung at the sheer delight on his daughter's face. His very own Tinker Bell, with her golden hair in a high ponytail on her head. She danced beside the float, her smile bright, and she looked every bit the part of a happy, healthy child.

And right by her side, looking just as happy and giving a nod to their spring performance, walked Cinderella, except instead of pixie dust, she was handing out small packages of some sort. He couldn't quite make them out, but they looked like little golden bags. Her red hair piled on top of her head featured a silver crown, similar to the one she'd worn on her dinner date with Alec, and the gown bloomed out around her in a shimmery hue of pale blue.

Penelope embraced her part, her pink smile on full display as she strategically approached families lining the road and gave the golden bags to the children.

On several occasions, Penelope leaned over to give Iris guidance; all the while, his little girl stared up at the woman with a look of unadulterated pleasure. Matt's internal arguments against pursuing Penelope hit a snag. What did Iris need most? Could it be the same thing that his heart wanted?

"What . . . h-how?" came Alec's stuttered response.

"Magic, I'd say," Matt responded without one hint of a smile. "She is fairly teeming with it."

Alec opened his mouth as if to respond, but merely turned to stare back at the parade.

"How on earth did Emblem get ahead of her, is my question?" grumbled Grandfather. "I called and made the arrangements myself about placement, and I was assured we'd follow directly behind Avontur."

"You knew about . . ." Alec blinked, waving toward the float. "This?"

"I'm assuming she didn't divulge the information to you at dinner?" Matt pinched his lips tight to keep them from curling with a bit too much pleasure.

"She . . . she mentioned a surprise"—Alec shrugged—"but I never imagined something so . . ."

"Marvelous?" Matt finished, his grin breaking free. As marvelous as the creator.

The float passed, and pasted on the very back hung a large sign that read:

Celebrating 100 Years of Magic
Become a part of The Darling House story too

And beneath was listed the phone number and web address in bright red.

Had she thought of everything?

"Actually, Grandfather," Matt added, keeping a peripheral view of his brother, "I believe the placement worked better than even you planned. People had a stark comparison between the two companies. And ours celebrated the community, which is something Emblem has never quite grasped."

"Unless it was only a certain part of the community." Grandfather huffed.

"And . . ." Alec finally seemed to find his voice. "Darling invited everyone."

Something in Alec's face caught Matt's attention. Perhaps he'd come to the realization, as Matt had done only a few days ago, that the community loved The Darling House, and The Darling House needed to find a way to love them back. To bring back the magic it once fostered among the streets of Mountcaster and beyond.

"She's actually going to save the theater," Alec whispered, staring back in the direction the float went. "Impossible."

"'Impossible things are happening every day,' I hear," Matt said, quoting Penelope's earlier phrase from Cinderella, and then he placed his hand on his brother's shoulder. "But actually, we're all going to find a way to save the theater. Penelope's outside perspective—"

"And gumption," added Grandfather.

"—has started a trajectory we hope will resurrect the theater we grew up loving."

"We—" Alec started to respond, his gaze distant.

Matt softened toward his younger brother. He'd borne his grief alone, refusing to talk about it. He needed his family. Maybe he was beginning to realize that too.

"Exactly." Matt nodded. "The Gray family and the community that loves us."

Text from Matt to Penelope: I have no words for the magnificence that was the Darling float today. You were marvelous.

Penelope: Wasn't it wonderful? Oh, Matthias! I almost told you about it ahead of time so you could witness how much the community theater loves your family and The Darling House. So many people pitched in their time and money to make this happen. You should be so proud!

Text from Alec to Penelope: I have no idea how you planned the float, but it made a huge splash today. Did Mark come up with the idea? I know he's an excellent woodworker.

Penelope: It was my idea, but Mark took my idea and helped turn it into reality. (Look how neat reality can be sometimes.) He, Dani, and Lucas were vital to today's success! Wasn't it a great surprise?

Text from Matt to Penelope: Sorry I'm just now responding to your text from yesterday, but you must know I am tremendously proud and grateful. BTW, I'm planning to have a meeting with the theater group next week to make some changes for our upcoming season. Grandfather, Gwynn, and I had a long talk last night about it. I would have brought you into the conversation, but when I phoned you, you never answered.

Penelope: I was rewarding myself with a trip to Chocola for their Chocolate Strawberry Dream, and then I went home for a bubble bath. Glitter is very hard to remove, in case you didn't know. Well, you probably found out when Iris took a bath. I should apologize, but she WAS a fairy so glitter was necessary.

Penelope: BTW, I've had the Chocolate Strawberry Dream almost enough times to figure out the recipe. I've made it four times so far and each time I'm close, but not quite.

Text from Alec to Penelope: Are you going to be at the theater tomorrow? I'd love to learn more about all your other plans. Has *The Sound of Music* come through?

Penelope: I'm planning to be there, and no, not yet. But I'm going to keep trying.

Alec: Don't hang your hat on it, princess. What you've done already has made enough of a difference, don't you think?

Text from Grandpa Gray to Penelope: You were the belle of the ball yesterday. Thank you for all you're doing for our Darling.

Penelope: You of all people know what a pleasure it was for me. Just wait until they see the best surprise of all, right?

Text from Penelope to Alec: A good difference, but we need a showstopper to ensure we keep an upward trajectory.

Alec: A touring company this late in the season? Even your magic doesn't have that power.

Penelope: You really know how to make a girl feel hopeful, Mr. Pessimist.

Alec: I'm just trying to temper your expectations.

Penelope: I'd rather be hopeful and disappointed than to have tempered expectations. That just sounds like eating generic chocolate instead of the name brand.

Text from Matt to Penelope: You're taking the day off tomorrow, right?

Penelope: Why would I do that? We have an opening weekend!!

Matt: Penelope!

Penelope: I'll trade you my fifth attempt at the Chocolate Strawberry Dream for a little favor??!!?? (insert heart eyes)

Matt: What favor? (insert grumpy eyebrows)

Penelope: I just snort-laughed, which regularly wouldn't be a noteworthy occasion, but I may have scared the kid sitting beside me in the restaurant. Anyway, I'll tell you next week after opening weekend. It will be a surprise.

Matt: The Chocolate Strawberry Dream better be worth it.

Penelope: Oh, it will be. You can totally trust me. (insert batting eyelashes)

CHAPTER 16

From: Penelope Edgewood
To: Luke Edgewood, Izzy Edgewood, Josephine Martin
Date: October 5
Subject: Plays and parades

You guys! *My Fair Lady* has had an AMAZING opening weekend!!!
Matt said that all of the shows were sold out! SOLD OUT!
Grandpa Gray said they hadn't had sold-out shows in several
years. The team is meeting on Monday to discuss some of the
renovations, which will begin, in part, this week, but in full after
next weekend's shows. Narnia rehearsals will be happening then,
but the reno crew plan to work around them. It's all so exciting!
And it's giving me so many ideas for The Ashby Theater!!! I've
emailed JMC some photos of The Darling House and some of my
ideas, just to see whether she'd be open to them. (And yes, I still
plan to wait and give her an answer later in the month.)

Oh, BTW, I'm attaching the video Grandpa Gray sent me from
the parade. Just ignore the talking in the background. It's
Grandpa Gray, Matthias, and Alec. Well, Izzy, you may not want
to ignore the talking. The accents are fabulous. Alec is much
more pessimistic than I realized. Grandpa Gray is adorable. And
Matthias, well, he's my ally and friend. In fact, he actually takes
my thoughts and ideas seriously without doing one of those eye
rolls some men give me when I talk. It's so infuriating. Luke does
it, of course, but deep down I believe he has partial faith in me
(please don't clarify this if I'm wrong on my assumptions, Luke).

Anyway, Failte Feis reminded me of the parade back home, though Mt. Airy doesn't have any royalty . . . and has a lot more dogs in the parade. When I get home, I'm getting a dog, just so everyone knows. And my own place, especially if I'm going to have such a very grown-up job.

Luke, I asked Grandpa Gray about the stage floor since I have no idea what *ash* is unless we're talking hair color, and Grandpa Gray said yes. Then I told him about what you do and showed him some photos. He's very interested in your skills. He says there are fewer and fewer stonemasons in Skymar and lots of people want to take preexisting buildings (like outbuildings or old houses) and turn them into vacation rentals. Tourism is a HUGE industry here. Along with fishing, textiles, energy things, and . . . reenactment weaponry. Seriously. Grandpa Gray said that Skymar is one of the top countries in the world that creates historical weaponry often used in movies. Cousin Jude would be ecstatic. I'm determined to find him a jeweled dagger just for fun.

This week Kinleigh is coming to help with the rehearsals for Narnia and we're going to discuss her future as an intern. I'm so excited to start the training process with her like JMC did with me.

Penelope

PS: Is it strange to want to hug Grandpa Gray, Iris, and Matthias every time I see them? They are my favorite people in Skymar!

. . . .

From: Izzy Edgewood
To: Luke Edgewood, Penelope Edgewood, Josephine Martin
Date: October 7
Subject: Re: Plays and parades

Penelope! The float was amazing! I can't believe you designed one even better than the one you created for The Ashby Theater during your gap year. I don't know how in the world you were able to make Cherry Tree Lane on the back of a trailer look as if Mary Poppins was going to show up at any moment. That Bert was probably the best one I've ever seen in any performance!

Why did Alec seem so surprised that all these plans are actually working to save the theater? I adore that Grandpa Gray and Matt were so pleased! And Iris is the most adorable little fairy I've ever seen. I could see her as Goldilocks with all of her curls.

• •

From: Luke Edgewood
To: Izzy Edgewood, Penelope Edgewood, Josephine Martin
Date: October 7
Subject: Re: Plays and parades

I never knew that the professor in Narnia was the same one in *My Fair Lady*.

Weird.

He must have stopped breaking out in song by the time the Pevensie kids showed up.

PS: Send Gramps my contact information. Maybe I can at least give a virtual consult or two.

Text from Penelope to Luke: You are such a dork.
Luke: How old were you when you stopped praying for your
    Hallmark hero to show up? Oh wait, I think you still do.
    Hmm . . .

Penelope: That was a very old diary entry.

Luke: Yes . . . very old. Last year?

Penelope: Any proof has been burned.

Penelope: I also deleted the photo you just sent. I thought
I threw that Christmas ornament away three years
ago. Do you just keep things like that around for use as
blackmail?

Luke: I didn't have any brothers growing up, Penny-girl. I
learned to be resourceful.

Skymarian Theater Troupe

From: GK
To: JA

I cannot believe what you did with the float at the Failte Feis! It was
a perfect way to reintroduce The Darling House to the community.
From what I heard in the crowd, it was the talk of the parade. I
think what our community needed most was a reminder of places
like The Darling House and loves like the music and magic of the
theater.

Ah, that's right. You're not a native European, so some of our
words, I imagine, are novel to you. But it seems that you've fit right
into the heart of Skymar, so that's what matters most.

I'm glad you've found friendship among the Grays. I'd heard
the elder brother is standoffish, but with the right type of person,
I'm glad he's proving "worth knowing." Single dads can be rather
unusual, I understand. Careful of heartbreak and such, but if a man
has loved faithfully once, it gives a hint he is willing and able to do
so again. I've always thought that winning a heart like that would
be worth it. A rather romantic notion, isn't it?

From: JA
To: GK

You came to the parade!! Oh, how wonderful! Did you come to talk to any of the theater group? I wish you'd approached me. Since you know who I am but I don't know who you are!

I'm so very proud of the parade and all the people involved. We made the news! Which, of course, is great publicity, whether for good or bad, but I prefer it for good, don't you? There is something to be said for "Popular" as Glinda sings in *Wicked*, especially for business. I don't mind being a behind-the-scenes person, but you can't let your business be behind the scenes. That's why I've been trying to create more ways to be visible. Out there!

The blog I started has been a hit. I've been trying to share funny recipes people have created from different musicals, like Hunchback Galette and Romanov Fudge. Plus I've been featuring an interview with each of the community theater peeps once a week, to build some visibility for them too. We have an amazingly versatile and experienced group, and Dani said they've added ten new people to the in-person group in the last three weeks. I think it's excellent that two of the community theater members are a part of the board of directors for the theater, because they really bring practical voices into the meetings.

Did you know that The Darling House ball is going to happen this year too?! The board (in concert with the Grays) have already begun preparations for a masquerade ball to celebrate the centennial of the theater. Isn't it perfect?!? A ball celebrating a theater where we all come in costume!!! (I'm not ashamed to say I came up with the masquerade idea. I love dressing in costume.)

I'm taking the day off tomorrow so I can go adventuring through Fiacla. It's my birthday and I don't want to spend it alone in my house or working at the theater. Exploring will be not only a great diversion but a real treat.

BTW, have you ever heard of Earnest Stevenson? He's an artist who is up-and-coming for theatrical art. His work has an illustrated vibe. Kind of like Al Hirschfeld for the modern day. (And Earnest always slips the name of his puppy, Sam, into every creation so that the viewers have to find where it's hidden.) Anyway, I introduced him to his now-wife back at the North Carolina School of the Arts, so I'm going to call up a favor and have him create some promo material for Darling. Ohhhhh, I'm so excited.

Penelope took her time getting out of bed, enjoying the leisure of a day off. From the sunlight blinking through her window, the day promised to be a pretty one too. She'd chosen one of her favorite blouses to wear—a flowing green confection with puffed sleeves—and wrangled her hair into a ponytail, complete with a matching green bow. With some quick work, she slid into some jeans and tennis shoes, ready to bike to Elowyn's Tower first.

Her phone blinked awake from charging overnight and the first two messages blared to life:

Happy Birthday, Penny-girl. You're my favorite baby sister.

She grinned at Luke's message. *He thinks he's so funny.*
Izzy's followed.

Love you big, birthday girl! I hope your day is fantastic. Will call this evening.

Both must have stayed up late enough to send them so that she wouldn't receive them until morning. Her grin spread as she walked downstairs and munched on a breakfast bar while she packed her backpack for her day.

It wasn't so bad spending the day alone. After all, she'd been with people all week long. And there were plenty of things to do alone on a beautiful island. She slipped down on the stool and sighed.

She'd never spent her birthday alone before, so it was a rite of passage, so to speak. Wasn't it? Very grown-up and mature. She reread the texts and then, without hesitation, ordered the shoes she had saved in her cart for two weeks. Both pairs.

Happy birthday to her!

She'd just slung her backpack over her shoulders when a knock sounded at her front door.

She glanced at her phone. Barely nine o'clock. Who could possibly visit her at nine in the morning in the middle of the week?

A massive bouquet of all sorts of flowers greeted her as soon as she opened the door.

"Happy birthday!"

Behind the lovely bouquet of various flowers appeared the adorably grinning face of Iris Gray.

"Oh my goodness," Penelope exclaimed, taking the flowers into her arms. She looked over at Matt, whose wide grin paused her thoughts a moment. Had he gotten a haircut? He looked . . . well, rather handsome. Maybe it was the smile. Or the navy turtleneck. There was something academically swoony about men in turtlenecks and jeans. "How . . . how did you know?"

"Gwynn mentioned something about it, so I checked your paperwork to confirm the date. Iris wanted to surprise you or I would have rung first." He gave a one-shoulder shrug and winked. "*Perhaps* I would have rung. Though you *are* rather fond of surprises."

A rush of warmth spread through her chest, like an internal hug. She stepped back so they could enter, and Iris smiled up at her as she passed.

"Daddy let me choose the colors and I said all of them."

Penelope laughed and placed a kiss on Iris's cheek. "They're perfect. In every way." Her gaze came up to Matt's. "This is such a wonderful surprise. I . . . I don't remember telling Gwynn about my birthday."

"She can be rather tricky at sussing out information from people." His expression gentled in a way she'd never noticed before. It made her keep staring for some reason.

He cleared his throat. "So Iris and I thought we'd make a day of it in your honor." His gaze landed on her backpack and his smile faded. "Did you . . . already have plans, or were you wanting to be alone?"

"No!" She softened her quick cry with a smile. "I mean, I was planning to spend the day alone, but I'd much rather have company." She lowered to Iris's level. "Especially this kind of company." She ran a hand over Iris's head and the little girl vaulted forward to wrap her arms around Penelope's neck. Penelope breathed in the sweet scent of strawberries from her hair. Oh, how she loved this little girl!

And Penelope hadn't realized how very much she'd wanted company on her birthday until just now. The idea of it being Matthias and Iris only made everything better.

"Well, then—" Matt gestured toward the car. "We have a rather lovely day planned, if you're up for it?"

"A picnic at the Vandermeer and then a walk by the beach," Iris added, bouncing up and down with a little clap.

"Vandermeer?" Penelope looked up at Matt for clarification as she stood, but he merely shrugged again.

"You'll just have to trust us." He held out his hand and Iris imitated him on Penelope's other side. "Do you, Miss Edgewood?"

She burst out with a laugh, taking each hand in one of hers. "I certainly do."

Matthias opened the door for both of the "ladies," as he called them, and then took his place in the driver's seat.

"I knew she would say yes, Da," Iris announced when he started driving, and her chin tipped with her smile. "Penelope loves us."

"I do," Penelope said, glancing back at the little girl and then catching Matthias's look as she turned back around. His gaze held hers for a second before she pulled her thoughts back together. "Sweet surprises and company are two of my favorite things. The very best of birthday presents."

Jazz marked the background music. Sinatra and Bublé. Matthias probably did that for her too.

They drove in a direction Penelope hadn't gone before, away from Mountcaster or Ansling. To the south. And their conversation consisted of Iris recounting all her favorite birthday memories and then her favorite parts of the parade until she grew quiet, humming to the music.

"I do have a parade question," Matthias said.

She relaxed her head back against the headrest and looked over at him. "All right."

"What did you give away in those little bags you distributed? The phone rang all day yesterday with inquiries, but Evelyn only smiled and told me to ask you or Grandfather." His brow quirked. "But Grandfather said he'd leave the surprise to you."

Penelope burst forward in her seat. "Classes." She squealed. "There were some sweets and a card with the upcoming productions through summer, and then there was a coupon for classes. And if people called to show interest in Darling featuring classes again, then they would have their names put down for a 20 percent discount on the first set of classes offered."

"Classes?" Matthias shook his head, one expressive eyebrow pointed skyward. "Who is planning to teach these classes?"

"Haven't you realized how many people you have around you with amazing potential?"

"You're right." His grin split wide. "I do. They just seem to have been gently prodded to become more demonstrative in their potential."

"Positivity is highly influential, Mr. Gray." She gave a shrug topped with a not-so-innocent smile. "Gwynn volunteered to start with the voice class, along with Gloria. Dani offered to teach an audition course for those interested in learning how to try out, and Mark said he'd teach something about set design. Lilith is going to teach beginners dance, and Grandpa Gray volunteered to teach an advanced waltz class."

"Grandfather?"

"He did." Penelope giggled. "It's amazing. Once he embraced the life he still has left to live for his family and theater, he jumped all in."

"He's done that with the business side too. Taking things back in hand." Matthias shook his head as if the news surprised him. "I'm afraid you're going to inspire me out of a job."

"What do you mean?"

"Well, if Grandfather takes back his previous responsibilities, then all I'll have to manage are the finances. He's already taken back his previous work overseeing the donors and working with the board of directors." He chuckled. "That may sound like a handful, but it's nothing compared to what I've been juggling the past few years."

"I'm sure there's plenty to do." She watched the passing scenery of green fields and jagged mountains growing nearer. "You love the theater, too, don't you?"

He hesitated enough for her to notice. "I appreciate it as a place my family loves, a place of history and talent, but I was more invested in the entire production because I was working alongside family." He nodded. "I'm realizing more and more how much it means to the people who perform on a regular basis, and how they can become like family, to an extent."

"You didn't know that before?"

"I was so close to the theater and the business of it, I don't think I'd ever stepped back and seen the . . . house view, if you will. As someone watching the performance and recognizing how it all works together to create something memorable."

"That's a great way to think about it." She rested her head back against the seat again, basking in the comfort and sweetness of sharing this drive with her . . . friends. On her birthday. "It's something I learned when I worked at The Ashby Theater because we had a little crisis there—kind of like here—and had to revitalize."

"Ah." He raised a brow and sent her a look from his periphery. "You've had practice saving places before."

She liked the notion of saving places, rescuing dreams and people. It sounded very heroic. "Well, I don't know if *saving* is the right word, but maybe loving a place back to life? Or loving a dream back to life?" She shrugged. "It's what sent me in the direction of marketing *and* theater, instead of performance. Besides, despite my obvious emotional flexibility, I didn't have the superb talent for performing that's required to make it big." The ocean came into view along the road. Just glimpses. And a smaller town, all cobblestone and lantern-lined roads. "And, well, to be honest, I want a family, so I chose a different path."

His quiet drew her attention to him. His attention shifted back to the road. "Do you regret it? Not pursuing performance? Broadway?"

"No." She'd spent a lot of time thinking and praying about the decision, but the past two months had only proven her choice was positively perfect for her. She was doing exactly what she was meant to do, professionally. Introducing others to theater. Educating them. Bringing the classics back to the forefront of people's minds while giving the old a new shine for a new population. "I'm doing exactly what I feel professionally called to do. I love it." She looked over at him. "What about you? What would you want to do if you could do anything?"

"A few months ago, I don't know what I would have said. But now?" His gaze flickered back to her, searching, and then he gestured with his chin toward the window. "Well, right now, I'm going to take you and Iris on one of our favorite walks."

Hmm . . . deflection? Well, she'd just have to save that particular investigation for another day.

The parking lot was nothing more than a little dirt patch near a thick wood of evergreens.

"It's the best place ever, Penelope!" Iris danced alongside her. "Da says it's our special place and we only take special people to see it."

"Do you?" Penelope looked up at him as they entered the forest on a little trail weaving between the trees. He carried a basket and the wind tossed a few strands of his hair over his forehead in a look of disarray. She decided she rather liked that look on him. It made him seem less put together and serious, though she'd come to realize he wasn't *so* serious.

"It's a public footpath," he whispered. "Anyone can find it."

"You're supposed to just say yes, Matthias," she whispered back. "Only special people come here with you."

His grin crooked and his gaze roamed over her face in such a way her breath grew a little shallow. He really believed in pulling out all the stops for a special birthday, because she sure felt special at the moment.

"Then yes. Only special people."

They walked on and talked about the day and Penelope's favorite birthday memories, including the time Luke rode a camel first in order to show her that she could fulfill her birthday wish of riding a camel. They'd been eleven and seven. He'd walked funny for a week.

Iris shared how her last birthday party had been at the very spot to which they were walking, and they'd stayed until dusk in order to catch fireflies.

The image of Matthias running around with a giggling Iris catching fireflies settled in her heart like a perfectly sung note. Right. Sweet. The type of family memory she'd embrace too.

After holding Penelope's hand for part of the walk, Iris took off after a rabbit scurrying past, leaving Matt and Penelope following at a slower pace. Birdsong twittered overhead and a gentle breeze rustled the leaves, carrying the cool scent of pine. The simplicity brought its own magic and she breathed it all in, the feeling of . . . well, she wasn't certain, but it made her want to linger and sing and sigh all at once.

"You do realize how much you've made a difference here, don't you?"

Matthias's deep voice blended in with the setting around her, offering a deliciously warm mix within the slight chill in the October air. A perfect sound. Hot chocolaty.

"I'm happy I've been able to help." She smiled up at him, pushing back a strand of hair that had fallen loose from her ponytail. "It really has been one of the most delightful experiences of my life so far."

"Even with all the troublesome Grays?" The twinkle in his eyes inspired her chuckle.

"I'd have to say the troublesome Grays have been my favorite part. People are what make the difference in our lives most of all." Her thoughts dove into her doubts. "But, Matthias, there's something I wanted to talk with you about."

His attention zeroed in on her face with such intensity, she almost forgot what she was going to say. How strange was that?

"Yes?"

She drew in a breath, garnering courage. "I think someone is stealing our ideas for Darling and giving them to Emblem."

He came to a stop, turning completely toward her. "What?"

She gestured for them to keep walking, and when he didn't move, she slipped her arm though his to urge him along. Iris didn't need to worry about this. "I dismissed the idea at first, but the longer I'm here, the more I realize all the instances can't be coincidences."

"What instances?" He'd lowered his voice to match the tone she'd set.

"The website designs, the box seats, the newspaper ads, and then . . . the float?"

"The float?" He almost stopped again, but she tugged him forward, glancing around them to make sure no one was within earshot. It was unlikely that a spy followed them to the Vandermeer—whatever that was—on her birthday, but she'd watched enough mysteries to be suspicious.

"I just assumed Emblem had already secured a spot in the parade when Grandpa Gray signed us up, but then I overheard the Emblem folks arguing at the parade about how their appearance was a fast decision. And that they hadn't planned on even being at the parade until a few days before."

"Which would make sense seeing as how the presentation was so . . ."

"Uncreative?" She waved at Iris, who'd stopped in front of them to pick an orange leaf off the ground, and the realization that this little scene in her life looked very much like a family moment almost distracted her. She gave her head a shake and pulled the current conversation back to the forefront of her mind, pocketing that unexpected thought for later. "Grandpa Gray said that floats receive their placement based on the size of the donations—a sacrifice Grandpa Gray made along with pulling a few strings of his own."

"He knows everyone."

"Right, which is why he thought we'd be closest to Avontur or that other company nearest the royals."

"And you think someone tipped off Emblem from The Darling House team?"

"But who would? Not Grandpa Gray or Gwynn, surely."

"No, I can't imagine either of them ever doing anything to wound the Darling. And Gwynn practically lives and breathes love for the place." His gaze fastened on hers. "Did Alec know?"

Alec? No, surely not him. He was family. "I hinted at something about the parade, but wasn't specific. The theater troupe knew, but if it were one of them, then it would have to be someone different for all the earlier times. None of them knew about the news interview or the web designs or the other things."

"Have you told anyone of your suspicions?" He'd stopped and turned toward her.

"Only my family, but I'd thought about mentioning it to Grandpa Gray."

"Good idea." Matthias nodded and threaded her arm back through his to continue walking. "He knows so many people and I'm certain you can trust him above all others."

"Except you." She grinned, giving his arm a little squeeze with her own. "You're my closest friend I have in Skymar."

He stopped again, searching her face. "Am I?"

The admission pooled through her with welcome warmth. Despite his being older, and certainly wiser, and having a daughter, she valued his friendship more than anyone else's here. He just fit in her heart so well. "You sound so surprised."

He tipped his head as if in thought and then continued their walk, his smile gentle. "Honored, more like."

Something inside her bent, shuddered, and then expanded as if welcoming in a feeling so big that it needed more space to reside.

She searched his face as if he would explain it to her, but his tender expression only confused her even more. What was happening? She blinked her attention back to the path up ahead, but her mind raced with an impossible notion. Was she falling in love with Matthias Gray? Friendship took on a very different definition: deeper, sweeter, and topped with a few delicious tingles.

"We're here!" called Iris with a giggle—a sound as at home among the forest as the other woodland noises. "We're here!"

And whatever spell Matthias Gray had cast on her heart released as she turned to the little girl. "Are we?"

"Come, we'll show you," Matthias said, taking the lead in tugging their linked arms forward.

They followed Iris through a last veil of trees and the forest fell away to reveal the most magnificent waterfall she'd ever seen. It plunged over the cliff and across a deep gorge from the field in which they stood, so high a few birds even flew below the waterfall's origin spot. Maybe Penelope had stepped into a storybook!

"Vandermeer."

She looked from Matthias to the falls and back.

Everything felt too big to take in. The view, the possible mole, this realization about her feelings for Matthias. But as the latter idea sank deeper into her heart, she embraced it.

She wouldn't have noticed him a year ago in her world of busyness and college fun. Not with her silly list of what she thought she wanted, but the truth in her heart began to form more clearly in her head. She'd been so focused on some crazy definition of a leading man that she'd forgotten some of the best characters played the secondary roles. And sometimes, they should've been in the spotlight all along.

Her heart squeezed against the thought. She couldn't fall in love with Matthias Gray, could she? He was six years older than her. There was no war. And she was returning home in less than two months.

CHAPTER 17

A perfect day.

That's how Matt would describe this particular Tuesday of his life.

He'd had a few before, but not in a long time, so the presence of this one glowed a bit brighter than the ones before. But that's how life seemed to work. By comparisons. Seeing the good more clearly and with more gratitude when placing it next to more shadowy memories. Or in this case, setting one relationship next to another.

This hopeful, intelligent, and lovely woman riding beside him toward home shone a clearer light into how broken his relationship with Deirdre had been. How one-sided. How much he'd changed to suit her demands or whims. How he'd come to dread entering the house at the end of the day to one of her tirades or criticisms. Nothing ever seemed good or right or . . . happy.

But spending time with Penelope was wholly different and . . . beautiful.

Penelope never seemed jealous of Iris's presence but instead pulled his daughter into conversations without a hint of exasperation. She painted the world with melodies and joy—he couldn't help but grin—as much a real-life fairy-tale heroine as anyone he'd ever known. Her arm had slipped through his with such familiarity, as if she'd always belonged beside him. Her laugh came quickly and often, and he hadn't realized how much he craved someone looking at him the way she did. Like he wasn't a second choice or a failure but . . . important to her. Her friend? Yes, and his heart wanted even more. The impossible more.

How strange a turn of life.

He'd never have expected to be drawn to her, and yet it was almost as though she matched him like no one else. And as he'd looked down into her lovely face after she'd called him her friend, he wondered for the first time whether her heart felt the same draw. A flicker of something in her eyes. A change in the way she'd touched his arm or the way her gaze lingered in his.

His chest deflated. But how? How could it work? He lived here. Iris's life and family were here. And clearly, Penelope longed for home. But Iris came alive under Penelope's care. So did he.

Was he a fool to pursue something that could very well break both their hearts?

"You never know," came Penelope's voice in the car as she spoke to Iris about the possibilities of performing as a princess in a musical one day. "The biggest dreams are the ones that take the most risk, but they're worth it, Iris. You may just have to make it through the hard things first."

So he took those words to heart. *Risk. Worth.* The two words went hand in hand. He would never do anything to hurt his daughter, but what if loving Penelope meant the best for all three of them? Could that be true?

He pulled the car up to the cottage.

"This has been the very best day. I just don't want it to end." Penelope smiled over at him, the green of her blouse bringing out the same color in her eyes. "Would you and Iris like to come in for dinner? I make homemade pizza for my birthday every year and, well"—her teeth skimmed over her bottom lip—"I'd love for you to join me in the making and the eating."

"What do you say, Iris?" He held Penelope's gaze as he turned his head toward the back seat. "Pizza and Penelope?"

"Yes, yes!" Iris had already unbuckled her seat belt and opened the door.

And the perfection continued with laughter and flour and

Penelope's special care for Iris. He saw what his life *could* be. A family. A future. But the possibility of thousands of long miles hung between reality and hope.

"I made a fifth try of Chocolate Strawberry Dream." Penelope winked at him.

"Ah, I see the way of it." He nudged her with his shoulder as he kneaded the pizza dough. "You only wanted us to stay for this favor of yours."

"No." Her eyes grew wide and then she smiled. "The favor is the bonus. Having you both here is just . . . well, right." She shrugged. "But I won't ask the favor until dessert so I can sweeten you up and secure a yes."

He chuckled. "You're a very poor negotiator, you know? Laying all your cards out for everyone to see."

"It's true. I'm not very good at subtle." She finished grating the cheese into a bowl while Iris worked the dough for her own little pizza. "I'd much rather be honest. It makes everything less complicated."

Yet another reason to love her.

"You mentioned during our picnic at the Vandermeer that you'd worked in theater since you were very young. Was it at this Ashby Theater you mentioned?"

"Mm-hmm." She nodded, tossing a little extra flour on Iris's mat to keep the dough from sticking. "Mom started me there to help me get over my shyness, and it worked a little better than she'd hoped, I think." She laughed, her eyes dancing. "I fell in love with the place, the magic, and Mr. and Mrs. Crenshaw. They became like an extra set of grandparents to me."

"The owners?"

"Yes, and theater fit so well that soon I was working there during high school and teaching acting camps during summer breaks. I worked full-time as an assistant to Mrs. Crenshaw during my gap year too."

He spread out the dough on the pan while Penelope helped Iris with hers. "Was there a reason you took a gap year?"

Her palm went to her shoulder almost as if it were second nature and then she turned to Iris. "All right, Iris, I grated enough cheese to make these the cheesiest pizzas ever known in the history of Skymar. Dip your hand into that bowl and sprinkle all the cheese you want."

She moved closer to Matt, bringing the homemade sauce with her, and began spreading it across the dough. "My friend Erin." She'd lowered her voice for his ears only. "She was diagnosed with an inoperable brain tumor our senior year of high school. The doctors gave her a year, so . . . well, I decided college could wait but time with her couldn't." Her eyes took on a glossy sheen, the familiar appearance of grief. "Her mother was on her own and the medical demands could be pretty tough, so I helped take care of her."

She cleared her throat and kept spreading the sauce. "Erin made it through the spring production of *Alice in Wonderland* and then"—her whisper shook, but her smile bloomed in a captivating way—"she moved on to the very best wonderland of them all."

Air lodged in his throat at the new revelation about this beautiful woman. Yes, she knew grief. Wounds. The gaping scar of a missing life. And yet her grief held an inner glow of acceptance and even joy. A true understanding of the greater wonderland, indeed.

His palm rested on her back. "I'm so sorry, luv."

She smiled her gratitude at his comfort. "But that year taught me so much, not just about life and grief and hope but about the business and inner workings of the theater, and it only secured my course of study when I started college." She pushed the cheese bowl in front of him with a little sniffle, smile still intact. "As much cheese as you can stand, Mr. Gray."

He held her gaze. Did she realize what a unique and beautiful person she was? His parched heart swelled beneath her . . . joy.

He tipped his head toward the bowl, brow raised, his throat tightening a little. "The cheesiest in the whole history of Skymar?"

She gestured toward the mound of cheese topping Iris's pizza. "Probably second cheesiest."

His chuckle broke free, and he made the decision right then that he'd do whatever he could to pursue a relationship with Penelope Edgewood, because he was certain neither he nor Iris could find anyone more positively perfect for them than her.

Penelope put the pizzas in the oven and then turned toward them, her hands together, a light in her eyes that he was beginning to see as a possible warning of ideas to come.

"Now, as a birthday rule"—she raised a finger—"while the pizzas bake, we take a dance break."

His "What?" sounded at the same time as Iris's "Yay!" Without waiting, Penelope turned toward her phone, and immediately "'S Wonderful" by Tony Bennett sounded through the room. She raised her brows and danced in his direction, but stopped just before she reached him. His pulse vaulted into a hip-hop. Dancing and romance? Was he ready for it all?

Before reaching him, she turned to Iris and pulled her into a little dance, shooting a wink in his direction. He tipped his head, his grin slowly growing wider.

Baiting him? Very clever.

She had no idea he was already hers. Hook, line, and sinker.

She batted her eyes up at him and took Iris into a modified, kid-friendly swing dance. Iris only giggled and Penelope allowed Iris to spin her around with or without rhythm, but Penelope's skills still showed. Her fluid movements. Her style. The way her body naturally moved to the music.

The next song came on. He'd heard it before. What was it? "Dance with Me Tonight"?

"Iris, I think we should get your dad dancing, don't you?"

"Yes, yes!" She sounded thrilled, hopping up and down, hands clapping.

Penelope started snapping to the beat, rocking side to side as she watched him through narrowed eyes. "Of course, he might be too afraid to try." She tsked and shot Iris a wink. "What a shame."

Iris giggled. "Da's not afraid."

Well, right now Matt wasn't too certain about the accuracy of his sweet girl's statement. His heart hammered in his chest like a conga drum, but the rest of his body responded to Penelope's request before his mind fully caught up. He stepped forward.

"Ooh, he's pushing up his shirtsleeves. This looks serious." Her eyes gleamed alive, drawing him another step forward. "Probably a good idea to keep it serious, Mr. Gray. You don't want to have too much fun."

Yes, he wanted this. All of it. For himself and Iris. Wherever the story led. He at least needed to try.

"That's quite enough, Miss Edgewood." He leaned in and caught her hand, pulling her into him. "How's your Lindy Hop?"

Her mouth opened with her smile, and as they moved in time with the classic swing dance, Iris twirled alongside them, pausing at times to clap her hands and laugh.

Penelope took his cues, giving a twirl here, swivel there, rock step, triple, and a swing out.

"You're smiling an awful lot, Mr. Gray," she said breathlessly as he spun her around. "Almost as if you enjoy dancing or something."

His only response was a grunt, which likely looked ridiculous while wearing a grin he couldn't shake.

"It makes me think about that favor of mine."

They rocked back from each other as he watched her face. "I believe there was some dessert involved first."

"Trust me, the dessert will be worth it."

Pulling her into a swing out was his only response.

"You know Jamie Carson?"

"Mark's son? From the theater troupe?"

She nodded, continuing to keep in step with him. "His dance instructor broke his hip and Jamie has a performance coming up for college placement and possible scholarships."

Matt nearly lost his step. "Penelope."

"I know you used to teach dance."

One of his brows rose without his consent.

"Don't give me that look. I've been going through the archives for two months. I've seen the flyers and the class list." She drew close on her next rock step, one of her eyebrows hitched high. "And the awards."

His frown won for a second, until she slid back into his arms again, dragging the intoxicating scent of mangos with her.

"Four weeks," she added, her hand in his, her gaze pleading. "That's all. Twice a week."

The music bled into a slower song and they shifted their style.

"You Were Meant for Me," sung by Gene Kelly. He kept one hand at her waist, the other palm pressed into hers. She naturally closed the distance, swaying to the music, those eyes of hers imploring.

"I think you need to do this, Matthias."

Matthias. His frown softened. He knew she was right. And the small bits of dancing he'd done between the time he'd waltzed with her until now proved it. His body missed it. So did his heart.

He sighed out his fight. "Only if we keep it a secret for now."

Her entire face bloomed with her grin. "Promise."

"And that means no one. Not even Grandfather."

"Cross my heart." She nodded. "Not a word."

"And that dessert?" He leaned close, breathing in her scent, his lips close to her ear. Her breath caught. Perhaps he could woo her after all? With dancing and kindness and Iris. "It better be worth it."

The oven timer sounded.

Penelope stumbled back from him, her cheeks glowing in a rather fetching way. As she searched his face, her palms came to rest on those rosy cheeks, and he immediately thought of Julie Andrews's response to dancing with Captain von Trapp the first time.

Penelope cared about him. In a romantic way.

And she didn't even know it.

The urge to laugh nearly sent him breaching the distance to her and taking her back in his arms.

"Time for the pizza," Penelope squeaked. She turned to Iris, casting a look back to him before turning for the kitchen.

He followed the ladies and began helping Iris set out the plates and cups while Penelope retrieved the pizzas.

This simplicity was his dream. Family. A woman who not only loved him and his daughter but turned any place into a real home.

Penelope had just set the pizzas on the table when a buzzing sound broke into Gene Kelly's singing.

"Matt, would you go ahead and slice those while I check this message?" She gestured toward the table. "I think it might be another birthday wish from home."

He complied, taking on Iris's massive mess of melted cheese first. "Oh no!"

Matt looked up. Penelope studied her phone, a frown pulling at her lips. "Not again."

Matt moved to her side. "What is it?"

"Look." She turned her phone to show him a message from Gwynn:

Someone's taking your ideas from the blog! How did they know about Romanov Fudge before you even posted it?????

A link showed for Emblem Studios, featuring a post called "Romanov Fudge: Tasty Treats Inspired by the Classics."

"What does that even mean?"

"I've been posting fun recipes on the blog inspired by certain musicals. This one, for *Anastasia*, was meant to go up next week, but Emblem's already taken it." She stared down at her phone, shaking her head. "How?"

"You've told no one else?"

"I don't even remember telling Gwynn, but I must have." She leaned back against the counter and then her gaze shot to his. "Wait. There is another person. Someone I've been emailing since before I arrived here. A member of the online theater group."

"The Skymarian Theater Troupe?"

"Yes, the one with Dani and Mark and the others. We've been private messaging for months. But I haven't told her many things. Only a few." She shrugged. "I think she's a 'her.'"

"What? You don't know?"

"I don't even know her name." She sighed, her shoulders drooping. "We kept with the anonymous rule for the group unless we reveal ourselves of our own accord. She never did."

"Then we have no idea who she is." He leaned beside her against the counter, their shoulders almost touching.

"All I know is that the initials she uses are GK."

Heat drained from his face. "GK?"

For Gene Kelly.

She nodded, staring down at her phone. "I don't know much else."

He trained his expression before she looked up. She pulled up a Skymarian Theater Troupe email for his perusal. "This one."

GK on STT. That was *his* former account. Had he never deleted it? With all that had been going on in his life during the last handful of years, it wasn't a priority. But clearly someone was using his former email, and that someone was sharing information with Emblem Studios.

As soon as Matt tucked Iris into bed, he made his way down to his computer. Who on earth would steal his STT account? Blast him for using the same password for his social networks for a century! Anyone close to him could likely guess it and tap straight in.

But who would care to take an account for a theater troupe? And why? It made no sense whatsoever.

He'd left Penelope with a smile before completing the brief drive home, assuring her they'd solve this dilemma together. And he'd meant it. They would get to the bottom of this little situation, but first things first, he'd change his password or delete the account altogether.

Emblem had been after The Darling House for the past few years. Even made a couple of ridiculous offers, too, but Grandfather would have nothing to do with them, and Matt couldn't blame him. They wanted to tear down the building and use the space for a more modern theater. They'd even offered Matt a lucrative job as a dance instructor.

Dance instructor. He almost grinned. His body still hummed from the energy of dancing with Penelope. The steps and unused muscles remembering their form . . . and the pleasure, especially with Penelope in his arms. In fact, she made everything a little better. She'd been right about another thing too. He'd allowed Deirdre to steal his joy for dancing and he wanted to rediscover it all. The simple pleasures of spending a day with his daughter and a beautiful woman. The delight of being part of the choreography of a musical. And the thrill of dancing and teaching others how to dance as well. He had allowed Deirdre to steal much more than his self-confidence, and it was past time to take back what he thought he'd lost.

Teaching Jamie would be his litmus test, of sorts. A dip back into the world of dance instruction.

He turned to his computer and scanned the screen. In the far-right corner, the red icon of STT waited. When he clicked on it, a long line of messages filled the screen. All between his account and a

JA. JA? Jane Austen? Then he read through the first few lines of the most recent message:

> There is something to be said for "Popular" as Glinda sings in *Wicked*, especially for business. I don't mind being a behind-the-scenes person, but you can't let your business be behind the scenes. That's why I've been trying to create more ways to be visible. Out there!

His lips parted into a smile. Not Jane Austen for Penelope, no. He'd wager his dancing feet that JA stood for Julie Andrews.

He skimmed through the previous messages, and the identification of the person using his account became perfectly clear.

Text from Matt to Gwynn: Why are you using my old STT account?

Matt's phone buzzed on the desk and his sister's photo popped up on the screen. *Ah! Caught!*

"Okay, I should have told you," she started in as soon as he placed the phone to his ear. "But I didn't want people to know it was me because Victor is still a part of the troupe."

Her ex-boyfriend?

"And to be perfectly honest, Matt, he was a little threatening when we broke up, so . . . well, I wanted to stay in touch with what the troupe was doing without giving away I was still a part of it."

The excuse made sense, even though he didn't like it. Victor hadn't responded well to Gwynn ending their relationship. At all. They'd even alerted the authorities at one point because he'd been following her.

"Hmm." He sighed. "So you just decided to hide behind my profile?"

"Your profile was so vague, anyone could hide behind it." He could practically hear her rolling her eyes, if that were even possible. "Dancer, accountant, likes long walks and good movies." She rattled off the list. "Besides, you weren't using it, and I only meant to hide behind it for a few emails, but then—"

"You liked the anonymity."

"Yes." He could almost envision her pouting. "It's not caused any harm for anyone and that's how I've been able to get to know how to support the theater troupe some more, even while away at college."

Thus, the reason she'd always known who was auditioning for parts before he did. And where the individuals worked. She'd been following them for months.

"And I suppose you're aware that Penelope has no idea *you* are GK or that GK is *my* account?"

"I didn't know it was her until a few weeks ago, and then I . . . well, I didn't know what to say."

He skimmed over the last few emails. "And you decided to play matchmaker, from what I see."

"If the sparks are flying, far be it from me to douse a flame." She chuckled. "And don't deny it. Other people wouldn't notice, but I'm your sister. She's good for you and you are for her."

"Since you're so excellent at noticing details, have you realized that someone else is possibly reading your emails to Penelope? Unless you're the one feeding Emblem Studios information?"

"Feeding Emblem information? Are you mad?" came her rather passionate response. "I'd never do anything to jeopardize my theater."

Matt nodded to himself. Of course she wouldn't. The fact that the theater had been passed down to the women in the family, in contrast to the men, made the theater even more precious to Gwynn. An idea first devised by their great-grandfather to ensure his wife had financial security during a time when estates went to men.

He skimmed through more of the email exchanges, grinning at some of Penelope's messages. "Can you come home this week?"

"I can leave after my last class on Thursday and be home before tea."

"Excellent. We need to go through the list of things Penelope believes has been taken from our ideas and see if we can put the pieces together. In the meantime, I'll try to find a way to discover who else has been logging into my account besides you, because if we can sort that out, we'll likely find our culprit."

From: Penelope Edgewood
To: Izzy Edgewood, Luke Edgewood
Date: October 15
Subject: The curious case of the theater spy

I've been so busy with the Narnia production, museum, marketing, and helping Grandpa Gray work through the ball plans that I've not had a lot of time to write, so I'm sending a quick update.

I sent my email to JMC accepting the job at The Ashby Theater. It seemed silly to wait any longer when I knew my answer. I texted Josephine after I sent the email. She called me right away and proceeded to both scream and cry for thirty minutes. It's clear she needs someone nearby to show the twins some excitement without the . . . Josephine-ness to it. JMC said she'd send me paperwork and plans within the next few weeks, and I'm glad, because right now I don't have the time to focus on that.

Next week, the whole team (Matthias, Gwynn, Grandpa Gray, Alec, Evelyn, and Dani) is getting together to discuss the strange goings-on with Emblem. (I just love writing the phrase "goings-on." It sounds very classic.)

Now more than ever, I'm determined to keep the museum a secret until I absolutely have to share about it, so Grandpa Gray ordered the locks changed on the entrance doors to the museum so only he and I would have the keys. There are irreplaceable artifacts in there, and it promises to bring in more donations to the theater. And though I can try to hide news about the museum, there's no way to hide it if we get a touring company to come. We HAVE to get the news out ASAP, though I've not gotten any hits yet. Lots of very nice rejections, but . . . rejection is rejection, even if it's very nice.

Even though Emblem stole my musical recipes idea, I'm still going to forge ahead. I've actually MADE the recipes. The recipe they put up after Romanov Fudge is inedible! That's what they get for cheating!! So I've added a few other things like "If you like ____, then watch this movie!" That's for Fun Fridays. I'll take any of your book recommendations, Izzy. I won't take Luke's movie recommendations, though. They'll involve war. Or death. Or people who speak in a Russian accent.

Anyway, I've got to run. Edmund Pevensie just fell over Mr. Tumnus, and evidently I'm still the only one with bandages, tweezers, or socks. Really, those should be staples for any theater person, especially the socks. You can stuff those into anything for additional umph. At least Dani is always prepared with batteries for mic packs.

Penelope

PS: Do you remember when Grandpa Edgewood told us to keep our expectations low so we wouldn't be disappointed? Well, I read a quote from *Anne of Green Gables* once (be impressed, Izzy) that said, "Mrs. Lynde says, 'Blessed are they who expect nothing, for they shall not be disappointed.' But I think it would be worse to expect nothing than to be disappointed." And I agree. I'm going to keep expecting magical things to happen, and I'll just deal with the disappointment. If we don't try, then we're definitely going to be disappointed.

• •

From: Luke Edgewood
To: Penelope Edgewood, Izzy Edgewood
Date: October 15
Subject: Re: The curious case of the theater spy

I'm sure Edmund blames Tumnus for all the trouble anyway.

And you say you like classic movies? My tastes are purely classic. Originals. I can practically hear the theme from *Superman* playing in my mind right now. And there is no war in that one.

PS: I'd keep an eye on Grandpa Gray for this whole spy business. Any guy who has classic shoes and a mustache should be on your radar.

Penelope stretched out her back after another long afternoon going through a few of the last storage boxes. She had to be getting close to some of the oldest ones, because most of the dates on the programs or playbills were in the 1920s. The costumes in some of the photos were stellar, not to mention the shoes. Penelope found a photo of Lorianna Gray in the most splendid pale gown that glittered like starlight. Those long white gloves just gave the entire outfit the perfect touch.

Penelope moved the closest box over to a table in the museum, just so she could stand while sorting through this one. A playbill of *Top Hat* from 1936 waited on top, followed by an actual top hat and scarf, purportedly worn by Fred Astaire. She breathed out a laugh. It seemed like every time she opened a box, she uncovered more treasures.

Nestled at the very bottom of the container sat a few framed photos instead of the loose prints she'd been used to finding. A woman who looked a whole lot like the photos she'd seen of Lorianna Gray stood beside a tall, dashing man, both in evening attire and standing in front of The Darling House. The display featured *Peter Pan* and *The Wizard of Oz.* Could those be Lorianna's parents? The original founders of The Darling House?

A small wooden case rested at the bottom of the box. Penelope carefully lifted it out and turned the brass clasp. Inside, two golden-framed photos waited. One with the couple from the earlier photo standing with a little girl, and the other was of a different and more regally dressed couple with what looked like the same little girl. A card rested in the corner of one of the photos, so Penelope opened it.

12 November 1933

Thank you for allowing Alaina the opportunity to play the part of Peter Pan in her first public performance. What an honor to celebrate a theater and a family we admire a great deal. May The Darling House continue the legacy of loving our community and bringing quality performances to Skymar.

Sincerely,

HRH

Penelope read it again. HRH? She glanced back at the little girl and the adults. Didn't HRH mean His/Her Royal Highness?

She did a quick Google search on her phone for the royal family of Skymar and scrolled back to the current family's grandparents. Diederik and Rowen.

Her pulse jumped into a gallop. This was them! Their daughter, the princess Alaina, performed as Peter Pan in 1933.

Penelope pulled the photo close. At some point in history, the Gray family had a fantastic connection to the royals! Oh, oh! She had to tell someone.

She jumped up from her place, grabbed her purse, and started for the door.

Grandpa Gray welcomed her into his office, and when she showed him her find, he rubbed at his chin like a very thoughtful Gandalf sort of character. Izzy would have appreciated the turn of her thoughts.

"My dear girl, this brings an idea to mind."

"Does it?" She moved to sit in a chair next to him.

"Indeed. I should have considered it before." He looked up from the photos. "How soon can you have the museum ready for a first viewing?"

She tried to tally her final plans. "My hope was to have it in place in time for the ball so we can give all the donors a preview, but if everything goes as planned, it will probably be ready the weekend before."

"Next weekend?"

She nodded. "Well, before *Peter Pan*, so if we wanted, we could even have a few days of public viewing before the show."

"Excellent." His smile spread to crinkle his eyes. "You said visibility is what we need, is that right?"

"Yes." But she wasn't quite sure whether to be excited or a little terrified at his ominous response.

"I have an idea for visibility." He winked. "From the very top."

He tapped the photo and then raised a brow.

"The royals?" She leaned closer, lowering her voice. "Do you mean they might come to the museum?"

"I'm not certain, but it's worth a request. I went to school with the king back in my day, and I think he'd appreciate seeing these photos of his mother and grandparents."

Penelope could meet a king. Or queen. In real life. Her posture straightened at the very idea.

"That would be amazing!" She squealed and pressed a kiss to Grandpa Gray's cheek as she stood. "You're definitely getting the hang of this visibility thing."

He chuckled and relaxed back in his office chair. "You bring excellent inspiration."

"Well, I hope we bring excellent patrons with all this hard work we're doing." She stood, her body humming with excitement. "I'm going to get back to work right away. Dani and Mark have promised to help me this afternoon with the placement of some items, but I've sworn them to secrecy."

"They're the good sort." He tapped his temple. "Good thinking."

And with that she rushed through the door, nearly mowing down Alec. He steadied her with his hands to her shoulders.

"What's your hurry, princess?"

That endearment had certainly lost its shine. "So much to do! It's all very exciting, just busy." She gestured toward the door. "Your grandfather is inside if you're here to see him."

"So you're finished with your meeting?" He waved back toward the room.

"Oh yes." She tugged the photographs against her chest and leaned closer to him, wiggling her brows. "More and more surprises, Mr. Gray. Beautiful surprises."

"Is there something I can do to help?"

"I know the set designers could use an extra hand on some last-minute repairs, but I've got all the help I need."

"For your secret project?" He waved in the direction of the museum doors.

"More for the *Peter Pan* set than my secret project." Her grin grew and she lowered her voice to conspiratorial tones. "But you're going to love the secret project. It's something to make our community and your family proud, Alec." She nodded. "And you should be so proud. This theater, your history. It's worth celebrating and saving. For so many."

His gaze searched her face, and then his expression turned sad. "I can't wait to see your surprises, Penelope. I hope they do all the things you think they will."

CHAPTER 18

Text from Penelope to Izzy and Luke: GK is Gwynn! Gwynn Gray! Matt told me today that she's been the one messaging me on the Skymar group all along! Using HIS former account.

Penelope: AND they both think that someone else has gotten into the account and read about my ideas!

Penelope: At first I thought Matt was saying HE was GK and I was confused because he didn't seem the type to have a shoe fetish, but then he explained. It seems she's known who I was for a few weeks but never revealed herself. I feel a little tricked.

Izzy: After pretending not to know about LOTR for . . . a decade? I think you can show Gwynn some grace. What do you think?

Luke: Do either of you know what time it is? It's five in the morning. I'm not supposed to get up this early unless I'm leaving for vacation or have recently become a father.

Izzy: Then don't sleep with your phone near you, smarty-pants.

Luke: I'm a whole lot smarter than y'all. Five in the morning.

Penelope: It's not five o'clock for me. I've been at work for a few hours now. That's when Matthias told me. This morning when we had scones together. I made strawberry scones and they were DELICIOUS!

Izzy: Oh, Penelope! If there is an Antoinette's near you, you MUST try their scones. They were the best scones I've ever had.

Luke: Oh look! It's still 5:00 a.m. It's amazing how both of
you can still drive me crazy when you're not even in my
house!

Penelope: It's a gift.

Matt loved this theater, but at the moment, it had taken away too much free time.

And by *free time*, he meant time to spend with Penelope. Between the rehearsals, repairs, and now dance lessons, an entire week had gone by with only a few conversations at work, lunch together after church, and two days of bicycling to work together. The meeting with the team about this possible "mole" in the theater brought no answers, except to increase everyone's caution about sharing information. He'd discovered the other log-in address but didn't recognize it, so he'd need to do a little more investigating. But whatever the theater ended up putting out for the whole world to see became fair game, for the most part.

However, not even the annoyance of Emblem's "cheating," as Penelope called it, had dampened the continued growth of The Darling House's business. Sales were up. Donations were up. And they'd had the most auditions for parts in *Peter Pan* than they'd had in more than ten years. Grandfather had taken over his old responsibilities, leaving Matt to keep the books, assist with repairs, and . . . dance?

He greeted Jamie Carson's da, Mark, with a handshake and a gesture toward the opposite chair in The Braw Bean. Matt had always liked Mark, but recognizing the man's passion for theater, and particularly The Darling House, only secured Matt's desire to teach his son to dance even more. It was strange how just agreeing to do this fueled Matt's yearning to dance again.

They'd just ordered coffee and a breakfast buttery when a

movement outside the window drew his attention. Bright teal. Ginger hair.

Penelope was outside the neighboring restaurant, peering into the windows.

He slowly lowered his coffee cup to the table and blinked. What on earth?

Her hair fell down around the shoulders of her long teal coat, and red boots peeked out from beneath the long multicolored skirt she wore. She stepped back, frowned, and shook her head, as if not finding what she was looking for, before moving on to the next set of windows. The Braw Bean.

"Isn't that your American?" Mark had turned around in his seat, likely to witness whatever had distracted Matt.

His American? Sounded nice, didn't it? "Excuse me, Mark. I'll be back in a trice."

"She's *maerk barry*, ain't she?"

Matt grinned over at Mark as he stood. *Weirdly wonderful.* "Aye, Mark. Aye, she is that."

Matt caught her attention as soon as he walked out of the café, and instead of rushing forward, as he'd expected her to do, she stood frozen in place, staring up toward his head.

"You're wearing a derby?"

"I am." He looked up at the bill of his cap and then back at her. "There's a *tousle* wind on today."

"Tousle?" Her eyes lit. "Does that mean blustery?"

"Aye." His fingers itched to tug at the scarf blowing around her neck, maybe just to pull her nearer. "Tousle."

"I love it when you use all those wonderful Skymarian words. They're positively delightful." She sighed and then bit down on her bottom lip with her smile, still eyeing his cap. "You look rather dashing and vintage in a derby."

The urge to kiss her nearly bowled him over. What would she do

285

if he lost all restraint and snogged her quite thoroughly right here on the pavement? He curbed his inner rogue.

"Well, thank you, miss." His smile unfurled and he tapped the tip of his hat. "And what has you bouncing outside the café window distracting me from my buttery this morning?"

"A derby and all those delicious words. What a wonderful way to start my day." He was nearly undone by the glow in her eyes as her smile bloomed even wider. How could he feel this much for her so soon? It was as if he'd been storing up a singular emotion just for her, and once he found her, the feeling nearly burst his chest wide open to get out. As if she truly was made for him.

Then her expression fell. "But I didn't mean to interrupt something important. Especially when food is involved."

He chuckled and waved back toward the window. "No, just breakfast with Mark about Jamie's dance lessons."

She waved at Mark through the window. "Oh, what's the word? *Braw*?"

"That will work." His grin slipped free again. "And the first lesson went well yesterday."

"Of course it did." Her chin tipped. "You're a professional and you love dancing. You just needed to be reminded of the latter part."

"And since you've started all of this nonsense, I think you and I should have another go at dancing, don't you?" He stepped forward, dusting off a little unused charm. "See about your tango or jive, perhaps?"

She copied his stance, though at her shorter height, she had to tilt her head back. "I'm game if you are. I've been told that my tango is particularly nice."

The idea of a tango with her added a little summer scorch to the blustery day. It was difficult not to charge full into a relationship with her once he'd made up his mind, but she clearly wasn't at the same place as he was. Not yet. But he hoped with a little more time . . . maybe? And then they'd have to sort out the rest.

She sighed and stepped back. "Maybe once things slow down a little bit? The past week has been so crazy I doubt I even have the coordination for a waltz right now."

"I'll take you up on that tango later then."

Her gaze drifted back to his cap, her smile so sweet he nearly breached the distance.

Pull it together, lad.

"I suppose you were peering in café windows for a different reason than to compliment my cap and tease another dance out of me?"

"Me tease another dance . . ." She caught his grin and paused, narrowing her eyes. "Your humor just keeps getting better and better. I would credit the power of my prayers, but I know how inconsistent I am, so we must have unearthed a dormant character trait."

He laughed and her smile spread wide again. Stunning.

"Anyway." She clapped her hands together like Iris when excited. "Guess what?"

"You finally taught the White Witch how to perform an evil laugh?"

"Not yet, but she *is* improving."

"What, then? You're nearly quivering from excitement."

With a little squeal, she grabbed the front of his jacket and tugged him down toward her so she could reach his ear, then she whispered, "We got *The Sound of Music.*"

"What?" The word burst from him.

"The theater for one of the touring companies' stops flooded, so they had to cancel that performance, which places them very near us and without a venue."

"We got *The Sound of Music?*" he whispered down to her, her face so close, her scent wrapping around him with such a hold he nearly lost complete control of his admirable intentions.

She nodded and he wrapped her in his arms and swung her around.

"Whoa, whoa." She laughed and pushed him back. "Now people are going to be curious, so the secret will be out for *everyone* to know."

"You'll have to get it out as soon as possible anyway."

"True." She released a sigh so large her shoulders bent. "This week has been the most remarkable of my life, I think! And this win will look great for my new job."

His grin froze on his face. "Your . . . your new job?"

"Yes, the founding director of The Ashby Theater asked me to come on as executive director." Her smile faded a little. "It's . . . it's unheard of for someone my age to get such a position, and I guess she sees my potential and already knows what I can do."

"Of course." He nodded, keeping a threadbare hold on his smile. "You're brilliant. Who wouldn't want you as part of their team?"

The news shouldn't hit him like a blow to the stomach, but it did. It meant time was running out. That she'd already chosen there over here. Another place over him. The old wounds tempted to resurrect, but he trained his expression and held her gaze. She was watching him as intently as he was her. Weighing his response. Waiting.

His heart ached in his chest, but those eyes, that smile, had become too precious to focus on himself. And he realized that he loved her. Truly and wholly, and he wanted the best *for her*. The spotlight on her own stage. Maybe he'd be a part of the production of her life, and maybe not, but first and foremost, he wanted her to shine.

"It is wonderful news, Penelope."

She lowered her gaze and reached up to pat the front of his jacket. "It is. Amazing."

"And you'll make miracles happen there like you have here."

Her attention shot back to his face. "I can come visit, you know? I have to return to see how *Cinderella* goes in the spring. It's one of my all-time favorite musicals."

His breath lodged in his throat, pressing down his words. "I'd like that."

Her brow creased as she watched him, almost as if she were trying to sort out something. "Me too."

Was she starting to care for him? Would she act on those feelings? How he wanted to sweep her into his arms and taste that smile. But this choice had to be hers. Not his. He came with a ready-made family and a life thousands of miles away from her home.

He needed her to choose him and for that to be enough for her, no matter where their futures took them.

"I think we should embrace what time we have left with you in Skymar." The words squeezed through his throat. "Not waste a day."

She searched his face. "Not one."

"So what if we start with dinner at the house tonight?" He offered a shrug. "I would try to cook something, but Da's cook is much better at it than me. We could ride together after work."

"That sounds great."

"I'll be a little late because of the lesson with Jamie, but would you mind waiting an extra hour?"

"Not at all." Her smile returned. "I have plenty to do."

From: Penelope Edgewood
To: Luke Edgewood, Izzy Edgewood
Date: October 22
Subject: A ball and Peter Pan

I can't believe I'm down to only six weeks left in Skymar! The time has gone by so quickly and, well, I'm not sure how I feel about it now that the end is closing in. It's not that I don't want to return home. I DO! I know I'm supposed to be back there, even if I'm struggling with that admission. It took going far away for months to realize that I really do love spending time with my family, and the comforts of home and The Ashby Theater and small-town Mt. Airy, but there are things here that I will miss terribly.

People I'm going to miss.

Matthias and Iris are at the top of the list. And Grandpa Gray. Those three, in particular, have become so very dear to me. What a strange thing, right? From the first meeting in the airport when Matt was all "Grumpy Gray" to now, when he's the person I look forward to seeing most every day.

And it's ridiculous really, because I'm not staying, but he makes me want to stay. I KNOW what that sounds like, but I can't embrace the idea of it because I'm leaving. And long-distance relationships are hard. And I really like kissing, and there's no way to do that long-distance. But would it be worth the long-distance non-kissing just to know he's on the other side of the ocean loving me? Ugh, he probably doesn't even think about me that way, but there's something . . . I don't know, in the way he looks at me now. Maybe he's just grown accustomed to my face, but he seems to find ways to come by my office or linger nearby or, well, I don't know. It's just all so confusing and if I KNEW what to do, I would just do it, but that's the tough part. Knowing and KNOWING.

Anyway, I'm swamped with getting all the marketing stuff up and out about *The Sound of Music* while also navigating Narnia's second weekend and helping with rehearsals for *Peter Pan*. The ball is next weekend and *Peter Pan* opens the following weekend. I'm living in the middle of all the magic and I love it. But there's a bittersweetness to it right now, like the end of the last performance. I might drive up to Skern and visit Brodie and his family again just because it makes me feel closer to you all. Not sure why.

Love,

Penelope

PS: The White Witch finally learned to cackle. I'm not sure why some people have such a hard time learning how to do that. It comes so easily for me.

PPS: I'm attaching photos of derby hats. I think Josephine should purchase one for baby Noah. Patrick might look nice in one too. I'd suggest Luke get one, but he'd roll his eyes and give an extra tug to his ballcap.

Text from Luke to Penelope: I hate long-distance
   relationships. But some people are worth it, Penny-girl. I
   don't know if the dancer is, but don't kick the guy off the
   stage without giving him a good audition.
**Penelope: Did you just make a theater analogy? Are you sure
   this is my brother?**
Luke: Izzy stole my phone. The only theater I'm interested in
   is the theater of operation in World War movies.
**Penelope: But I know you know what I should do. Even
   though I don't like it, you always seem to know. Or most
   of the time. Except when it comes to fashion or music.**
Penelope: Or movies.
Penelope: And sometimes restaurants.
Luke: I get it. I'm only great at things that matter.
Penelope: What should I do about Matthias? I want the truth.
Luke: "You can't handle the truth!"
Penelope: LUKE!!
Luke: This has to be your decision, Penn. Is he worth the risk?
   The risk of distance? Of wondering and waiting? Instead

of just looking at the list of what you want in a guy, maybe you should also think about what fits you best. Can you be totally you in all of your costume-loving, vintage, shoe-fetish, loud singing, talkative, silly quirkiness and know he's going to accept ALL of that because it's part of you? I'm not the best person for love advice, but if he fits all of that and is the guy you would choose, then he's worth the risk and the tough stuff that comes along with any relationship. Real love is like that. Sacrifice and joy. You may not know that answer yet, and that's okay. But if you DO know the answer, then maybe he's willing to risk things too.

Penelope: I don't know if he wants to risk things for me, Luke. He has a little girl to think about. His family is here.

Luke: Then maybe that's something you could spend the next few weeks figuring out. For you and for him. If the guy keeps trying to spend time with you, there's a good chance he's interested, Penn. As a single dad who cares about his daughter, he's not going to play games.

Penelope: I don't want to play games either. And I don't want to hurt Iris EVER. So maybe I shouldn't even try because there's a good chance someone will get hurt.

Luke: Which would be the greater hurt? Caring about each other openly but having to sort out logistics? Or knowing you never tried?

Penelope: Wow. I just groaned from the possible pain of the second option.

Luke: Then it sounds like you might have an answer.

Luke: BTW, joke's on you. I own a derby.

⸱ ⸱

From: Izzy Edgewood
To: Luke Edgewood, Penelope Edgewood

Date: October 23
Subject: Re: A ball and Peter Pan

Penelope!!! Oh my goodness! You are living your very own Maria von Trapp moment! Joyful, happy, singing young woman (not a nun) and handsome (is he handsome?), dancing, single dad. Do you see the similarities? It's perfect for you. Unless it's not. But from what you've mentioned on our video calls, he seems like a sweet guy.

But long-distance relationships ARE hard. Even though Brodie just left last week from visiting, I'm already missing him something horrible. I just keep reminding myself that I will move there permanently by Christmas and then I'll start a long-distance relationship with you guys. But I know it's the right thing for me. Kind of like I think you know that coming back home is right for you.

And that's the weird part about life. Personal choices.

It's sad that so many fiction books celebrate the woman who leaves all she's known to venture forth into the great wide world, but few praise the choice to love the familiar. To find joy in where you are and create magic nearer to the places you've always known. To me, they're both worth acknowledging.

But it is a big decision and if you don't know how he feels, then I'd take my time observing his responses. Because the truth is, either choice is a big deal. Either way, someone has to sacrifice. And SOMEONE will eventually have to move because . . . kissing and stuff like REAL LIFE.

On a different note, is there a way to view any of these performances online? I know that's become somewhat common in this day and age, but I didn't know whether The Darling House allowed for online purchases or not. I've heard of folks downloading a code to watch the film once and then they cannot access it again. Is Darling doing that? I'd love to see what you've been doing!

Are you going to send us a video of the museum too? I'd love to see it!

Love and prayers,
Izzy

The sound of "Moon River" filled the living room as Penelope curled up on her sofa to finish *Breakfast at Tiffany's*. A fire crackled in the small rock fireplace nearby, and she tucked her socked feet deeper into the blanket while sipping from a magnificent cup of hot chocolate. She'd taught Iris how to make homemade hot chocolate earlier that evening when she kept the little girl so Matthias could finish dance lessons.

After Penelope had helped Iris with her homework, they made sugar cookies and hot chocolate—the weather had turned cold fairly quickly over the last two days. Iris said the wind felt *snell*, which must mean biting, because that's exactly what it felt like to Penelope. Thankfully, Penelope knew how to start a fire and help with first-grade math. Making hot chocolate, baking cookies, and spending time with an adorable seven-year-old were just an added bonus.

Matthias had arrived in time to join them for cookies, his presence as warm and inviting as the baked scent lingering through the house. And each time their hands or arms touched, Penelope embraced the wonderful tingles of awareness at his closeness. She'd purchased a cedar-scented candle to keep on her nightstand just to sniff occasionally in order to work up courage.

Courage to make a very hard choice—loving him and Iris from very far away.

However long that far away may last.

Her attention returned to the screen as Audrey Hepburn, playing Holly Golightly, sat on the windowsill, guitar in hand, and George Peppard, with his excellently groomed hair, stared down at her from his window. And he smiled. The smile that let you know his heart was already gone. It belonged to Holly in all her ridiculousness. Penelope grinned.

And that character would later tell Holly these wonderful words: "People do fall in love, people do belong to each other."

She rested her head back against the couch. She knew she belonged back home for now, but could her heart also belong somewhere else? With someone else? Did Matthias smile at her like Paul smiled at Holly? Was he where she belonged, regardless of where that was?

Her phone buzzed on the side table, so she reached for it. Grandpa Gray's picture appeared on the screen.

"Hello, dear Grandpa Gray."

"Good evening, Penny-girl. I hope it's not too late to call."

She relaxed against the cushions at the sound of his kind voice. "Not at all. Just watching a movie."

"A good thing to do on a *baltic* evening like we've got tonight."

Baltic. Another word the Skymarians used for *frigid.* Matt said it was Scottish in origin.

"Did Iris bring you some of the sugar cookies?"

"She did. She gave me the one with the chocolate sprinkles since, as she put it, pink is for the princess."

"Referring to herself, of course." Penelope laughed. "Because she is."

"Most certainly." His warm chuckle sounded through the phone. "But that does transition nicely into the reason I called."

"Princesses?"

"Queens, actually."

Penelope turned down the volume on the television. "Queens?"

"And possibly princesses, too, I'd wager."

She turned off the television altogether. "What do you mean?"

He cleared his throat. "I've just gotten off the phone with His Royal Highness's secretary, and he and the queen will be driving from the airport tomorrow and wish to stop in to see the museum on their way to their Fiacla estate."

She sat up so fast her blanket fell off the couch. "What?"

"You'd mentioned having it nearly complete."

"Well, yes, I have—"

"And this would bring excellent visibility just before the ball and *Peter Pan*."

"It would, of course, but—"

"They hope to pop in between one and three in the afternoon."

She opened her mouth but only a squeak came out.

"And they'll likely bring one or two of the princesses."

And the princesses. Penelope was going to live a lifelong dream. Meeting royalty. Her brain immediately took inventory of every possible outfit she had in her closet.

"Penelope? I told them yes because one doesn't say no to the royals if at all possible."

"No, right, of course." She swallowed through the growing lump in her throat. Would a hat be too much?

"Do you think you can work on a social media announcement for it to draw attention? But keep it under our hats until midmorning tomorrow." His voice sobered. "We don't want Emblem to have time to cause mischief, if we can help it."

"Of course."

"And I'll phone my contact at the news station tomorrow as well."

"Great," she managed to whisper.

"There's no hiding the royal family stopping in front of The Darling House in Mountcaster. It will be news within minutes, so we might as well use it to our advantage. Are you ready for it?"

"Whether I am or not, I'll be there."

CHAPTER 19

From: Penelope Edgewood
To: Izzy Edgewood, Luke Edgewood
Date: October 28
Subject: The royals

I met the royals of Skymar!!! You guys!!! And let me just say, all the curtsy practice for playing Cinderella came in so handy. Because not only did the king and queen come to see the museum, but they brought their two eldest daughters. So I curtsied four times. Once when they showed up and once when they left. I may have a few other times in between, but I'm not sure because nerves took over.

They stayed for an hour, asking questions about the theater's history and about certain items in the museum. I'm so glad Grandpa Gray and Matthias were there, because they knew details and personal stories I didn't learn about in the archives. But everyone seemed impressed with the exhibits—special props, a few full costumes (and I even have the Peter Pan costume likely worn by the king's mother on display).

As tempted as I was, I did not ask the queen if she'd ever mattress surfed. Though, Izzy, I agree with your assessment. She DOES look like Julie Andrews. And she took my hand when she left and told me how "lovely" it was to meet me and that she "loved the shade of my hair." BTW, Izzy, she said she remembered meeting you. I think it was a good memory because her smile twitched as if she were trying not to laugh. Her daughters were as elegant as she was. The younger of the two, probably in her midtwenties, had a quieter but pleasant personality. The elder sister engaged in lots of questions and peppered in a few jokes too. She's the princess I've seen featured most in television interviews and things.

I think Matthias probably read my mind because he asked if the royals would mind posing for a photo. So I'm attaching a copy of the photo with me, Matthias, Grandpa Gray, and the king and queen. It's going to hang in the museum!!

Grandpa Gray had made a copy of the king's mother's photo and presented it to the king as a gift at the end of the museum tour. But you can imagine that from the time the royals entered the theater to the time they left, news had spread like theater gossip always does. I thought poor Alec was going to pass out from the surprise. He'd shown up when he saw a report on the news. Evelyn nearly did pass out, especially when the king approached her to thank her for providing refreshments for them. (They didn't realize that I'd baked the scones, but that's fine. It made Evelyn's day that the king spoke to her.)

But now the news about the museum is out. And I am so proud of it. I'm also attaching a video I made of it so you guys can see what the royals saw today. It officially opens next week, in time for the ball, or in this case, the Darling House Masquerade.

Grandpa Gray's house staff are already busy getting the unused ballroom ready! ACK!!

I still need to find a dress! Iris and I made our masks this past weekend. Needless to say, we're matching.

Penelope

PS: Matthias is handsome in a subtle way. I mean, it's not like he's trying or anything. He just is. I think it's because his eyes are so kind. That makes him extra handsome, I think.

PPS: And his smile. He has a great smile.

PPPS: And he has great hair. You know what I mean? Great guy hair.

· ·

From: Luke Edgewood
To: Penelope Edgewood, Izzy Edgewood
Date: October 28
Subject: Re: The royals

I'm glad all your hard work is paying off, Penny-girl, but I just don't get the fascination with royals. I mean, they're people. Rich and popular, maybe, but folks who have to eat and breathe to survive like the rest of us. Though I'll admit that anyone who can keep their posture that straight for so long has to have a solid grasp on perseverance.

"Great guy hair"? I'm going to leave that alone.

Luke

· ·

From: Izzy Edgewood
To: Penelope Edgewood, Luke Edgewood
Date: October 28
Subject: Re: The royals

Can you feel my blush from here? Oh my goodness, every time I relive that moment of criticizing her library, I feel my face burn to volcanic temperatures. Of course she remembers! She's a queen. I'm sure they remember all sorts of things from weird people they meet.

But the museum looks amazing, and to have a copy of that photo, Penn! What a treasure! Hearing Grandpa Gray speaking in the background with that amazing Skymarian accent! Oh heavens! Isn't it delicious? Was that deeper voice Matt's? PENELOPE!! His voice sounded like . . . what? Melted chocolate?

Izzy

PS: Your dress for this ball needs to be a stunner. That's all I'm saying.

Text from Luke to Izzy: "Melted chocolate"? You two are gross.

Izzy: Hey, if you know, you know.

Luke: Or you're just surrounded by lots of people who really don't know.

Izzy: Maybe you're the one surrounded by people who don't know.

Luke: I'm surrounded by dogs for a reason.

From: Penelope Edgewood
To: Izzy Edgewood, Luke Edgewood
Date: October 28
Subject: Re: The royals

He does have a great voice, doesn't he? Swooning for hours! I wonder if his kiss is as decadent as his voice? Oh dear, I shouldn't have written that. Not so much to protect Luke's virgin eyes but more to keep my thoughts from turning in the kissing direction of Matthias Gray! I can't think about him that way. I can't! I'm leaving. And he may not even care about me in a romantic way.

And, Izzy, the Captain von Trapp analogy did NOT help with my attempts to keep my mind in a neutral space. At all! Though, if I'm being completely honest, Matthias would look fabulous in those classic suits. ACK! Stop, brain! Stop!!

Clearly, me and neutral thoughts are not working.

On a different note, Alec was so complimentary about the museum. He said he'd never realized the lengthy and touching history behind the theater, and this visual representation really brought it to life. I'm not sure what to think about him. He seems more emotional than most girlfriends I've had. Back and forth. One moment debonair and charming, and the next kind of sullen. It's so weird. Anyway, he said that Grandpa Gray and the theater group should do something for me as a thank-you, but I really do just love doing what I get to do. I'm not sure why that surprises Alec so much, but I guess he hasn't experienced it before. I hope he gets a chance someday. I think he's just so caught up in his own . . . self, that he hasn't recognized what a great family he has and how important deeper things really are. Having money and looking great aren't the only ingredients for a successful life. Though, as a caveat, you all know how much I adore looking great. I mean, the shoes! And hats! And lipstick!

Matthias and I talked about that type of love this afternoon while we had tea together and went over final info related to our parts of the ball. I think, at one point, Matthias truly loved what he did (even accounting, which I find completely shocking), but he'd lost that love . . . until recently. And the dance lessons with Jamie have really changed things for him. I think he's even considering teaching classes again in the new year.

In fact, last night after-hours, I was leaving later than planned because I'd helped Kinleigh create a proposal for her internship. Anyway, I noticed lights on in the Gray Theater. Heard music too. I snuck into the back of the house and there Matthias was, performing the entire "Singin' in the Rain" choreography done by Gene Kelly. He even used the lamppost from Narnia. It was beautiful. I knew he could dance, but this . . . wow!

I snuck out before he caught me watching, but truly, y'all. He has a gift!

And really nice arms.

Penelope

PS: Luke, you have great hair. Thick and wavy. It's your beard that's the trouble.

<u>**Text from Luke to Penelope:**</u> I might point out that the king of
 Skymar has a beard.
<u>**Penelope:**</u> **Yes, but he actually trims his more than twice a
 year. You know, clean-shaven looks really good on you.
 Women adore a cleft chin.**
<u>**Luke:**</u> And now I will aim for a Gandalf beard forever.

<u>**Text from Penelope to Izzy:**</u> **You won't believe this! Grandpa
 Gray gave me a dress for the ball. And not just ANY**

dress! He took me to a special closet in his house filled with elegant, vintage-style dresses that used to be his beloved wife's and he asked me to choose one for myself.

Izzy: What? That's amazing. Is it amazing? I mean, I know you like vintage, but it's a nice vintage dress, right?

Penelope: Amazing. Better than I could have afforded, unless on consignment. And I couldn't make up my mind between three of them, so I asked him to choose. He chose the one his wife loved best. Isn't that THE SWEETEST THING EVER!! It makes me adore the gown and the man even more.

Penelope: Here's a photo I took last night, but of course, I need different shoes than my red sneakers.

Izzy: Penelope! Pale blue. It sparkles like starlight. You remind me of a redheaded Arwen. Wow! The color contrast is perfect.

Penelope: Don't you think silver heels would be superb? I'm going shopping during my lunch break to look nearby. Squee! A handsome man, a borrowed dress, and a ball!! I'm living a fairy tale.

The Gray House bustled with crowds of people once again, there to show faith in the Darling's success as much as in Matt's family. Friends, donors, business owners, artists, and even a few gentry, likely from Grandfather's connections.

Matt's gaze found Gwynn, dressed in astonishing red, as she assumed her role of hostess alongside Grandfather. Yes, the theater had a ready future on the horizon, especially when Gwynn took her rightful place at the helm soon.

Her theater. Her inheritance.

That had always been her dream.

And his dream?

His body relaxed into the realization of having found those long-lost dreams again. This setting only fueled the magic of it all. With the evening glow of sunset shining pinkish-gold hues through the tall windows and each door framed with greenery and twinkle lights, the room became its own fairyland, beckoning him forward toward his dreams. And—his grin deepened—perhaps his own happily ever after.

As a string quartet invited some of the more interested, dramatic, or gifted folks to use the ballroom for its original purpose—to dance—his gaze searched for his two favorite pixies.

He'd left Iris in Penelope's care, his little girl ecstatic with the idea of "getting ready" with Penelope—which seemed a mutual pleasure. Gwynn had convinced Penelope to plan to stay the night at the house so that she wouldn't have to walk back to the cottage after the ball, but they'd had little time to converse. Not with all the preparations. But he'd quieted his heart to the resolution of embracing each day of Penelope Edgewood's acquaintance, whether romance bloomed or they maintained their friendship alone. He rubbed at the center of his chest, where the thought of her returning to the States still ached like a bruise.

But she'd never planned to stay. The very idea of an internship meant temporary.

And she'd never sought out a romance with him, so the decision to initiate one had to be hers.

He turned his gaze heavenward, his thoughts ushering up a little plea. His heart couldn't link "temporary" with Penelope in any scenario of his mind.

He knew now. He wanted forever.

But how could forever work? He was needed here. She wanted to go there. It was an impossibility.

Yet he'd thought saving The Darling House an impossibility three months ago, until Penelope.

Until Penelope . . .

As if summoned by his thoughts, a flash of pale-blue and gold shone in his periphery. He turned, his attention immediately drawn to the little princess in red running toward him, her silver mask sparkling with copious amounts of glitter and a few crooked rhinestones. All of her blonde hair spun in myriad curls upon her head and a tiny little crown—the one he'd seen on Penelope's head before—nestled within those beloved curls.

"Daddy, I'm a princess." Her arms wrapped around his waist as she looked up at him. "Penelope let me wear her princess crown."

At Iris's mention of Penelope, Matt raised his gaze to the object of his thoughts. Penelope walked forward, pink lips in a broad smile and green eyes sparkling behind her silver mask. No, more like glided. Or something. He wasn't quite sure, except that the pale-blue gown she wore poured over her like liquid starlight, only pausing to hug various parts of her body in a rather fetching way. One side of the gown boasted a sheer long sleeve, while the other side showed her bare shoulder, complete with a generous sprinkling of freckles. She looked as if she'd stepped directly from a storybook, and his breath held in utter appreciation.

He dragged his attention from the distraction, heat branching from his increased pulse to his neck. Thoughts unraveled in dangerous synchrony about her lips and those curves and his need to hold her.

Yes, he'd moved well beyond friendship. *Well* beyond. And he needed to prepare his heart for the devastating possibilities.

All of Penelope's hair curled atop her head in a similar fashion as Iris's, and pink toenails peeked from a pair of silver heels. How could he deny fairy tales when he'd just stepped into one?

He faintly remembered Iris speaking and pulled his gaze back to his daughter.

"That was very kind of her to let you wear her crown."

"A little girl needs to wear a crown once in a while," Penelope added as she closed in. "And Iris has some catching up to do since her daddy had lost sight of fairy tales for a while."

His gaze came back to hers, unswerving. "I believe I've revisited my previous ideas about fairy tales, Miss Edgewood, and found I was wrong. You've more than proven your point. Where would we be without a little magic now and again?"

"Not in the theater, that's for sure." Her smile split wide. "And tonight, well, everything looks so enchanting."

His attention followed the lines of the gown again only to return to those beautiful green eyes of hers. *Indeed.*

"You certainly look the part." He waved toward her. "Stunning. Absolutely."

Her nose scrunched with her smile, and she leaned in, nearly derailing his self-control with her nearness and her scent. "This was your grandmother's. Can you believe it?" A soft laugh bubbled from her. "Grandpa Gray gave it to me."

His palm went to his chest. Yes, Grandfather saw it too. The joy and effervescence of his grandmother glowed in the person of Penelope Edgewood. The same beautiful soul. The same faith in people and dreams and . . . the impossible? "Quite fitting, luv."

The endearment emerged, every time, without premeditation. It simply fit her.

"You look wonderfully handsome in tails, Mr. Gray." She stepped back and studied him from head to toe, then her gaze stopped on his face. "Even with a crooked mask."

"A crooked—"

She reached up to straighten his simple black mask and her shoe hit his, sending her a little off-kilter. He steadied her with a palm to her elbow, but the movement kept her close. His palm slid up her arm, her skin cool and soft beneath his touch.

"All fixed," she breathed out, and her tone made him wonder. If the mask hadn't cloaked her full expression, would he have been able to see her attraction?

In a previous life, he'd have been more demonstrative, more certain. But after Deirdre and with the uncertainty of Penelope's interest, not to mention willingness to commit to a long-distance relationship, he doubted himself at all turns.

"Penelope!" someone called, their voice distant.

Penelope blinked up at him and then turned.

Grandfather marched forward with a small entourage of five people trailing behind, rather prestigious-looking folks too. "Dear girl, I have some local businessmen and artisans here who'd like a word with you about your marketing strategies." He waved toward his group. "May I pull you away for a moment?"

She glanced back at Matt as if waiting for him to respond.

What to say?

"Promise me a dance, won't you?" A lifetime of them, even?

Her smile quivered wide. "I would love that."

She shouldn't be disappointed about not dancing very much. Truly. The ball served a strategic business purpose: bringing together people who loved The Darling House, and not only showing appreciation but allowing these people to converse and deepen the bonds of community. Because communities worked together. And working together was what it would take to keep The Darling House existing as a for-profit theater for a very long time.

The masquerade had seemed like such a great idea until Penelope realized she wouldn't be able to make out Matthias's expression when he saw her for the first time. Of course, it was every girl's dream to leave a man speechless. Not forever, but a good ten seconds of gathering his wits after looking at her as if she'd stepped from a dream. That Cinderella moment or the Hallmark-princess moment.

She internally sighed. But he had told her she looked stunning, and he may have offered more if they hadn't been interrupted. When he'd caught her in her stumble and his palm trailed up her arm, all she wanted to do was lean in and give him full access to her lips for, like, at least five minutes. A vision of him in his tux flashed back to mind. Okay, maybe ten.

He probably kissed wonderfully well.

She fanned her hand in front of her face as she moved from one introduction to another, her internal temperature taking an uphill climb into dazzling proportions. What would Matthias do if *she* kissed *him*? Just to break the ice? After all, he'd been the one to have his heart betrayed and smashed. He might need a little encouragement in the kissing direction.

Grandpa Gray took her around the room, introducing her to various people, showering her with praise for her work. He'd even shared how he'd been in touch with JMC, after doing his own search for The Ashby Theater, and JMC and Grandpa Gray had engaged in a Penelope lovefest.

She glanced around the beautiful room, taking it all in. This life of magic and theater and parties was part of her future. She was doing exactly what she was meant to do.

Then why did she feel the teeniest bit of sadness?

She knew.

On the stage, the heroine got the family and the home and the dream too. But real life didn't always work that way. One happy ending sometimes had to bow to another. One had to become more important than the other. Her heart pinched. And her choice gave her two of the three. The dream job and home. Her eyes fluttered closed. But oh, how she wanted the knight.

"Are you up for a dance, princess?"

She looked around to find Alec standing before her, every bit the heart-stopping Chris Pine look-alike she'd fantasized about from the time she was fourteen. Tux trimmed to perfection. Hair in perfect waves. Smile, faultless.

But her heart failed to pitter-patter even once.

Funny how dreams changed when the heart finally knew what it wanted—and *needed*—most.

"I thought you said you didn't dance."

"I said I *didn't*"—he raised a brow and offered his hand—"not *can't*. But don't expect anything close to Matt's skill. I learned well enough to appease my mother, and even taught a few classes, but I'm no award winner."

She slid her hand in his and he drew her to the dance floor.

"You really are the belle of the ball tonight, Penelope Edgewood. Everyone's talking about you."

"It's the hair color." She nodded with a grin. "People always talk about troublesome redheads."

"You know it's much more than that." He chuckled. "I still can't believe all you've managed to do in such a short time. And Grandfather said you have one more miracle to reveal tomorrow in an interview with the local news."

"I do." She squeezed her shoulders up with excitement. "They'd asked for an interview about the return of the Darling House ball anyway, but Grandpa Gray and I decided it would be an excellent time to get the news out about a surprise, upcoming Christmas performance."

He stared at her, brows raised, and then his jaw slacked. "You didn't."

She gave a little squeal. "I did."

"*The Sound of Music*? How? That's utterly impossible."

"You keep using that word." She dipped her chin. "I do not think it means what you think it means."

Her quote from *The Princess Bride* took much too long to inspire his smile. "Then this calls for a definite celebration. As I said before, you deserve something remarkable as a thank-you for all you've done."

"I was just doing my job, Alec. And it was a pure delight. Loving what I do and having the opportunity to fall in love with the people here has been the biggest celebration for me."

"No additional recognition?" His tone almost mocked. "No reward?"

"Is that why you do what you do? For the recognition?" she challenged him. "There's something much bigger than that. You have a family who loves you so well. You have a history built on such beautiful people like your mother and grandmother." She leaned closer. "There are bigger and more beautiful things worth fighting for than the bottom line, the spotlight, and the rich connections."

"Very laudable, Miss Edgewood, but in reality, the rich connections make the world go round."

"The right connections make the world go round, Mr. Gray. *Rich* is a relative term—one which, if you define it the wrong way, may very well leave you alone and sad in the long run."

He stared at her as the song ended, his eyebrows so drawn, he actually looked a lot like Matthias when she'd first met him. Impressive eyebrows must run in the Gray family.

With a tip of his head, he released her and moved back into the crowd. Poor man! How had he gotten so lost in the glitter that he didn't even see the treasure he already had?

She paused on the thought. Had she been the same way?

"The night's coming to a close, Miss Edgewood, and I'm here to claim my dance."

Penelope turned to find Matthias at her side, his mask discarded, his hand outstretched. Her heart flip-flopped for a solid five seconds, this moment somehow solidifying itself in her mind for all eternity.

"Oh, I'm so glad you returned to the party after putting Iris to bed." She placed her hand in his, allowing every sensation an extra spot in her memory. Her fingers slid over the grooves of his palm until his fingers tightened around hers. "I thought I'd missed my opportunity."

"I couldn't let the evening pass without at least one dance"—he brought her toward him—"with you. The one who reminded me how much I love to dance."

And off they went, the rhythm, the synchrony, the fit. Everything paired together in a perfect match. If . . . if he cared for her as more than a friend, then she'd give up her negative view of long-distance relationships and fight to the finish to make this work.

So how did she uncover his feelings? Did she just ask outright? She swallowed the growing lump in her throat.

"There's a very good chance that The Darling House would be up for sale by now if it hadn't been for you."

Her gaze went to his. "I knew it was bad, but I didn't know how bad." She shook her head and searched his face. "And what would have happened to your family then?"

"Us?" He shrugged and stared down at her, the look so gentle. "I suppose I would have sought out an accounting job somewhere. Alec has his own business, so I don't expect his life would have changed a great deal. Grandfather likely would have been able to live off of his investments and what portion of the theater sale went to him. I suppose Gwynn would have been the most impacted by it all."

"Gwynn?"

"The theater goes to her as part of her inheritance." He looked over the crowd and she followed his gaze to his sister, who looked amazing in a deep-scarlet gown. "For generations, the theater has passed through the female line as part of our great-grandfather's attempt to ensure the women in the family had a way to earn their own money. Besides, as Grandfather tells it, Great-Grandfather believed women took better care of places anyway."

"And he knew women excelled at drama, no doubt."

Matthias's grin split wide. "I don't know. I've met a few dramatic men in my time."

Penelope couldn't help her gaze wandering to Alec on that comment. She turned back to Matthias, and the warmth of his palm on the small of her back fuzzied up her thoughts in the most wonderful way. "I love how special the inheritance is for Gwynn." A thought popped to mind. "I suppose, if the theater were sold, the money for the sale would go to her too?"

"I'm not certain." His brows pinched in thought. "A special situation in the inheritance contract allows for the widower of the owner to hold control of the theater until the next female in line is twenty-five, at which time she receives control of the theater. But if the situation becomes so dire that the widower must sell the theater, I believe the funds are split among the remaining nearest family members."

"So you, Gwynn, Alec, and Grandpa Gray would all receive an equal amount of the sale cost."

His gaze sharpened on hers. "What are you thinking?"

"I'm not quite sure." Her thoughts whirred around an answer she couldn't pin down. "Just curious, I guess."

They danced in silence a few more beats and then Matthias gave her hand a squeeze. "Do you still have that list you're making of all the places you wish to visit before you leave?"

"I do." Saying those words out loud to him nearly tickled alive her laugh. Very romantic words. *I do.*

"Would you allow me to see it next week? I'd love nothing more than to escort you on your adventures, if you'd like."

"That would be great!" She squeezed his hand back. "And ensure I don't get lost on the way."

"If we travel to the northwest mountains, we both may get lost." His brows wiggled. "The Skymarian Scots in those hills are worth experiencing for certain, and I can dust off some of my Scottish Gaelic."

"Oh, and I want to visit the Kirk of Skree. Izzy said it's a must."

"Certainly, and something we should do fairly soon before it gets too cold." He nodded. "The island is open to the elements, and winter is closing in." He held her gaze. "How does next week sound? Perhaps we could take the day off on Tuesday? Or Wednesday?"

She mustered up a bit of courage. "It's a date?"

His smile fell, his attention focused on her face. "Do you want it to be a date?"

"I'd like that."

He blinked a few times before his grin reemerged. "Aye, Penelope, it's a date for certain."

Text from Penelope to Luke and Izzy: Matthias and I have a date sometime next week. A DATE! I mean, it was a kind of date-ish conversation, and the word "date" was used in the right context, so I'm banking on it being a mutual acceptance of the same definition. EEE!

Luke: Do you even know what you write sometimes? I can give you the date that reading your confusing gibberish caused me a headache.

Penelope: Do you remember what Grandpa Edgewood used to say about headaches?

Luke: You think you're so funny.

Penelope: With a head like yours, it ought to hurt.

Luke: It wasn't funny from you either.

Text from Penelope to Izzy: It's not a sin or anything to sort of hold hands in church, is it?

Izzy: What are you talking about?

Penelope: Well, I was sitting next to Matthias in church this morning and had my hand strategically placed on the

pew between us, just to . . . you know . . . see if anything might happen. And near the end of the sermon, he reached down and wrapped his hand around mine. I didn't look his way to make a scene or anything, but I'm pretty sure I wore a really ridiculous grin for a while. Or the rest of the day.

Penelope: And just in case you ask, I was listening to the sermon. Mostly.

Penelope: And I know it's ridiculous to get excited about hand-holding like I'm some junior-high kid, but . . . well, it was HIS hand. And he took mine. And I'd been wondering and wondering if he was attracted to me at all, so . . . it mattered. God doesn't mind, does He?

Izzy: You do remember that God is all about love, right? I mean, there's a part in the Bible that says something about God being love, so as long as your priorities are in the right place, then I'm pretty sure hand-holding in church is not an unforgivable sin.

Penelope: I'm pretty sure my priorities jumped into dangerous territory only a few times . . . because, well, he has wonderful hands. But I assure you, I remember the sermon. It was about a man named Jiminiah.

Izzy: Cuz, you might need to work on those priorities again. Jiminiah? But also, God understands our human hearts and distractions, so . . . aren't we glad. Otherwise, I'd be in a heap of trouble every time I sit beside Brodie in church. He smells delicious.

Penelope: Thanks for the encouraging words, mostly. Matthias asked if I'd be free on Tuesday for the whole afternoon. We're going to spend the AFTERNOON together! And though I'm looking forward to more hand-holding, I'm anticipating a first kiss! AHHHH!!!! I KNOW

God doesn't mind the right kind of kisses. It's mentioned about fifty times in the Bible. I counted.

Izzy: You're weird sometimes.

Penelope: I started searching as penance for letting my mind wander a bit during the sermon once Matthias took my hand, and then I got curious. Um . . . if I ever doubted that God was okay with kissing, my doubts were allayed when my research took me to Song of Solomon. Whoa!

Penelope had just pulled her hands out of the soapy dishwater when her phone rang on the counter beside her. Alec's name popped up. Hmm. She raised the phone to her ear.

"Hey, Alec. Missed you at lunch after church Sunday."

He paused. "Yes, well, I had a meeting."

"That's what Matt said. Grandpa took us to that wonderful Italian restaurant on Marigold Lane. I'm pretty sure any place on a street named something as sweet as that has to be a great stop."

"Ah, he took you to Antonella's. Excellent choice."

"It was." She cradled the phone between her shoulder and cheek as she finished washing her teacup. "How can I help you this fine Tuesday morning?"

"Well, I just wanted to congratulate you on that great interview on Friday. You really know how to engage the audience."

"Thanks." She took the towel and started drying her teacup. "I'm really hoping the interview will have an even broader reach than the last time, now that we're more visible online."

"I imagine since you're the queen of the impossible, you'll receive an overwhelmingly positive response."

She chuckled, easing into the conversation with him. "Exactly what I want. All things that are overwhelmingly positive."

"Speaking of overwhelmingly positive, there's a bit of a surprise in the works and I've been tasked with ensuring you reach the right place at the right time."

"Surprise?" She returned the phone to her hand. "For me? I thought that was what Antonella's was all about."

"Antonella's was only the . . . appetizer, so to speak. It seems everyone took my suggestion to heart and got together after the ball to make a plan to properly celebrate you." A smile warmed his words. "Rarely do they take my words to heart, so I feel uncharacteristically justified."

"What did they plan? When?"

"You'll find out today, as a matter of fact. I think Matt ensured you took the day off?"

She glanced over at her clock. Matthias said he had a phone conference at the theater that morning but would see her after lunch for their date. Her jaw dropped. He'd been planning this all along? Ooh, he had been very sneaky with the surprise. She hadn't had a clue.

She looked down at her jeans and T-shirt. "But . . . but I thought I had a few hours before I needed to leave. There are important decisions to be made about clothing when surprises are involved. What time will you be here?"

"A half hour."

"A half hour? But Matt said we weren't meeting until after lunch."

"It's going to take a little while to get to where the surprise happens, princess."

Oh. She blinked and then her smile spread. How exciting! "Then you owe me a little secret-breaking for giving me such short notice."

Silence.

"I promise to act surprised. I'm very good at acting surprised, even when I know the truth."

"Fine," he groaned. "Grandfather reserved one of the best rooms at a top restaurant in Port Quinnick, but make certain to dress warm."

"You're taking me to Port Quinnick in half an hour?" she repeated, trying to sort it all out.

"Early enough that you can get a tour of the Kirk of Skree, if you'd like." He added, "Matt said something about meeting you there, but that's supposed to be a surprise too."

Matthias was planning to meet her on the Kirk of Skree? She pinched her lips closed to hold in her squeal. How romantic!

She felt the sudden urge to sing "I'm in Love with a Wonderful Guy" from *South Pacific*. Very island-ish. Of course, *love* might be a strong word at the moment, but her heart was definitely moving in that direction. "Well, *that* adds a bit more strategy to the outfit then. I need to look my best for my date."

"'Date'?" His sigh blew through the phone receiver. "Of course, the two of you! You're perfect, aren't you?" He groaned again. "Well, never mind. I'll see you in a trice. And don't forget your coat. Like I said, the coastal winds are baltic this time of year."

She ended the call and ran up the stairs to her room. For a split second, she thought about texting Matthias but then stopped. What would she say? If it was all a surprise, she didn't want to give anything away. Her teeth skimmed over her bottom lip with her smile.

A date on Skree and then a surprise party for her? It sounded like the perfect way to celebrate *Peter Pan* and *The Sound of Music* and, well, the possibility of falling in love.

CHAPTER 20

Matt searched through another set of emails and texts for the third time, looking for anything to give him a clue as to who had been giving information to Emblem Studios. He'd gone over things with Grandfather last night, after they'd learned of Emblem's latest scheme. Penelope had mentioned Earnest Stevenson in the last email to GK, so it was likely that the person logging into that account had seen it. But who could have done so?

He looked over his list.

Website design.

The people in those meetings were himself, Grandfather, Gwynn, and Alec.

Newspaper placement.

Again, the same people had been in that meeting, along with Evelyn.

The parade.

Gwynn, Grandfather, and some of the community theater. But Penelope had shared it in an email with GK.

And she'd shared Earnest Stevenson's name only with GK.

So the culprit had to be someone with access to the in-person meetings *and* GK account.

Matt's phone buzzed.

Text from Gwynn to Matt: Where are you right now?

Matt: In my office.

Gwynn: I'm coming to you.

He stood from his desk and walked to the threshold of his office to find Gwynn rushing down the hallway toward him. Her pale face and large gray-blue eyes sent his body into automatic defense.

"What is it? What's wrong?"

"Have you been here all morning?" She scanned past him into his office and then down the hallway, looking every bit the part of a scared rabbit.

"Mostly." He drew closer. "I helped with some of the set preparations in the main theater for a few hours and just finished a meeting."

"Then you wouldn't have noticed. Not if you didn't enter the museum this morning." She looked back behind her and shook her head. "Someone could easily get in and out of here without being noticed."

"What do you mean?"

"The museum." Her gaze fastened on him. "It's been vandalized. Half of the artifacts are gone."

"What?" He rounded her and took off at a run up the hallway.

The museum door stood open and evidence of the truth greeted him as soon as he stepped over the threshold. Broken glass. Empty walls. Displays left in disarray. Parts or all of the items missing. "How?" The word burst from him. "Why?"

He turned to find Gwynn behind him, her eyes watery, her bottom lip shaking. "Morale. To break us. Punish us?" She shook her head. "I know it can't destroy us, but it can certainly put every other immediate performance under a cloud."

"But how could our little museum hurt Emblem?" He ran a hand through his hair. "I don't understand it at all. And there was no break-in. The door isn't damaged."

"It's that visible representation of our place in the community, Matt." Her voice shook and she leaned over to remove a Mary Poppins hat used in a performance in the sixties. "And we've been advertising for people to visit it when they come to the *Peter Pan* opening in a few days. Nostalgia brings people."

"So someone's trying to hurt our reputation and steal our business." He scanned the room, his fists tightening on his hips. All of Penelope's hard work. "Who would do this?"

"I asked around once I saw the museum. Last night, Dani was working late and he saw someone leaving the theater with some big boxes in tow."

He spun back around to his sister to find tears making silent trails down her cheeks.

"Alec," she said.

"Alec?"

"I phoned Grandfather." She wiped at her face with her hand. "His museum keys are missing."

All the information from the emails and the meetings came together. Alec? At the heart of it all? Against his own family? Why? What sort of hatred could fuel him to do such a thing? What could he possibly gain by the theater's downfall?

"Why . . . why would he do this?" Gwynn's voice finally broke and Matt crossed the space to her, taking her into his arms.

She wept against his shoulder as the ache of betrayal burned through him. Why, indeed? And then the realization dawned, deepening the wounds.

The money. If Emblem bought The Darling House, then not only would Alec receive a portion of the sale, but—Matt's shoulders slumped—would he receive some sort of payoff from Niles Westing too?

"We're not ruined, Gwynn." Matt ran a hand down his sister's back. "Our hard work and a bit of Penelope's magic have done such good, not even this is going to ruin our trajectory. The theater will be all right."

She nodded into his shoulder.

"But do you know where Alec might be?"

She looked up at him and shook her head. "Grandfather said he left after breakfast but didn't mention where he was going."

"Then we need to see if we can find him, because then we can retrieve the museum items, and perhaps it's not too late to save Alec from choosing to do something even worse."

A mix of large, fluffy clouds and brilliant sunshine filled the big sky. The sky always seemed so big on this island, but perhaps it was because the sea hovered on the horizon at every turn. It was one of the most beautiful places Penelope had ever seen, and she'd definitely be back.

She *had* to come back. Especially if she got up the courage to tell Matthias how she felt about him and he reciprocated. She should tell him tonight after her surprise party. Or . . . perhaps during their romantic meeting on the remote Kirk of Skree. A shiver of delight shimmied up her shoulders. Oh yes! Then they'd have a month to date and see if long-distance could work. Was worth it.

She already knew it would be for her, *if* he reciprocated.

He and Iris already had her heart.

She'd always dated guys very close to her age—those in high school or college with her—but a relationship with Matthias Gray, a friendship with him, had been different from the start. More settled and right. Adding Iris into the mix only made everything sweeter.

Maybe she *was* living a Maria von Trapp story.

"You're terribly quiet," Alec said as he drove them along a coastal road. "Everything all right?"

She turned to him with a smile. "Just enjoying the beauty of Skymar. This is such a great drive."

"It is." He cleared his throat and gave the steering wheel a pat as he'd done quite a few times on their drive. "Though sometimes this place can feel rather small."

"Really?" She rested her head back against the seat. "I can't imagine it ever feeling small with a sky like that."

He offered a humorless chuckle. "Perhaps it's the people, not the place, then?"

"What do you mean?" Penelope's experience with the locals had been mostly fantastic, except for the occasional grumpy store clerk or creepy theater owner.

"There are times when you need to breathe." He focused ahead, his frown deepening. "Like people are placing you in a box with what you ought to do and you don't fit."

She stared at his profile, weighing his words with what she'd learned about him so far. "Is that how you feel about The Darling House? Like you're not a part of that world?"

"I don't know if I've ever been."

She studied him. "That must be difficult for you."

Her comment appeared to open some door in his internal dialogue. He gave a strong shake to his head. "Everything revolves around that theater. Our jobs, our conversations." He slammed his hand against the steering wheel with a little more force. "And since Mother and Grandmother died, it's been stifling. Like their ghosts are everywhere."

She was beginning to understand a little better now!

She placed a hand on his arm. "You hide your grief pretty well, don't you?"

"What?" He shot her a look, his frown deepening. "What do you mean?"

"Maybe you do feel trapped in The Darling House, but I wonder if it's more that you're trying to outrun the hurt you're still feeling from losing two people you love so much so close together. That can't be easy for anyone."

"But that's been years ago."

"Grief doesn't have an expiration date, Alec."

He remained silent.

"People take up places in our hearts and our lives, and when those people are gone, we have this space left." She settled back into the seat. "Sure, memories may fill up some of the space, but they're never enough to completely take away the pain. Ever. And no amount of work, or praise, or money is going to fill the space left behind that only they were meant to fill."

"Then how do you get on with life—like everyone else in my family—when you have a gaping hole in the center of who you are?" He nearly growled out the words.

"I'm no expert." She shrugged, almost feeling the ache in his heart. "But embracing your grief—and the fact that it's okay to grieve—is one thing. A very good thing. Talking about those people is another." Her smile spread. "I love talking about the people I've lost because it means they were here and alive and were a part of making me who I am. Somehow, it makes their space in my heart seem not so empty." Her eyes burned a little. "I pray, too, but I know that's not for everyone. It helps me, though."

He swallowed so hard his Adam's apple bulged.

"And if you really don't want to be a part of the theater, I think your grandpa would be more than willing to hear you out. He loves you, Alec. So much."

He snorted a response.

"Maybe he wasn't able to hear you before because he was lost in his own grief, but I think he's able to now."

"You think?" He shook his head. "No, I'm not certain. Not when he knows everything."

"Love has a way of being much bigger than we imagine."

He shot her a look but didn't respond.

"You won't know unless you try, and I'm betting on your grandpa's love over any doubts you have." She said the words as much to herself as to him. "We can play scenarios of the what-ifs all we like, but there's no way of knowing for sure without putting on our brave pants and just going for it."

He looked back at her, his face wrestling with some expression between a smile and a frown. The frown won, unfortunately.

She allowed the quiet to settle between them and turned to take in the view of the countryside. Poor Alec. Perhaps he could find his way through his grief if he would just talk to his family, or maybe even get a little counseling. Penelope knew it helped her out a lot after Erin died.

The road twisted down through green hillsides, framed on one side by snowcapped peaks and the other by the gray-blue sea. Even with the windows closed, Penelope could almost smell the salty air and feel the "tousle" wind against her face. She'd grown to love so many things about this world of Skymar, memories she placed next to some of her favorites in her mind.

And then some buildings came into view. Brightly colored ones, row upon row in stairsteps along the water's edge. Her smile spread at the idyllic scene. Port Quinnick. Online photos didn't do the real thing justice. The town was even cuter in person and a little more expansive than she'd expected.

Shops lined the streets—a quaint mixture of old and new. She spotted two charity shops and an antique store.

"How much time do we have before the party?"

He pulled to a park along the street and checked his phone. "About two hours." He grinned, but the smile didn't reach his eyes. "Plenty of time to explore Skree before the party."

Why did something seem weird with him? "I do love exploring."

"I'm sure Matt will enjoy taking you through the village after the party, but we'll want to visit Skree first to make use of our daylight. The place is filled with Skymarian history about the three monk brothers and their quest to build churches worthy of their worship."

"Really?"

His smile softened, looking more authentic. "The ruins of the other two brothers' churches are farther inland, but the youngest chose the most unique spot of all, and legend has it his choice saved hundreds of lives when the Vikings raided Skymar."

"Oh!" Penelope unbuckled her seat belt and tugged her cloche hat tighter against her head. "I think I read about him online. Something about hiding the villagers within the rocks on Skree?"

"Yes, his rock church on Skree. It's fascinating, truly."

"Well, I'm excited to see it." She pushed open the car door. "Are you ready?"

He didn't answer but stepped from the car, staring down at his phone as he rounded to her side. "Could I catch up with you?" He raised his phone. "I've had three business calls from the same number and I need to take this." His expression turned apologetic. "It may be a little while, so you could go ahead and get a start. I've seen it plenty."

"All right." She looked back down the lane toward the water.

"Just follow the lane." He gestured in front of her. "You'll see the Kirk of Skree signs. Look for the Skree dock and that will lead you to the land bridge."

"Land bridge. Got it." She nodded, tugging her purse over her shoulder and moving in the direction he'd pointed. Right. Why wouldn't there be a land bridge? Skree was a small island off the mainland of Port Quinnick. You had to get to it somehow, and she preferred land to water. Definitely.

Her pace slowed a bit and she looked back the way she'd come. Alec sat in his car, his darkened profile angled down toward his phone. An unsettling agitation swirled in her stomach. Was Matthias planning to meet her at the bridge? Or on the other side?

She shuddered with the pure delight of the idea. That would be a very romantic thing to do, and she felt that if Matthias Gray *really* cared for a woman, he'd have all sorts of wonderfully romantic notions. Then it would make sense for Alec to "pretend" to have a business call so she'd make the walk on her own!

How exciting!

She increased her pace, adding a little hop to her step.

A direct walk to the path for Skree proved difficult. Well, not physically difficult, but around almost every corner, charming shops with nooks of temptation slowed Penelope's descent toward the sea. An actual millinery on one corner. A vintage clothing store on the other. But the notion of romantic moments with Matthias helped her shun the temptation and forge ahead.

Skree cleared in her view as she neared the coastline, bigger than she'd expected, its rocky mountains jutting up in the distance like teeth. And then there was the land bridge, which stretched long and a little narrower than she'd expected. What a strange sight to see this slip of earth pressed with the ocean on both sides, like Moses parting the Red Sea.

She drew in a deep breath for courage and thought about kisses.

And at least she didn't have to take a boat, because not even the idea of Matthias's kisses could get her to the island then.

She paused. Well, maybe *that* particular motivation could overcome the idea of sea monsters. Kisses were powerful in fairy tales for a reason.

A small building clung to the edge of the shore, a few boats—some with motors and others powered by oars—docked nearby with the words "Kirk of Skree" in bold blue alongside the likeness of a strange sort of sea creature. Her feet faltered. She stared up at the menacing likeness as she passed below the sign and entered through a bright-blue door into a small shop. A guttural roar exploded through the room as the door opened, some sort of recorded monster sound instead of a welcome bell. She drew a step back toward the threshold as if some enormous dog waited in a corner of the room ready to devour her.

What was this place?

The small building featured a few bookshelves, a counter, and a massive replica of a greenish-gray sea creature hanging from the ceiling behind the counter, its large mouth framed by pointy piranha teeth. Red eyes bulged from the sockets in an unnerving stare toward anyone entering the shop.

Penelope froze on the spot, held captive by the red-eyed creature, her worst nightmare staring back at her, unmoving.

"*Dia dhuit*," came a deep voice from her left.

She blinked out of her catatonic state and scanned past two boat-shaped bookshelves, which held merchandise including miniature boats, some stone-church replicas, and varied sets of toy sea creatures. She flinched.

"Aye?"

Penelope shuddered back to attention and found a hulk of a man rising from a chair near the counter. With each second, he grew taller. White hair poked in all directions from his head and even encircled his face, making him look like someone who'd been shocked by electricity. He wore a red shirt, fitted to his round belly, and a pair of massive black rain boots pulled up over yellowish pants. A pipe poked from between his grin as smoke curled around his rosy cheeks, dissipating above his head and just below the sea monster. He reminded Penelope of what Santa Claus might have looked like when he first got out of bed in the morning after a tumultuous night's sleep or a wrestling match with the reindeer.

"Excuse me?"

His bushy brows took flight. "*Americaugh*."

Ah, she'd heard that dozens of times since arriving in Skymar. "Yes, I'm American."

"You're here to visit the kirk, eh?"

"I am." Penelope pulled her gaze away from the sea monster again. Were those eyes following her, or was it her imagination? She swallowed through a lump in her throat. Probably just her imagination.

"You'll be wantin' a map then to find your way. Nice walkin' trail to the kirk." He lumbered behind the counter and slapped a pamphlet down for view. "And you'll want a *keilig* with ya for the crossin'."

Penelope studied him for a moment, trying to make sense of this new word. "Keilig?"

"Aye." He leaned forward, propping his elbows on the counter before twisting a pudgy finger around a nearby display of necklaces and key rings intricately woven with marbled and colorful stones. "Keilig. Made from the Skree stones. To keep you safe."

Penelope studied him through squinted eyes. "I need a keilig to keep me safe from a church?"

"No, not from the kirk. From the Kronimara."

She'd heard a lot of words in Skymar, but not that one. And for some reason, she didn't like it.

"Kronimara?"

Her gaze settled on the shelf nearby where replicas of a sea creature waited for purchase, then she looked above the man's head as the red-eyed monster stared back at her. "Mara" meant sea. Did "Kroni" have something to do with monster? She cleared her tightening throat. Surely not.

"The holy stones keep ya safe from him, so you'll be sure to take 'em with you across the *brune*."

Brune? Bridge. Right. There was a land bridge. She didn't have to take a boat. No need for worries.

A smile quivered into place and she laid her money on the counter for the map, then pulled down one of the keiligs.

"You know the story of the Kirk of Skree and Elerk the Younger, eh? When Elerk brought the folks from the mainland to Skree, they was protected from the Viking raid, aye?"

"I've heard about it." From Izzy after her trip. Penelope pulled at the map, but the man caught the corner of the paper, unyielding, his eyes sparkling with mischief.

"And those folks were protected by the Skree stones and the Kronimara."

She gave the map another tug. "But I heard the Vikings didn't try to get to the islanders who were hiding in the kirk on Skree."

"Oh, now they did. The Vikings crossed the brune but dinna return from Skree." His gaze shot back to the keilig. "The creature knows who belongs and who doesna belong."

Her fingers tightened around the keilig. Visions of Matthias waiting for her on the other side of the land bridge, roses in hand, maybe even a string orchestra, fought against the desire to run.

"Okay, so I'll just get one more." She tugged a lovely pink keilig off its hook to add to the blue one she'd already taken. "And maybe just another." A green. Her gaze shot back to the Kronimara and she offered a nervous laugh. "Seven is a good, solid biblical number. How about that?"

His grin broadened beneath his thick mustache. "Very good idea, *beaunig*."

Beaunig? What was that? Bird? Or fraidy-cat?

"And you'll want to return by three o'clock." He tapped the map. "The tide comes in then."

She looked down at her phone. It was barely noon. "No problem there." She'd find Matthias, have their confession of feelings for each other, exchange a few heel-popping kisses, take a walk to the Kirk of Skree, and find her way back arm in arm with time to spare. "Thank you so much for these." She raised the keiligs and they clinked together like glass coins. She began digging through her purse for money, but the Santa man held out a hand and shook his head to stop her.

"Just to be warned, beaunig. Kronimara bubbles beneath the water before he strikes." The Santa man wiggled his brow. "But hold up the keiligs and he should see you as a friend, not a foe."

"Hold up the keiligs." She nodded, searching his face and hoping, deeply hoping, the mischievous glint in his eyes proved of mythical proportions.

She stared down at the keiligs as she exited the shop. Sea monsters were not real. She shoved the stones into her purse. And even if they were, they didn't like to be seen, so they lived far out in the ocean. Except for the one she saw as a child. It hadn't been far out in the ocean.

She squeezed her eyes closed for a moment and drew in a deep breath.

Stop it, Penelope. Fisherman Santa was only teasing you. She looked down at the keiligs protruding from her bag. But being safe instead of sorry was an excellent rule for life. Especially near the ocean.

The small tract of land connecting the mainland to the island created a bridge of sand and rock more than half a mile long, according to the information on the map. Waves washed up on either side dozens of feet away, but gave a strange sort of walking-on-water feeling. She released the tension from Fisherman Santa's foreboding words and drew in a deep breath of the cool, salt-sea air.

She would be just fine.

More than fine. She was meeting Matthias.

And she did love surprises.

Matt met Grandfather and they called the police to obtain some guidance on what to do. Stolen keys for a family-owned theater? Sharing information obtained from family emails with another company? All small charges and, at the moment, not helpful in solving the real problem.

Grandfather encouraged Gwynn to take the rest of the day off.

"Someone needs to tell Penelope," Grandfather said, sinking into his desk chair. "Is she working with the rehearsals today?"

"No, she took the day off because we had plans this afternoon."

Grandfather's brows rose. "Plans?"

"A date, Grandfather." Matt released a sigh. "Penelope and I were going on a date after my meeting."

A smile replaced his grandfather's frown. "I had high hopes the two of you would realize what a good match you are." He clapped his hands together and rocked back in his chair. "She's good for you, Matt. She's been good for all of us, but especially for you."

"I know. It just took me a while to see it."

"Well, now that you know, don't let her go. Whatever the cost, my boy." He nodded, folding his arms across his chest. "She's brought you to life again and lavishes Iris with love. Ah, she reminds me of your grandmother."

"Aye." His smile softened at the sweet resemblance. "Me too."

"Would Penelope know anything about where Alec might be, you think?"

Matt looked down at his phone. "I sent a text half an hour ago just to check in with her but haven't gotten a response."

"I just don't understand any of this." Grandfather rubbed a hand over his closely trimmed beard. "Why would Alec do this?"

"I don't know for certain." Matt paced the length of the room, his jaw sore from the tension in it. "His business wasn't going as well as he'd hoped, and he's talked about moving to England for a fresh start."

"He hasn't liked being in the theater for years."

"Not since . . ." Matt breathed out a long breath. "Mum and Granny."

Grandfather looked up. "He could have asked for help and I would have given it to him. He didn't need to do this."

"Perhaps he didn't think he could. Not with finances being what they've been." Matt shook his head. "But that's no excuse, Grandfather. None. Not for this behavior—hurting the people closest to him?"

"No, and there are consequences for it." He leaned back in the chair. "But I want to understand. I want to help him."

"I want to hit him," Matt growled, and he folded his arms across his chest. "He deliberately tried to destroy the theater. For the money, perhaps? He'd get enough from the sale of the theater to start over somewhere else. No matter how many broken people he left in his wake."

"He's not been the same since your mother died. More erratic. Less involved in family affairs." Grandfather looked up, the lines on his face deepening around his eyes. "Money is one reason. Running away may be another."

A slight twinge of regret settled in Matt's chest, but he ignored it. "I'll find my compassion later, Grandfather. Right now, I want to set things right and beat a little sense into my brother's head in the process."

Matt's phone buzzed and he pulled it from his pocket. Alec's name showed on the screen.

He met Grandfather's gaze and brought the phone to his ear. "Where are you?"

"Penelope is on Skree," came the simple sentence.

"Skree? What?"

"You'll need to collect her." His tone sounded almost cryptic.

"From Skree?" Comprehension began a slow thaw. "Alec, what have you done?" Matt met Grandfather's gaze. "There's no internet connection on Skree. No one can reach her. Is that why you took her there? Alec, what is happening?"

"I'm sorry, Matt." His voice shook. "I didn't know it would go this far. Once I was in, he—" Alec released a huff. "Tell Gwynn I'm sorry. Grandfather too."

Something in Alec's voice paused Matt's accusations. "Alec, if you need help, we are your family. We will help you."

"Not now. It's all done now. I can't go back."

"Alec." Matt held his grandfather's gaze. "We'll work it out. Together. Whatever it is."

"She's not hurt," Alec continued as if not listening. "I just needed her out of the way and without phone access. Niles didn't want her contacting the touring—"

"Niles?" The heat left Matt's body. "What is he doing with the touring company? Alec?"

"I'm sorry, Matt. If I could change things now, I would. I'd change it all." He groaned. "Blast, you wouldn't understand."

"Why don't you give me a chance to try."

Silence followed his comment and then Alec cleared his throat.

"Penelope won't make the Skree boat."

And the call ended.

The Skree boat? Matt's eyes fluttered closed. No.

"What is it?" Grandfather stood from his chair.

"I need to get to Penelope, Grandfather." He rushed to the doorway. "I'll call you on the way to tell you what's happening, but we need to locate Alec."

"I'll keep trying." Grandfather nodded, putting his phone into his palm. "Go."

CHAPTER 21

Nothing had prepared Penelope for the rugged beauty of the Kirk of Skree. The pamphlet called the island by its old name, Eileen Colbh, which meant Island Pillar, and once she stepped onto the rocky soil of the ancient shore, she realized why. Sharp, pillar-shaped rocks, jutting upward like towers of teeth, rose into the cloudy sky in all directions, framing the back—or oceanside—edge of the islet. The ground rose toward the rock towers, so she took the well-worn trail, and once she topped the initial hill, she peered down into a lush, green world hidden behind the "teeth" in what appeared to be some sort of crater. For some reason it reminded her of Jurassic Park. A vision of the Kronimara came to mind and she quickly shook away the thought. Nope.

Had those pillars helped create part of the legend of the Kronimara? The jaws leading to the island? She sent a smile to the pillars. Not so frightening after all.

Matt was nowhere in sight along the shore, so she continued forward on the walking trail. The largest tower of rock soared from the center of the "crater," and as she neared it she recognized shapes of windows and doors etched out of the rock. Evidence of walled gardens and other buildings lay scattered around the area in broken stone and faded pathways. A waterfall spilled from one of the rock outcroppings into a creek encircling the main edifice. Elerk the Younger had built his kirk inside the caves of the rocks. Skree stones, in their beautiful array of colors, decorated different parts of the outside of the tower, highlighting the entrances and windows. Worn stairs and passageways led through the caves up to two overlooks: one toward the open sea and another facing Port Quinnick.

Once inside the tower, with its high ceilings made of stone, she frightened a group of locals nearby that she hadn't noticed when she burst out in a boisterous rendition of "Climb Every Mountain." After she made a sheepish apology, the locals seemed to realize her American status and quickly began a conversation before heading on their way.

Penelope took so many photos that her phone blinked a warning of reduced storage space. Every little turn introduced a new view or discovery: intricate wall paintings, faded with time. A few earthen vessels left for display. Carved-out watering places, which looked like ancient bathtubs or sinks. Hidden flowers within the caves, lit by a skylight hundreds of feet above. A tiny waterfall between the crevice of the rocks that dripped into a man-made basin inside the tower. An overgrown graveyard littered with stone crosses in various degrees of artistry and decay.

The design was remarkable. Unfortunately, there was no internet access, so sending copious amounts of photos to Izzy and Luke was out of the question until later. Oh, but what photos!

When the rain began a gentle shower around her, Penelope looked down at her phone for the time. An hour and a half? She'd already been there for an hour and a half?

She glanced around her.

And no Matthias. Perhaps he'd gotten caught in traffic or something. Maybe she'd beaten him here.

She moved back toward the land bridge, tugging the hood of her coat over her head. Or—her stomach dropped—what if he'd changed his mind about dating? She gasped at the thought. It was a huge decision. She was leaving. He was staying. He had to think of Iris. Maybe he didn't think Penelope was worth the risk.

She stumbled out into what had earlier been a sunny field dotted with picnickers and kids playing along the creek side, and her face went cold. The place was completely empty.

Empty? Her heartbeat pulsed into a gallop to match her increasing pace along the path. Where did everyone go? It was as if they just disappeared. As she climbed the hill to the land bridge, she attempted to pick up a phone signal, but her service displayed nothing. Not even a blip.

The sky grew darker, looming above the "teeth" with an angry darkness. She rushed into a jog.

At the top of the hill, a whimper slipped from her lips. Instead of a wonderful walkway of sand from Skree to Port Quinnick, a swell of gray-blue waves and an eerie mist separated her from the mainland. The land bridge was completely gone.

She shuffled forward to the edge of the water, peering into the fog for any sign of the port. Lights. Sails. Even the sea monster shop with Fisherman Santa would have been a welcome vision.

But everything lay shrouded in fog. Everything except the dark, endless sea.

At the very thought, a large *splash* sounded to her right, a sliver of silver coming into view before disappearing beneath the roily depths. Penelope shuffled a step away from the water and shook her head. *Nothing but a fish.*

Sea monsters weren't real and Luke was always right.

She studied the size of the ripples the creature left behind and swallowed through her tightening throat. *But that was an awfully big fish.*

Her attention dropped back to her phone, willing the service bars to at least flicker enough for her to send Matthias or Alec a text. Another splash sent her gaze to the right. Something very flipper-like curled beneath the gray waves, followed by a stream of bubbles.

A chill funneled through her. Bubbles! What had Fisherman Santa said?

An image of the Kronimara from the shop flashed through her mind.

Perhaps having a very good imagination wasn't always the best thing for real life. She pinched her eyes closed, drew in a deep breath, and then dug into her purse. Her fingers hit upon the keiligs and she pulled out all seven of them, holding them in the air like a cross toward a vampire. She'd only watched *Dracula, the Musical* once, but she knew the drill.

"Back!" She raised the keiligs higher. "Back, you foul beast!"

Another large spray erupted off the water's edge as if angered by her declaration.

Oh, wait, she was supposed to be a friend. "Nice sea monster?" she whimpered.

After surviving life with her mom's cooking, her dad's jokes, Luke's teasing, and Arnold Brown's horrible performance as the Phantom of the Opera, it made perfect sense to die on a foreign volcanic island by the fangs of a mythical sea creature she'd feared her whole life.

This was what she got for loving drama so much!

Just as another splash nearly brought her to her knees, two other noises drifted on the breeze toward her. A rather intimidating growl and . . . the sound of her name. Fisherman Santa hadn't said anything about the monster knowing her name! And weren't sirens the ones who called out names or something?

Her name drifted back to her again. The voice was closer. More recognizable.

And sounded very similar to her favorite dancing accountant's.

The growl morphed into the rumble of . . . a motor?

She rushed forward to the water's edge and peered into the fog.

Something white pierced the mist in the distance. And then a small boat came into view.

Her breath released into a sob-like laugh. Leaning forward at the bow of the little boat sat a wonderfully familiar man, emerging from the fog as if from a dream. He halfway stood from his seated position, her misty-eyed gaze meeting his concerned one. She shuffled a few steps forward, keeping a death grip on the keiligs and her rising bout of hysteria.

But he was real. And coming for her.

Matthias killed the motor and then jumped from the boat into the creature-infested waters, tugging the skiff to shore before marching toward her, his rain jacket whipping around him. She'd never seen his features so hard, so . . . unyielding. Well, except maybe on that first day in the airport. And another time during one of her bike riding debacles.

"You're all right."

His voice broke her from her stupefied pose and she rushed forward, burying her face into his chest. Without hesitation, his arms wrapped around her, holding her against his warmth, encasing her with his touch and his smell and his rescue.

She didn't want to let go.

At first, the sense of safety held her there, assuring her that she wasn't going to die from some horrible nautical attack, but as her fear subsided, she stayed for a different reason. Something deeper and sweeter. She *wanted* to stay. Right here. With him, all wrapped and warm against him, because it was *him*.

He released a long sigh and then pulled back. His warm palms slipped to her cheeks as he searched her face. "Thank God, you're all right." He pressed his forehead to hers, his lips curving upward. "I thought I'd lost you to either the local fishermen or the vengeful mermaids."

She shook her head, giving his jacket a little tug to hold him close and trying hard to keep her voice steadier than the rapid fire of her pulse. "I've only been introduced to a sea monster, no mermaids yet."

Those impressive brows rose. "Please don't tell me you believed a word Bram said. He's a fisherman! You can't fall for their tales, luv."

"Fall for—" She caught the glimmer in his eyes and narrowed hers. "I saw lots of bubbles under the water and held up all seven of my keiligs to keep whatever it was at bay."

His laugh burst out as he slipped out of his jacket and held it over her head. "I imagine the seals were quite curious about your behavior then."

"Seals?"

"Indeed. Usually they stay on the far side of the island near the open sea, but when the tide comes in, they'll swim around to portside, leaving bubble trails in their wake. Those are the only visiting sea creatures around Skree, I'm afraid."

Fishermen! She shoved the keiligs back into her bag. "And I suppose *Bram* is the name of Mr. Fisherman Santa in the sea monster shack?"

"'Fisherman Santa'?" His laugh broke through again. "Yes, and he's known all around for his attempts at terrifying newcomers. All in good fun."

"Well, it certainly worked on me."

He paused, his gaze roaming her face with such tenderness she really wished he'd just bend a little and kiss her.

Her bottom lip wobbled in response. "You came to find me."

"Of course I came to find you."

"In the rain." The words shivered along with her body.

He paused in his turn toward the boat and lowered the jacket. With a gentle touch, he brushed his thumb across her cheek, dashing away a rebel tear and every ounce of hesitation she felt in finding happily ever after with him. His expression sobered. "If I'd known what Alec was doing, you wouldn't even be in this predicament."

The warm tingles from his touch chilled. "Alec?"

"We'll speak of it once you're warm and dry." He took her hand and tugged her a few more feet toward the little boat.

The boat!

Over the deep, dark, turbulent water.

"I can't." She froze. "I . . . I can't do boats, Matthias."

He turned back to her, his hands settling on her shoulders. "We can't stand here in the rain until the tide goes out either, luv." The endearment took on magical qualities, almost as if it carried a little courage along with it.

Or maybe that was the feeling of coming down from the high of a near-death experience.

She shuffled forward another step, failing to keep the tiniest whimper from escaping.

He sighed and turned back to her.

"Here's what I want you to do." His warm hands framed her cheeks. Was he going to kiss her? That would be a fantastic distraction from sea monsters and boats.

"I want you to close your eyes and trust me to get you to the other side."

"And . . . and what about the sea monsters?"

His lips tilted ever so slowly. "I'll fight them all, if I must."

The feeling that had been fluttering in and out of the shadows of her heart stepped into the spotlight. Love. She loved Matthias Gray. All her excuses crumbled. Every doubt dissipated. What did she care about sea monsters when there was such a man?

Her very own hero. "No, I think . . . I think I can handle it, if you're with me."

"All the way across." He gave her hand a little squeeze and then helped her into the boat.

With a quick start of the motor, he took his seat next to her, tugging her close to his side as he steered to the mainland.

She pulled the jacket up so that it covered both of their heads and then she rested her cheek against his shoulder. The closeness helped the raincoat cover more of both of them, or at least that was the excuse she liked best.

The hushing sound of the waves ushered her forward like a gentle applause, as if the world proudly acknowledged her bravery at overcoming her fear and her wisdom at coming to the right conclusion. She'd conquered the boat. And she loved Matthias Gray. Not just liked. Not just wanted to date for a trial period. But . . . loved. For keeps.

She sighed against him. With all the hard stuff about the theater behind them, all she had to do was convince him to fall in love with her and then navigate a long-distance relationship.

A knot lodged in her throat. How hard could that be?

What had he just said? She stared at Matthias's profile as they took the hour drive back home.

"Alec has been the one sharing information with Emblem?"

"All along." Matthias nodded. "We think he was after the money from the sale, but after speaking with Niles Westing—"

"Speaking?"

"Fine. Threatening." He cleared his throat, his neck tense. "I discovered Alec was also getting a considerable stipend from Niles with each new bit of information he leaked."

"And then he vandalized the museum?" Her voice broke, but she caught her emotions before they dipped into hysterical. *Don't think about it. Don't think about it.* "Well, the theater is in a good place despite the vandalism, so that's the most important thing. And we can recreate it if we can get the items back."

He didn't respond and her heart dropped.

"And nothing from Alec since?" From the way Matthias described their last phone conversation, paired with her last conversation with him, Alec sounded . . . troubled.

Matthias fisted the steering wheel, his answer slow in coming. "Grandfather texted me when I arrived in Port Quinnick to say he'd finally gotten a response. He's safe, but wouldn't commit to a meeting or divulging any information. He just"—Matthias swallowed so hard she heard it—"wept."

Wept? A little of her frustration dimmed. She'd seen this type of behavior before in a teen boy she'd taught in one of her acting classes. He'd lashed out in irrational ways for attention or answers or whatever he thought might stop the pain, instead of working through the grief in healthy ways. When he'd finally been confronted with what he needed most, he wept like a baby.

"He needs counseling, Matt."

"I know." He shook his head. "It still doesn't excuse his behavior, but . . . it makes it more understandable."

She relaxed back in the seat, heart heavy, and looked out onto the darkening horizon. Wait, what? She leaned closer to the window. Why was it so dark so early? Her gaze dropped to the digital clock in Matthias's car.

"It's three thirty?" She looked down at her phone. "But . . . but my phone says it's only two. No wonder I missed the tide."

A growl rose from Matthias. "My brother."

"What do you mean?"

"Was there any time you left your phone in the car with him?"

She paused, thinking through the morning. "Only when I went into one of the rest areas on the way." She shook her head. "By the way, Skymarian rest areas are much cuter than ours back in the States. And you can get some shopping done. That's crazy."

"Our service stations are fairly nice." His smile softened when he looked at her but then hardened again as he turned back to the road. "And you left your phone in the car then?"

"Do you think he changed the time on my phone?" She gasped, a sudden burst of fire rising in her cheeks. "What a villain move!"

"And deleted any messages, I'd say, because I'd sent a few."

"What?" She opened up her recent missed notifications. "Oh my goodness, Matthias. I had three calls from Case Townley." She looked back at him, the warmth in her cheeks draining just as quickly. "He's the manager for the touring company."

"That's the other thing, Penelope."

Her nose started to tingle with the hint of tears, even before he spoke.

"When I spoke to Niles—"

"No!" The word erupted from her. "No, he didn't."

"They bought out the touring company."

The words hit like a bullet to her chest. She gripped the door for something to hold on to.

"I'm so sorry." She barely heard him, her brain still trying to comprehend the horribleness. "Niles took advantage of the fact that the company hadn't mailed in the contract yet, and since Alec knew exactly how to contact them . . ."

"Emblem outbid us." The words raked over her tightening throat. "But the verbal agreement should have held them. Ohh. And they couldn't get in touch with me to confirm because I was out of service on Skree. How could Alec do this?" She shook her fist. "This makes me so mad. Business is business. They should have honored their commitment, no matter what Nasty Niles dangled in front of them." She turned to him. "How horrible! Not only did they steal a production from us, but the whole ordeal will overshadow *Peter Pan*."

She pressed her head back against the seat and closed her eyes to try to keep the tears from coming. What were they going to do? Even if sales were up, this kind of hit could follow them for a while. Damage future sales. Hurt their fragile reputation.

"The Darling House can't keep their word" kind of thing.

And word of mouth made a difference in this business.

Matthias dropped her off at the cottage, his somber mood a mirror image of her own. But he'd tried to encourage her to rest for the night, saying they'd work things out tomorrow. That something could be done. That it would all be fine.

But she wasn't fine. And she barely made it into the cottage before all the tears broke free.

She stumbled to the couch, pulling the blanket up against her chest as a sob heaved through her.

After all their hard work? After building up all the community support and hype, to have someone from the inside mess so many things up all at once?

Text from Penelope to Luke: I need to talk to you. It's important.

Luke: How important?

Penelope: Like the time John Crestwell tried to kiss me important.

And her phone immediately came to life. She brought it to her ear and dropped onto the couch.

"Okay, sis," came her brother's familiar, grumpy voice. "What's going on?"

Talking to Luke had helped.

At least enough to get her through a crying fit so she could think clearly and breathe without shaking all over. And she'd prayed, too, since if past experience proved true, God didn't mind snotty faces and partial-syllable blubbering. He was supposed to understand things like that.

Matthias had called her later to check on her, the sadness in his voice nearly causing her to start crying all over again. And the whole Alec part of it all weighed everyone down. It was one thing to have a jerk in the family, but it was quite another thing to have something really horrible happen to said jerk. At least in Alec's most recent communication with Grandpa Gray, he'd offered to meet with him.

And when she'd told Matt about the conversation she'd had with Alec, more of the why behind all he'd done seemed to come to light.

Sleep hadn't come for hours, and when her alarm sounded, she hit Snooze and stared at her ceiling.

Peter Pan still opened in a few days. The centennial celebration of it. And she needed to assess the damage to the museum. She groaned and rolled over to face the window. She couldn't just lie here all day and cry about things. The best actors knew that the show must go on. Life still moved forward. With or without *The Sound of Music*.

She squeezed her eyes closed and the laughing face of eerie Niles Westing appeared in all its horribleness. Her skin hummed with the heat of fury. Giving up now would only let Niles Westing win. Her entire body revolted.

She sat up. What was she thinking? This was the Elle Woods against Callahan moment. The von Trapps against the Nazis. Dorothy against the witch. The Beast against Gaston.

She would not let Niles Westing win without a fight.

But how? How could she fight him?

What did The Darling House have in its arsenal? She squeezed her eyes closed.

Well, they had a theater, which was a start.

Good visibility right now, so capitalizing on that would help, if there was anything to put out there.

An excellent community of support, especially after the ball.

She nodded. Three very concrete and positive things.

They needed another solid production to bring in revenue if they planned to continue to overcome the deficit from the past years. And if Emblem stole their December production, they had to find something else to put in its place to keep Darling's reputation intact.

Somehow, they needed to find a production to put in its place.

She reached for her phone and pulled up her texts. Earnest Stevenson had sent her one of his show cards the night before. She groaned. The show cards for *The Sound of Music*. She pressed a palm to her stomach and looked over the attachment. Fantastic show cards. Perfect for the production they *weren't* having.

She paused on the thought.

Wait. She looked back at the show card and then shoved away her covers, hope pushing her from the bed.

Maybe there was a way to rescue this moment.

Text from Penelope to Matthias: Where are you?
Matthias: I'm at the office.
Penelope: I'm on my way.

Text from Penelope to Luke: I have an idea for how to save
  the production.
Luke: Do you realize it's one in the morning?
Penelope: I don't know if it will work, but I have to try. I can't
  let Nasty Niles win.
Luke: Nice villain name there. Fight, Penelope, fight! Now I'm
  going back to sleep.
Penelope: "To survive a war, you've gotta become war."
Luke: I have never been prouder of you than at this moment.

CHAPTER 22

Penelope burst into Matthias's office to find it completely empty.

Her momentum stumbled along with her feet. He'd just texted her that he was at the office. Of course, "at the office" meant basically anywhere in the theater, so she should have been more specific.

Then the sound of movement drew her attention down the hallway. One of the storage-closet doors stood wide open with light streaming into the hall.

Had someone come back to steal *more* from the museum? She tiptoed toward the closet, her hand reaching down into her purse for her little bottle of hair spray. She'd seen it used in place of Mace in a movie once. And this was extra-strong hold, so it would probably sting even more than regular hair spray.

With a slow step to the edge of the door, she readied the hair spray in one hand and a brush in the other and then peered around the frame.

Matt sat on the floor of the closet in a black T-shirt and jeans, boxes in various levels of disarray around him, his hair a little disheveled too. Penelope lowered her weapons and rounded the corner.

"What on earth are you doing?"

He looked up at her, some sort of shield in his hands. His gaze flicked to her weapons. "Arming myself against your hair spray?"

Her grin spread into a chuckle—a much-needed one. She returned her items to her purse. "I thought you were the museum thief come back to finish the job of utter Darling history destruction."

"Not quite. I was trying to search through our inventory for any replacements we could make to the museum items. All your hard work shouldn't be wasted." He pushed up from his position, his body stretching to his full height. He looked really good in a black T-shirt. Especially with those shoulders. And forearms.

And he was trying to find new museum items for her, when he should have been sorting out the entire musical debacle. How sweet could this guy be? She shot a look skyward with a little prayer tagged on. Surely they could make it through a long-distance relationship, right?

He was completely worth the effort.

And more.

He stepped close enough to surround her with his delicious cedar scent, his gaze searching her face. "How are you?"

And every thought she'd devised to share with him puttered into a ball of mush in her brain. Heaven help her. She really wanted him to kiss her. After all the crazy and pain of the past day, a good kiss from him might be the best medicine of all—her attention dropped to his lips—actually, she was pretty certain it would be.

"Penelope?" His palm moved to her arm, drawing her attention back to his eyes.

"Yes, right. I'm good." Her thoughts began to clear and reconverge around her. "Actually, I'm better than good." In fact, she'd conjured up, mulled over, and plotted the whole Darling House salvation story in her head during her bicycle ride to the theater. "I refuse to let Withering Westing win."

Matthias's expressive brows rose to attention.

"And I have an idea for how to salvage this. Maybe. But we could certainly use some fairy dust. I mean, there are a lot of things to worry about. Believe me. I've been expertly worrying about them all the way over here on my bicycle, which is likely why I almost killed three people. Maybe four, if you count the old woman in the leather boots wearing a burka."

A burst of air came from him. "Quite an entrance. Are you sure you're not in theater or something like that?"

She exhaled a breath she felt like she'd been holding all the way from the cottage. "My brain's been really busy. And my worries aren't helping." She brought her palms together, almost in prayer, and steadied her shoulders. "Do you think there are enough quality actors in the community theater who have performed *The Sound of Music* before? I know Mrs. Carrington played Mother Superior about ten years ago."

"Wait." His jaw slacked. "Are you thinking we pull off our own production of it?"

"If we can?" She looked around the closet as if searching for answers. "By the time we get the word out, we'll have only about three weeks to prepare, but if most of the actors have played their parts before, then that helps with memorizing lines and with some of the placement issues."

"Then we'd need set work and choreography." He snapped his fingers, his smile crooking so wonderfully that her mind almost dipped into kissing thoughts again. "But some of the sets from *My Fair Lady* could easily be modified for *The Sound of Music*."

"That's right." She laughed, relief pouring out through a sigh. He saw the vision. Believed in her idea. "Perfect."

Her fingers twirled her ring around and around, spinning, kind of like the feeling in her stomach. She loved him. In the middle of all this insanity, she'd fallen in love . . . with a wonderful guy! And now, with everything in chaos, all she wanted to do was let him know. In a very tangible, lips-tingling sort of way.

She knew kissing him wouldn't fix the fact that they didn't have a production ready, and the museum had been vandalized, and one Gray brother was missing. But it certainly wouldn't make any of those things worse. And she felt confident she'd feel a whole lot better afterward. Matthias probably would too. *Probably.*

Besides, she'd been told she wasn't a half-bad kisser.

She wet her lips, attempting to work up the courage to just tell him. Then chickened out. "And we already have the show cards from Earnest."

"I saw." He waved toward her. "You sent them to me. They're amazing."

"The touring company's name isn't on them, just the show." She twisted the ring some more. The word *kiss* wasn't such a hard one to say, right? *Matthias, how about a kiss?* "So why not use them if we can?" *Or maybe a few kisses? Stopping at one just seems like a poor use of the opportunity.*

His gaze flickered to her fingers and then back to her face. "Getting the sets ready in time will be a challenge, but if we have enough people willing to help, I think it's doable."

"Good, good. Yes."

"And Dani's wife could enlist some help to ready the costumes, I'm sure." Matthias's smile kept growing bigger, adding more confidence to her plan. "We can try to drum up some extra funds for that."

"You really believe this can work, don't you?" She blinked back the sting in her eyes.

"If I've learned anything from knowing you, it's never to underestimate your ideas. Or . . . the impossible." His head tilted to the side, studying her busy fingers. "We're working through this, luv." He caught her hand in his. "Things are already looking worlds better in the past five minutes, so what else is worrying you?"

"Do you want a list?"

"If that will help allay your fears"—he gave her hand a squeeze—"then give me a list."

The list was rather large at the moment, so she attempted to clear her mind of the less important items. "Well, I'm nervous about us not being able to pull this show together in time." She tugged her hand from his and began pacing across an uncluttered path in the small space.

"But I think we have a solid plan in the works already."

She nodded toward him. "Right."

"And once we get Grandfather, Gwynn, and the community theater involved, we'll have a better idea of the timeline."

She paused her pacing. "Do *you* think it's possible?"

His gaze never wavered. "I do."

Her heart gave a responsive shudder to those two words. Very romantic words.

"And I'm worried that all we've done to save The Darling House is ruined."

"Now, Penelope." He edged closer to her. "I know what the numbers look like, and even if we can't get *The Sound of Music* out, I think we still have a fighting chance to make it into another season stronger than we were before you came."

"That's good to hear." Her smile tempted a release. "And Alec? Is he going to be okay?"

"He's agreed to meet with Grandfather tomorrow." Matthias's expression sobered. "I take that as a very good sign. And I've messaged him as well. He's not saying a lot, but at least he's responding."

"But Gwynn's not reaching out to him?"

"She's too hurt by his actions to reach out right now, or at least reach out in a good way."

Penelope nodded. "I get that. And Grandpa Gray?"

"He'll be fine, luv."

The word *luv* possessed some sort of calming ability, because she drew in a deep breath and eased her stride, tossing a grin at him. "I'm worried about wrinkles from worrying too much."

His smile made a slow spread across his face, lighting his eyes, and she nearly stopped walking altogether to appreciate it. She continued talking before she lost her nerve. "I'm worried that I'll leave here and never know what it's like to have kissed you." Her eyes shot wide, and she looked away. "Or that I'll never see Iris perform onstage, or—"

"What did you say?"

She spun around, facing him. Sort of. Though she looked every other place in the closet except at him. "I'll never see Iris perform onstage?"

"Before that." He stepped closer.

Heat erupted in her cheeks, her eyes, her forehead, and even her ears. "Worry wrinkles?" The words barely reached a whisper and there was no way she was lifting her eyes to him, even if he'd once again stepped within smelling distance. And he smelled good.

"Penelope." The way he spoke her name somehow caused an explosion inside her. Like New Year's Eve fireworks combined with the feeling she always got when she heard the overture for *The Sound of Music*.

The single word weighted with meaning. Intention. Maybe even a little hope, kind of like the need beating through her. He moved so close his shirt took up her field of vision.

"I . . . I think you should kiss me." She cleared her throat. "I mean, if you want to."

He didn't respond, just shifted even closer. She stared quite forcibly at the collar of his shirt and then became a little distracted by his very attractive neckline.

"I . . . I didn't mean to sound bossy. It's just that I think you're wonderful and—"

He moved then, cutting off her words. His palms smoothed against her cheeks, framing her face, and with a little nudge, he tipped her face upward.

Her gaze locked with his, all stormy and blue and tender.

"Aye," he breathed, lowering his head nearer. "I *want* to kiss you, Penelope Edgewood." Without one more hesitation, his mouth captured hers.

All worries shrank into nonexistence as soon as their lips made contact. Warm, controlled, and completely annihilating any former kissing practice in her history. The gentleness in his initial touch brought her forward. His hands slid back from her cheeks to brace her head, his lips taking firmer control. As if it were the most natural thing to do, her palms slipped around his waist to smooth up his back, feeling the muscles beneath his shirt shift as she did.

He kissed like he had all the time in the world to do so. Like he enjoyed every millisecond. Like a *man* instead of the boys she'd dated in the past.

His lips moved with a controlled sort of passion, leaving her breathing shallow and her mind a little curious about what his uncontrolled passion might feel like. Her body tingled from the scalp southward. Have mercy!

This kiss was practically perfect in every way. Better than she'd imagined, but maybe that was because her heart understood more than it had before . . . and was ready for all of it. To try harder and love bigger and dream with more clarity about who she was and what she *really* wanted most. What really *mattered* most.

And she wouldn't have known that until she found it in Matthias Gray.

The kissing lingered, intensified. They stumbled back together against the closet wall, her fingers fisting in his shirt and bringing him along with her. A pleasant rumble-like sound reverberated through his chest, and for a second the kiss took a deliciously dangerous turn, before he drew back.

Her breaths shuddered, her mind completely blank except for the utter delight of the memory of his lips on hers.

His thumb trailed over her cheek, his smile a little softer and his lips a lot more delightful than they'd been a moment ago. The feel of Matthias Gray's kiss might be the best secret she'd ever uncovered in her whole life.

"I think you may have just calmed all my worries for the rest of my life."

One of his brows rose, his gaze roaming her face as if he liked what he saw. No, more than liked. Something sweeter and more endearing than just "liked." "*All* your worries?"

His touch slipped to her chin, causing her to have difficulty fully comprehending his question.

She shrugged and hoped her expression looked as innocent as she attempted to make it. "Well, maybe not all. I could do with some more help calming the pesky things."

With a crook of his smile, he made a thorough attempt at calming her fears. In fact, when he'd finished kissing her, she felt pretty certain the theater would become a world-famous venue, Iris would perform as Glinda on Broadway, and worry lines were a thing of the past.

"Now, Miss Edgewood." He touched his forehead to hers. "I have an idea inspired by you."

She blinked him back into focus and tried to remember any hint of a conversation they had prior to the moment his lips kissed away all her worries . . . and effectively had her planning their courtship, wedding, and house by the sea.

Okay, maybe not by the sea. But somewhere just as lovely.

"What do you mean?"

He tipped his head back, keeping her body close to his. "You've reminded me what a force of support we have in our community. How much the people love this theater and want to see it succeed. And I think we should honor that."

"Yes, of course we should." His hands rested against the top of her hips as if they already belonged together. In a comfortable "you're mine" kind of way that she found almost as distracting as kissing him.

"Let's promote our community theater troupe as much as possible in every venue we have. Celebrate them everywhere. We are Mountcaster's theater. Fiacla's theater. Let's not only use the people from this place but also enlist businesses to share the news, touch base with all those who came to the ball, reach out to local businesses we could feature onstage somehow. Furniture from Craig's, clothing from Marcia's. Let's make it the *people's* production."

"That's brilliant." She rested her palms against his chest. "I mean, we've already been building that connectivity over the last few months; now we can capitalize on it."

She loved Matthias Gray. Repeating the thought brought another smile.

He listened to her, valued her ideas, and danced with her. With the additions of a wonderfully sarcastic sense of humor, an adorable daughter, and the ability to kiss like a . . . well, like a perfect gentleman who reined in just enough passion for just the right time.

Her throat closed up for a second and her gaze dropped to his lips again.

"Audrey Hepburn has a fabulous quote for this moment."

"Does she?" His words surfaced low, raspy.

"'I believe in kissing, kissing a lot.'" Her voice dropped to a whisper as his lips drew closer again. "'And I believe in miracles.'"

"Well, I'll happily oblige the first one." His lips trailed her cheek, slowly slipping closer to her mouth. "And we'll work together to make the second one happen."

She'd have melted to the closet floor if he hadn't been holding her up, because he took the time to appreciate the first part of Audrey's quote quite thoroughly.

He pulled back rather suddenly. "I think I know what we need to do next."

"You were scheming while kissing me?"

He chuckled and took another taste of her lips. "Kissing you likely inspired my creative thinking." He took her hand and tugged her toward the door. "Here's what I think we should do. Take your idea to Grandfather while I ask Dani for his help on some things."

"All right."

"And if you don't mind, I'd love to take you out to dinner tonight on an actual date and we can make more plans."

Her smile bloomed and she squeezed his hand. "I'd love that too."

"Good." He bent and kissed her once more, lingering and warm and oh so wonderful, before he dashed down the hallway toward the stage.

Penelope watched his retreating back until he disappeared from view and then she closed her eyes with a sigh. "Supercalifragilisticexpialidocious."

Text from Penelope to Izzy: Remember what you said about
    the right kiss with the right guy?

Izzy: Oh. My. Goodness! What happened?

Penelope: Now I understand why they're so powerful in fairy
    tales. I can't go back to anything less after this.

Izzy: Exactly.

Penelope: And I know it's not going to be easy, but he's
    worth it, Iz. Whatever "it" is. He's worth it.

Text from Alec to Matt: The museum pieces are at the boathouse.

Matt: Do you want to meet me there so we can talk?

Alec: I'm not ready for that, but at least I could try to make
    one thing right.

Matt: You're still meeting with Grandpa tomorrow?

Alec: Yes.

Matt: I'm sorry I was so lost in my own grief that I didn't
    recognize you needed a friend.

Alec: That wasn't your responsibility. Tell Penelope that I'm sorry.

Matt's faith in Penelope's ability to create miracles proved solid.

Well, Penelope's ability along with the help of several dozen other people.

357

The opening weekend of *Peter Pan* went off without trouble. In fact, it outperformed any production of the past four years. Whether it was from the added publicity of the vandalism and news of Emblem "stealing" Darling's show, or the fact that everyone's hard work had paid off—or perhaps some combination of the two—Penelope and Gwynn, with a little help from Iris and Matt, put the museum back together at record speed, just in time for opening night.

And after a meeting with some of the community theater members, the idea of performing *The Sound of Music* was beginning to take shape. Whether they could pull it off in three weeks was yet to be seen.

But at least the main response showed more excitement than terror, which, as Penelope reminded him, "usually led to a healthier and more positive outcome." Matt no longer attempted to curb his grin when Penelope came to mind, even with their uncertain future. He couldn't remember ever feeling so . . . happy in love.

The simple fact she reciprocated with so much . . . enthusiasm—his neck warmed at the thought—only made the budding relationship even better. And they found ways to show their mutual affection on a regular basis, even if it included storage closets and "helpful" trips to the kitchen or office together. Evidently, kissing practice calmed his worries, too, because he'd even taken up humming again. Iris's smile and laugh came in droves, proving all the more that this little trio was well worth the future heartache distance was sure to bring.

Alec returned to his apartment in town but kept away from the family, even though Matt continued to reach out to him. Grandfather mentioned something about Alec seeking therapy and "needing time," so Matt kept his distance. As long as Alec was talking to someone, Matt would wait for his brother's timing. The initial sting of his betrayal had waned, and now all Matt wanted to do was find a way to heal together, even though Gwynn still wanted nothing to do with Alec.

With a set in need of modifying and few hands to get the job done, Matt grabbed his hammer, left his office, and started for the theater doors, when a scene ahead of him stopped him in his tracks. In the reception area connecting the office spaces with the other parts of the theater stood a stranger, a small bag at his side. And from his overall appearance, he looked every bit a foreigner.

A red-and-black flannel shirt showed beneath a heavy jean jacket. Dark hair covered his head and framed his mouth. He seemed to take in his surroundings with a careful eye, studying various parts of the ceiling all the way down to the baseboard. At the clip of Matt's footsteps, the stranger turned. There was something familiar about the shape of his eyes.

"May I help you?"

"Yes, sir." He tipped his head. "I'm here to see Penelope Edgewood."

His American accent held curls of an Appalachian dialect more pronounced than Penelope's.

Matt's grin grew as he approached. "You wouldn't happen to be Penelope's brother, would you?"

A light came to the man's dark eyes. "I am." He offered his hand. "Luke Edgewood."

"Yes." Matt took the proffered hand in a sturdy grip, his grin continuing to grow. "I've heard so much about you."

"Heard a lot about you too." The man held Matt's gaze. "Mostly good."

Matt immediately relaxed at the teasing in Luke's tone. "I could say the same."

Luke's smile stretched wide. "Well, now, then she's trying to fool you if she's saying mostly good things about me."

"It's a nice surprise to have you here." Matt waved toward him and his bag. "Penelope didn't mention you were coming."

"That's probably because I didn't tell her." He shrugged a shoulder, one dark brow hitching northward. "She likes surprises."

Matt's laugh burst out. "Indeed, she does." He had a feeling he and Luke would get along just fine. "Follow me."

At first glance inside the massive room of the museum, he didn't see the charming redhead, but then a grunt sounded from the nearest corner behind an expansive Cinderella dress used in a performance during the 1970s.

The skirt of the dress moved of its own accord.

"Ah, got it." And from behind the skirt crawled Penelope, her hair in a lopsided ponytail.

"Seems about right." Luke nodded, his voice low.

Matt bit back another laugh. "Someone's here to see you."

With great pleasure, Matt watched awareness dawn on her flushed face.

She looked up with a welcome smile, then her attention moved to Luke, and her smile fell into open-mouthed astonishment before she covered her mouth with her palms and ran forward, burying herself into her brother's chest.

Luke stumbled back from the impact and rolled his gaze heavenward before looking over at Matt as if Matt understood the current "drama." Yes, he'd been on Luke's end of an emotional response before. Plenty of times. But there was no mistaking the man's care for his sister. To travel all the way to Skymar. No, no doubt at all.

"What are you doing here?" Penelope pulled back, tears streaming down her face. "I can't even believe it." And then she burrowed back into his chest.

"I can leave if you want." He heaved a massive sigh. "Especially if you're going to make a mess of my jacket."

She jerked back. "Don't you dare. I haven't seen you for over three months!" She laughed and just stared at him for a few seconds before shaking her head and turning to Matt. "This is my brother."

"Yes." Matt chuckled. "We've met."

"I'm so glad to see you." She sniffed while giving the front of his jacket a tug. "But why?"

He captured a piece of her rebellious hair between his thumb and finger and lifted it off her damp face as if he were removing a bug. Very brother-like. "I reckon y'all could use some help with getting the sets ready for *The Sound of Music*, and I had a few weeks free to come."

Penelope laughed again and turned those glowing eyes on Matt. "He came to help us, Matthias! Isn't he the best?"

Matt gave a nod, happily being a bystander for this sweet and somewhat comical reunion.

"Now dry up your face and show me where I'm going to be the most useful." Though the words came out a little disgruntled, the twinkle in Luke's eyes intensified. "I can't help anybody if I'm soaked to the skin from all your crying."

"We're almost done for the day, Luke, and I'm sure you'd like to settle in." Matt gestured toward Penelope. "What do you say I order pizza and we meet up at Penelope's to talk things over?"

"I have an extra room in my cottage, Luke. You can stay there." She squeezed his arm. "It's a great shade of blue."

Luke stared down at her. "Well, I'm sure I'll sleep loads better knowing that." He turned to Matt, amusement flickering in his eyes. "If you're sure it won't help to start today, then I'll take you up on that offer. It'd be good to get a general idea of what's needed so I can use what time I have the best."

"Excellent." Good man. Smart. "And I'll bring Grandfather with me. I feel certain he'll appreciate meeting you since he was once a builder too."

"And you'll get to meet Iris." Penelope beamed. "I just bought her a new princess hairband that she wears nonstop."

"More princesses." Luke drew in a deep breath, his shoulders expanding as if preparing for battle. "Perfect."

Luke was here! And *The Sound of Music* was slowly, and a little shakily, coming together—at least as far as the cast went. And when Penelope recommended Iris play the part of Gretel, it took only a few minutes for Matthias to give in to the idea. The little girl had the talent and interest, so why not give her the experience on her family's historic stage? What a memory to appreciate later!

Luke and Grandpa Gray hit it off splendidly, sharing all sorts of builder-y types of information. There was a discussion about some property Grandpa Gray had that he'd wanted to renovate into holiday rentals for years and hadn't had the time. Luke even put Grandpa Gray's contact information into his phone, a huge show of compatibility. He only had fifteen contacts in there. She knew. She'd checked his phone dozens of times. Incognito, of course.

And a much more serious and somber Alec began a slow reentry into the theater's work, behind the scenes. Grandpa Gray worked out some kind of community service agreement to ensure Alec received the consequences of his choices, but it also left room for healthy reconciliation. Which Penelope hoped helped to not only heal Alec but make him an even better person. He'd started going to counseling, too, initially as part of his agreement with Grandpa Gray, but if Penelope guessed right, he'd end up continuing the sessions for himself. And the cast and crew welcomed him in without a hitch, which probably helped him return with more dedication. Well, everyone welcomed him back except Gwynn. She'd barely looked at him, let alone talked to him.

Luke jumped right into the work, connecting with some of the other men, especially Mark, who appreciated Luke's skills and work ethic. Penelope had always known her brother had a great deal of potential for socializing, but she'd never realized how much until watching him join in with the crew. Maybe it just took the right people for him to exchange his grumbly-ness for chattiness. Well, the word *chattiness* was going a bit too far. At least he was speaking in full, non-sarcastic sentences.

And Penelope nearly started crying all over again every time she'd turn a corner or glance onstage to find him there. A part of home had come to her. It caused the ache for that familiar place to somehow grow and shrink at the same time.

The second weekend of *Peter Pan* proved another sellout, with Mr. Carrington giving the welcome speech and sharing how his father had been in one of the earliest performances of the show. The board of directors set up hors d'oeuvres outside the museum before and after the performances, and people went through all the paraphernalia, leaving donations in a designated spot as they went. Something about the nostalgia and a look at how the community had supported Darling all these years created additional buzz and morale to push forward toward the uncertain *Sound of Music* performance.

Penelope was cleaning up in the museum the week following *Peter Pan*'s final performance when a pair of arms came from behind and wrapped around her middle. The welcome scent of Matthias's cologne along with the warmth of his body melted over her with wonderful belonging.

"We've not had much time alone lately." His words pearled near her ear and she leaned her head back against him, reveling in his hold and the tingles his voice sent through her.

"Any ideas on how to change that?"

His lips pressed into her hair. "Gwynn is taking Iris shopping for a Gretel dress this afternoon and offered to drop Luke off at the cottage. What do you say to dinner?"

She turned around in his arms. "A dress-up kind of dinner?"

The way he looked at her made her feel as if she already wore a beautiful gown instead of leggings and a baggy sweater. How could she leave this? Him? Iris?

"Would you like a dress-up dinner?"

Her eyes stung. "Actually, I don't care as long as I can spend the time with you."

"Oh, luv." His finger and thumb went to her chin. "Words directly to my heart." He drew in a breath. "But I believe you'd appreciate a little dress-up after all your hard work, and I know a lovely place to take you where we can enjoy a view, a quiet place to talk, and"—he gave his brows a wiggle—"perhaps some dancing?"

And so it was.

She wore a flirty red dress with a ruffle at the knee and he donned a suit and tie. Penelope felt as if they'd stepped into a movie, especially when the car pulled up to a manor house overlooking the sea and the sound of live jazz spilled from the windows. They were ushered to a quiet corner of the restaurant with windows offering a view of rocky cliffs and an endless horizon. They ordered. Danced. Ate. Laughed. And danced some more. It was the most perfect date she'd ever had, because it was with him.

And perhaps because she'd grown enough to know what "right" felt and looked like.

"I don't think I've ever had this much fun in my life," Matthias said as they shared a decadent chocolate dessert.

"Me either." She dipped her spoon into the creamy mixture. "And I have had a lot of fun in my lifetime." Her gaze came back to his. "But you're the best. Ever."

And with her declaration, the inevitable slipped into the conversation. The topic they'd skimmed around for weeks as they'd shared quick dates, many with Iris along, and momentary (yet delicious) closet kisses, definitely without Iris along.

An unspoken understanding passed across his features and he released a sigh, drawing her hand into his as they sat across the small table from each other. Her breath squeezed in her throat, eyes beginning the same threatening burn she always felt when she began counting down the days to her departure.

His brows pinched as he smoothed his fingers over hers. "You must know that I'm determined to try to make this work. You and me. Even after you leave."

"Me too." Her voice scratched over the words.

"And I realize it will be a sacrifice for both of us."

"I . . . I could stay, Matthias." She searched his face, her vision blurring. "I'm sure if I told Jackie the reasons, she'd understand. She's already heard so much about you and Iris."

He looked down at their hands, his breath coming slowly. "You can't know how much it means for me to hear you say that." He brought her hand up to his lips and then met her gaze. "And I would love for you to stay."

Her heart shook in her chest with the suddenness of the change in her decision. There was no doubt she could find joy working at The Darling House under Gwynn's direction and living in Skymar . . . so far from home. Even if she needed to adjust her plans, she could do it. For them. Of course she could.

She'd thought about it dozens of times. With a deep breath, she embraced the choice. "I don't want to leave you and Iris, and I'd have the least to give up."

"I don't know if that's necessarily true, luv. You have a once-in-a-lifetime opportunity to make your dream come true."

"But you're a once-in-a-lifetime opportunity too."

"You shouldn't have to make that choice, Penelope." His smile gentled and he gave her fingers another squeeze. "There may come a time when you do, but not right now. I've had opportunity to practice many things I've loved and have come to know myself better over the past few years. And enjoyed the support and love of my family in the process. You need that too." He shook his head. "If you stayed in Skymar, you'd be staying for me." He drew in a breath as if garnering some courage. "And I want you to stay for *you*. No regrets."

"But when people love each other, they make sacrifices."

His grin slanted in such a sweet way. "You love me, do you?"

The declaration had slipped out with such ease, she didn't even realize she'd never spoken it aloud. She'd written it in her journal plenty of times. "I do."

"Funny about that." His gaze met hers. "I feel the same. And because I love you, and because I *know* you, I realize your heart still longs for home and your family. And that is good and fine and right."

"But I want to be with you too." Her throat closed around the words. How could she have both? She couldn't. Not in the same place, and her heart felt like it was ripping apart.

"So here's what we're going to do." He held her gaze, his brows taking a determined dip. "We're going to enjoy the time we have left together here in Skymar. We're going to succeed in having the best performance of *The Sound of Music* that this theater has ever put on." He swallowed hard. "And then you're going to go home and celebrate Christmas with your family, lavish love on your niece and nephew, and begin this new job of yours."

"And you?"

"I will be here to help Grandfather and Gwynn sort out Gwynn's new role in the theater and reconnect with Alec." His gaze roamed her face with such sweet adoration. "And I will ring you and write you often, and find ways to fly to North Carolina."

"It would be easier for me to come here," she added quickly. "A ticket for one instead of two."

He cleared his throat and her heart lurched at the idea of him reining in his own emotions. "We'll make this work."

"We will." She knew the statistics about long-distance relationships, though. She'd looked them up. Four times, in hopes of a different answer with each new search. Very few relationships survived. Of course, at first everything seemed like it would work, but over time, one or the other grew tired of waiting.

She stared into the eyes she'd grown to love so much and squeezed his hand as if making a promise to herself that this would be one of the successes. She didn't know how, but she was determined to beat the odds.

A few miracles would be welcome too.

CHAPTER 23

Matt stood just behind the curtain with Penelope at his side, both peering out on the stage for the opening night of *The Sound of Music*. If miracles were on the menu for the past three weeks, The Darling House had gotten a full feast.

Of all people, Alec had been the one to secure the nearly impossible rights for them to perform *The Sound of Music* when a touring company was performing it in the same city. With all his connections, he'd pushed to make it happen as a sort of olive branch. And the rights holders, once they heard the story of what had happened, agreed. Miracle number one.

But the bigger miracle had been in the slow progress Alec was making in working through his grief and reconciling with his family. He still had a long way to go in earning Gwynn's trust, but Matt had seen him begin to love spending time with his family and the theater again, and that was a good indication of the trajectory of his heart. Because his business had suffered from his actions, he'd sold his apartment in town and moved back in with Grandfather, a good place to share in grief and healing together.

Collecting all the necessary and qualified actors to perform such demanding roles in such a short period of time proved an amazing feat of faith on the part of their community theater. People came together, pulling from all their connections across Skymar, and not only did they succeed, but they created an even stronger network among other independent theaters across the country. Which is likely why the production sold so well.

Community.

Penelope had reminded him that community was community,

no matter on which side of the ocean one lived, and the stronger the community, the more miracles happened.

To add icing on top of the cake, so to speak, Grandfather had sent a very special invitation in hopes of surprising not only the opening night crowd but also a certain ginger-haired beauty Matt had grown to love more and more with each passing day.

Now, as Matt and Penelope peered out on the stage, Grandfather made a brief welcome and then gestured, with a bow, to the side of the stage. From out of the shadows walked Her Royal Highness Queen Gabriella.

Penelope looked over at Matt, her eyes wide. He'd memorized her expressions, but he knew there were thousands more yet to see. He wanted to know them all. She'd become part of his heart, one of his family.

"We tried to get as close to Julie Andrews attending as we could."

She caught her laugh in her palm and then wrapped her arm around his, rocking up on tiptoe to plant a kiss on his cheek. "You're practically perfect, Mr. Gray."

"Practically?" He raised a brow.

Her brow lifted to match his. "You don't really want the pressure of being perfect, do you?"

"No, indeed." He laughed and brought their entwined hands up to his lips.

As the queen spoke, Matt glanced out over the full house. After years of living in the shadows of grief and uncertainty, this beloved place had come back to life, filled with the magic and joy of creativity and hope. He glanced down at Penelope. Much like his own life. And when someone found hope and joy again after thinking all had been lost, that someone found a way to hold on to them.

He caught sight of movement nearby and saw Luke's grin as he assisted in moving some of the sets into position. Over the course of the three weeks, the closeness of the siblings' relationship proved all the more why Penelope returning to the States was the right choice for her. That family connection. And despite Luke's quieter personality, Matt and Luke had gotten on very well. In fact, he would even consider the man his friend, and good male friends weren't easy to find.

"This performance has been a collection of a great deal of hard work, heart, and vision despite difficult and unexpected circumstances" came the queen's voice. "It is also an example of one of the less recognized beauties of Skymar, and that particular beauty is her people—a wonderful and eclectic group of individuals who love the creativity intrinsic to our culture and strive for ways in which we can celebrate that creativity through the arts."

Applause arose from the crowd and Penelope squeezed his arm again.

"It is a lovely thing to embrace the future while also cultivating an appreciation for our history, and places like The Darling House have shown us over time that both the past and the present can live in harmony and bring people of all ages together to inspire the future."

More applause.

"I would be remiss in expressing our appreciation if I did not introduce to you the two people who have been at the helm to make this performance possible. They've also created a way to celebrate the past through their museum, a history of which even our family has been a part. Let us welcome Mr. Matthias Gray and Miss Penelope Edgewood."

Penelope looked up at him, her face paling. He stood frozen in place. His gaze shot to his grandfather, who stood on the opposite side of the stage behind the curtain. The smile on Grandfather's face bloomed and he gestured Matt forward. Matt drew in a breath and, with a little tug, brought Penelope along with him to stand beside the queen.

The rousing cheers rose to a fevered pitch. He caught sight of a few locals in the orchestra pit sounding off their instruments with their own praise, and he chuckled. The past and present blended together and promised a beautiful future.

Penelope reached for his hand, and they stood basking in the spotlight together.

And Matt embraced the uncertainty of it all.

He trusted Penelope with his and Iris's hearts, so all he had to do was sort out how to keep their new little family together.

Much later in the night, after the performance and following celebration with the cast, crew, and donors, Matt drove Luke and Penelope to the cottage. Luke disappeared inside, making some excuse about being exhausted from all the singing and general happiness of theater people, but Matt knew it was to give him and Penelope some privacy.

He took the short walk from the car to the front porch slowly, arm in arm with Penelope, the contented exhaustion of a job well done soaking through him. Instead of following her brother inside, she paused, looked up at him with a sleepy smile, and slid down to sit on the steps.

"You're going to freeze out here," he murmured, his protest a bit half-hearted. The idea of revisiting the spot where he'd first realized he was falling in love with her somehow felt appropriate for such a night.

"I have on my fuzzy coat," she answered, tugging at the thick collar of her long black coat. "I'll be fine as long as we snuggle."

How could he refuse such a fetching invitation? He lowered to sit beside her and she linked her arm through his, resting her head against his shoulder and bringing the wonderful scent of her hair.

"We did it," she whispered. "And it was wonderful."

"It was," he rasped in response as he embraced her nearness. "We make an excellent team."

She looked up at him. "We do."

And he couldn't wait any longer. He cupped her face in his palms and tasted her lips. She hummed against his touch, encouraging him to linger. Her fingers twined into his coat, pulling him closer, giving him full access to her lips and cheeks. He nuzzled the spot where her ear met her neck, warming at her tremored response.

And she gave with as much passion as he did, one hand moving to slip into his hair.

It was a kiss that spoke more than words.

Of longing and believing and trusting the end would be worth the wait.

And in the back of his mind, a realization began to dawn. What if his idea of home had changed?

Penelope hated goodbyes. Of any kind. Even after dog-sitting for a week and having to leave any new furry friends with whom she'd created a bond.

But *this*. This was heart-wrenchingly worse.

It wasn't as if she'd never see Matthias or Iris again. She knew that—in her head anyway.

And it wasn't as if she couldn't jump on a plane and be back in Skymar in seven hours to have tea with Gwynn and Grandpa Gray.

Logically, it all made sense.

But logic didn't change the fact that once she got on the plane for home, a very different scene of her life began. Her role in this beautiful world of Skymar and The Darling House moved to memory instead of being a part of her every day. The movie nights and bicycle rides with Iris stopped. The moonlit walks and dancing dates with Matthias stopped.

Matthias.

He walked on one side of her while Luke followed on the other as they moved through Skymar International Airport. She was so distracted that not even the giant replica of the Kronimara upset her. Well, not very much.

Matt pulled her bag behind him, but she was determined to keep hold of his other hand as long as she could.

"I'm gonna go on through security, Penn." Luke put out a hand to Matthias. "Matt."

"I'll text over the photos of Grandfather's properties he'd like you to consider. The ones you didn't have a chance to visit while you were here." Matthias took his hand. "Assuming you're still interested in the job."

"I am." Luke gave a nod. "I'd appreciate learning from your grandpa. He's got some top-notch woodworking skills."

"March, then?"

Luke nodded. "See you then." He gestured with his chin toward Penelope and lowered his voice. "If not before."

Penelope breathed out a hopeful sigh. There was no way she'd be able to wait three months to see Matthias and Iris again. Maybe February? For Valentine's Day.

She frowned. But that was still two months away.

She internally whimpered.

Two months? Why did it feel like forever right now and a split second when planning for a performance?

Luke sent Penelope an encouraging wink before moving on to security and disappearing into the crowd.

She turned toward Matthias but couldn't look up. Saying goodbye to Iris had already left her with a red nose and completely mascara-less. She stared down at the buttons of his jacket, her eyes filling with tears all over again.

"At least we'll see each other on the screen." He brushed a thumb across her chin. "Every night if we can."

She nodded, words lodged in her throat. And she was usually so good at talking.

"Penelope."

The way he cradled her name drew her gaze to his.

"I'm in this to the finale." His grin tilted in the way she loved so much. "Whatever it takes. You know that?"

"I know." She breached the gap between them and buried her face into his shoulder, her arms holding tight. "But I want you within hugging distance." She looked up through blurry vision. "And kissing distance is nice too."

His grin spread and his gaze roamed over her face with such tenderness, it smoothed like a caress. With a dip of his head, he brushed his lips against hers.

"I'll see you soon."

She pushed up a smile. She had to be strong. This was the choice she'd made. And it was the right choice. But why did right choices have to hurt so much sometimes? Weren't they supposed to be the easy ones? "And we'll both be busy with Christmas."

"And then you're starting your new job."

She framed his face with her hands. "All those times before when I thought I knew what love was." She shook her head. "I was so wrong. Because this is so much more than the fairy tales, and even if I'm going to have to deal with the painful side of love, I'm so grateful I get to experience the sweet side too. Somehow, as weird as it sounds, it makes the hard parts worth it."

"Love is worth it all." He brought his smile to meet hers again, lingering a bit longer, and then he pushed her bag toward her. "Now, you take care. And phone me when you arrive home, won't you?"

"Maybe before."

"I'll keep the phone close by."

She rose on tiptoe for one more kiss. One last hug, her fingers reluctant to release the lapels of his jacket.

And then she stepped into the security line. He waited, watching her until the crowds blocked him from her view, and then she breathed out a prayer. That the magic of this romance would overcome any harm caused by distance. If anything was strong enough to breach thousands of miles and dozens of days, it was love.

Luke moved out of the way so she could take her seat by the window. She wasn't quite sure what to say or do, so she slumped in the seat and stared at the tarmac. Rain had soaked the ground and a thin fog swirled around the jagged mountains in the distance. Those were Steinndunn Fells. She sniffled. Matthias and Iris had taken her hiking there.

Her breath shivered out. The reality of everything probably wouldn't hit her until the plane touched down in North Carolina and the distance became concrete.

"The queen wasn't so bad."

She turned to her brother and gave a weak chuckle. "That's a big statement coming from the guy who doesn't think much of royalty."

"I have other things to think about than people who don't even live in my country, let alone my town, Penny-girl."

They sat in silence, and she leaned her head onto his shoulder.

"And as much as I hate to even think about it, let alone say it"—he shook his head—"I think you're positively perfect for Matthias Gray."

She raised her head and looked at him. "High praise from the overprotective brother."

"Yeah, well, I couldn't have you going off and falling in love with a foreigner no one in the family had laid eyes on, could I?" He gave his head a shake. "Didn't fit the big brother rules at all."

She chuckled and wiped at her eyes. "You know, you could have left four days ago, Luke. Gotten back home." She rested her head back against his shoulder. "Why did you stay?"

Silence greeted her question, and then he drew in a breath. "I didn't think you needed to fly home alone, little sis."

She pinched her lips tight against a sob and squeezed his arm. "Thanks, big bro."

Matt finished up the work in his office and started a walk-through of the theater to ensure everything was locked up before the Christmas holiday began. Since graduating, Gwynn had taken over as liaison to the community theater group and overseer of marketing. She'd also jumped all in with the business side of things, surprising everyone with her vision for the Darling. She'd truly stepped into her calling, her dream.

Grandfather's last meeting of the year with the board proved a room filled with unanimous encouragement. Everyone approved upcoming productions for two years in advance, something they hadn't done in a long time.

But now there was momentum. And hope.

And business to go around.

And Matt was left wondering where he fit in this world. With Grandfather back at the helm, Gwynn diving into her role as executive director, and Dani and Mark supporting in various ways, he found, for the first time in the history of working in this theater, he wasn't . . . well, needed. Not exactly. Of course, he continued to do the finances, but the cogs of the theater were running well, and his hands felt free.

He paused in his walk toward the Carrington stage doors. Free for what?

His heart thrummed with a possibility he'd only dreamed about since Penelope's departure. But could it be a real possibility?

Matt secured the stage doors and passed by the museum on his way to the Gray stage. He'd underestimated how much he'd miss Penelope on a daily basis. Her ridiculous singing in the mornings— well, actually any time of the day.

Her happy talking.

The way she brightened any room she entered.

Her love for his little girl.

He couldn't seem to go anywhere without missing her.

It was ludicrous, really. He should be able to master the feelings and counsel himself with the same words he'd given her. But he ached for her.

Video calls were at least something. Three times a week and texting or phone calls in between. But it teased him, like the photograph of a place once visited. A paper replica without scent or touch or vista.

His smile spread despite the ache. But he'd rather have her in his life in video-call form than in no form at all, so he'd take what he could get for now.

A faint light shone from beneath the door of the Gray stage and Matt slipped quietly through the door. One lone light shone down on the empty stage, tossing a faint glow out into the house seats. Matt's attention caught on a single person sitting among the seats near the front of the theater.

Was it Gwynn?

He squinted into the dimness. Alec?

Matt moved down the center aisle and paused at the end of the row where his brother sat, waiting for an invitation to join the pensive moment.

"My business had been failing for a long time." Alec's voice came softly toward him. "And I . . . I wanted to work here, be a part of the Darling like I always had, but I just couldn't. It hurt too much."

Matt moved through the row to take the seat beside his brother.

"When Niles approached me one day with the idea of trying to buy this place, I thought, *That would fix everything for me, wouldn't it? I would have money and wouldn't have to face this place every day.*" His voice broke.

Matt rested his palm on Alec's shoulder and Alec shook his head.

"But the problem wasn't the theater. It was me." He looked over. "First Mum, then Gran. I felt like I couldn't breathe inside these walls. Their absence took up every space."

"I felt it too."

"I don't think I had the words to describe what I was feeling before now." He cleared his throat. "The counseling has helped me understand, but before, I was just . . . angry. Angry that those two beautiful people were taken from us."

Matt nodded, his eyes squeezing closed from the hurt still close to the surface. "It didn't seem fair or right, and we were expected to go on with our lives as if this catastrophic thing hadn't happened."

"But you did go on." Alec turned his head toward Matt. "Why couldn't I?"

"We all grieved in our own ways, Alec." Matt blew out a long, slow breath. "Mine didn't cause the difficulties yours did, but it was still there. Closing off my world. Reframing my thinking. I gave up dancing and laughing because I was so buried in my grief." He shrugged. "But I think you felt you lost this place—this magical world—and you love it as much as Gwynn."

"And that made me angry too. Angry that a place I'd loved so much would now become like a tomb to me."

"So you fought like a drowning man."

Alec nodded, his face tense from trying to control his emotions. "I'm sorry for all the pain I caused. For not seeing that this place wasn't to blame. My family wasn't to blame. That I needed to understand my own pain, my own loss."

"I don't know that I would have come out of my pain like I did if it hadn't been for Penelope." He held Alec's gaze. "But I think we're all better for where we are now, don't you?"

Alec leaned forward, hands braided before him.

"Don't waste time, Matt." A small smile softened Alec's features. "I'm learning the value of a second chance. You have one now. With Penelope. You should take it."

<u>Text from Penelope to Matthias:</u> **I'm sending a pic of the twins in their reindeer costumes I bought them. Would you show Iris? I know she'll love them.**

<u>Matthias:</u> Iris says they are the cutest reindeer she's ever seen. BTW, the Christmas gift for Iris just arrived in the post, but I've told her she has to wait for Christmas to open it.

<u>Penelope:</u> **Ooh, it got there early! You know what it is? A Just Like Me doll! A doll specially designed to look like Iris, with all the gold curls! And I bought the princess dress to go with it. AHHH!!!!**

<u>Matthias:</u> Are you certain you bought the doll for Iris?

<u>Penelope:</u> **Hush. Of course I did. There's a magic wand in there too. That goes with the dress. And a crown.**

<u>Matthias:</u> Thank you for outshining any possible gift I could give her this year.

<u>Penelope:</u> **I'm farther away. I have to make a bigger impression since I can't be there in person.**

<u>Matthias:</u> Luv, you are forever impressed upon the minds of me and Iris. I assure you.

<u>Penelope:</u> **Are we still on for our usual video chat tonight? I may have a red nose when we talk because we're getting ready to drive Izzy to the airport for Skymar. I almost booked a ticket along with her and it's only been a WEEK since I saw you! Ugh.**

<u>Matthias:</u> I'll await your call, with or without the red nose. And just keep in mind, you begin your coveted position on January 2. You'll love it.

<u>Penelope:</u> **I'm pretty sure I love you more, but I can't back out on JMC now. She's announced it in all the local papers, which means my name is toast if I don't follow through. Everyone loves JMC. And the Ashby!**

Matthias: You are exactly where you're supposed to be, luv. See you tonight.

Text from Matt to Luke: Would you have time for a phone call today? I'd like to enlist your help on a certain project.

Luke: If the project involves transforming my pathetic sister from this mopey person to her happy self, I'm all in. I never thought I'd miss her singing, but her silence is a hundred times worse.

Matt: I'm not certain what "mopey" means, but I get the general idea. However, I think my plan may prove useful to the both of us.

Luke: I'll call you in five.

From: Izzy Edgewood
To: Luke Edgewood, Penelope Edgewood, Josephine Martin
Date: January 9
Subject: Missing you

I know it's been only three weeks since I left, and I still know I'm exactly where I'm supposed to be, but I'm missing our winter movie nights a whole bunch. Brodie has been a sweetheart, and when I was having a day of missing you all, we drove to Fiacla to visit The Darling House. Oh, Penelope, what a beautiful theater. And everyone I met just sang your praises. You are so loved here. And Brodie was right, of course—somehow being around people who know you made me feel better too.

Grandpa Gray was a darling and Gwynn is a fun take-charge sort of person.

I can't believe you're coming to Skymar in March, Luke. The idea of you being here about the time I REALLY start missing home is just wonderful. I know Brodie would love to show you his home of Waithcliff. Pictures really don't do it justice.

Penelope, didn't you start your new job this week? What was it like to be back at your childhood theater in such a new position? Matt said you were really excited and have already hit the ground running by going through inventory and meeting with local businesses. (BTW, I really liked Matt. And Iris was adorable. She was wearing your old princess headband. Matt said she only takes it off for bedtime, bath time, and church.)

Josephine, now I realize why Penelope was always asking about the twins! Do share photos!

Love you all,
Izzy

PS: I almost missed you all enough to pull out the photos of our camping trip through the Smoky Mountains. Almost.

. . . .

From: Luke Edgewood
To: Izzy Edgewood, Penelope Edgewood, Josephine Martin
Date: January 9
Subject: Re: Missing you

You've been gone three weeks, Iz. And you have Brodie. Surely you can't miss us *that* much. Those photos are reserved for real emergencies, like . . . never.

Luke

PS: Brodie will talk some sense into you.

• •

From: Penelope Edgewood
To: Izzy Edgewood, Luke Edgewood, Josephine Martin
Date: January 9
Subject: Re: Missing you

More like he'll KISS some sense into her! And then she won't miss us at all.

It's been wonderful to be at the Ashby and to know I've been brought on to make a difference. AND that I have the power to make that difference. It would be practically perfect if I didn't miss Matthias and Iris so much. But we've gotten into a good schedule of video calls (just like you and Brodie used to do), and since I have your relationship with him as a positive example, it's definitely helped with the distance and . . . uncertain future.

I have NOT cried every day. I've gotten it down to maybe three days a week.

And I still smile. Luke's telling people that I left my smile in Skymar! That is NOT good PR for an executive director of a theater!

Your message made me miss everyone in Fiacla so much more! Aren't they just a wonderful group of people?

JMC and I are meeting with the board in a few minutes to discuss which musicals we plan to feature our first year. EEEE!!! I'm bringing every Julie Andrews / Audrey Hepburn recommendation I can. You can never go wrong with Julie Andrews or Audrey.

Penelope

PS: Doesn't Matthias have the best eyes?

Text from Josephine to Izzy: I just wanted to let you know that I miss you. I think Penelope's personality energizes the twins much more than yours. You had a calming effect, especially since you chose to read books to them instead of sing musicals. I came in on her singing "The Phantom of the Opera" the other day, and I am certain it took the twins longer to go to sleep than usual.

Izzy: Was it a Tuesday night? They usually have a hard time going to sleep after you take them to whatever baby yoga you've enrolled them in.

Josephine: It was Tuesday, but it wasn't because of the yoga. *The Phantom of the Opera* is terrifying. A man wearing a mask in a basement? When she saw my horror, she kindly changed to "I Could Have Danced All Night," but then she started crying, kissed the babies, and left. She's much too attached to those musicals.

Penelope stood and stretched out her back from an afternoon of sorting through another series of boxes stored throughout the Ashby. And though Jackie had offered to send someone to go through the boxes for her, Penelope felt that she needed to be the one to decide what was useful or not. Some people didn't understand how something as simple as a clothes hanger could easily be transformed into a theater-worthy addition, not to mention lovely little discoveries like costumes, hats, and myriad props.

Besides, staying busy was good for her.

It kept her mind from thinking about Skymar and her fingers from looking up flight details.

She couldn't afford a flight just yet, neither financially nor time-wise, but boy oh boy, when she could, she was jetting right over to enjoy some Iris hugs and some Matthias kisses. At least she got to see them on video calls. That was something! Of course, she'd known separation was going to be tough, but she hadn't fully grasped the ache.

But having this job had been wonderful. And spending time with Josephine, the twins, her parents, and Luke had made the transition so much easier.

Right.

Like she was exactly where she was supposed to be.

But how could that fit at all?

Functioning long-term with her body in one place but her heart in the other proved to be an exhausting dance number. But she would do it for as long as she had to, because when you found something as wonderful as this, you held on.

And she was holding on for keeps.

Even from afar.

Her shoulders slumped. Very far.

But Matthias seemed all in too. Even over the last month of long-distance messages and video calls. Unless he was faking! He *did* work in a theater!

She rolled her eyes to the beautifully embossed ceiling of the Ashby. *Stop it, Penelope.* Her brain was her own worst enemy some-times. It didn't help to dive headfirst down the rabbit hole of disastrous possibilities. It only caused her to bake way too much food for a single woman to eat.

Her phone vibrated in her pocket, and she pulled it out, noting she had only another hour before closing up the theater.

Her smile spread across her face as she noticed the author of the message, but then her smile dropped when she read it.

> **Text from Matt to Penelope:** I'm sorry, luv, but something has come up and I'm going to have to miss our video call tonight.
>
> **Penelope:** Is everything all right?
>
> **Matt:** Yes, very well. In fact, I was hoping we could reschedule our chat for a little later?
>
> **Penelope:** Sure. Tomorrow?
>
> **Matt:** If we can still have it this evening, I'd prefer that.
>
> **Penelope:** It's going to be super late for you.
>
> **Matt:** That's all right. It will be worth it to see your lovely face.

She shook all the sad-ending thoughts from her head and closed a few more boxes, glancing at the list of things to do on her clipboard. She and Jackie had already hired an office manager. And they were interviewing two potential candidates for facilities manager tomorrow. Then there was the need for an overall coordinator between the community and the theater. Plus a few teachers so they could get classes started to generate additional revenue. Ugh. And speaking of revenue, they needed to look into hiring someone to help with managing the finances.

Her brain started to ache, so she turned the clipboard over and dusted off a few of the lovely bonnets she'd found in storage. Had they been used for some Oscar Wilde or Jane Austen play? *The Pirates of Penzance*? She gasped. Or maybe even *Les Misérables*?

Had the Ashby ever performed *Les Mis*?!

"Penelope."

Penelope turned at the sound of Jackie Crenshaw's voice coming from somewhere in the distance. The woman's silhouette shone in the theater doorway, the house lights too dim to make out her face.

"Yes?"

"I've had an unexpected meeting come up with a possible donor, so I need to leave a little early tonight."

"Well, what a wonderful surprise." Penelope stepped to the edge of the stage, squinting into the dimness. "We've had so many interested folks."

"In no small part due to you, dear girl." Jackie's response straightened Penelope's spine. She'd spent the first few weeks designing a new website for the theater and reaching out to some of her own contacts.

"But since I'm leaving early, I need you to do something for me."

"Of course," Penelope answered, cupping her hand over her eyes to get a better view. "I've already locked up the back doors."

"Excellent, but actually, this is something completely different. One of our possible new hires is stopping in for a tour of the theater. Would you mind sticking around to give the tour?"

Penelope started for the stairs. "Of course, but what position?"

"One of the teaching positions," Jackie called back. "There's no need to come back here, dear girl. I must be off. But I told him to meet you here in the theater."

Penelope stopped. "One of the teaching positions?"

Him? She didn't recall seeing any male applicants for teaching positions, but evidently she'd missed one.

"It all happened quite suddenly, but I think he'll be a good fit for what we want. And I have no doubt you'll convince him that the Ashby is the right place for him." There was a lilt to her voice. New donors were always a delightful surprise. "All right, I must run. Thank you for doing this, dear girl."

And off she went without another word.

Penelope shook her head and returned to her boxes, the front lights illuminating the space. She placed the boxes for discard nearer the stairs and the ones to keep back toward the curtain so she could have them moved to the appropriate storage room for later. Since the museum idea had worked so well for The Darling House, she'd planned to incorporate it at the Ashby once she made it through a few more storage rooms. The theaters were about the same age, after all, and both had such rich histories.

She'd just stacked the last one atop the other two when a soft sound filtered in through the house speakers.

Music? She looked toward the sound. Strings?

She stepped forward on the empty stage, searching the darkened theater, the music drifting into recognition. She knew this song.

Gene Kelly.

Her pulse took an upswing as the song continued. "You Were Meant for Me" from *Singin' in the Rain*.

Had someone gone into the sound room? Was there a glitch in the system?

She frowned. And why would Gene Kelly be the glitch? He should never be a glitch.

And then one of the house doors opened, allowing a sliver of additional light into the back of the hall. A little shadow burst forward down the aisle at a full run, a giggle paired with her approach.

That giggle sounded incredibly familiar.

Penelope blinked as the shadow took form on the stage steps. Iris?

A gasp shot from her as the little girl barreled into her stomach. Penelope sputtered through a few incoherent responses and then succeeded in muttering, "What . . . what are you doing here?"

The little girl looked up, her face wreathed in smiles. "Seeing you, of course."

"Of course." Penelope shook her head and laughed, leaning down to pull the little girl into her arms. "And I'm so very glad to see you. Hug you."

Penelope buried her face into Iris's neck and breathed in her soapy scent, her eyes burning as she continued to do something that sounded like a half sob, half laugh. Lob?

Over Iris's shoulder, Matthias came into view, emerging into the light of the stage.

"I don't . . . This is—" She lost control of her laugh again. "Am I dreaming? Because this would be a really great dream and a horrible thing to wake up and find isn't real."

"We couldn't wait another day to see you."

His voice sounded real. And the look he gave her appeared much more real than her dream last night.

"I can't believe this." Her smile grew as he closed in. "Are you sure I'm not dreaming?"

His warm scent surrounded her just before his arms. He pressed a quick kiss to her lips as Iris released another giggle. "No dream, luv."

She tipped forward into his arms, another . . . lob sniffling out as she pressed her face into his shoulder. "You're really here?" She pulled back. "How long do you get to stay?"

"What if we discuss that over dinner?"

"That would be amazing. Dinner. Here. With me." She paused and looked down at her watch. "But I have to give a possible new hire a tour of the theater first and they should be here any minute. Would you mind waiting around for me?"

Iris started to talk, but Matthias shook his head at her and then winked.

Penelope looked from him to Iris and back again. What was that for?

"A possible new hire, you say? What sort of job?"

"A teacher, I think." She studied his face, his eyes sparkling above a veiled grin. "Jackie wasn't very clear on the details, but I'm supposed to give him a—" She froze, and her breath caught. "A tour of the theater."

No. It was just a coincidence he'd shown up at the same time as the interviewee, right?

But then how did he get the music to come on just as he entered? Iris's giggle resounded again.

"Matthias?"

He slipped his arm around her waist and spun her into a dance. "What would you say if I told you I enlisted your brother to obtain Mrs. Crenshaw's contact information for me?"

"Luke knew about this?"

"And I contacted Mrs. Crenshaw regarding a position as a dance instructor and accountant for The Ashby Theater?"

She opened her mouth but nothing came out. She'd mentioned those needs to him a few weeks ago. But . . . how?

"And Mrs. Crenshaw took a look at my résumé, connected me to you, and offered me the job on the spot?" He shrugged a shoulder with his growing grin. "She helped with the music too."

"You're . . . you're moving here?" She stumbled to a stop in the dance. "To be *here* with me?"

He nodded. "With you." He gestured toward Iris. "We are."

She looked from Iris's bright smile back to Matthias, trying to match what she was seeing with reality.

"Daddy said families need to be together and that's why we came. We want to see if you will be a part of our family. Right, Da?"

"And the only way we can make certain that's the direction for us"—he searched her face—"is to be in the same place at the same time."

Their family? Her heart mamba-ed into a yes, but she stumbled back. "But what about The Darling House and your family there?"

He tugged her toward him again, his warm palms framing her face. "I can help with the finances remotely, but my grandfather and siblings know where my heart belongs. It's here, with you." His grin peaked. "You, dear Penelope, were definitely meant for me."

"But . . . are you sure?" Penelope tightened her hold on him, his face blurring in her vision. "You're upending your whole life for me. I don't want you to have any regrets."

"I would only regret not starting forever with you as soon as possible."

Her bottom lip dropped. Was that a line from a movie? Because if it wasn't, it certainly needed to be.

"Kiss her, Da." Iris pulled at the bottom of his jacket. "People always kiss at this part of the story."

"Oh, Iris." Matthias's attention never left Penelope's face. "I plan on kissing her in every part of the story."

"That sounds very fairy-tale-ish to me, Mr. Gray."

"Aye." But his response came out a little breathlessly as his lips found hers, and she caught hints of happily ever after sneaking between those vowels. "For certain it is, luv."

. . . .

From: Penelope Edgewood
To: Izzy Edgewood, Luke Edgewood
Date: January 21
Subject: Once upon a time

Izzy,

Matthias is HERE! He's moving here! Not here as in Mt. Airy but here as in the general location, to be near the Ashby. Oh, it was all so romantic, involving a sneaky plan between Luke, JMC, Matthias, and Gene Kelly. Ooh, but it was all so deliciously romantic and the BEST surprise ever!

Can you believe Luke helped plan it? Luke is even letting Matthias and Iris stay with him until they find a place. A place for a family! EEEK!!!

Gotta run. I have a DATE!!!! In PERSON!!!

Penelope

PS: I think Luke is a romantic way deep down inside.

PPS: WAY DEEP DOWN INSIDE.

PPPS: All it's going to take is the right type of fairy-tale princess for him.

· ·

From: Izzy Edgewood
To: Penelope Edgewood, Luke Edgewood
Date: January 21
Subject: Re: Once upon a time

WHAT? This is amazing, and I'm sure it will be even more amazing if you'd finish the story!

How was Gene Kelly involved? Is the Ashby haunted by his ghost or something, because I'm pretty certain he's no longer dancing on this side of eternity.

I think this really deserves a video call. Immediately. So you can FINISH THE STORY!

Izzy

PS: I'm so glad you didn't tag Josephine on this. The idea of setting Luke up would be like offering her free babysitting, a day at the spa, and a nap. I can see her salivating right now.

· ·

From: Luke Edgewood

To: Penelope Edgewood, Izzy Edgewood
Date: January 21
Subject: "Why Are You Pushing Me?"

I'm deleting this thread, ladies.

No fairy tales or princesses for me.

And I'm looking more forward to getting over to Skymar so I can outrun Penelope's or Josephine's matchmaking habits.

Luke

PS: Now, Penny-girl, go enjoy your own fairy tale and leave my solitary reality alone.

PPS: Izzy, don't get any ideas. I'm not afraid to use ninth-grade prom photos as blackmail.

Acknowledgments

This book was an interesting mix of introspection and downright fun. Introspection in looking at different ways grief and brokenness affect people, how joy is a choice, how important it is to look beyond a first meeting to get to know someone, or to see how a generous and joyful heart can impact the lives of others.

But it was also fun to bring the characters to life. To watch the sunshine/grump trope grow into a tender romance with a tiny Maria von Trapp twist. To revisit the wit, ridiculousness, and sweetness of family. And to show a depth to a "happy" character who may be misperceived by readers as well as the people she meets . . . without her losing her occasional silliness and (let's face it) one irrational fear. I hope you know the joy of having someone like Penelope in your life. Or maybe you *are* someone like Penelope.

Happy characters don't often get their own stories. They're usually relegated to the role of a supporting character who brings in the comic relief (and there's nothing wrong with that). But I was extra glad to get to bring Penelope's story to the page.

If I may, I'd like to rephrase Audrey Hepburn's famous quote a little. Instead of "Happy girls are the prettiest," I say, "Joyful hearts make the prettiest people." There is something attractive about a person who throws joy around like confetti. So this book celebrates those people who add that extra bit of light, love, and positivity to the world . . . and to the people who love them, even in all their . . . theirness.

There are a lot of people who bring joy to my life and have helped bring Penelope to the page. I won't remember them all, but I'd love to thank Joy Tiffany, Beth Erin, and my street team, as always. A shout-out to Alissa Peppo for sharing such excitement about my creating a musical-loving heroine. A big thank-you to my dear friend Jennifer Boice, who listens to me work through stories as we walk at "Poop Park." I am so thankful for Becky Monds and the team at Thomas Nelson who have continued to pump positivity and faith toward me and these stories. I can't imagine a more amazing team! And for my agent, Rachel McMillan, and her undying optimism and loyalty.

This is the first acknowledgment page I've written since my dad passed away, and I'd just like to say that there has been no bigger cheerleader for me and these stories than him. He and my mom have believed in me my whole life (even when they didn't always understand about my imaginary friends), and I'm so thankful that through their love, I learned about the joy of the Lord—a joy that leads from this world to the next (no matter the circumstances).

Thank you to my husband who allows me time to write in the evenings after the day job . . . and attempts to try to understand about my imaginary friends. And to my five "joy-bringers." I can't imagine life without you as a part of it.

"May the God of hope fill you with all joy and peace as you trust in him, so that you may overflow with hope by the power of the Holy Spirit" (Romans 15:13).

Discussion Questions

1. Theater is a big part of this story. Do you have a favorite musical or play? Why do you enjoy that particular performance?

2. As we grow, we often develop deeper understandings of big emotions, like love and forgiveness. How do Matt's and Penelope's definitions shape their decisions in the early part of the story versus in the end?

3. Is there a certain character in this story with whom you identified the most? One with whom you really didn't?

4. Penelope really struggled with people making assumptions about her because she was a generally happy person. Have you ever drawn the wrong conclusion about someone's personality on first meeting, only to realize later how very different at the "heart" they truly are?

5. I adore how Penelope's joyfulness first shocks Matt and then begins to grow on him. At what point in the story did you notice a shift in the way he began seeing Penelope? And how did that shift in his opinion begin to change him?

6. Penelope talks about choosing joy. Do you believe it's possible to choose joy? How have you done so in the past? If you are a Christian, what biblical promises help support your ability to choose joy despite circumstances?

7. Humor is a big part of this story. How did humor help grow relationships in this book, and how did it help the characters deal with life? How has humor helped you in the past?

8. How do you think joy and happiness are the same? Different?

9. Grief is a powerful emotion. It can really shape our thinking, thus leading to a change in our behavior. Matt and Grandpa Gray closed themselves off from the world. Alec "ignored" the pain and tried to smother it instead of face it. How have you faced grief in your life? What is the Bible's perspective on grief, and how can that perspective bring comfort?

10. Matthias and Penelope have a discussion about Matt having a "gratitude" problem. How can gratitude change our perspective and behavior, even when we're grieving?

From the Publisher

GREAT BOOKS

ARE EVEN BETTER WHEN THEY'RE SHARED!

Help other readers find this one:

- Post a review at your favorite online bookseller

- Post a picture on a social media account and share why you enjoyed it

- Send a note to a friend who would also love it—or better yet, give them a copy

Thanks for reading!

LOOKING FOR MORE GREAT READS? LOOK NO FURTHER!

THOMAS NELSON

Since 1798

Visit us online to learn more:

tnzfiction.com

@tnzfiction

AVAILABLE IN PRINT, E-BOOK, AND AUDIO

THOMAS NELSON

Since 1798

About the Author

Michael Kaal @ Michael Kaal Photography

Pepper Basham is an award-winning author who writes romance "peppered" with grace and humor. Writing both historical and contemporary novels, she loves to incorporate her native Appalachian culture and/or her unabashed adoration of the UK into her stories. She currently resides in the lovely mountains of Asheville, NC, where she is the wife of a fantastic pastor, mom of five great kids, a speech-language pathologist, and a lover of chocolate, jazz, hats, and Jesus.

You can learn more about Pepper and her books on
her website at www.pepperdbasham.com.
Facebook: @pepperbasham
Instagram: @pepperbasham
Twitter: @pepperbasham
BookBub: @pepperbasham